THE FIFTH VERTEX

by
Kevin Hoffman

Illustrations and cover art by
Eli Neugeboren

ISBN: 0990647919
ISBN-13: 978-0-9906479-1-1

Follow Kevin Hoffman
on Twitter @kshmusings and on Facebook and Goodreads

To Isabella,
whose insatiable appetite for wonderful characters and the
amazing worlds they inhabit inspired me to finish this book.

To Waldron
DOVEC'S COVE
FUR
PIROGANI MINES
KEST
VALLEY OF THE DEAD
RIFFSLAG RIVER
GREAT EASTERN DESERT
DRAGONSPINE MOUNTAINS
TANIS
BLACKPORT
GREAT WESTERN DESERT
WHITEPORT
ORDA
MIDEAN SEA
NOVESH
ROVESH
DRAGONSPINE MOUNTAINS
N
W
E
S
Legend
Built Road
City
Mountains
River

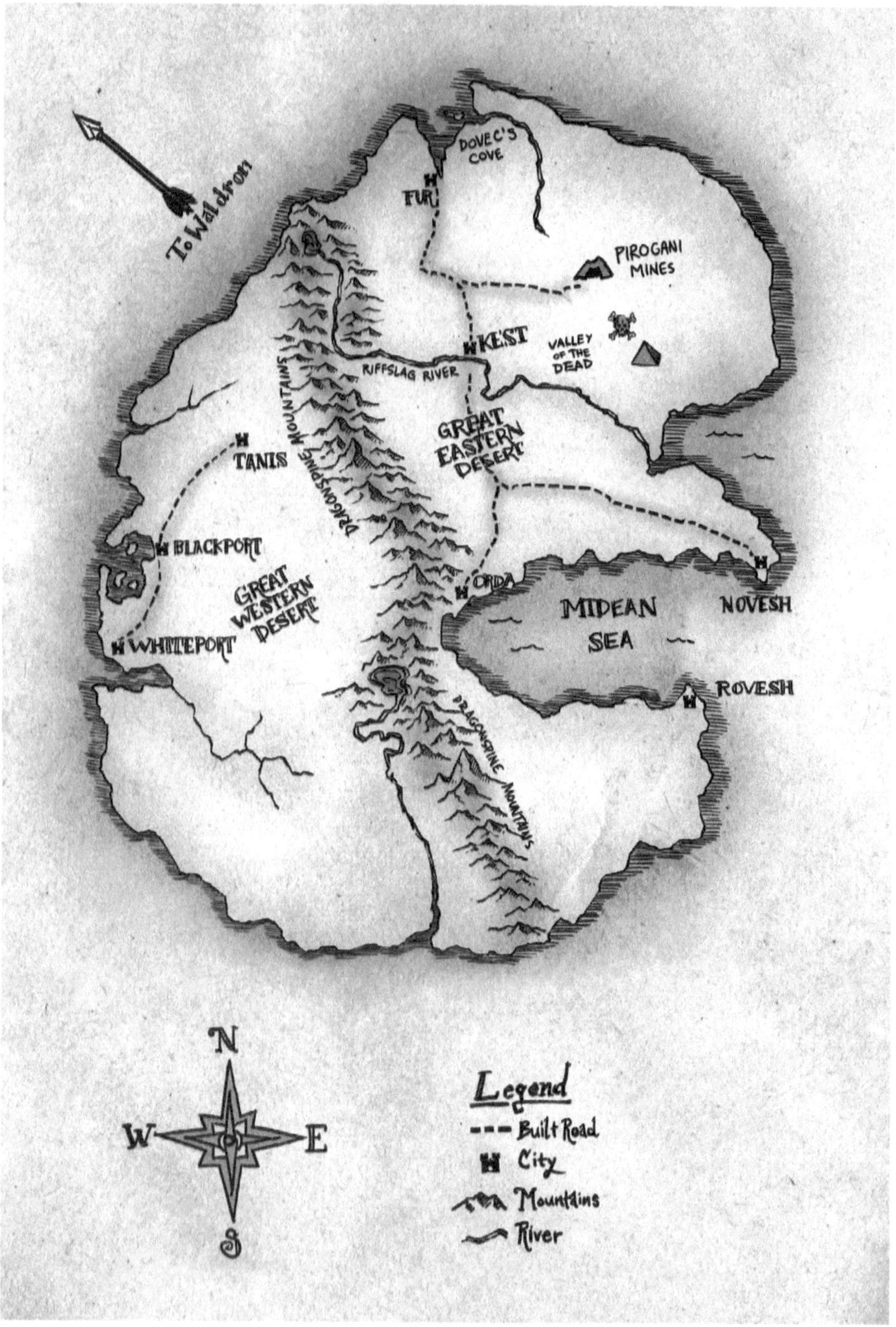

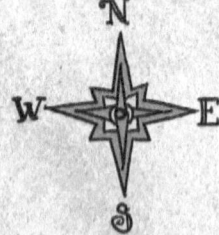

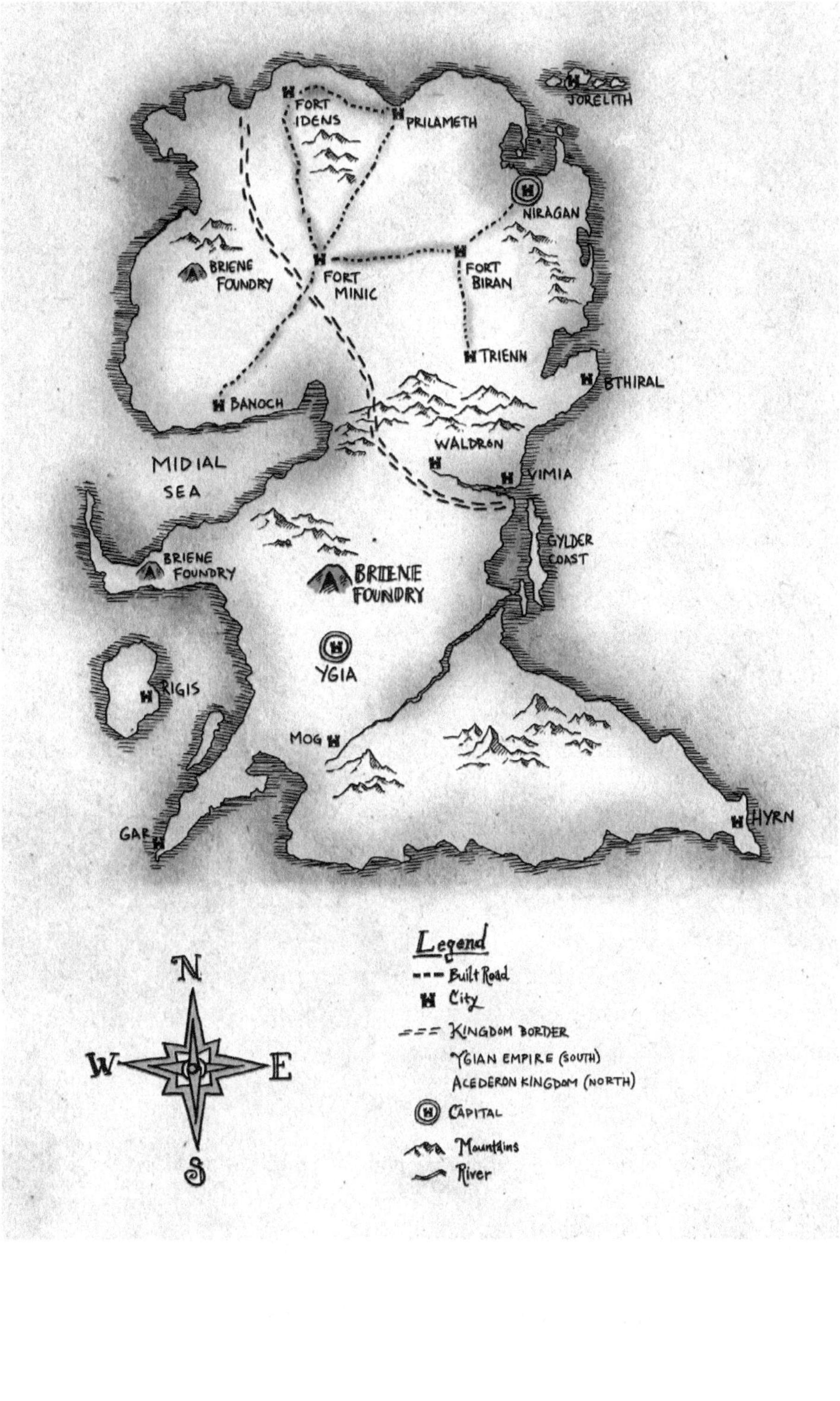

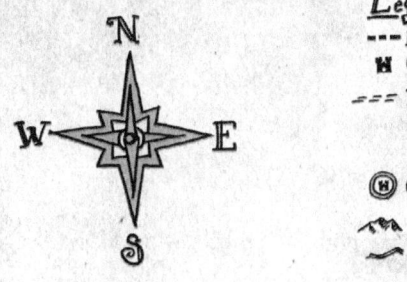

FORT
IDENS
PRILAMETH
JORELITH

NIRAGAN

BRIENE
FOUNDRY
FORT
MINIC
FORT
BIRAN

TRIENN

BTHIRAL

BANOCH

MIDIAL
SEA
WALDRON

VIMIA

GYLDER
COAST

BRIENE
FOUNDRY
BRIENE
FOUNDRY

RIGIS
YGIA

MOG

HYRN

GAR

N
W E
S

Legend
- - - Built Road
H City
=== Kingdom Border
Ygian Empire (South)
Acederon Kingdom (North)
(H) Capital
Mountains
River

Chapter One

Urus Noellor wondered what it felt like to die.

He leaned over the edge of the roof. Below, the glowing orange spiderweb of sunstone buildings and cobbled walkways spread outward from the palace, pushing back the cold dark of the moonless desert night.

Nestled along a strand of the luminous web of Kestian streets, the student barracks, by now filled to bursting with celebrating graduates, shone like a beacon of shame. Here on the roof, all was silent.

But even if he were among the graduates, Urus still would not be able to hear the cries of joy or the shouts of victory. He would never again be among those warriors.

He climbed onto the flat parapet and straightened his clothes—a futile gesture. The simple white tunic and pants of a novice were torn and bloodied from the day's attempt at defeating the gauntlet, the last rite of passage into adulthood for all Kestians.

He had failed.

The wet, stiffened cloth clung to spots of dried blood on his knees and elbows, bruises leaving purple and yellow patterns on his olive skin. Even his long, straight black hair hadn't escaped, tangles and knots glued to the back of his neck with a mixture of blood and dried sweat.

None of that mattered now. It would all be over soon. He was just one step away from relief in the afterlife. He would never be at the vanguard leading a charge to victory, nor would he even be at the rear.

No, he was doomed to a life away from the battlefield, and to a Kestian, a life without battle was no life at all.

He closed his eyes, took a deep breath, and teetered, about to step off the roof. A firm hand gripped his shoulder.

Urus flinched, then cursed himself for flinching. His mind returned to the gauntlet, returned to the scene where he'd faced off against a boy a hand shorter and two stones lighter. The boy had come close to landing a blow to Urus's face. Urus had flinched then, like he had done since he was a boy, and his opponent wasted no time in using that instant to defeat him.

Urus knew whose hand it was on his shoulder before he turned. He knew the strength and confidence of that grip, the grip that belonged to the commander of the First Fist of Kest, second in command of the entire city, and his uncle.

Urus stepped back off the parapet and turned to see his uncle looking down at him with an awkward smile, his face clean, his salt-and-pepper beard neatly trimmed, and his fine silk tunic the golden, gleaming opposite of Urus's tattered uniform.

His uncle folded his arms across his chest, making horns with one hand, the sign looking like a charging bull mid-stride. It was the name sign his uncle had given Urus the day he had come to take him from his father.

Urus loved that sign. It was one of the few things in the world that made him feel special, and it represented his identity more than any spoken name ever would.

"Get into a mess playing with Goodwyn today?" Uncle Aegaz signed, his hands moving rapidly as he mouthed the words. His eyes had that uneasy look they always had when trying to relate to his nephew.

Urus frowned. *He doesn't know.*

As usual, the man was too busy doing important things like keeping the city safe and being a war hero to know what was going on in Urus's life.

"Today was the gauntlet," Urus signed, wishing he could look away. "I failed."

Aegaz looked stricken, eyes wide with surprise. Urus couldn't tell whether he was more surprised that Urus had failed or that he didn't know about the event.

"That's all right," his uncle began with slow and gentle signs, as if trying to force feelings of reassurance out through his fingertips. "You still have two more attempts."

Urus scowled, his feelings of self-loathing and despair shifting outward to anger at his uncle, a man so busy he could barely tell what day of the week it was.

"Uncle, I failed my first attempt two weeks ago, and the second just this past Fastday."

Aegaz stared at Urus for a moment, letting the impact of the statement sink in. He looked horrified.

"But that means tomorrow you will be—" Aegaz signed, cut short by Urus's hand.

"Culled," Urus signed, trying to keep his anger in check.

"I am so sorry. I don't know what to say."

Urus shrugged. "There is nothing for it. It's done and my fate is sealed."

"There is still life in Kest for the culled. There are plenty of professions in need of young men like yourself. Why, even today the trade guild expressed interest in you," Aegaz signed, trying to force a smile.

"No!" Urus shouted aloud, startling both himself and his uncle. "Life as a culled is not a life. Life without a sword at your side is not worth living."

"That's not true," his uncle countered.

"It is and you know it. Where is Falk, the boy culled at last year's ceremony?" Urus asked. He knew the answer but asked anyway, the pain growing in the pit of his stomach, feeding on the sadness and anger.

"He died a month after the ceremony," Aegaz signed.

"He didn't just die. They found his body a day's ride from the city gates, buried up to the neck. The crows had eaten the rest to the bone."

Aegaz shifted his weight from one foot to the other, unsure of what to say.

Urus gave in to the despair, and it filled the emptiness within him. "You should know better than anyone. It doesn't matter what the law says about the culled. No one will accept me or even speak to me after tomorrow. My life is over."

"We will find a way, Urus," Aegaz signed. He leaned forward hesitantly as though he might attempt a hug, but stopped short.

"I just need to be alone for a bit," Urus signed.

"Just come inside with me—"

Urus cut his uncle off again. "Please, I need to be alone."

"All right," Aegaz signed, looking defeated. "I'll put on some of your favorite stew. When you're ready come inside we can talk."

His uncle turned to go, giving Urus the "I love you" sign before disappearing through the small wooden hatch leading down into the palace.

Urus let the pain well up inside him until it pushed the tears out, his nose running. He gazed through the fog of his tears back down at the glowing street and wondered if he would feel any pain before he died. He climbed back onto the parapet.

Aegaz's standing in the palace would be threatened by being the guardian of a culled. No true warrior would ever take his own life, but there was no shame in a culled doing so.

There's nothing I can do that would be more shameful than my own existence, he thought.

He took a deep breath and closed his eyes. He was ready to go, ready to end his life before it got any worse, end it now rather than spend the rest of it as some worthless cook watching everyone else bask in the glory of the battlefield.

He held his hands out in front of him and signed a prayer to Hol, the Protector: *Hol, protect and shield me in the afterlife. Though I may not deserve your notice, I beg for your benevolence.*

Urus stepped forward and fell from the roof.

He squeezed his eyes shut, his imagination conjuring up an image of a vast battlefield below, the desert sand red with the blood of his enemies, the sky black with the smoke of their burned villages. This was the dream of all Kestians, and he still wanted that dream, even in death.

The impact came without warning.

He slammed into the ground, though it felt more like the ground swung upward at his face like a hammer. Pain radiated throughout his body then vanished a moment later.

He wiggled a finger, then another, then wiggled his toes. He tapped the ground to make sure it was solid and he wasn't floating somewhere in Hol's realm.

Opening his eyes, he half expected to see fantastic scenes of the afterlife only described by books or traveling bards. Instead he saw the hard cobblestones glowing beneath him, only a few steps from the palace wall, some of which had sunken deep into the ground and cracked in half.

He looked at his hands and, for a moment, thought he saw tendrils of blue smoke drifting up from his fingertips. He shook his head, inspected his hands again, and the smoke was gone. It must have been a vision brought on by the blow to the head.

He jumped to his feet, surprised that he could even stand.

Maybe this is the afterlife, and I'm a ghost, he thought.

He certainly didn't feel dead.

Would I even know I was a ghost if I was a ghost?

He took a few steps back and craned his neck to look up at the palace roof. The height was tremendous. How he could have been foolish enough to jump from up there, he couldn't imagine.

Then he saw the silhouette, a dark outline of a man cast in the soft orange glow of the palace stone. Urus knew the man from his outline alone.

It was his uncle, his arms held in the sign of the charging bull.

CHAPTER TWO

He was alive.

Somehow, inexplicably, he was alive. Nausea and pain wracked his body, but he was alive. The fact that he didn't know why he was alive bothered him even more than having survived the fall in the first place.

Urus staggered over to the palace's side entrance, clutching his stomach and hoping he wouldn't throw up. Staying close to the luminous stone wall, he avoided the gazes of those wandering in the courtyard still celebrating the Winter's Long Night festival, which had fallen the night before graduation this year.

It wasn't hard to stay unnoticed. He wore the white uniform of an acolyte, and by now everyone knew that he was to be culled. Decent folk didn't look at or speak to the culled.

He waited for a break in the traffic spilling down the glowing stairs, then scurried up through the massive doorway and darted left, hugging the wall, hoping to circle the outskirts of the east foyer without bumping into anyone.

The celebrants, their drinks in hand, their weapons slung from their hips or backs, filled the hall nearly to capacity. No one in Kest attended a party without their finest, most polished weapon, and the more important the person, the fancier the weapon they brandished.

He watched the band in the far corner: a fellow on a lute, two older men with gray beards and thinning hair pounding drums, and a chorus of women singing. He could feel the percussion rhythm through the floor, but had no idea if the rest of the music was any good. The smiles on the faces of people bobbing their heads and swaying their hips told him the tune was at least passable—or they were too drunk to know better.

Having never heard music before, he didn't feel he was missing much, though his best friend Goodwyn's family certainly seemed to enjoy it, playing their instruments nearly every night after supper. Supper at his home was a lonely affair, with Urus usually reading himself to sleep before Uncle Aegaz came home.

Urus had made it nearly halfway along the wall when a shift in the crowd sent people dancing in his direction. He panicked, searching for an escape route, but saw none. Instead, he ducked and swam upstream through the crowd, staying low and whirling through the gaps as dancing partners separated.

By the time he made it to his destination—a narrow and barely noticeable iron spiral staircase—he had only knocked over two people and spilled as many drinks. Finally, after so many failed tests, he had completed a successful mission. He might not be able to fight as well as any other child in Kest, but nobody passed without notice like Urus.

A fitting talent for a culled, he thought.

He breathed a sigh of relief and started up the stairs, his relief turning to fear as he pictured his uncle, waiting upstairs in their apartment, and the talk he couldn't avoid having. As scared as he was of that conversation, it was still better than being stuck in the middle of all these people, dancing and celebrating their amazing lives, lives that were all better than anything that might lay ahead for him.

He slogged up two more levels, then stopped when something in the distance caught his eye. Two men stood at the end of a hallway having a heated conversation. He knew what his uncle had told him about eavesdropping, but one of the men was just about as tall and pale white as Urus had ever seen. There was no way he could resist that temptation.

He hopped off the spiral staircase and sidled along the hallway, keeping to the shadows. Neither man seemed to notice him.

He recognized the shorter of the men as High Shaman Kebetir, the third most powerful man in Kest after the emperor and his uncle. Urus didn't care much for the man, but Aegaz hated him with a passion, ever since the day he brought Urus to live with him after his father died.

The men gestured wildly, but both tried to keep their voices down. Despite the agitation on their faces, they were still whispering.

That just made him even more curious.

"—our arrangement," said the tall man, his skin a ghostly white and hair somehow even whiter. He wore simple brown robes with the cowl pulled back.

Urus had seen white men before, but none as interesting as this one. Thankfully both spoke Adosian, the common language of the continent of Ehmshahr. Of all the spoken languages he knew, Urus found Adosian the easiest for lipreading.

"I am not the one who altered the timeline," said Kebetir.

"It was ours to alter to begin with," said the other.

The two turned just enough so Urus could no longer read their lips. Then Kebetir, pacing, pivoted back toward the stairs.

"—won't let you ruin my chance," the shaman said.

The pale man put his hands on his hips and towered over Kebetir like a father scolding his misbehaved son.

Urus had never seen anyone treat the shaman like that. It was as frightening as it was satisfying.

"…planning…blood mages…" was all Urus could read on the High Shaman's lips.

The white-haired stranger took a sudden step toward Kebetir, and Urus tensed for the blow that he thought might come next. But the stranger merely stopped and peered into the dark shadows that enshrouded Urus.

"What?" asked Kebetir.

"We are not alone," replied the stranger.

Still swathed in shadow, Urus leapt over the iron railing and fled up the spiral staircase to the next floor. He couldn't be sure that he had been quiet about it, so he kept on climbing as fast as he was able, treading as lightly as he could on the stairs.

He had made it nearly to the top of the stairs at the fifth floor when he tripped and caught his weight against the wall. His hands burned as the rough stone tore and scraped his skin.

He examined the blood on his palms. At least now he knew he hadn't survived the fall from the roof because he couldn't bleed. He had one answer and a thousand more questions, and he vowed not to give up until he had answers to them all.

He paused at the top of the stairs, checking to see if he had been followed. After a few moments, Urus convinced himself that he hadn't been spotted and stood up.

Kebetir was up to something, that much was certain. His uncle should know that Kebetir was scheming, but if he told him, Aegaz would find out he'd been eavesdropping again.

The back of the fifth floor was a vast open room filled with a menagerie of dead animals, souvenirs from the epic hunts of past emperors, all stuffed, mounted, and posed to look just as they had in their natural habitats, only dead.

Urus cut diagonally through the displays, slowing to pat a lioness on her head and enjoy the soft feel of her fur. Her name was Leonora; at least that was the name he and Goodwyn had given her when they were younger and used to sneak in and play hunter-and-game. Urus usually ended up as the game, a little cub hiding under his mother surrounded by a roomful of vicious animals and one cunning hunter.

The truth was he had spent more quality time with the dead lioness as a child than with his real parents or his uncle. He wished he could curl up into a ball and hide under the strong, proud lion mother protecting her cubs, but he had to get home and deal with what had happened, face what he had tried to do.

He sighed, gave Leonora and each of her three cubs a farewell pat on the nose, and left the zoo of petrified animals behind, heading for the staircase leading to the level where the emperor's personal staff, including his uncle, had their apartments.

As he rounded the last step at the top of the stairs, he passed beneath a gas lamp whose flame flickered and struggled to stay alight.

Urus grinned. *Finally a problem I can fix*, he thought. It didn't hurt that it would give him an excuse not to head straight home. He dashed down the stairs and back into the menagerie, grabbed a stuffed monkey, and carried him back all the way to the fading lamp.

Standing on the monkey's eerily stiff shoulders, Urus unscrewed the brass fitting from the wall and pulled off the glass dome. Hard, black soot covered the tip of the brass pipe, just as he'd suspected.

Spitting on his finger the way his uncle had taught him, he flicked off the dark crust and the lamp flared again to its former brilliance. It had taken Urus three straight weeks of begging and annoying his uncle before the man had finally relented and showed him how the gas lamps throughout the city worked and where their fuel came from.

He still hadn't figured out how they stuffed all those animals in the zoo room with no smell of decay and how they kept the lioness' fur so soft after all these years.

He returned the stuffed monkey and slogged home, sucked back into the morass of pain and regret he felt and the looming fear of what his uncle might say. He hoped he might find another broken lamp or out-of-place tile that needed fixing. But there was no delaying the inevitable this time. He soon found himself staring at the door to his home, on the other side of which would be his uncle, no doubt fuming with anger over what he'd done.

He was about to turn the bronze knob when the teak door swung inward, revealing Uncle Aegaz, standing in the shadows on the other side.

Urus stood in silence, gazing at him across the portal. He felt a wave of shame and sadness, his throat tightening and pain welling up in his chest, hot tears escaping down his cheeks. He yearned to hug him, to reach out and squeeze his uncle as hard as he could, squeeze all the pain and suffering out and let Uncle Aegaz make everything better the way he always did, but humiliation locked his arms at his sides.

Urus took a step forward and waited, half expecting to be hit.

Aegaz simply stepped aside and waved Urus to the table.

Urus sat, wrapping himself in the smell of the spiced stew and the red and white embers keeping the kettle warm. It was a good, comforting smell.

The apartment, like all the others in the palace, was small and spartan, with just enough furniture to accommodate the two of them. The only decorations were antique weapons resting on wall brackets and Uncle Aegaz's sword belt on a peg near the door.

"We need to talk," signed Uncle Aegaz, sitting on the bench opposite

Urus.

Urus gulped, barely managing a nod.

"I failed you," Aegaz signed.

"What? That's crazy," Urus started but Aegaz held up his hand.

"Let me finish."

Again Urus nodded.

"I may not be your sire, but—"

"Thank Hol," Urus interjected, shrinking back when Aegaz gave him a look.

"But I am responsible for you. It is my job to give you a home, to raise you properly, to teach you what you need to know. I haven't done my job." Aegaz sighed. Urus wasn't sure if it was the light or the situation, but the wrinkles on his uncle's face looked more pronounced, the fatigue circles under his eyes darker than usual.

"This isn't your fault, Uncle," Urus pleaded while shoveling stew into his mouth, too hungry to wait until they were done signing to eat.

Aegaz leaned back on the bench.

"I've always thought of you as the son I could never have. I have to keep you from harm and see that you grow up strong and right and turn into a great Kestian, even if you aren't a warrior."

"Stop making this your fault, Uncle. It hurts to see you like this."

Aegaz leaned forward and signed, "And it doesn't hurt me to see you try to kill yourself?"

Pain ravaged Urus's heart—pain for what he was putting his uncle through and shame for his own cowardice and despair.

Aegaz swept his hand toward the open window that overlooked the city below.

"This city—I gave everything to it, to keep it safe and the people in it, to keep our enemies at bay." Aegaz shook his head. "All that time I should have been paying attention to you, keeping you safe, keeping you from... from..." Aegaz couldn't finish.

"Uncle, don't," Urus said, reaching across the table to hold his uncle's hands.

"I need to make this right. I will make this right."

Everything Urus had done to get to this point flashed before his eyes: the despair and loneliness of his childhood; the joy when his uncle came to take him from the brute who was his sire; the desolation at his failure to become a warrior. Gazing across the table at his uncle, he realized how little any of it mattered.

"It will be right, Uncle. I don't want to…to…do that…not anymore."

Aegaz nodded firmly. "This isn't going to get better overnight," he said. "We have a lot of work to do, and I have some changes I need to make. But first, there is something else we need to talk about."

Urus cocked his head, eyebrow raised.

"By Ishimani's tears boy, haven't you wondered how you survived that fall?"

"It's all I can think about. It's driving me crazy. Did you—" Urus paused, idly stirred his stew, then looked back at his uncle. "—see what happened?"

"I saw enough."

Urus tried to wait patiently. Tapping his foot and fingers didn't help.

"This is going to be like the gas lamps, isn't it?" Aegaz asked, the faintest hint of a smile struggling to break through the sadness on his face.

Urus nodded as hard as he could. "Worse."

"Your family, our family, on my father's side, we have always had this—I don't know what to call it—ability. Maybe it's magic; maybe it's something else."

"Magic ability? What kind? Like Sorcerer Fal and the Dragons or more like Rahab and the Thousand Ogres?" Urus asked, his mind latching onto some of his favorite stories. The worlds he entered every night in his books offered him an escape from the ugly world in which he spent his days.

"No, not like any of those; at least I've never seen any evidence for it. And besides, Fal and Rahab are just characters from books," Aegaz signed. He stroked his chin with one hand, stirring his stew with the other, deep in thought.

Finally he put the spoon down and signed, "There are symbols, carved into stone in some places in the world, even here below Kest. These symbols are old, older than any city still standing today. When a son from our bloodline touches one of these symbols, the symbols glow."

"So that's it? Our family can make things glow?" Urus signed, disappointed. When he thought of magical powers, making shapes light up in stone wasn't the first thing that came to mind. No, he wanted fireballs and wingless flight and to be able to conjure whole turkeys with an incantation, like the wizards from his favorite stories. Magic could make him powerful, powerful enough to defeat any of the graduates—maybe even any warrior in Kest.

The prospect practically made him salivate, especially the part about summoning turkeys. He leaned forward on the bench, the pain and emotions stuffed down beneath the excitement of a new puzzle to work out.

"Up until tonight, for as far back as we can trace the history of the radixes—that's what the journals call people like us—that's all we've been able to do," Aegaz signed, pausing to rap the side of the kettle again. "When you jumped off the roof tonight, you...landed...in a pool of that same light. It even splashed, like water. I can't remember reading about anything like that in any of the family journals, but I don't read ancient Kestian as well as you."

"So our family's magic saved me from the fall?"

"I think so. There is a room below the dungeons, on the other side of the cistern, a room with a stone slab in the middle with ancient writing on it. It has journals written by my father, his father before him, and so on through the history of Kest itself. I will go there tomorrow and see if I can find any mention of the sort of thing that saved you."

"Let me go with you; I want to see the journals!" Urus pleaded, grabbing his uncle. This was definitely going to be worse than the gas lamps. No way in Hol's realm would he be able to sleep tonight, not with a mystery like this in his head.

"Tomorrow is the graduation ceremony."

"You mean the culling," Urus signed, his mood souring.

"Now look, Urus, there is more to life than being a warrior. Master Villus from the trade guild told me they could use a good translator, and you know more dialects of tradesign than anyone in Kest."

"I want to be a warrior!" Urus shouted loud enough so he was keenly aware of the strain and vibration in his throat. He jumped to his feet, knocking the bench over. "I'm not going to be some stupid translator!"

His uncle frowned. "This is an important duty, not a stupid one. You'll see. I will be there for the culling; then afterwards I will go with you to see

Master Villus. We'll do it together."

Aegaz got up and walked around the table, reaching for Urus. But before he could hug him, his head snapped toward the door. Hugs weren't something that came naturally to his uncle. Urus knew exactly what that head turn meant.

"Don't answer it," Urus begged. He didn't want to be alone.

Aegaz glanced sadly from the door to Urus and back.

"I have to answer it; it might be important," he signed and dashed to the door.

I'm important too, Urus thought, but said nothing, watching his uncle again ready to drop everything to take care of the city and everyone else in it; everyone except Urus.

Aegaz answered the door to a member of the First Fist in full battle gear, his black and red tabard pinned to his body with two swords strapped to his back and two short swords sheathed at his waist.

The soldier crossed his arms over his chest and saluted, then delivered his message. Whatever it was, Urus couldn't read it on the man's lips and Aegaz certainly didn't like it.

His uncle grabbed his sword belt from the peg near the door, strapped it on, then looked up at Urus, eyes bloodshot and moist with tears.

"I have to go. You know I wouldn't go if it wasn't important," he signed.

"I know."

"We will talk more about this tomorrow," Aegaz signed, and then he was gone through the door, his lieutenant in tow.

Urus poked at the kettle of stew, taking a whiff of its aroma. The now-empty room held little evidence that his uncle had ever been there.

Urus was alone again.

Chapter Three

Cailix urged her wheelbarrow forward, plowing a narrow trench through the fresh powder of the early morning summer flurry. The snow had nearly covered her load of lava rocks in the time it had taken to get from the quarry back to the monastery.

She banged the head of the wheelbarrow against the thick wooden doors twice, then waited for one of the monks to admit her, shivering under her heavy wool coat.

The door opened, and as she rolled her burden into the warmth of the monastery's antechamber, the monks disappeared without a word back into the sanctum's quiet depths. Shedding layers, she peeled off the wool overcoat, then tossed her cloak aside and shook her hair free. Tresses the color of red wine hung to her waist, cinched in even bunches starting at the nape of her neck.

She wheeled the rocks from the antechamber into a vast, domed room ringed with recessed fireplaces that warmed the desks in the center of the room piled impossibly high with books and scrolls.

This was the great room where the monks spent most days and nights, transcribing and worshipping the written word almost as fervently as their pantheon of deities. Iron vents covered holes in the gray stone floor, crisscrossing below the grid of desks and tables, a faint orange glow blooming up through the slats.

The heat of the volcano was all that kept the city of Naredis and everyone within from freezing solid. The room, like most of Naredis, had the scent of a noxious cocktail of burned wood and rotten eggs.

Cailix was glad it was summer; otherwise she would have needed a heated wagon to do her chores. The natives always said the only difference between winter and summer in Naredis was how long it took to freeze to death.

"The floor is no place for your cloak, child," remarked one of the monks without looking up from his work. She was sure these monks had supernatural sight—they always knew where she was and what she was doing.

"Sorry, Brother James," she said in her sweetest, most apologetic voice. A few days after they had taken her in from the orphanage, she'd learned that the monks loved the sweet and meek tone, so she practiced it often. If the monks were happy, that meant she stayed warm and well fed and out of the orphanage.

After hanging up her cloak, she started her rounds, tossing a few of the lava rocks into each of the fireplaces to keep them warm without choking the monks on wood smoke. In the winter, the monks sealed this room off because it was too difficult to heat, everyone huddling instead into a smaller chamber three stories below, closer to the heat of Mount Kebel's core.

As the wood ash and sulfur smell filled her nose, the memory of the adventure of getting to the quarry and back vanished and she settled back into the humdrum routine of keeping the monks warm, their tea brewed, and their meat pies hot. She had just finished tossing the last rock into the last fireplace, her mind already filled with places she wanted to explore later that day, when the chamber door burst open, the sound of dense wood banging against stone reverberating off the ceiling.

Cailix's ears rang.

Standing in the open doorway in white robes were three tall, slender men with short cropped hair, their fair skin bronzed by the warmth of some faraway climate. The only color Naredis turned people's skin was blue.

"We have come to speak with Brother Toyce," said the middle of the three strangers, stepping forward. None of them bothered to close the door, which infuriated Cailix. If they left it open much longer, the monks would get cold and she would have to stoke all the fires. The whole place would fill up with smoke and her day would be ruined.

"I am Brother Toyce," said one of the monks, rising from behind a pile of books, his head barely reaching above the top of the stack.

Finally, the two men at the door slammed it shut.

"At long last," said the leader, snaking his way through the stacks toward the monk, his bright white robe flowing over the dark stone floor like some ghostly train dragged behind an apparition. "You would not believe how long we have been looking for you."

Cailix blinked as she saw the man's bare, sandaled feet.

Sandals, on the top of Mount Kebel! The very idea was ridiculous. Even at the peak of a midsummer's day, bare skin could freeze outside in a matter of minutes.

"I am honored that you have sought my counsel, stranger. What may I call you?" said Brother Toyce, bowing slightly, his face flushed. Cailix couldn't tell whether it was from the cold or from taking the man's words as a compliment.

"Anderis will suffice." The man's face wrinkled as he smiled, baring the most perfect set of teeth Cailix had ever seen. "And then you can fetch what I have come for."

Books and tables obscured her view, so Cailix inched her way toward the middle of the great room, ignoring the whispered pleas of the other monks to stay back.

"We have many fine books here, works of fiction, historical archives, trade routes, maps—"

Anderis raised his hand to cut the monk short. "I seek a map, but not just any map. I seek *the* map," he said, beaming, as though the monk should somehow know which map he meant.

Toyce's face remained calm. "You will have to be more specific, my Lord Anderis. We have an entire floor below this one dedicated to maps of the world."

"I am no Lord, monk," Anderis snapped, as his friends at the door stifled their laughter.

Cailix didn't get the joke.

"I seek the oldest map you have. In ages past it was called the Woan Map. Before that it was called the Map of Doors. Before that it was called Hulgoth's Pyramid, before that the Sigilpost Guide, and before that—"

"Ruorc's Earthly Vertices," Toyce added, a wide grin on his face. "We have all heard this fairy tale before. One would be more likely to find a grand wizard riding a golden dragon out of this fireplace than the Woan Map."

Anderis's smile vanished.

"You can drop the act, Brother Toyce. We know this map is real. We know who gave it to you and we know you have it here. Brother Todwynn sent his regards only moments before his death."

The color drained from Brother Toyce's face, his eyes wide, mouth slack-jawed. Cailix's eyes widened as well. Toyce was the head of the monastic order and could issue orders and scold disobedient children like no other. She had never seen him put off guard by anything or anyone, not even Naredis's Regent.

"Give me the map, Brother Toyce, and my friends and I will be on our way."

"Never," Toyce snapped, brow now furrowed, jaw and fists clenching. *This* was the Toyce Cailix knew, and it looked as if he was going to give this stranger a good tongue-lashing.

"If you know what this map truly is, then you know what I am capable of doing to obtain it," Anderis said, towering over the short monk.

"I know this map, and now I know what you are," replied Toyce. "We have all taken an oath to protect the location of that map with our lives, as did our fathers and their fathers before them. We will tell you nothing."

Cailix drew in a wary breath. She wasn't particularly fond of the monks, but they did take her in when the orphanage discarded her and they were her only source of food and shelter. Something bad was about to happen to that, and she didn't know how to stop it.

Anderis smiled. "Oh, you'll tell me everything; you have no choice in the matter. You do, however, get to choose the degree of pain involved in the process."

He reached into his robe and drew a knife from a sheath on his hip.

"Decide now, monk. Are you going to talk or will your blood?"

Cailix decided that she wasn't going to stand around and let these men bully the monks. Maybe if the brothers saw her defiance, they would quit being so monkish and fight back.

"No!" she shouted.

She hurled herself at Anderis shoulder-first, slamming into his chest. Despite the man's height, he went down pretty easily. The sounds of bone cracking when he hit the floor startled her. If he had broken anything, the man in white didn't let it show.

"Insolent girl!" he hissed, grabbing her and rolling over so he knelt straddling her chest, his knife poised at her throat.

"Leave her alone!" called Brother James, several of the other monks echoing his plea.

Her plan might actually be working, she thought. The monks sounded defiant, and they easily outnumbered the strangers. All they had to do was throw a few chairs or some of their giant manuscripts or start stabbing people with quills and it would all be over.

"If any of you move from where you stand I will feed this child's blood to the volcano, understood?" Anderis said, his icy gaze fixed on Cailix's face. His chest heaved as though he had just run a race, veins bulging from the surface of his neck, sweat beading on his arms. Cailix couldn't remember the last time she had seen anyone sweat in Naredis.

The man in white looked older and more frail than when the trio first arrived. If it weren't for the knife at her throat, she figured she might actually be able to overpower him.

"Give me the Woan Map now. Then I let the girl go," Anderis snarled, no longer bothering with his calm facade.

"We took the oath. You could kill us all and we would not deliver you this map," answered Brother Toyce, his voice shaky as he tried to sound determined.

Cailix studied the man who had clothed and fed her for the last few months. Their eyes met, and she knew that he meant what he said. Toyce would rather die, and let her die as well, than let these men have a simple map.

Well, she wasn't about to die today, least of all for some stupid map. What could possibly be so important about a map that monks, of all creatures, would sacrifice their lives for it? What could Anderis find with such a map that was so terrible?

Anderis's face contorted with anger.

"Then we will do this the difficult way," he said, standing up. He had to push off against a knee to stand upright, like an old codger without his cane.

He nodded toward Brother Toyce, and his companions grabbed the monk, binding his hands behind his back and delivering him on his knees to Anderis.

None of the other monks made a move to stop them.

Anderis turned his back to Cailix to stand over the monk. If they were going to die anyway, then she wasn't going out lying down crying like a baby.

She pounced.

She landed on Anderis's shoulders, and the man collapsed, his limbs folding and bending at odd angles. Again she heard the sound of bone cracking.

This time he screamed, loudly.

"Get them, there's only two!" she screeched, pointing at the two shocked henchmen.

She hammered a few more blows into Anderis's chest from her perch on his shoulders, looking around for support from the monks.

All of them were on their knees, hoods drawn, chanting in prayer. Rather than jumping at the chance to help her vanquish the men in white, the monks were praying.

Just like everyone else who'd ever said they would take care of her, the monks had lied.

Fine, she thought. *I'll just have to take care of myself, as always.*

Before the two henchmen could react, she leapt from Anderis onto the first, climbing up his frame and locking her legs around his neck.

Hollering, she pulled his hair and pounded her fists on his head. This one didn't collapse under her weight, and she didn't hear any bones break. With one hand he reached up, grabbed her by the scruff of her neck like some little animal, and threw her against one of the desks. She gasped in pain as she landed on her back and bounced off the desk.

She rolled onto the floor, fighting for breath, sucking in but not drawing any air. Finally her lungs expanded and she took a breath, just as her attacker kicked the desk over on top of her, burying her under a pile of wood and books.

"This is ridiculous," snapped Anderis. Again he stood and brushed the dust off his robe, with no sign of broken bones or injury. "Who knew the monks kept wild animals as their servants?"

Wild animal, indeed. She would show them just how wild once she got out from underneath the desk.

"Well, Brother Toyce, since you refuse to tell me where the map is, then your blood will have to tell me," Anderis said, holding his knife to the monk's neck.

"No!" Cailix howled, helpless to intervene as Anderis stabbed Toyce's throat, spilling his blood onto the stone floor.

The leader of the men in white kneeled in the spreading pool, his robe soaking up the blood like fresh paint on a canvas. He dunked his hands in the thick, red liquid and stared into Brother Toyce's dying eyes, both men facing each other on their knees.

"The Woan Map," Anderis whispered.

Brother Toyce's eyes rolled back and blood gurgled out of his mouth as Anderis's henchmen held him up.

Then Toyce spoke, but with Anderis's voice. "Accounting archives." Cailix wasn't sure if she was watching a dead man talk or some kind of crazy magic. It was a gruesome sight and she probably should have looked away, but she stood transfixed, mesmerized by the power Anderis wielded.

Anderis splashed more of the blood up onto his arms and rubbed it on his face. Toyce, or whatever that semi-dead thing was, continued. Her protector and benefactor was dead and nothing Anderis did to his body would change that. She had to survive.

"Regency coffers log, Common Era 412, Harvest Record 23B," Toyce's lifeless body spoke with Anderis's voice.

Anderis gave a short laugh.

"They hid the most valuable map in the world in the most boring set of archives nobody ever wants to read." He stood up and let Toyce's body drop. "Clever, except they left it defended by a handful of pacifist monks."

"What did you do to Brother Toyce?" Cailix yelled.

Anderis waved his men off, and they disappeared down the staircase leading to the archives. He paced idly through the room, flipping through the books and manuscripts. It was a while before he spoke again.

"You have such spirit and fight for a young woman. Why do you not cower in the corner and cry for your mommy like a normal child?" Anderis asked.

"I'm not weak like them. I don't have a mommy or a daddy. Nobody comes to hold me and sing me stupid songs when I cry."

"What a terrible shame."

"It isn't shameful at all. If I'd been crying in a corner I wouldn't have found out that you're a brittle old bastard who can barely stand without breaking his bones," Cailix said, spitting in his direction.

"Perhaps, but then you wouldn't have ended up stuck underneath a desk watching as I bled your benefactor to death."

"You'd have killed him anyway. I'd rather have my dignity stuck under a desk than be without it, hiding in a corner."

"What a fascinating little creature you are," Anderis said, an amused, appreciative look on his face.

"Come closer and say that again."

She was sure that any of the men could kill her as easily as they had Brother Toyce, but that didn't matter. What mattered was not showing any sign of weakness. If you showed weakness, others preyed on you, and she was nobody's prey.

Anderis had opened his mouth to reply when the henchmen returned. One carried a giant tube sealed at both ends with wax under his arm.

"Is that it?" Anderis asked.

"We found it right where the monk said," replied the man who had knocked the desk onto her.

"To think that after all this searching, we would find it buried in some accounting archive below a monastery," said Anderis.

One of the men broke the wax seal, withdrew the ancient parchment, and unfurled it onto a desk, knocking aside a pile of books to make room.

Anderis gasped. "The Woan Map. Finally."

It drove Cailix mad that she couldn't see what was on the map, what was so important these men would kill and the monks would die for.

"Somehow I thought it would be harder to find. Seems kind of foolish to leave it unprotected down there," his companion remarked.

Anderis's eyes widened, a look of shock spreading across his face. "The map gave itself up too easily. The seal in the wax, was it a sigil?"

His companions shrugged, fumbling through the broken wax.

"No! Not after all this time and work!" Anderis shouted. "Mirol, the map was warded! I'm going to need your blood."

"What?" Anderis's companion asked, taking a step back. But even from where Cailix lay, she could see the man didn't stand a chance. Anderis's knife slit Mirol's neck open. Rather than spilling down, the blood flowed outward, spraying a fine red mist all over the map just as the paper started to burn. Some of the spray shot past the table and onto her face and hands.

As Anderis held his hands over the map and whispered something, Mirol's exsanguinated body dropped to the floor in a heap. All the while, the remaining monks continued praying, not making a move to stop their attackers.

"Did you save it?" the remaining white-robed thief asked.

Anderis nodded. "The blood preserved the image before the parchment burned. Go get a blank scroll."

As the thug departed in search of a scroll, Cailix felt the heat of the blood dripping down her cheeks and sticking to her fingers. Her heart raced and the heat seemed to transfer from the blood to her body, warming her from head to toe. She was fascinated by the sight, the smell, and the texture of the blood. It was intoxicating.

The henchman returned with a large scroll. They unfurled it and pressed it down on the pool of blood on the table. After a few moments of rubbing and pressing the paper to the wood, they lifted it, revealing a mirror image of the map, drawn entirely in blood. Cailix couldn't help but marvel at the beauty of it.

"Put it over there to dry for a moment," Anderis said.

"And the monks?" the henchman asked.

"Kill them all, and make sure the girl watches."

He nodded. Cailix lay there in silence as the man paraded the monks before her, stabbing each through the heart, piling their bodies there so that was all she could see. Their blood ran down the woodgrain in the floor toward her, soaking into her clothes. It took the henchman just a few minutes to kill all twelve remaining monks.

Anderis rolled up the scroll and slid it into the original map tube. Then the two men turned to leave without another word, as though she didn't exist.

The monks were dead. Without them, she would have no way of surviving in the harsh city. She had already been cast out of the orphanage. With nowhere left to go, the only thing in doubt would be whether the hunger would kill her before the cold.

"Wait," she cried before the men reached the massive doors.

They stopped, Anderis looking back across the chamber with a raised eyebrow.

"Take me with you," she said.

Anderis chuckled, but he said nothing. Instead, he walked back to the overturned desk and squatted atop the pile of monk bodies, resting his weight on the balls of his feet as though he were an agile young man.

Cailix couldn't figure him out. One minute he was as brittle and broken as an old man, while the next he perched like a cat, ready to pounce.

"After we just killed all the monks and left you like this?" Anderis gestured at the mess weighing her down, "Why on Emys would you want to come with us?"

Cailix met Anderis's gaze, unflinching, and said, "Because I'll die without the monks to provide for me. I am a good servant and can earn my keep and I don't want to die out here in the cold."

"Truly the strangest creature I have ever encountered," he said. "If you were just a year or two older, you would have fetched a king's ransom as a whore over in Whiteport."

Her stomach turned at the thought. It turned at the thought of being near this man, too, but she had to be patient and bide her time. Planning her revenge would be enough to fill her stomach and keep her warm at night.

"I wonder," he said, his head cocked to the side.

He drew his knife and reached for her arm, twisting her hand back so the blood vessels in her wrist bulged.

"No, I can be a good servant, I promise! Don't kill me!" she pleaded.

He poked the tip of the blade into the palm of her hand then held the wound to his lips. She could feel him sucking blood from her palm; a warm, disgusting sensation that she would never forget.

When he was done he licked his lips and made a clicking noise, like the nobles did when they tasted the really expensive wines.

Abruptly, he stood up and exchanged looks with his man by the door.

"Get her out from under there. She's coming with us."

CHAPTER FOUR

The steamy air below the arena reeked of sweat and dung. Performers and graduates alike crammed into the narrow tunnels and staging areas, sharing the limited space with elephants, caged tigers, and a host of other trained animals. But the audience didn't know or care how hot or foul-smelling it might be below the arena floor. The dramatic effect was what they craved, the different acts of a performance surging up through the trapdoors hidden beneath a smoothed coating of desert sand.

Rather than building the arena from a valuable trade commodity like sunstone, it was instead made from the cheap and plentiful sandstone. Nor could they run gaslamp lines out that far, so torches lined the walls, providing just enough light to avoid animal or performer collisions, and more than enough smoke to add to the burn already festering in the lungs and eyes from the foul air.

Urus stood at the bottom of a ramp two levels below the arena, staring up at the hindquarters of an elephant contributing more than his fair share to the odor of dung in the place. He could feel the wood floor bouncing as performers channeled their anxiety into warm-up jumps and rolls, holding back their performances just enough to avoid slamming into the ceiling. Urus had already seen enough and the ceremony hadn't even started yet.

A group of graduates squeezed past him and up around the elephant, the metal grommets in their leather armor glinting in the firelight, their fresh new tunics swaying regally, untouched by the faintest hint of dirt or stain. The boys and girls paid him no heed. The only hint they saw him at all were the short steps they took to get around him on their way up the ramp.

He smoothed his clothes, garments that would scarcely qualify as a uniform. An oversized beige cloth tunic and pants hung from his sinewy body, the pants dirty and stained from use, his bare feet just as dirty. While he still fussed with his tunic, another bevy of graduates stampeded through the narrow staging tunnel, knocking him down on all fours into a warm mound of fresh elephant dung.

Being dead can't possibly be worse than this, he thought.

Still on the ground, trying to extract himself without getting more dung on him, he saw a well-shined pair of boots approaching with the relaxed, confident gait of a trained warrior. Urus immediately knew who wore those boots. He could tell just from the way they moved that they belonged to his best friend Goodwyn.

Goodwyn was every bit as tall and narrow as Urus was short and muscled. The few training bouts Urus had won had been with strength, while Goodwyn's speed and ability to out-think his opponents had left him undefeated since his twelfth birthday.

"Last time I checked, dung wasn't part of your performance uniform," Goodwyn signed after helping Urus up. Goodwyn and his uncle were among the few non-merchants in Kest who knew tradesign.

"At least you have a uniform," Urus signed, admiring Goodwyn's freshly made dark red leather armor with shining metal studs, the dye alone costing as much as the rest of the suit. "This is prisoner cloth. Funny how the acolyte uniform is the same as the war-prisoner outfit used in the reenactment."

"It's not that bad."

Urus knew that placating look, the awkward grin Goodwyn used every time he felt the need to apologize for winning some accolade while Urus fell further behind the others. He gave his friend's uniform another appraising look, noticing a bronze pendant hanging from his neck.

"That's new," Urus signed, then pointed at the pendant.

"It's nothing."

"It doesn't look like nothing. You've been turning down courtship proposals from all the most beautiful girls for months now. Did one of them finally hook you? What was it, did she beat you in combat or just soften you up with ale?"

"I said it's nothing," Goodwyn snapped. He scuffed the ground with his boot then, unslung a chain and shackles from his shoulder and held them out to Urus, his mouth turned into a grim frown.

"They sent you to shackle the culled?" Urus asked.

"I have to check the ropes and chains for all the procession lines."

"But that's a job for the new First Fist recruits," Urus signed, the realization of what was happening only hitting him after he put his hands down.

Goodwyn shifted his weight from one foot to the other, saying nothing.

"You got picked, didn't you?" Urus grabbed the shackles and threw them down. "Answer me!"

Goodwyn nodded.

"If you got picked, that means my uncle knows," Urus signed.

"Your uncle is the one who selected me."

"And you wait until you're about to put me in chains for the ceremony to tell me this?"

Urus couldn't believe that his friend would do this. He was used to being jealous of Goodwyn's accomplishments, but nothing had ever stung more than his friend trying to hide this from him like he was some weak, pathetic little creature who couldn't handle the news.

Worse, his uncle had taken the time to personally select his best friend for service in the First Fist, but still couldn't even finish one conversation with his own nephew.

"I'm not going to apologize for my achievements, Ury."

"I've never asked you to, but you could've told me. We're supposed to be friends."

"We may be friends, but I've wanted this all my life and I'm not going to let you hold me back."

The air went out of Urus's lungs, pressure squeezing in on his heart like a hammer-blow to the chest.

Goodwyn's eyes bulged wide.

"So I hold you back, do I?" Urus signed. He snatched up the shackles and clamped them around his wrists. They were props, but looked real enough to complete the illusion that he was a prisoner of war.

"I didn't mean it like that," Goodwyn signed.

Urus held up his hands, rattling the shackles in front of his friend's face. "I know what you meant. Being shackled to someone like me could ruin your chances to be the hero you were meant to be."

Goodwyn glanced over his shoulder back up the ramp, his head cocked to one side. Someone must have been calling him.

"It's starting and I have to go. Look, Ury, I'm sorry about what I said. Maybe after the ceremony we can—"

Urus cut him off before he could finish. "You go on, *hero*. Go and listen to the crowds cheer your name. Don't let a culled like me hold you back." Unable to hold back the tears, little rivulets carried salty dirt down his cheeks.

Goodwyn opened his mouth to say something but stopped. He shifted his weight, lifted his hands to sign something, and gave up on that as well. He stood there looking sorry and angry and even a little guilty for a few moments before finally running back up the ramp.

There Urus stood, covered in dung and chained to the back of an elephant, given the role of playing a prisoner of war in a ceremony to honor those talented enough to have graduated. All the magic that had somehow saved his life the night before hadn't helped him as a warrior, hadn't helped him pass the gauntlet or avoid being culled.

What good is a magic you can't use? Urus thought.

When they were younger, he and Goodwyn had dreamed of standing on a hilltop, overlooking a battlefield as victorious generals. Now Urus figured he would be cooking stew for the soldiers while Goodwyn stood alone on that distant hilltop.

He wanted to be happy for his friend. Goodwyn deserved the honor of being in the First Fist, and there wasn't a Kestian alive who could match him in single combat. But right now all Urus could see was a mundane future helping negotiate worthless trades. He would rather clean up elephant manure on the battlefield than be a translator miles away from the action.

The procession started, thankfully giving him something to do other than think about his future. He made his way up the ramp, following the lumbering elephant through the maze of landings and corridors. The first performers were already a few minutes into their routines before daylight hit him.

The stadium held more people than Urus thought possible. Nearly every citizen of Kest and every visiting trader or diplomat had crammed into seats with barely enough room for their drinks in oversized ceramic mugs made just for the occasion.

The smells of roasting meat, spices, and mouthwatering pastries filled the city. Most holidays could come and go in Kest with little pause or concern, but Kestians started preparing for the next graduation ceremony before the debris from the previous one settled. Were it not for the stench drifting up from his clothes, the aromas wafting into the tunnels would have made him hungry.

The younger warriors went first, giving combat demonstrations to show off their rapidly growing skills with training blades and staffs. Kestians didn't use shields, seeing an unarmed hand as a wasted attack. Instead, many of their sword hilts had defensive metal plates that were so big they seemed to swallow the arms of the little fighters.

So far no one seemed to notice him, their attention focused on the children performing dazzling feats of gymnastics and martial arts.

After the first few hours of the ceremony, Urus's legs cramped. He stretched and shifted but nothing seemed to help. He couldn't decide which annoyed him more, the pain in his legs or the boredom. Finally his elephant moved. It was time for the part of the drama where the prisoners of war were paraded in front of the citizenry as trophies of glorious victories from far-off lands, showcasing the strength of Kest's armies.

There was only one prisoner this year.

As the mock battlefield shifted, the groups headed off to the side while the solo performers made their way into the center ring. The elephant dragged Urus in a full circuit around the arena, assuring that every citizen of Kest got a good look at the boy who wasn't good enough to be a warrior—to be a true Kestian.

The solo performances were so much fun to watch, Urus almost forgot that he was watching from the ass-end of an elephant. A few of the most skilled graduates each got to give a demonstration in their specialty, some performing feats of archery, others showing off their speed or strength. Goodwyn, the most gifted warrior in the class, performed last.

As a pair of children from the earlier performances carried an ornate box between them to Goodwyn, the vibrations of the crowd's cheers and stomps went silent. Goodwyn opened the lid and withdrew its contents with the reverence one might show for a holy artifact. To the warrior caste, the weapon inside was as close as an object could get to holy. It was a *suzur*, a twenty-foot length of barbed metal chain, at one end a heavy spiked mace and at the other a long, curved blade. Goodwyn gripped the leather-wrapped wooden handle in the center of the weapon and let the chains unravel.

Most people just called the weapon "the stumper" in honor of the missing limbs that invariably resulted from the weapon's use, even by the most skilled soldiers. Suzurs were as renowned for killing their wielders as they were their enemies. Goodwyn was the only graduate brave—or foolish—enough to wield the weapon, let alone specialize in it.

He started by hurling the mace end of the chain to shatter pottery targets filled with bright, multicolored sand, each resting on wooden posts at different heights. The audience rose to their feet, clapping and clanking mugs in salute after Goodwyn broke three targets with one swing.

Urus had seen Goodwyn practicing this routine and knew what was coming next. The audience was in for a spectacle. All of the children who had performed earlier formed a line, each carrying a heavy burlap bag. Goodwyn nodded to the first child, who stepped forward and threw the bag as high in the air as he could.

This was the first day of his life as one of the culled, and Urus was getting a taste of what it felt like to have everyone in Kest ignore him while they stared in awe at the spectacle of his friend's skill.

Goodwyn wrenched his right hand and the chain lashed out at the bag. The blade at the tip sliced through and spilled colored confetti into the air, which swirled high above the spectators in the cool afternoon wind.

One line of children separated into two small groups. Then more lines appeared, then more, of graduates and even some of the battlemasters and other adults, who finally formed a circle of queues around Goodwyn like rays shooting from the sun.

Each line passed bags from supply carts inward to the circle around

Goodwyn and his whirling blade and smashing mace. Bag after bag flew into the air and Goodwyn cut through them all, even with a half dozen bags in the air at once.

He spun and rolled and turned his slashing blade into a dancer's prop, no one able to escape the lethal beauty of his skill. He threw the blade into the air and the bags seemed to fall toward his weapon, as if landing on the blade by random chance. Goodwyn was in one of his rhythms, a dance where he knew every move his opponent would make before they made it. It was what made him impossible to defeat and what made his performance so mesmerizing.

Urus was so enthralled by the performance that he almost didn't notice the two groups of First Fist slowly making their way around the outside of the stadium, heading away from the performance and toward him. At first the movement started as a flicker of red in the corner of his eye, but as they drew closer they stared back at him, the only people in the stadium not watching Goodwyn. He had no idea what the First Fist could possibly want with him, but it couldn't be good.

The closer they drew the more worried he became, his mind careening through a list of all the things he had done wrong that might warrant a visit from the First Fist. He thought of the cookies he'd taken from the palace kitchen; the ale he and Goodwyn routinely smuggled from the storehouse behind the Victor's Chalice; and all the other mischief the boys had a penchant for getting into.

His mind returned to the fall from the palace roof and he wondered if he had somehow broken a law, either by jumping or by surviving. Maybe they knew about his family's magic and the shaman wanted to interrogate him.

Then a truly terrifying thought occurred to him: Had High Shaman Kebetir seen him? Were the First Fist coming to arrest him for spying on the man's conversation?

His heart raced, his chest tightened, and sweat poured from his head as the men approached. He looked for a way out, but he was still shackled to an elephant's hind end and had nowhere to go. The rapt audience focused solely on the performance. If he made a move to run, everyone would notice.

"Urus Noellor," the first man to arrive said aloud, "you're to come with us."

Urus held up his chained hands and tilted his head at the elephant, forcing a smile.

"I'm kind of in the middle of something," he signed, dragging his chains as he made each word.

The men shared a laugh at his expense, pointing to the dung on his clothing and sneering at his chains.

"You play a good prisoner," remarked one of the men, who stood close enough for Urus to see and read his lips. "It suits you."

"What do you want with me?" Urus asked, relenting and speaking aloud. The men chuckled again.

"Not only does he fight like a baby, he talks like one too."

The insult didn't hurt. Urus had long ago developed a thick skin when it came to his speech problem.

The leader of the group leaned in so close to Urus's face that he could smell the spicy meal the man had just eaten on his breath. "Boy," he said, "if it were up to me I would drag you and all the other culled outside the city walls, bury you neck-deep in the dunes, and let the crows feast on your eyes."

Urus swallowed, wondering if this man had been responsible for what happened to the last boy to be culled.

"But instead we've been ordered to fetch your worthless hide, willing or no. So you're coming with us."

"I beg to differ," shouted Battlemaster Guren, hopping a wall and stepping out of the center ring.

"This is First Fist business, Guren, do not interfere," shouted one of the soldiers. His gaze, still fixed on Urus, held nothing but contempt and disgust.

"I don't care if it's your business or the goddess Ishimani's business, this boy has yet to be culled and you'll not take him," ordered Guren, towering over the two smaller soldiers in his polished armor, brandishing one of the most jewel-encrusted swords in the arena. Battlemaster Guren was outranked only by Uncle Aegaz, Kebetir, and the emperor himself.

"Then cull him so we can get this over with and back to the celebration," snorted the leader of the group.

Guren nodded, strode over to one of the many ceremonial pyres burning throughout the arena, and pulled a metal rod from the fire.

Urus blanched.

It was a branding iron.

"Off with your shirt, crowfeed," snarled Guren.

Unsure of what to do next, Urus held up his hands, jiggling the chains.

"Funny boy, eh?" Guren snapped. "Take his damn shirt off."

The First Fist soldiers ripped off Urus's shirt, re-opening his stinging gauntlet wounds as it tore.

"That's better," Guren said, standing in front of Urus. "On his knees."

The soldiers kicked the back of Urus's knees, and he dropped like a stone, a cloud of dust billowing up around him as he landed. The vibrations from the crowd had stopped. Goodwyn had finished his performance and all eyes in the stadium were fixed upon Urus.

Guren held up the branding iron, a circular symbol that contained four inward-pointed triangles and another circle within it: the symbol of the culled.

"Urus Noellor, I pronounce you culled. Hereafter you are not a man, you are not a boy, not a soldier, not a citizen. You do not exist and have no rights or privileges in this city. Like the captured war prisoner you portray, you will be fed and clothed and sheltered and nothing more, hereafter a burden on those in this city who perform their proper Kestian duties."

Urus closed his eyes, clenching his teeth and fists. He knew what was coming next and imagined it might be more painful than surviving a fall from a rooftop.

Guren pressed the red-hot branding iron into Urus's chest. For an instant he felt just pressure, then a searing sting, then unbearable scorching heat. He smelled the skin rupture and burn, saw the hair on his chest catch fire, smolder, and give off a noxious smoke. He was glad that he couldn't hear the sound of his own scream.

"Now you can take him," Guren said, tossing the iron aside and walking away.

Urus's eyes rolled up into his skull, his mouth sagged open, and the world faded into darkness.

CHAPTER FIVE

Urus awoke to a myriad bright, multicolored lights and fuzzy shapes, his eyes unable to focus. His knees hurt and dried blood clung to them, but his chest hurt more.

The memory of the First Fist coming for him flooded his mind, shocking his blurred vision into crystal clarity. He remembered Guren searing his chest with the branding iron, remembered the pain right up until he passed out, unable to bear it.

Gingerly touching his chest, he found that it had been smeared with a foul-smelling mud, probably made by the shamans—they were always trying out new muds and pastes that they claimed could cure everything from headaches to broken limbs. But there was nothing this mud could do to change his situation or dull the pain, no matter how pungent the odor.

All eyes in the room were upon him. He stood and lifted his head. He was in a room crowded with people, all staring at the spectacle of his burnt, bare chest and wrinkling their noses at the stench. Urus couldn't blame them. He didn't know which smelled worse—the burn or the mud. At least most of the dung had been removed when the First Fist tore his shirt.

This was no ordinary collection of random gawkers, however. Ogling Urus were the most powerful men and women in the city. They filled a large square chamber, most wearing their full combat gear. Even the shamans wore their decorative feathers and bone necklaces.

To his left stood his uncle and to his right a collection of members of the First Fist and equally high-ranking members of the shaman caste.

In the center of the room knelt a man who was as tall on his knees as many of those standing upright, his strange gray skin highlighted by his bald head and a thin shock of white hair springing from his chin like the last remnant of a once-proud beard. He wore a peculiar blue woolen shirt that rippled in waves like the slopes of sand dunes, the shirt covered by a long, simple woolen cloak. His hands were bound behind his back and to his ankles with thick rope.

Aegaz signed, "Are you all right?"

Urus nodded tentatively. There was nothing all right about him or his situation, but he put on a brave front for the sake of those watching. He might not be a warrior, but he could still pretend to be as brave as one.

Fear and panic hit him in waves, his heart pounding. Instinctively he searched for the nearest exit, the panic doubling when he could find no obvious doors or windows, just solid sunstone not yet glowing from the sun's descent into night.

The focus in the room shifted to the back as a piece of the wall detached itself and receded, allowing a tall man with shoulder-length gray hair to step through, his body covered in bright red plate-mail armor, a thin cape hanging to the floor behind him. The gathered crowd dropped to one knee and bowed their heads, their gaze fixed on the floor in front of them, an elbow resting on the other knee. Urus painfully followed suit.

Emperor Kaled had arrived. As close as his uncle was to the man, Urus had only seen him a few times in his life.

"Your Imperial Majesty," Aegaz began, still kneeling and making sure Urus could see his lips move, "this is hardly a matter that requires your attendance. We can interrogate the prisoner without posing any risk to you."

Kaled eyed Aegaz, his face wrinkled with age and scarred with the marks of countless battles. Even at his age, the man had never lost a duel, not even to Aegaz.

"I will decide what is and is not of import to me, Commander."

Aegaz bowed. "As you wish, Majesty."

Kaled waved his hand. "Proceed."

The assembled company stood. Relief washed over Urus as everyone looked away from him and to the prisoner. High Shaman Kebetir stepped out of a rift in the throng of important-looking people and stepped toward Urus, brilliant feathers hanging from the hair in his topknot.

As Urus and Kebetir locked gazes, he wondered if he had been caught, if the shaman knew it was he who had been eavesdropping in that hallway the night before.

"What's happening?" Urus signed to his uncle, focusing on him and trying to ignore everything else in the room.

"This is madness. This *culled* creature has no business here," Kebetir protested, his decorative feathers flapping as he waved his arms.

"You know we need him here, Kebetir," Aegaz said.

"Urus," he signed, "we found this man in the dungeons. The guards tried to subdue him, and the shamans shot enough darts in him to put an elephant to sleep. That just slowed him down enough so we could capture him."

"If the First Fist hadn't gotten in our way, we would have taken him ourselves," Kebetir protested.

The emperor watched the exchange with a distant look, seemingly unaffected by the tension between the warrior and the shaman castes.

"This is why you had to leave last night, and why you weren't at the culling?" Urus signed.

Aegaz nodded. But Urus didn't care about prisoners or anything else to do with his uncle's job. His uncle had promised to be there and he broke that promise.

"Stop coddling the brat and put him to work; important matters await," Kebetir said, eyes darting tentatively between Aegaz and the emperor.

Uncle Aegaz had always said that what he and the others did in the emperor's court every day was like a game, a game with very high stakes. Urus didn't understand this game. He just wanted to get out, to get out of Kest and away from the shame.

"The point is that he doesn't seem to speak any languages we know," Aegaz signed. "I showed him some tradesign, and he replied in an old dialect from Orda. All I could manage to understand was when he spelled his name, Murin."

"Orda? We haven't seen a trader from that far south in years," Urus signed, the conversation starting to take his mind off the officers in the room and the throbbing pain from the burn on his chest.

"We need you to translate for us," Aegaz signed with a sad, apologetic look. His eyes never dropped to Urus's chest.

"Why can't you get Master Villus to translate?" asked Urus.

"Master Villus has fallen ill," Aegaz replied. "The poor man can't even get out of bed, and we're changing his sheets twice an hour from the sweats."

Aegaz finally looked down at Urus's festering brand, barely concealed by the mud poultice. He spun around and spoke to one of his men. Urus couldn't make out any of the conversation, but the soldier glanced back at Urus over his uncle's shoulder and nodded once.

A moment later one of the emperor's attendants arrived with a clean white linen shirt, the scent of fresh flowers and soap wafting from it. The attendant handed the shirt to Urus, who quickly put it on, glad to have the culled brand hidden. He didn't know whether they wanted the symbol hidden for their sake or for his.

"Your boy has the chest of an ox to fit so snugly into one of my shirts," Kaled said. "It is a shame one so strong lacks the skill to become a warrior."

Aegaz swallowed and clenched his fists but said nothing.

No one ever doubted Urus's strength, only his ability to use it to be anything other than a strong, clumsy failure.

"On with it then," Kaled said, breaking the awkward silence. "Ask this Murin what he was doing in our dungeons."

Urus faced the prisoner. The old man hadn't moved from the spot the entire time, his dark green eyes focused on the emperor.

Urus made the sign for *prison*, as Orda's tradesign dialect had no sign for dungeon, then the signs for *within* and *why*. Urus always thought it crazy that a language created for trade had so many local dialects, practically defeating the purpose.

"I was looking for something," replied Murin. His hands moved slowly, the huge dose of shaman sedative in his system preventing him from making fine gestures.

Urus turned to the emperor and signed the prisoner's reply in standard tradesign.

"No, boy, say it out loud. I don't know the tradesign."

"He says he was looking for something," Urus said aloud. Then he winced, waiting for the inevitable comments about his awkward speech, or that he'd been too loud or too quiet. Everyone except Goodwyn and his uncle made fun of it. It was the reason he only spoke aloud as a last resort.

"Looking for what?" asked Kaled, paying no heed to Urus's speech problem.

Urus relayed the question and awaited the answer. It was a long time in coming.

"I must have the recipe for whatever was in those darts. The effect is…" The prisoner studied Urus, his brow furrowed, his green eyes moist. "A blessing."

"Blessing? He should be dead by now. No one should be able to survive that much of the extract," Kebetir said.

"Silence, shaman, I am handling this interrogation," Kaled snapped. "Ask him what he was looking for again. We don't have time for swapping recipes like handmaidens at the market."

Urus asked again.

"I seek a door," replied Murin, Urus barely able to keep up with the man's use of old and outdated signs. He wasn't sure if he had meant *door* or *opening*.

Those in the room exchanged curious and confused looks. Some bent to whisper in others' ears, but Urus couldn't make out what they were saying.

Kaled raised a hand again, silencing the whispers in the room. His face turned cold and serious. "Surely you could have found a door closer to your own home, somewhere near the top of the world from the look of your skin. Why seek a door in Kest?"

"This is ridiculous. Obviously he has no intention of talking under normal circumstances," Kebetir said, seeming as agitated as the emperor was calm. "My men can interrogate him privately using our own methods. We will have answers before nightfall."

"You doubt my ability to interrogate a prisoner, High Shaman?" Kaled asked, his face still a mask of calm.

Kebetir blanched as Kaled turned again to the prisoner. "Explain this nonsense about a door or I may actually let the High Shaman have his way with you."

"This is no nonsense. For me, this search has consumed the last—" the old man paused, as if reconsidering his words. "—many, many years of my life. Somewhere beneath Kest lies what you might call a door but it has many other names. A more accurate name would be to call it a *vertex*. It was put there two millennia before the first brick of Kest's foundation was set."

Kaled raised an inquiring brow toward Aegaz and a few others in the room, his trusted advisors.

"There is nothing below Kest but the dungeons and the cistern," he said. "The only structures older than Kest for a thousand miles are the pyramids in the Valley of the Dead."

Murin sighed, his huge chest heaving. "This is no ordinary door. It may not even look like a door at all. It might look like a slab of flat stone or perhaps just a boulder. It would have writing on it in a language no living person today would recognize."

Urus recognized that description; it was the stone Aegaz had described. If there was a chance he could resist going to that vault before, it was gone now. His mind raced with possibilities, conjuring up images of ancient books of magic and dragons and power and puzzles, just waiting for him to solve.

"And why do you seek a simple slab of stone, and why sneak into our dungeons like a brigand instead of asking our aid directly?" asked Kaled.

"I must find it before the Order does," Murin signed.

Again Kebetir stepped forward. "Highness, I must protest. All this talk of doors and ancient ruins is madness. This prisoner is beyond your capabilities. Please, let me take him and use a special potion on him so—"

Kaled cut him off with a sweep of his hand. "One more interruption from you, shaman, and I will make sure that you are taught your place."

Kaled returned his focus to Murin. "What order?"

"The Order of the Sanguine Crystal," Murin began, having to spell out much of the phrase because the old tradesign dialect simply lacked the right words. "They are all that remain of a race of people called the Ibumai, but most historical texts simply call them blood mages."

Urus watched Kebetir's eyes grow wide at the mention of blood mages.

He said those words last night, Urus thought. Had the shaman's frustration and interruptions all been intended to keep the prisoner from mentioning them?

"I have never heard of these blood mages," said Kaled.

Urus began signing Kaled's words, as he had been doing throughout the interrogation, his heart beating hard in his chest, his skin slick with sweat. Between his worry over eavesdropping on Kebetir and the insatiable need to get inside that vault and see those journals, he could scarcely breathe.

As he signed the words for *blood* and *mage*, his fingertips grew warm and thin blue arcs of light shot from fingernail to fingernail, creating an eerie azure spiderweb.

He stopped short. Murin stared at him, a single, white eyebrow raised.

The warmth and the blue light—it was the same blue light that had saved him from jumping off the palace roof, the same light that his uncle said was some kind of family magic.

Had anyone else seen it?

Murin addressed the emperor as he signed. "You would not have heard of them. The Ibumai were believed extinct over a thousand years ago. The Order is all that remains of their kind. They are a fanatical people, and their mere existence poses a danger to the entire world."

"What would such supposedly dangerous people want with a door? You do realize how ridiculous this all sounds."

Murin nodded. "It is what it is. I must find the vertex before they come. It must be moved before they can destroy it."

Kaled shook his head and turned to Aegaz. "What do you make of all this nonsense about doors and mages, Commander?"

Urus watched as Aegaz scanned the crowd, his gaze resting on Kebetir. There was definitely something very strange going on with that shaman and Aegaz knew what it was. Urus could barely hold still. He needed to talk to his uncle and go find that vault.

"I've never heard anything like it, sire," Aegaz said, making sure Urus could see his lips as he spoke.

"If the Order destroys the vertices, it will be the end of our world and countless others," Murin signed.

"Countless others? What does that mean?" Kaled asked.

Before Urus could sign Kaled's words, the door to the chamber burst open and a pair of scouts cloaked in sand-colored fabric raced through the crowd. They skidded to a halt before the emperor, dropping to one knee.

"You had better have good reason for interrupting," said the emperor.

"Majesty, this couldn't wait," said the first scout, panting.

"Report," Aegaz commanded.

The scout turned to Aegaz and gave a slight nod. "Commander, the fires of an approaching host were spotted on the horizon to the east."

"How big a host?" Aegaz asked.

"Three blades, maybe more," replied the scout.

That's not so many, Urus thought. *A group that small won't even get close enough to Kest to see the gates.* The Kestian army was divided into groups called Blades and Fists, a fist being a group of fifty soldiers and twenty Fists to a Blade.

Kaled straightened. "What fool would bring such a small army to attack Kest, especially from the east?"

"Majesty, there's more," said the second scout.

"Out with it," Kaled urged.

"There are three other armies. One approaching by boat on the river, sailing south toward us. The other two approach from the south and west. They come at us on all fronts."

"How many?" Kaled asked.

Murin sagged and shook his head. The scouts exchanged uncomfortable looks.

"How many?" Kaled demanded again.

"From the fires and ships we could see, we guess maybe a hundred blades. There could be more beyond the horizon we couldn't mark."

"That's twice the population of this city," Aegaz muttered.

Urus had never seen anything approaching fear on his uncle's face before, but his wide eyes said everything. Kest had never been taken, and it was a city filled to the brim with the most fierce warriors in the world, but it had never before faced an attack from so many enemies on all sides.

Kaled pointed to Aegaz, his mouth set in a grim line, "The defense of Kest is in your hands. Do what you must to get everyone ready, then meet me at the command post as soon as you can."

Aegaz nodded, then spun toward his second in command. "Avery, wake everyone up, sound every bell, open the armories. Within thirty minutes I want every cook and cobbler in Kest wielding our best steel. Understood?"

The lieutenant bowed, thrust a clenched fist to his chest, and darted from the room. A moment later, a cacophony erupted that Urus was glad he couldn't hear. Men and women barked orders, arms waved, and people raced in all directions with clear purpose. He sighed. These were warriors, real warriors, and they all knew what needed to be done to defend the city and defeat their enemies.

"Get the prisoner into the dungeon; we will pick this up later. We will show these enemies why no one has ever been foolish enough to lay siege to my city," Kaled said, then swept from the room.

Two guards grabbed Murin and dragged him across the floor, much the same way they had dragged Urus into the room.

Aegaz dodged the oncoming crowd to stand in front of Urus.

"Urus, you need to talk to the prisoner again," he signed. "If he knows what that stone slab is in the vault then he might know about our magic."

"Kebetir knew about the blood mages," Urus blurted, only partially aware of what his uncle had said.

"What?"

"I was reading Kebetir's lips last night, and—"

Aegaz cut him off. "I've warned you about eavesdropping before."

"This is important," Urus pleaded. "Kebetir was talking to someone about blood mages, last night, before anyone interrogated the prisoner."

Aegaz scanned the room, checking to see if anyone was watching their conversation, even though no one else in the room knew tradesign.

"I've been suspicious of that man for a long time, and he has resented our control of this city for years. He wants a shaman on the throne, not a warrior."

Aegaz watched the door. Urus followed his gaze. Murin had pulled away from the guards and was yelling to the departing emperor.

"This is the work of the Order! They bring the armies to your city. You must not let them destroy the vertex!" he shouted. It took a moment before Urus realized why he had been able to read the gray man's lips. Murin had shouted in perfectly lip-readable Kestian.

As the guards regained control of their prisoner, Aegaz told Urus, "Find out what he knows about the stone. If Kebetir is in league with these blood mages, and they're after the stone, then we have to stop them no matter what."

Urus nodded.

"I'm counting on you," Aegaz signed.

That's what scared him most. More than the blood mages, more than Kebetir, Urus feared disappointing his uncle.

Chapter Six

"Where are we going?" Cailix asked, trudging through the fresh coating of snow on the road, hugging her heavy wool cloak tight to keep warm. She couldn't help but stare at Anderis's sandaled feet, which despite walking for several hours in snow hadn't succumbed to frostbite. He seemed immune to the cold.

"What does it matter so long as we continue to move away from that blight of a city?" Anderis replied with a wave back at the barren, white landscape dotted with dwarf willows and tundra pine that separated the travelers from Naredis. Anderis's companion had gone ahead hours ago, though Cailix didn't know why. It bothered her that she didn't know where the man was or why he had gone.

"I just like to know where we're going," Cailix said. She looked back the way they came, up at the distant peak of Mount Kebel, its steady plume of foul-smelling smoke ever rising into the clouds. "I want to know what's coming next."

"I'll bet you do," said Anderis with a smile, puffs of steamy breath escaping from his nose. "Keep up, I have important business to attend."

With the sun unable to penetrate the thick clouds and fog at the top of the world, telling direction by the rising or setting sun was impossible. Cailix knew they were headed south by their slow, winding descent out of the mountain range. Jagged, rising peaks and impassable glaciers blocked all other directions.

They plodded on through the cold and harsh wind for another several hours until at last Anderis stopped short, holding up a closed fist. Several times she tried to make conversation, asking him questions about his power and, more specifically, why his bones seemed to snap like dry kindling at one moment and then be strong as steel the next. Anderis answered none of her questions.

"Don't move," he whispered after a long, silent period of slogging down the road.

"Why not?" Cailix replied, not bothering to whisper.

Teacher or jailor, no matter what he is I won't let him control me. Not completely, she thought.

Anderis flashed her a big smile. It seemed forced and artificial, like all of his emotions.

"Because it is time for your first lesson," he said, still grinning.

They stood in the center of a shallow depression in the snow, the faint tracks of wagon wheels the only hint that the road even existed. The permafrost spread out in all directions, interrupted only by short, fat evergreens and tiny shrubs.

"I know you felt the call of the blood," he began. "Back in the monastery I saw it take hold of you. I saw the hunger for it in your eyes. You are as much a blood mage as I am, girl."

"I don't know what you're talking about," Cailix blurted, though she knew the man was right. She had felt it. The smell of freshly spilled blood had called to her like water to a dying man in a desert.

Anderis lunged, punching her in the face. He swung hard, the blow lifting her up out of the snow and throwing her back. She landed in a heap on a prickly bush. Thankfully her skin was so numb from the cold that she didn't notice the pain from the thorns.

"I am the teacher now, girl. That is the first and only lie which I will allow you. Lie to me again and I will flense you right here and leave your innards to feed the white wolves."

"I," she stammered. "I'm sorry. You're right. I wanted the blood. It was all I wanted. Nothing else mattered."

Anderis took a step back and clapped lightly. "Now we are making progress," he said.

She touched her eye and winced. It would be swollen and any number of hideous colors tomorrow. A tiny bit of blood dripped from her nose. It ran down over her top lip and touched the front of her teeth. The blood smelled like hot iron—like *power*. She licked the blood from her teeth, secretly hoping more would come.

She looked up and saw Anderis staring at her, a smug smile on his face. *Did he see me licking the blood?* she wondered.

"Look around, tell me what you see," her new teacher said, resting his hands on his hips.

She did as she was told and took in the desolate scenery. "Nothing," she said.

"That borders on another lie," he wagged a finger at her. "Look around and tell me what you see that is important to you."

She sighed, kicked at the snow and took another long, hard look at the dead world around her. She was about to repeat her previous answer when she did notice things, important things. These were the kinds of things she noticed everywhere she went.

"I do see something," she began. "There's a broken tree branch behind you that has an end sharp enough to use as a weapon. I can see the wagon ruts in the road even with the snow on top. The trees are taller far to the south so the climate is better there. There are two kinds of poisonous berries nearby and three edible ones. We are a half day's jog from Naredis."

"What does all that have in common?" Anderis asked, beaming with pride.

"It all helps me survive," she replied without hesitation. "Everywhere I go I know the exits, the entrances, the dangers and safe spots. These things tell me how I could kill you and run away."

Anderis nodded, ignoring her comment about murder. "Now close your eyes and tell me what you *feel*."

She did as she was told, again thinking this was a foolish exercise. Eyes closed, she listened to the snow-dampened quiet of the mountainside. She heard the wind blow and the beat of her own heart.

"Stop listening and *feel*," Anderis said.

She felt the *thump-thump* of her heartbeat. Before long it became the *thump-thump-thump-thump* of two heartbeats, beating out of sync. Without knowing how, she knew the second heartbeat belonged to Anderis. She could *feel* the blood coursing through his veins as easily as she could her own.

She gasped aloud when she realized what was happening. A moment later she felt another heartbeat, this one beating much more rapidly.

"A rabbit," she said. "I can feel a rabbit. I don't know how I know it's a rabbit, but it's a rabbit, and a big one. It has a strong, fast heart."

"Keep your eyes closed and point to it," Anderis said.

Cailix thrust her finger out without hesitation. She knew exactly where the rabbit was. "There," she said. "Maybe ten meters."

Anderis chuckled. "Do you know it took my last pupil a month to learn this simple technique?"

"You need to pick better pupils," Cailix quipped, opening her eyes.

"Indeed I do," he said, stepping closer. "Now for the real lesson. Why do we feel no remorse in the killing of these rabbits?"

"Because people eat rabbits," she replied. "That's a stupid question."

"Is it? You have remarkably little patience for one who has survived so many trials. Men kill animals for food, but also for pelts, hides, bone, all sorts of things. But man also destroys and kills without using anything of the corpse. Why?"

"War. Men fight wars."

"And?"

"Murder. People kill each other."

"Ah, now we're getting somewhere. Why do people kill each other?"

"That's another stupid question. People kill each other because they're mean, or stupid, or both. And some people just deserve to be killed," said Cailix, hoping Anderis would know the last bit was meant for him.

Anderis shook his head and paced back and forth for a moment before continuing. He seemed like a different person entirely when teaching, completely unlike the murderous brute that slaughtered the monks for a map.

"It is much more basic than that, so simple that none ever stop to think about it. We kill rabbits because we need to eat. We kill men because we need something from them, or they are keeping us from something we need. We fight wars because our enemies occupy the land we need."

Cailix listened, genuinely interested in the lesson now.

"There is no good and evil, no right or wrong. There is strong and there is weak. There is no bad, there is only *need*. If you have what I need and I am stronger than you, I will take it. That is the end of it. *That* is the nature of the world and nothing more. I am not evil for killing those monks. They had what I needed, they could not stop me from taking it, so I took it."

"But you killed them for that stupid map," Cailix growled. "You could have just taken what you needed and left them in peace."

"Perhaps," Anderis said with a nod. "Why did you come with me? What did you *need*?"

"I needed to survive and I wasn't strong enough survive on my own," she said, pausing to think a moment. "I wasn't strong enough to kill you."

"Excellent," he said. "Now for the second half of the lesson. We need to eat. That rabbit is meat. It being alive interferes with our needs. We're going to kill the rabbit, but how? You have no spear, no bow, no sword."

"I can use blood magic?" Cailix asked, eager to test the power Anderis claimed she had.

If he teaches me blood magic, I can use it to kill him one day, she thought.

"But what form? You could bleed yourself dry, using up your power to summon a fireball to burn the rabbit. You could conjure a storm to suck up your prey and knock it against the ground. You could hurl rocks at it. Blood is a rare, precious commodity and must be used wisely. How would you use your power to fetch us dinner in this cold, miserable wasteland?"

Cailix studied the rabbit. It remained blissfully unaware of potential predators as it chewed incessantly on a tiny bit of vegetation. The creature probably spent its energy foraging all day for the smallest pieces of greenery. It was a boring, miserable existence.

I would lose my mind if my life was as boring as a rabbit's, she thought.

Suddenly an idea occurred to her.

She touched her nose and felt a bead of blood form on her fingertip. It was just a single droplet, but instinctively she knew what she could do with even one drop. The droplet lifted off her finger and floated in the air before her.

"Wha—" Anderis gasped. "I haven't taught you that yet! How did you —?"

Cailix smiled. Confusing and angering Anderis amused her. Controlling the blood felt invigorating and made her feel powerful, and she liked that. She focused all of her concentration on the tiny droplet of blood. Then, building up all that focus and power like fanning a flame with a bellows, she released all that energy focused on the blood drop.

It shot through the air, covering the distance between her and the rabbit in the blink of an eye. The blood drop hit the rabbit in the center of its eye with so much force that it punched through the eye and burst out the other side, bits of eyes and brain splattering onto the snow beside it.

Without making a noise or ever getting a chance to flee, the rabbit simply flopped to one side and died.

"That was—" Anderis said, eyes wide and breathing heavily. "That was simply amazing. There are fully trained blood mages who cannot control their power with such precision!"

Cailix shrugged. "It just felt right to me. To survive you have to conserve your energy, in case you need more later. This felt like the same thing—kill the rabbit with the smallest effort."

Anderis stepped toward her and grabbed her shoulders, grinning from ear to ear. "You will make a fine blood mage one day."

"I thought mages were men," Cailix said. "Don't you mean blood witch?"

Anderis beamed proudly down at her, "I suppose you're right. I have never trained a female blood mage so I never thought about what one would be called. But, you *do* need a new name. Cailix is the name your weak, insignificant caregivers gave you. From now on I will call you Aerlissa."

"What does that mean?" Cailix asked. Seeing the joy this man got from teaching her showed his weakness. She now knew what pleased him, and so now she knew how to manipulate him and get from him what she *needed*. She needed power, and power meant survival.

"Aerlissa is a name from ancient history, from a war thousands of years ago. She was a fierce soldier and an even more vicious commander. The name comes from an ancient tongue long forgotten. It means 'bringer of death'."

Anderis smiled again, "Much better than Cailix, yes?"

"Yes, much," Cailix lied. It was then that she decided she would exploit Anderis's weakness. She would learn everything he had to teach, learn how to be a blood witch, and then she would kill him.

CHAPTER SEVEN

The gas lamp taunted Urus. It hung atop the arched entryway over the stairs, framing the darkness below, reminding him that few of his usual tricks for compensating for deaf ears would work in the pitch black of the dungeon.

He clenched his fists at his side. The dungeon was a rat's warren of interconnected tubes and hallways on four different levels. The only light in the dungeon came from lamps in sconces, providing just enough amber glow for prisoners to see their food and water. Any enemy attempting to get in or out of the dungeons might die of thirst or madness before reaching their goal.

How do the guards know where to go? Urus wondered.

He crept down the lamplit stairs, wading into the pool of darkness. Taking one deep breath before stepping out of the last ember of light, he stepped forward.

A hand gripped his shoulder, startling him. He jumped and stumbled back, barely avoiding a fall. After recovering his balance, he saw Goodwyn trying his best to stifle a chuckle. He was in full First Fist uniform, red sash hung over his leather jerkin, his suzur slung around his waist, chains resting against the rigid leather guard that kept them from slicing Goodwyn's leg.

"What are you doing here?" Urus signed.

"Helping you," Goodwyn mouthed. Barely visible in the murky light, Urus could see that his friend cradled a neatly folded set of padded armor in his hands. Two heavy spiked maces rested atop the dark brown leather.

"I don't need your help," Urus snapped aloud.

"Really?" Goodwyn flashed Urus a sardonic smile. "You're culled. The guards are as likely to throw you in your own cell as they are to let you speak to a prisoner."

He shoved the bundle into Urus's arms. "Put these on."

For a moment Urus considered refusing out of spite and anger. He hated that Goodwyn always made so much sense. The idea of descending into the dungeon alone really had been a stupid one, but it was worse that Goodwyn knew it.

"With that on you can pass as an acolyte in the First Fist, like me. We might be able to talk to the prisoner that way. They won't recognize you as long as your—" Goodwyn paused. "As long as your chest is covered."

"Far better than my plan," Urus said aloud, pulling the padded leather jerkin over his shirt, its metal studs glinting in the torchlight. The poultice finally seemed to be doing some good as the pain from the branding barely bothered him anymore.

"It was your uncle's plan, really."

Urus froze. "My uncle's? He sent you down here? He doesn't think I'm good enough to do this on my own, does he?"

"It's not like that. He said you had to get in to see some mysterious prisoner and that I could help."

"I don't know why I should be surprised. Lately you get to spend more time with him than I do," Urus signed, hands a blur in the dim corridor.

He picked up the maces, appreciating their weight. He swapped them so the heavier of the two was on his left, his strong side. Satisfied, he slipped them through the loops on his belt.

"Maces?" he signed. "Couldn't have brought something with a little more finesse?"

"I never took you for a finesse fighter," Goodwyn replied with a wide smile.

Urus gave him a look but didn't disagree. As jealous as he was of his friend and angry in general, he simply couldn't stay mad at him.

"Urus, I saw what they did to you," Goodwyn said. "During the ceremony. I—"

"I don't want to talk about it," Urus replied. "Truce?" he signed, then held out his arm.

Goodwyn nodded, grabbing hold of Urus's arm up past the elbow. They clasped firmly in the typical warrior greeting and then let go.

"Grab the mace end of my suzur; I'll guide us through," Goodwyn said, unraveling some of the weapon and handing Urus the mace.

"Who's going to guide you?" Urus asked.

Goodwyn just smiled and spun around, disappearing into the darkness. A moment later the suzur chain jerked taut, tugging Urus forward.

They ducked into the dungeons, and Urus's mind recoiled, the absence of sight and other senses almost too much to bear. For a few minutes he held onto the tiny scraps of remaining light from the lamp at the entrance, but that quickly faded until it was darker than the darkest night and, other than his grip on Goodwyn's suzur and the occasional scrape against a stone wall, there was nothing.

He focused on the smells to keep from panicking. He smelled smoke, tea, and coffee, all probably from the fires kept by the guards in the cell blocks.

They turned corners, descended stairs, turned more corners, and climbed back up even more stairs. Even with a light and a map, Urus was sure he would never be able to navigate this maze alone. How was Goodwyn doing it?

As he wrapped his mind around that new puzzle, he slammed into Goodwyn's back. His friend had stopped short. A finger pressed up against Urus's lips, and he knew instantly something was wrong. Goodwyn took his hand in the darkness and spelled into it, "K". Then he spelled "E". Then a "B". Two more taps in his hand to let him know he should be able to figure out the rest of the word.

Kebetir.

Kebetir was in the dungeon!

Goodwyn pulled down on Urus's arms, and they knelt together, careful not to make a sound. Panic threatened to take control of him. It was in a situation just like this that he had failed in his last attempt at the gauntlet. Unable to hear, Urus could never detect the other students sneaking up on him, nor could he tell if he had made a sound.

Goodwyn pressed his hand into Urus's chest. He wasn't sure if it was to help keep him calm or to let him know to stay still. Either way, he was glad for it. The touch of something, anything, down here in the dark was welcome.

They waited for a while, the darkness stretching time and making the wait agonizing. Urus's knees ached and his lower back throbbed. Sweat crept down his neck and soaked outward through his shirt, triggering an itch that demanded to be scratched.

He resisted, barely. Even the quiet shuffle of the leather armor might give away their position.

Finally, Goodwyn helped him up and spelled again into Urus's hand: *FAST.*

Urus made a fist and tapped Goodwyn's hand twice. He grabbed the mace end of the suzur again and Goodwyn was off, this time running at full sprint.

They ran fast enough so that Urus struggled to keep his breath. Goodwyn veered and twisted, knowing exactly when to turn and which way to go, despite the complete darkness. How many times had he been in the dungeon that he could find his way through it so well?

Finally a tiny bobbing light appeared in the distance and they swung toward it. Once the light expanded outward from a pinprick to a circle to reveal a hallway, they could make out the shapes of iron cells, a large fire pit below a chimney hole in the ceiling, and two guards.

They slowed to a walk, hoping to look casual, as though they had every right to be there. Urus let go of Goodwyn's suzur, resting his hands on his own mace pommels for reassurance, assuming the "Remig Stance" named after the weapon master who stood on the ramparts, hands on pommels, glowering at the students all day long. Of all the people in the palace, Weaponmaster Remig always seemed the most like he belonged there. Urus even tried to look angry and squinted his eyes like Remig.

The guards started as the two stepped out of the darkness.

"What's all the commotion? You boys know what's going on topside?" asked the first.

They must be wondering about the armies, Urus thought.

"You come to relieve us so we can get topside and do some fighting?" asked the other.

Urus and Goodwyn exchanged looks.

"Yes, we have," Goodwyn said. "You guys get to have all the fun while we acolytes get stuck on guard duty during all the real fighting."

"It's okay, boy," said the first guard, clapping Goodwyn on the shoulder, already on his way into the hallway. "You'll get your chance at real action someday. You'll be safer down here anyway."

The guards ducked into the hallway and left the boys alone in an empty cell block, staring across a cook fire through iron cell bars at the prisoner.

The tall man raised a white eyebrow but said nothing.

Urus spun Goodwyn around, unable to contain himself any longer. He had to know. "How did you do that?"

"What?" Goodwyn said.

"How did you get us through the tunnels?" Urus demanded.

"I don't know, really," he replied, looking a little uncomfortable. Goodwyn appearing uncomfortable was a rare experience. "It's like how I know where people are going to attack when I'm fighting. I just knew where the right hallways were."

"You just knew? That's your explanation?"

Goodwyn nodded.

"One of you open this door; we do not have much time," Murin said in such fluent Kestian that even in the light from the fire Urus could read his lips.

"If you speak Kestian so well, why did you make me translate an old tradesign dialect?" Urus asked.

"I only know Kestian because you do, and now the shaman drug is wearing off," Murin said, as if that should make total sense.

"We didn't come down here to free you, we came to ask you questions," Goodwyn said, standing tall, hands on his hips. He looked every bit the warrior of the First Fist Urus had always wanted to be.

"There is no time for that. The Order has four armies under their boot heels at your doorstep. To control four armies there must be at least a dozen Ibumai here, and they all want the same thing."

"The door?" Urus asked.

"It is so much more than that. We do not have time for this. You have to let me out so we can get to the vertex and move it, or at least protect it."

Urus approached the cell door, gazing into the tall man's dark, blank eyes, wondering just what his game was. Urus trusted very few people, always expecting they would turn on him, make fun of him, or exclude him from something. But despite every instinct and ounce of common sense he possessed yelling at him otherwise, Urus believed Murin was telling the truth. There was a sadness, a deep sorrow behind those strange eyes that just couldn't be faked.

Murin was holding something back. Urus saw something so terrible that the stranger couldn't bear to deal with it. It tore at him constantly, like a million poisonous bugs stinging his very soul, so excruciating it made Urus's own inner turmoil seem petty in comparison.

"Stop that," Murin said.

"Stop what?" Urus asked, still mesmerized by the images floating through his mind, as though they were inspired by the emotions Murin held in check so deep within. In his mind, he stood on a cold shoreline, buffeted constantly by giant waves of sadness, torment, and guilt. In this vision, wailing spirits surged up from the waters and attacked Murin, screaming.

"Stop!" Murin snarled, gripping the cell bars, sweat beading from his forehead.

Urus took a step back. "I'm sorry, I-I didn't know I was doing anything."

"You were within my mind," Murin said. "That should not be possible."

"I wasn't trying to do anything," Urus said aloud, suddenly self-conscious. He switched to signing and glanced at Goodwyn. "My uncle said we need to find the door and protect it."

"He did?" Goodwyn said, shocked.

Urus slipped the key into the door and unlocked it with a firm twist. As the giant man stepped out of the cell, Urus half expected him to draw a weapon or cast some spell and kill them both. How could he trust someone he was so afraid of?

Murin stopped and regarded Urus. "Have your hands had any more spontaneous emissions?"

"What does that mean?" Goodwyn asked.

"My fingers," Urus began, "I saw blue sparks coming out of them while we were in one of the chambers behind the throne room."

"Was that before or after you started drinking?" Goodwyn said with a grin. When neither Urus nor Murin seemed amused, Goodwyn fell silent.

Murin shook his head, marveling. "I have had a hundred lifetimes of days filled with nothing but empty time, and now on a day when I have none to spare, I meet a sigilord and a quiver in the same place.

"A what and a what?" Goodwyn asked, his impatience obvious.

"The door. Goodwyn, you must lead the way," Murin said, pointing back into the dark hallway from which they had come.

"Why would I know where the door is?"

Murin sighed, tilting his head slightly. He tilted it again to the other side, eyes flitting back and forth.

"The commander and the shaman leader are both in the tunnels now. Time grows short. You must lead us to the vertex, Goodwyn."

"How?"

Murin grabbed Goodwyn by the shoulders and stared into his eyes. Again, Urus's mind conjured up images of flames erupting from his dark eye sockets or Murin opening his mouth and sucking out Goodwyn's soul like the witches did in the storybooks. Urus angled himself to see Murin's words.

"Close your eyes and imagine that you are fighting. Your opponent is a stone with writing on it, the image of which is in my own mind and now in yours. Anticipate its movements as it tries to conceal its location from you. Follow those tricks to the source."

"I can't. I don't know what you're talking about or why you think I can do this."

Murin smiled, a look that seemed very alien on that gray face. "Now that you have seen your quarry, you cannot fail. Simply guess at every turn and we will find it. It is what quivers do; it is what you do now."

"This is stupid."

Murin ignored the comment and pointed to the hallway.

"Mace," Goodwyn signed. Urus took hold of the mace at the end of the suzur's chain, and once more they plunged into the darkness.

At first Goodwyn seemed unsure and tentative, but after a few turns he broke into a full sprint and they ran, presumably with Murin behind them, weaving and dodging through the dungeons. Urus couldn't tell if they were simply backtracking the way they'd come or taking a different route to some new, probably very dangerous, part of the palace's underbelly.

Goodwyn skidded to a halt, holding up a hand. Urus stumbled into his friend, and with grace that belied his size Murin rose up onto his toes and hugged the wall, his robe barely touching Urus.

"We're at the cistern," Goodwyn said, turning toward them. "There are people in boats down here."

Murin took a step and peered over Goodwyn's head, looking around the corner. "Loderans."

Urus squeezed between the two to get a better look.

The cistern was a massive natural cavern supported by Kestian-carved sunstone arches and pillars, the stone above drawing just enough sunlight during the day to allow the structure to glow below in the cavern.

At least a dozen boats moved over the shallow waters, rowed by men nearly as pale as the stranger Urus had seen arguing with Kebetir, large axes and swords on their backs. Most of them sported thick blond or red beards, long, scruffy hair, and a seemingly permanent scowl.

"We have to go back. We have to warn everyone," Urus signed.

"They can handle themselves, and they will have their hands full defending the city walls. We have to get to the vertex before the Loderans find it," said Murin.

"Who are the Loderans?" Urus asked.

"Northerners, from nearly as far north as men dare live. I cannot imagine what it took to get them this far south. We cannot let them find the door."

"It's on the other side of the cistern," Goodwyn said, pointing.

"I still don't know how you're doing that," Urus signed.

"And I don't know why your fingers glow blue."

"It was more of a spark than a glow."

"Children. The door. Now," Murin urged.

Goodwyn frowned. "How are we supposed to get there?"

"Let's take one of their boats," Urus suggested. Goodwyn and Murin exchanged looks of disbelief, but neither suggested a better alternative.

"What?" Urus asked, noticing Goodwyn staring at him, mouth agape.

"Nothing, I just—" Goodwyn paused. "Let's go."

They crept out of the hallway and waded into the water, far into the cistern. Most of the boats had pulled up on the shore, their rowers getting ready to enter the dungeon. They waited for the last boat, a straggler rowed by three Loderans.

"Wait until the last group heads into the dungeon; then we can just take the boat," Urus signed.

They waded further into the cistern, staying clear of the boats coming ashore. Urus could barely breathe as the water rose to his chin. He hung from a piece of jagged stone on the bottom of an arch, his mouth just inches above the surface. He waited in the dark water for the last boat, with its strong, veteran warriors, to moor, knowing that he was not up to the challenge. Murin could just stand up and scare the Loderans out of their wits while Goodwyn cut them in two with his suzur. There was nothing for Urus to do except watch.

After an eternity, the last of the Loderans scuttled their boat, hopped onto the carved shoreline and disappeared into the dark dungeon tunnels. Urus, Goodwyn, and Murin swam in slow, quiet strokes until they could touch bottom, then stalked up to the back of the canoe.

Murin held the boat steady while Goodwyn deftly slid on board. Urus clambered up over the edge and plopped onto the center bench with far less grace and poise. He flailed like a turtle on its back until Goodwyn pulled him upright.

There's a reason desert folk don't like boats, Urus thought.

Murin pushed the boat away from the shore with one giant leg and hopped into the boat as effortlessly as Goodwyn had.

As they set oars to water, making for the other side of the cistern, the canoe owners reappeared on the shoreline. They reared their heads back, bellowing something in a strange language.

The three picked up the pace, rowing frantically. The Loderans splashed into the water and swam out after them. Urus had never seen anyone swim so fast, especially men that size.

It took only seconds for their attackers to overtake the boat. Still in the shallows, the men leapt out of the water. Murin and Goodwyn reacted instantly, daggers sliding out of Murin's sleeves and into his hands, Goodwyn unleashing the suzur.

Urus froze.

His companions caught two of the men as they came over the bow, then gently let their bodies slip below the surface, dead before they splashed into the water.

The third man leapt toward Urus, axe high above his head, ready for a death swing. Deep within, Urus knew that he couldn't stay still. He would be dead and cleaved in two before anyone could stop the Loderan.

Act or die. React and you're already dead, Weaponsmaster Remig always said. Since Urus had already pretended to be him once tonight, he did what Remig would do.

Attack.

Steadying himself with one hand on the edge of the boat, Urus swung his mace up with the other. He slammed the spiked weapon into the Loderan's face before the man could bring his axe to bear. The axe dropped onto the water, flat-side down, making a splash that no doubt echoed throughout the cavern. The Loderan tumbled backward out of the boat, making an even bigger splash.

Murin reached into the water, his face strained. With a single, swift jerking motion he finished off the man Urus had so sloppily failed to kill.

War and battle were part of the Kestian way of life. Urus had never killed anyone and, unlike all other Kestians, he didn't want to start now, despite the lives of everyone in Kest being at risk.

"Some of them will have heard the splash," Murin signed in standard Kestian tradesign. "What happened to your oar?"

Urus blinked. In all the commotion he hadn't noticed it slip out of the iron ring and into the water. Surviving had been his only priority.

Murin handed Urus one of his oars. "Row, fast," he urged, signing to Goodwyn, who had managed not to lose either of his oars.

Goodwyn rowed, pushing on toward the far side of the cistern. Urus looked back at the shoreline near the dungeon, suddenly nauseous. He wasn't sure if it was the fight or the motion of the boat.

Attacking straw men with dull weapons was easy enough, but fighting a real man with a real weapon who probably had a real family was something Urus hadn't been ready for. Maybe that was why he'd deserved to be culled. All the instructors and students told him that he lacked the "killer instinct" and now he knew what they meant.

He was a liability in battle.

"How much farther?" he asked aloud, hoping he'd managed to keep his voice down to a whisper.

Goodwyn shrugged. "I'll know when we get there."

Murin chuckled. "I had forgotten how amusing it is to be in the presence of a quiver."

"Enough mystery," Urus said. "You're going to tell us what a quiver is."

Before Murin could answer, the cavern shook. Pieces of rock cracked away from the cave ceiling and crashed into the water. Jagged black lines spiderwebbed through the glowing yellow arches and aqueducts.

Urus watched in awe as twice more the cavern shook and waves formed in the water. He looked again at the far shore. Two four-man boats were pushing off from the dungeon entrance and were headed their way.

"What was that?" Goodwyn asked.

"Ballista. Kest is under siege," Murin said, eyeing the stalactites, their razor-sharp tips ready to plummet down and kill anything below them. "Keep rowing." He stabbed the water with his own oars.

Again the cavern shook. This time whole stalactites broke from the ceiling and dropped. One of the arches supporting the cavern ceiling twisted and snapped in two, taking half of the aqueduct with it, setting the water churning.

"None of the attacking armies have siege weapons that can do this kind of damage," Murin said, furiously rowing now. "The Loderans certainly did not bring catapults with them when they left the north. The Order is behind this."

They frantically paddled the boat to the far shore, no longer concerned with staying quiet. One of the boats following them had been destroyed during a tremor and the other was short a man and having trouble steering around the fallen debris.

"Up there, in that cave." Goodwyn pointed to a dark spot ahead, then leaped out of the boat as it slid ashore.

Urus squinted at the spot in the distance, but it just looked like a dark smudge on an even darker canvas of browns and blacks.

Murin swung his legs over the boat and stood up as if the water were just a puddle. Urus stumbled over the edge and dropped like a stone into the shallow water. Finally, on all fours, he managed to gain dry ground. He would much rather feel clumsy on land than flailing in the water.

Following Goodwyn's lead, the three made their way into the dark spot that did indeed turn out to be a cave, the only light the soft glow of the cistern sunstone filtering in from the cavern. Murin grabbed Urus's hand and pulled him further into the chamber. Urus lunged forward and tripped over something, hand scraping against stone as he fell. A cool blue light enveloped the chamber, seeming at once to come from everywhere and nowhere in particular.

"Where did the light come from?" Urus asked.

"You," Murin said, facing a slab of stone in the center of the room. Though only a hand thick, it ran from floor to ceiling. "Fascinating."

"What do you mean, it came from me?"

"You triggered the light. This chamber was originally built by the sigilords," said Murin.

"Once we get out of here, you're going to explain all of this stuff. You're not making any sense," Goodwyn told him.

Urus stood up to look at the slab, but his eye was immediately drawn to a shelf carved into the stone wall at the back of the chamber, a shelf filled with thick, leather-bound books.

"Books," Urus gasped and ran for the shelf, plucking the first book off like ripe fruit dangling from a low tree branch. He held it in his hands and turned it over, taking in that wonderful musky smell of old hide.

He tried to open the book but its cover wouldn't budge, held fast by a golden clasp. Chiseled into the clasp was a symbol, an expert carving of a circle, within it two hook-like shapes on top of a square. All the books had the same clasp with the same symbol.

"Open it," Goodwyn said.

"I can't, it's locked somehow," Urus replied. "I'll bet these are the family journals Uncle Aegaz said were down here. He said there might be clues about our magic in them."

"Your magic?"

"Boys, we are here for the vertex," Murin said, stepping between them and the bookshelf.

Still clutching the book, Urus stepped closer and examined the stone slab. It was covered from top to bottom in strange writing, carved with unbelievable precision deep into the stone and then colored with some kind of dark blue dye. For a stone as old as Murin said it was, the etched writing showed little sign of aging or erosion.

"Why do these Sanguine Crystal people want this door?" he asked.

"They want to destroy it and all the others. We cannot allow that to happen," Murin replied, running his fingers methodically along each row of writing, white eyebrows furrowed.

"There are more doors?" Urus asked.

"Five in all," Murin said, still inspecting the stone.

Goodwyn paced around the stone slab. "How can we keep them from destroying it? There are four armies attacking Kest. All they need is another of those tremors and this stone will crumble."

"Precisely," Murin said. His head jerked to face Goodwyn. "That is *exactly* what they are doing. If they bring this whole place down, they will not have to find the vertex; it will simply crumble when the chamber collapses."

"Vertex?" asked Goodwyn.

"Can we not be here when that happens?" asked Urus simultaneously.

"We need to move it." Murin leaned into the stone with his shoulder. "Help me see if we can slide it out of place."

Together they strained and pushed but the stone didn't budge. Eventually they stopped, worried they might crack or crumble it themselves while trying to force it out of position.

"I need a moment to consider this problem," Murin said, stroking his scraggle of a beard and circling the slab.

Urus took another look at the writing, then walked to the far side to study it. From there he could see past the stone slab, outside into the cistern, beyond the water to the faint orange glow of the dungeon entrance.

Uncle Aegaz was in that dungeon somewhere, and so was Kebetir.

The writing was every bit as beautiful as it was indecipherable. There were distinct units, probably symbols, but he didn't know if they stood for letters, sounds, or words. He hoped they didn't stand for sounds.

As he scanned the stone for patterns, he stopped at a symbol that looked oddly familiar. The lines carved into the stone were in the same position as the tradesign symbol for the word *open*, like two open hands touching, palms up, each with fingers outstretched, thumbs pointing in opposite directions.

He touched the symbol, and a blue arc surged from the symbol to his fingers.

Urus gasped aloud and stepped back.

"What is it?" Murin asked.

"My fingers," he said, pointing at the symbol. "They did that thing again."

"You must not touch anything else, do you understand? Especially not any of those symbols. The consequences could be dire."

Urus nodded. As he looked back at the symbol, again movement beyond the stone caught his eye. There, far away on the shore at the dungeon entrance, he made out the distant, but familiar shape of a man. It was Aegaz, running, splashing into the water, the Loderans in close pursuit. At the head of the group of Loderans, Kebetir charged into the water after him.

"Uncle!" Urus yelled, pointing. Murin and Goodwyn's gaze followed his finger to the shoreline. He watched helplessly as Kebetir leapt onto Aegaz's back, plunging something into his uncle's neck. They both went down in a splash, Kebetir on top.

"No!" Urus shouted, reaching forward, stumbling against the stone. A searing heat ran from the stone through his palm, all the way up to his shoulder. The *open* symbol flared bright. The brilliant blue blossomed, growing until it was the only thing he could see.

Suddenly the whole world was only blue light and heat and pain.

CHAPTER EIGHT

"Stay close and pay attention, Aerlissa," said Anderis, his hands clasped behind his back as they waited before the great iron door. Cailix had spent the better part of the morning following her new custodian from the surface through the caves below the mountain. She was hot, sweaty, and covered in soot, while Anderis seemed unaffected by the climate, his white garments pristine.

"My name is Cailix," she quipped. The only thing that infuriated her more than the uncomfortable journey was that insufferable alias.

"Cailix was the name given to you by insignificant fools who did not know your true potential. Aerlissa is a new name for a new person, a strong and powerful young woman."

"Yes, master," she replied in the way he liked. He was no different from the monks. All she had to do was figure out what motivated him and she could manipulate him.

Anderis gave her a skeptical glance. "Watch and learn, Aerlissa. People respect power, and when you have power, you are beholden to no one. With power, you do not have to rely on anyone for what you need; you simply take what you desire."

Cailix nodded. She had never considered what life might be like without relying on others. Before the monks she'd been in an orphanage, before that the ward of a minor noble whose territory extended only to the end of his farmland. She had few memories from the time before that. She knew nothing of the parents who had left her as a baby on the front steps of a church.

A cog in the center of the door spun. Then, with a great sigh and a belch of foul-smelling air, the door rolled to the side, slowly disappearing into a slot in the side of the cavern. From the size of the iron door, Cailix expected to see some giant or troll lurking behind, but instead there stood an odd-looking little man. He stood two hands shorter than she, wrapped head-to-toe in thick, soot-stained leather, a pair of tinted goggles strapped on top of a smooth black helmet.

"The assistant will take the blood witch to see the foreman now," said the little man in a voice deep enough to belong to someone twice his size.

"I've told you people to stop calling me that," Anderis said. Then he straightened his immaculate robe and continued, "Lead on. I am pressed for time."

The little man ushered them through the door and they descended further below the mountain, rounding countless spiral staircases and ladders.

"Have you ever seen a briene before?" asked Anderis as their diminutive guide knocked and waited for another door to open.

"If that strange little man is a briene, then no, I haven't."

"Don't let their size fool you. They are as strong as two upworlders, but their real power is building. We are about to enter the foundry. Pay close attention to what you see in there. The briene are clever beyond words and, with a little guidance and prodding from us, build machines most of the world has never seen before."

As if on cue the foundry door opened out at the top of a chamber so vast and tall that Cailix almost forgot she was underground. Lit by the red glow of molten metal, there seemed to be no need for lanterns. Stairwells and scaffolds interwove in a tangled web of steel and iron, briene filling every nook and cranny of the place. Huge cauldrons hung from chains near the ceiling of the foundry, their bottoms aglow with the heat of the molten ore within.

Machines spread out across the floor, contraptions of all sizes and shapes, some like metal chariots and giant dragonflies, others with shapes that gave no clue as to their purpose.

"This way," their guide shouted over the cacophony of hammer banging and ringing steel. He hopped into an iron bucket strung from a massive cable that ran the length of the foundry's ceiling. Anderis followed and lifted Cailix in after. Wasting no time, the little briene stood on tiptoes to grab the top of a giant lever and pulled it.

The bucket creaked into motion, rolling below the cable as it soared above the foundry. After passing over the cauldrons filled with molten ore, they drifted above an area where flashing blue-white lights arced between enormous steel tubes on opposite sides of a catwalk. A pungent odor like burning sand permeated the air.

Cailix ogled the activity in disbelief. She was accustomed to people who spent most of their lives indoors, but that was just to escape the cold. Never in her wildest dreams had she imagined an entire underground city of strange little blacksmiths and machine-makers. She almost smiled before she caught herself. If she let Anderis see something that pleased her, he could use it against her.

When the ride was over, they climbed out of the bucket and up a final set of stairs, stepping into the foreman's office that was, like everything else around them, clad in shiny metal. Unlike the foundry floor, the foreman's office had glass windows and soft chairs and even a desk made of wood, the only once-living thing Cailix had seen since arriving.

"The blood witch has brought a guest," said the foreman, a man who stood just a hair taller than their guide. He didn't wear the goggles she had seen all the others wearing. His eyes were a brilliant gold color and even seemed to glow a little bit. "The foreman was not expecting a guest."

"She stays," Anderis said, his tone firm.

It felt odd, hearing someone actually insist that she stay. Even the monks never seemed to care one way or the other if she was around, except for when the rooms got cold or the coffee ran out.

"Business, then," said the foreman, sitting down at his desk and pouring himself a drink of something thick and black.

Anderis straightened his robe, its bright white color standing out like a beacon in the dark pit below the mountain. He shot a quick glance at Cailix and nodded. He wanted her to pay attention. He seemed to enjoy having someone to whom he could impart all of his little lessons. He had been giving her lectures for the two weeks it had taken them to get from Naredis to wherever it was they were now.

Another weakness, she thought. *He likes being the smartest, most powerful person in the room. That should make it easier to kill him.*

"The briene have produced all of the equipment the blood witch has ordered except five buzzwings. The buzzwings will be ready in two days."

"And the manpower?" Anderis asked.

"That too. All will be ready in two days."

"And in position within striking distance of Waldron? We must attack in two days."

The foreman nodded. "All will be in place, so long as the blood witch has held up the blood witch's part of the agreement."

"I have. You will have everything you asked for in two days. I will hand it to you personally just before I give the order to attack."

"The foreman has a question." The man sipped his thick, black brew. Whatever it was, it smelled amazing, and Cailix was suddenly very thirsty.

"I have time for one and then we must be going," Anderis said.

He treats these people as if their only value is what they can do for him, Cailix thought, studying the briene foreman and his funny goggles, aromatic drink, and strange grammar. *Another weakness.*

"The foreman has placed scouts all around and below Waldron. They do not move to attack. There are no signs of excavation. They make no attempts to steal the briene's foundries and mines. This is not as the blood witch described."

Anderis sighed, then bent over the foreman's desk, hands clenching the edge tightly enough to scrape the finish.

"You stick to what you do best, building things and taking orders, and we will do what we do best. We have sources inside Waldron to confirm their plans. They *will* destroy you if you do not destroy them first."

"But there is no proof—" insisted the foreman.

"Need I remind you that were it not for the gifts and knowledge we have shared with you, your people would have starved to death last year during the drought. You *owe us*."

"The briene are indeed indebted to the blood witches, but—" the foreman said, unsettled, putting his cup down and pacing behind his desk.

"But nothing. That is the end of this conversation. You will proceed with the plans or we take back all that we have given. Then you can sit back and watch as what little remains of your people wither and die like cut vines in the sun."

A long, tense silence passed between the two as the foreman struggled with his conscience and Anderis fought to resist the urge to kill a pest.

Finally the foreman dropped heavily back into his chair and said, "The blood witch did not need to come all the way down to the Myddenhold to ask the foreman for a status update. All is and will be as the blood witch requested."

"Show me the device," Anderis said.

"The device is not ready yet," said the foreman, his tone suddenly shaky, his eyes wide.

Anderis wheeled on him. "I did not ask if it was ready. Show it to me now."

The foreman stood and walked to the wide panel of glass, through which he could supervise the operations of the entire city. Cailix didn't know what they were building, but they were building a lot of it, and fast.

He pointed. "Up there."

Anderis walked to the window, Cailix following, and they both looked up through the glass.

Suspended from a dozen massive black chains, a shiny golden ball hung just below the chamber ceiling. Hundreds of briene worked busily around it, poking it with their firesticks. Thick rods of varying length jutted out from nearly every open space on the surface of the sphere.

"The foreman does not understand this."

"The foreman doesn't have to," Anderis said, wincing as he involuntarily lapsed into the briene speech pattern. "You built it to my specifications?"

The foreman nodded, then poured himself some more of his black brew and returned to the window. "It will do as the blood witch asks, but the catalyst required to activate it…even the briene cannot generate this much power."

"You let me worry about the catalyst," Anderis said.

"The blood witch uses blood for catalyst. This will take a lot of blood. If the device is activated without the right catalyst, it will not reach full power."

"Understood," Anderis said, turning away from the glass.

"Is there anything else?"

"I will need the services of a few more of your men, for some labor above ground."

"This was not part of the arrangement. The blood witch takesthe foreman's forgemasters for the blood witch's foundry, making the foreman draw extra shifts. The blood witch takes too many."

Anderis bent over the little man. "I decide what is too many. Since you need men to make your deadlines, I will settle for one worker."

He shot Cailix a meaningful look. She didn't know what sort of meaning she was supposed to read into that look, but it definitely seemed important. Who was this new protector of hers, really? she wondered.

Anderis was the outsider, the only one like him for miles, surrounded by a city of people who could turn on him in a moment, and yet he walked among them as though he owned the place. Maybe this was another lesson about power and respect, or maybe just power.

Do they really respect Anderis, though? Cailix thought. *Or is it just fear? Is there a difference?*

The foreman raised his hands. "All right. The foreman will send a worker to the upworld gate to meet the blood witch, but when this campaign is over, the foreman wants the foreman's forgemasters back."

"Thank you, foreman. You will be compensated."

"The foreman just wants the blood witch to stop taking the workers. Or maybe just to never come back."

"I would like nothing more than to never see this dirty hole again, foreman," Anderis said, waving for Cailix to follow him.

They left in silence, weaving their way back through the foundry and up the seemingly infinite number of stairs and ladders until finally reaching the steel door that marked the edge of Myddenhold.

For a city, it seemed to be missing a lot of city-like things that Cailix would have expected to see. There were no inns, no houses that she could see, no schools, not even any kind of fancy building to hold the nobles or the lawmakers. For that matter, she hadn't seen any children either. Anderis was silent, staring up the cave shaft toward the daylight as they waited. A few minutes later a briene emerged and closed the upworld door behind him.

"The foreman has sent the worker to assist the blood witch," said the briene, giving a little bow.

"Dig a hole." Anderis pointed to the soft dirt ground.

The worker shrugged, then gave them each a questioning look before dropping to his knees, pulling two trowels from specially made holsters on his belt and digging. Cailix was used to seeing men with sword sheathes on their belt, but the briene wore tools and gadgets with just as much pride.

"Stand next to it," Anderis said as the worker finished, having produced a hole about two hands deep and just as wide.

The briene nodded and stood next to the hole. Anderis shrugged in his robe, thrusting his hands forward. A little dagger appeared in his hand and, with no hesitation, he sliced open the worker's throat.

He held the gurgling worker over the hole until his heart stopped pumping blood out through the wound in his neck. It seemed to take forever, and Cailix marveled at the sheer amount of blood that came out of the little man's body. The hole was now filled with dark red briene blood.

Anderis tossed the body aside like so much refuse and bent down in front of the blood pool.

"This, Aerlissa, is what power looks like. Never forget this lesson: The lives of those who do not have power belong to those who do, to do with as they see fit."

Cailix nodded in silence, horrified and in awe at the same time. There was so much blood, and that poor little man might have had a family, though she couldn't remember seeing anything that passed for family in the depths below. She could smell the blood; the smell of a cold anvil in a smithy. Even though she knew where it came from, she found the odor electrifying and breathed it in deeply as she stepped closer to the pool.

"So the workers the foreman sends, they're not actually working for you," said Cailix. She knew the answer, but wanted to know how Anderis would respond.

"Oh they're working for me, all right," Anderis said with a smile, an expression that looked alien compared to his natural state of concentration or anger. He dipped a finger into the pool and swirled it around, creating a spinning current. The faster it swirled the more the slough of blood changed color, from deep to light red to almost the color of clear water. "Just not the way the foreman thinks."

"And Waldron isn't really planning on invading their foundry, to steal their resources?"

Anderis chuckled. "Of course not. That is your next lesson: Find what motivates people and use that to exploit them. The briene won't fight for just any cause, but they will fight to defend their homes and their precious mines."

She definitely knew that lesson, and she intended to use it against Anderis as soon as she was able.

Cailix bent, gazing through the now-transparent blood. On the bottom of the pool she could see the ceiling of a white marble chamber, suffocated by ivy and hanging candles. A moment later a face appeared, an ancient face, all wrinkles and pockmarks and black mustache. The face appeared to be leaning over something, as though it were looking down the same way Cailix and Anderis were looking down. The effect made her a little dizzy.

"You have news," the face said. The sound didn't quite match up with the lips, and the water rippled as if vibrating with the speaker's words.

"I do, my Lord," Anderis said, bowing to the image in the undulating puddle.

The being's dark eyes focused on Cailix. "I see you have brought your pet."

Cailix bit her tongue, holding back a torrent of insults she had ready for pockmark man.

"The briene will be ready in two days. The siege will proceed as planned."

"And the map?" asked pockmark.

"It was warded, but I used a blood veil and captured the inverse of the map."

"A blood veil? Where did you get enough blood?"

"I had to take it from Mirol. A loss to be sure, but the map needed to be preserved," Anderis answered. Cailix thought she could detect a faint crack in his voice.

He's afraid of the pockmark man, Cailix noted to herself.

"There was no other suitable source?" the face in the pool asked, seemingly unaffected by discussing the murder of their cohort.

Anderis gave Cailix a look, then gazed back into the pool. "No."

"Because it was for the Woan Map, I will let you live, this time. Disappoint me again, however, and I will skin you alive and let all of your blood go to waste. Am I understood?"

"Yes, my Lord."

For all of Anderis's claims of power and control, Cailix watched him cowed by his superior. If she was going to have power, she wanted the power of the man on the other side of the pool, the one pulling all the puppet strings.

"What of our operation in Kest?" Anderis asked.

"There were some complications, and we encountered far more resistance than we ever thought possible, but all is well," said the older man.

"So the vertex has been destroyed?"

"Yes, the first ward is broken."

Anderis exhaled a sigh of relief. "This is heartening news."

"I am trusting you to deal with the others. Do not fail me."

"I will not fail, my Lord." Anderis stood as the pool grew opaque and then returned to its original color, the face of his superior replaced by still, cold blood.

CHAPTER NINE

Urus blinked.

He had closed his eyelids a moment before, when a brilliant blue light enveloped the world. Now, when he opened them, he stood on a smooth stone road sloping up along the side of a cliff, carved like a notch into the rock face, with wide columns of stone left along the original cliff face for support. The gaps between the columns looked like vast windows that opened out to the sky beyond, dotted with small tufts of slowly drifting clouds.

The damp and oppressive air was so hot Urus felt like he was breathing the steam over a hot bowl of soup, only this air held no aroma of soup, only that of thick foliage and warm, damp soil.

He found Goodwyn at his side, also taking in the scenery, looking just as confused and disoriented as he felt. Urus still clutched one of the books from the room with the stone slab, its ornate lock still clasped shut. He stuffed the book between his leather vest and the acolyte's jerkin, hoping he might find a way to pry it open later.

"By Ishimani's tears, Urus, how did we get here, and where is here?" his friend said aloud.

"I don't know. I saw Kebetir attacking my uncle on the shore. Then the room flashed bright, and then we were here."

"The commander will be fine. Kebetir doesn't stand a chance against him."

"I hope you're right," Urus signed. "I'm worried, though. About him, and Kest, and everything else."

Goodwyn ignored the statement and stepped to the edge of the road between two of the thick carved support columns and looked down. He turned to Urus and signed, "I can't see the bottom." He leaned back and craned his neck, looking up at the cliff. "Nor the top. Who builds a road into the side of a mountain like this?"

Urus thought about it for a moment. "If this is the only way in or out, and there's a castle up there somewhere, it's probably the most defensible position around, with even more natural defense than Kest," Urus said aloud, not feeling self-conscious about his speech when Goodwyn was the only person who could hear him.

Urus felt a pang of pain. Kest was under attack, and they might as well be on the other side of the world. He looked past Goodwyn into the crescent-shaped canyon beyond. Huge needles of stone rose from the invisible depths, poking through layers of clouds, impossibly covered in thick green mosses. A few of the needles even had a tree or two growing on top. Through the mist, dark silhouettes of enormous birds circled over the canyon. It was a beautiful sight, beyond anything he had ever seen or read about before—the air was so wet and everything was so lush and green.

So much water! There's so much water you could practically squeeze it out of the air, Urus thought. Life in the desert taught one to appreciate every drop of water.

"Where's Murin?" Goodwyn asked.

Preoccupied by what had just happened and the change in scenery, Urus hadn't even noticed Murin's absence.

"Maybe he's nearby," he said. "I don't know how it's supposed to work, but maybe the door didn't put us all in the same spot. Or maybe he got here first and started walking."

Urus studied the road again; it sloped down the side of the mountain to the left and climbed up it to the right.

"Let's pick a direction and go. Standing here isn't doing anybody any good," said Goodwyn.

"Up then," Urus signed. "If Murin got here before us he's probably up there, and if he gets here later, we can wait for him. Plus, someone up there might be able to tell us where exactly 'here' is."

Goodwyn nodded, and the two started walking up the road, finding that it took a great deal of strength and concentration to ascend the steep slope on the dew-slicked stone.

"So what do you think he meant by all that stuff about the doors?" Goodwyn asked.

"I don't know; none of this makes any sense. I didn't think any harm could come from a block of stone. But a few days ago I didn't think magic was real and look at what's happened since then."

"Yeah, nothing good," said Goodwyn.

The two were soon covered in sweat, their leather armor sticking to their bodies and making it twice as hard to walk. Urus still felt like an impostor, wearing the First Fist uniform. The slope was so severe that the road was carved into switchbacks. Urus couldn't imagine the amount of work that had gone into making such a thing. Cutting a road into a cliff seemed harder than quarrying sunstone to build the Kestian palace.

"What if they're not friendly up there?" he asked, mesmerized by the giant bird shadows in the sky above the canyon.

"Only one way to find out."

"Murin said the Order was after all the doors, not just the one in Kest, right?"

Goodwyn nodded.

"What if there's a door here, and that's why we showed up where we did? The Order could be on their way to attack this place, too."

"Or they could already be here." Goodwyn stopped to let the statement sink in.

"I don't like any of this, Wyn. This isn't like when we got lost exploring in the Valley of the Dead. We're lost, and we don't even know how lost we are or if we can get back or if there's even a city to go back to."

Goodwyn crossed his arms over his chest. "Kest has never fallen and it never will. When we get back we'll see the heads of those red-bearded invaders and all the others on pikes in the square."

Urus glanced out at the sky and the crescent canyon and noticed the birds again. He pointed. "Are those birds getting bigger or closer?"

They squinted through the mist. The dark, winged shapes were definitely getting bigger. As they moved closer, Urus could make out more details, like long, skinny legs and arms.

"Those birds have arms," Goodwyn said, echoing Urus's own thoughts.

The creatures soared on the hot updrafts, coming ever closer. Urus thought it odd that they never flapped their wings, only glided on the currents.

"Those aren't birds," Urus signed. "Those are people with wings."

"That's ridiculous," Goodwyn signed unconvincingly.

One by one, five bird-men pierced the veil of clouds and emerged in clear, sun-drenched sky. Each was clad helm to boot in brilliantly gleaming bronze-colored armor that looked far too thin to be real bronze. Their cloaks spread wide over their backs and stretched taut like wings.

As they approached the road, each reared up like a horse, their cloaks deflating and folding inward. Each bird-man expertly transitioned from glide to fall to walk, making the whole process look as easy and natural as a bird landing on a perch.

"They're talking to us," Goodwyn signed.

"What are they saying?"

"I have no idea; I don't understand the language. Their face guards being down isn't helping."

The armored bird-men gesticulated and waved their arms. Urus thought it odd that they bore no weapons, at least none that he could see.

"They're yelling," Goodwyn signed.

"I can see that," Urus replied.

"This isn't going to end well," Goodwyn started, pushing Urus down the hill a little. "Stay behind me."

Urus bristled. "I may be culled, but I can still fight."

"It's not that. You just need to be right there for the next minute. Trust me."

Urus didn't understand, but then he didn't understand how they had found the stone-door room, and he didn't understand how Goodwyn had managed to navigate through the dark maze of the dungeons either.

He took a step down the slick stone slope and readied himself for battle.

The bird-men's flailing grew more intense. Urus watched Goodywn's mouth moving, trying to placate the strange men.

Unable to think of anything to say, Urus tried the standard tradesign for "peace". The bird-men exchanged looks, then returned to their yelling, heads bobbing and arms waving.

Urus held up his hands, showing his palms to indicate surrender or submission. This must have infuriated the bird-men, because they stopped yelling and charged. The first two to arrive seized Goodwyn by the arms. The third hung back, and the other two circled around and sprung at Urus.

Urus pivoted to his right, facing his first opponent. The bird-man raised his gauntleted fist over his head for a knockout blow. Urus surged upward, grabbing his elbow and wrist. He twisted the man's arm back, carrying him backward, bending him over until he fell.

Without waiting for his opponent to recover, Urus whirled and caught the other man in the throat, gripping the soft tissue not covered by armor between his thumb and forefinger. For all that armor, the joints still had to be soft to let the wearer maneuver. Those joints, as the battlemasters used to say, might as well be giant bullseyes.

The second opponent dropped, grabbing his throat and gasping for air. Urus turned and kicked the first man in the head as he attempted to regain his footing. The other thing the battlemasters used to say was that men in heavy armor were like men wearing turtle shells; knock them on their backs and they are just as helpless.

Urus looked to see how Goodwyn was doing just as a glinting armored body flew through the air, close enough to his head that he felt the metal pull against his hair. If Urus had been standing a few inches further uphill, he would have been dead and likely headless.

Clearly Goodwyn did not need any help.

Within seconds, Urus and Goodwyn stood over a pile of rolling, injured bird-men, their armor shining on the outside but the wearers soundly defeated and bruised on the inside.

Urus bent and pulled the helmet off one of the downed soldiers, hoping that perhaps being able to look the man in the eyes might help. He had to hold onto the hope that this was just a misunderstanding and these soldiers weren't the Order or working for them, like the armies that besieged Kest.

The bird man's helmet came off easily, revealing the pale white face of a young boy beneath long, sweat-soaked blond hair. The boy looked to be a year or two Urus's junior.

"They're just boys," Urus signed.

"Your hideous face must have scared them into fighting," Goodwyn responded, forcing a grin.

Urus extended his hand to help the boy up, hoping this gesture wouldn't be as easily misunderstood as his first attempt.

Tentatively, the boy accepted his hand, and Urus hauled him up. The others managed to right themselves and stand, each removing their helmets. All five of their attackers were younger than Urus and Goodwyn.

Before anyone could say anything, not that it would have been understood anyway, four more cloak-winged men landed on the road, these bearing long, curved swords fastened to their hips. One of the new arrivals stepped forward, this one wearing several multicolored stripes of fabric across his breastplate. He pulled off his helmet and held it in the crook of his arm, a welcoming smile spreading beneath a blond, short-trimmed beard and mustache.

He said something that Urus couldn't make out by lipreading. A quick glance at Goodwyn confirmed it wasn't in any language they understood.

Urus shook his head, then repeated the tradesign symbol for "peace".

This time the leader of the bird-men shrugged. At least they could finally agree on something—that they had no clue what the other was saying.

He tried to speak again, each time in a language Urus couldn't read on his lips and that Goodwyn didn't understand. Finally, on the third attempt, the boys recognized Adosian, the common language of the continent of Ehmshahr, home to Kest.

Goodwyn and Urus exchanged encouraged glances and nodded they understood.

"Two boys from Ehmshahr are certainly a long, long way from home. I am sorry for the way my cadets treated you. They mistook your appearance for enemies," said the man in slow, broken Adosian.

Urus and Goodwyn looked at each other, wondering what might have antagonized the boys. Urus's gaze stopped at Goodwyn's suzur and the two full dagger sheaths on the sides of his boots. Then he remembered the two maces hung from his waist and similar daggers in his own boots. Compared to standard Kestian gear, the boys were poorly equipped and barely carrying any weapons. The pair would have no trouble being admitted to most holy shrines wearing those weapons.

We look about as intimidating as a pair of mice, Urus thought. But he noticed that even the adult soldiers only bore a single weapon, which seemed odd.

"No harm done," Goodwyn said, also in Adosian, forcing a polite smile.

"To you, perhaps. My cadets may need a few days to recover, though I imagine their pride hurts more than their bodies," the leader said as his cadets took up positions behind him, avoiding eye contact with the newcomers.

Goodwyn introduced himself and Urus. "We mean no harm."

"My name is Knight Marshall Corliss Tudell. Welcome to Waldron," he said. "Come, you can tell me your story on our way up to the city. We have a long walk ahead."

CHAPTER TEN

"Magic?" Corliss scoffed after listening to their tale. "Look, boys, I enjoy a good story as much as anyone else, but I am a busy man and don't have time to waste on bards' tales like this one. Magic is a fairytale, a myth, the bedtime stories you tell your children. I've seen a jester turn an egg into a chicken, but we all know it's just a trick." Corliss focused mostly on Goodwyn as he spoke. That was fine with Urus. So far he hadn't needed to speak, and that was just as well. He just wanted to find a way back to Kest and to his uncle and get out of this hot, strange wet place.

"It's the only explanation we can think of, sir," Goodwyn said. "One minute we were in Kest, the next we were here."

Corliss shook his head. "You didn't just climb down out of the Dragonspine Mountains, fly over two weeks of rough riding through the desert to Blackport, then sail four weeks from Blackport to the Gylder coast, then travel uphill through forests for two more weeks to get here—all in the blink of an eye. There's a reason only a handful of people in Waldron know Adosian, and that's because Ehmshahr is just too damn far away. Magic or no, what you're saying is impossible."

"How can you say magic is impossible when you and your soldiers fly like birds?" Urus said, unable to hold his tongue any longer. He hoped Corliss would understand, as even without his speech problem, his Adosian was terrible.

Corliss cocked his head and studied Urus, eyebrows furrowed. "Sorry, your accent is very different from your friend's and your Adosian is as bad as mine. We don't fly, we glide, and there's nothing magical about it. The cloaks have spines in them made from the bark of a tree that only grows at this altitude. When spread out, our cloaks let us float on the currents."

"How do you learn to do it?" Goodwyn asked.

Corliss winked and flashed a little smile. "Same way the birds do. We throw the cadets off a cliff."

Urus could not think of anything to say in response to that.

They walked a while longer in silence, the armored cadets taking up positions ahead of them. While the cadets might have been able to find updrafts to get back up to the city, part of their punishment for breaking protocol had been to walk the rest of the way up. In that heat, wearing that armor, the cadets must have been roasting.

"Cadets or not, there's no excuse for the way those boys fought," Goodwyn signed to Urus.

"It did feel too easy," Urus admitted. Even though the boys were younger and hadn't been trained by Kestians, it felt good to win for once. Urus rarely won his practice bouts, and those he did were usually by brute force alone.

Corliss glanced over at them out of the corner of his eye, watching their hands as they signed, but said nothing.

By the time they turned up onto the third switchback, Urus's thighs burned and knees ached, his lungs struggling to breathe in the thin, high-altitude air. Maybe this was why the cadets were so poorly trained; they didn't need to fight to defend the city, as most attackers probably gave up climbing the road before ever getting there. He paused, gazing up the road, amazed by what he saw. As the road ascended, the mist thickened until it finally smothered the road beneath a thick, puffy white cloud.

Corliss turned and faced the boys. "Surely the legend of the Sky Gate of Waldron has made it even as far as your homeland?"

Corliss was visibly disappointed when the boys shook their heads.

"The cloud above us is always there, except for a few hours a day in the middle of summer. The main gate to Waldron, the Sky Gate, sits above the cloud just the right way so if you approach the gate from the air, it looks as if

Waldron itself rests upon the clouds."

The boys gaped up at the cloud.

"Clearly not enough bards or traders visit Ehmshahr if you haven't heard of the Sky Gate. It is considered one of the most beautiful sights in all the world."

"Can we see it?" asked Goodwyn.

Corliss's face grew grim. "All in due time."

He turned back to his cadets and gave an order in their native tongue. The cadets bowed, their arms out to their sides, the tips of their helmets and outspread cloak making them look like giant vultures. They headed up the road, the cloud dulling the shine on their armor, then rendering them dark silhouettes, and finally swallowing their forms entirely.

"All right, now that I've sent the cadets back to their barracks, you can stop this foolish game," Corliss said in Adosian, facing the boys with one hand on his hip, the other resting on his sword hilt.

Goodwyn frowned. "What game?"

"You can't possibly expect me to believe that you caught some magic transport that whisked you straight out of Ehmshahr and all the way here. Though I must admit, the fact that you're from such a distant land adds a certain flavor to this attempt that I wouldn't expect from Noah. He truly has outdone himself this time."

"What we told you is the truth, every bit of it," said Goodwyn. "We don't know how we got here and we're just trying to find our companion. And we don't know who this Noah person is."

Corliss waved his hands, shouting something in a foreign tongue. Urus didn't understand a word of it and just shared a confused shrug with Goodwyn.

"Very well done, pretending you don't speak Erubis. Noah really has picked a fine pair this time. But it won't work. I'm onto your game, and the moment I turn my back on you boys, you'll try to slit my throat and send my head back to Noah in a Solstice Day gift box."

"Master Corliss, I swear that we don't know this Noah," Urus said, struggling with the words, unsure if he was shouting. "All we know is that our city was under siege when something...something magical, brought us here. Our companion, a tall gray-skinned man with white eyebrows, is missing and might be waiting for us in your city."

"A gray man? That's rich. Just admit it; you are spies working for Noah, the leader of the thieves' guild, a man who has been trying to assassinate me for years."

Urus had no idea what Corliss was talking about, but the situation felt as though it was about to get very ugly if he couldn't prove that their story was true.

He held his hands out before him and concentrated. He thought back to Murin's interrogation, when the blue smoke had drifted up from his fingertips. He thought back to the time he had jumped from the palace roof and the blue glow had saved his life. He squinted and clenched his fists, then wiggled his fingers and shook his hands. Eventually he felt the strange yet familiar surge of heat in his fingertips and he smiled, awaiting the light and the smoke, sure that the proof of magic's existence was about to appear.

But no smoke came, and no blue light emerged.

There was no magic. It had worked when he didn't know it was there and it had worked when he didn't want anyone else to see it, but now that he needed it to manifest, nothing happened.

"And what was all that about?" Corliss asked.

"I was trying to show you the magic that brought us here. I—I think it comes from my fingers."

Corliss snorted. "How much of a fool do you take me for? Magic fingers indeed. I suppose you arrived on the Gylder coast on the back of a dragon, then?"

"I guess if I were you, I would think we were lying too," Goodwyn said, looking crestfallen. He glanced at Urus's fingers and then hung his head.

"Hand your weapons over," Corliss said, drawing his sword.

The boys relinquished their weapons and watched in silence as Corliss strapped the maces to his sword belt, carrying the coiled suzur in his right hand. He handled the weapon as if it were a snake that might bite him at any moment.

"Walk up the road. You boys take the lead. If you make any sudden moves, I will cut the two of you in half. Just because you beat my cadets doesn't mean you stand a chance against me."

He led the boys at sword-point up the remainder of the road, the cloud gradually smothering them in its warm, wet embrace. For a moment all they could see were their hands, both blindly tripping over their feet, only to be hauled back up again by Corliss's steely grip.

As they emerged from the mist, Urus gasped at the sight of the Sky Gate. A massive pair of arched black stone gates were set into the ivory-and-gray colored mountain, a peak hewn into smooth walls by decades of meticulous carving, with jagged ramparts, narrow window slits, and soaring towers. Blue vines and creeping yellow-leafed trees grew up and over the walls and sprouted from spots of rock and soil carefully left unmolested. It truly did look like a city floating on the clouds. Urus stood staring until Corliss urged him forward.

As Corliss approached the gates they swung outward. Even though he couldn't see them, Urus figured there were lookouts on the walls nearby who had marked their approach and ordered the gates open. A group of armed soldiers filed out of the gates and stood talking to Corliss in their unintelligible language. These men were older, stronger-looking, and carried themselves like seasoned veterans. Urus did not want to get into a fight with this group.

The men cast scowls and sideways glances between Corliss and the newcomers, occasionally chuckling as Corliss no doubt recanted their wild tale of magical travel.

When Corliss waved them forward, they complied, coming to stand before the group of soldiers. Urus felt very small and very weak beneath their penetrating stares.

"I haven't the slightest idea what to do with you two," Corliss began, clearly irritated by having to speak Adosian in front of his men. "If you were strangers who just arrived here, you would be homeless and without money, so we would be obligated to hand you over to the care of the church. But since I think you were sent by Noah to kill me, I should put you in the stocks by the courthouse and let you rot there."

"But—" Goodwyn tried to interject, but Corliss held up a hand.

"Since you haven't yet tried to kill me, I have no evidence that you are assassins. You see my dilemma? I know you're going to try to kill me, but I can't arrest you until you make a move."

"We weren't sent to kill you," Urus said. His words drew curious glances from Corliss's men.

"Yes, this one talks a little strange. I've never heard the like before," Corliss said to the soldiers.

One of his men spoke up. The soldier's eyes had that warm, wet look that so many parents had, like his uncle's always did.

Corliss raised an eyebrow and studied Urus as though seeing him for the first time. "Pallis here once had a deaf uncle he says talked funny like you. You aren't deaf, are you boy?" he asked in Adosian.

Urus wasn't sure whether to answer out loud, to nod his head, or to sign.

He wouldn't get a chance to decide.

Up the road beyond the gate and in the city, amid a crowd of vendors and customers packed into a street market, a man stood out among the crowd. While men and women in brilliantly colored clothes haggled and traded, this man wore drab gray cloth, heavy black boots, and was drawing back on his bow, aiming an arrow at Corliss's back. He made no effort at all to blend in with his surroundings. Even from this distance, Urus could see the menace and intent in his eyes.

"Archer!" Urus shouted, realizing only after that he had shouted it in Kestian. With no time to repeat the warning in another language, he leapt forward, sweeping Corliss's legs out from underneath him and pushing him to the ground.

Urus didn't have to tell his friend what to do. Goodwyn was already off and running, driven by the killer instinct of a true Kestian. He had grabbed his suzur from Corliss, dodged to the side, and was now charging through the market, chasing down the bowman, unraveling the suzur a little more with each stride.

Peddlers and customers alike screamed and shied away, giving both men a wide berth. Urus rolled off Corliss, only to be slammed back to the ground, a heavy knee planted on his neck as the rest of Corliss's men charged off into the market. He couldn't tell whether they were chasing Goodwyn or the archer.

Rope cinched around Urus's wrists and two soldiers hauled him to his feet.

"I saved you! The bowman in the market was trying to kill you!" Urus shouted, again in terrible, slurred Adosian.

"You disappoint me. Up until now your lies have been so well crafted. I name you an assassin, then you knock me down so your friend can steal his weapon back and escape?"

The Knight Marshall stood up and his men dropped Urus on the ground before him, hands bound behind his back.

"I'm not lying! Look," Urus said, thrusting his head to the left, in the direction the arrow had flown as it sailed just inches from Corliss's head.

There, stuck feather-deep in a wooden hitching post, was the arrow.

"Well, I'll be dipped in pitch." Corliss spat. He issued an order with a gesture Urus hoped meant "release the prisoner."

The men didn't move. The faint vibrations he felt through their hands told him they were talking, and probably quite loudly.

Corliss repeated his order, sharply.

His men complied. As they untied Urus, Goodwyn emerged from the crowd, dragging a bloodied and beaten man behind him, three of Corliss's men following with their swords drawn.

Corliss shouted something at his men, clearly frustrated.

One of the soldiers responded, though again Urus was unable to make any sense of the language.

"In Adosian," Corliss said. He also seemed to make an extra effort to allow Urus a clear look at his face while speaking.

"I said, this man here," the soldier pointed to Goodwyn's prisoner, barely conscious and bleeding from both eyes, his nose, and mouth, "took a shot at you with one of those new bows the tinkers have been making."

"One of Noah's men?" Corliss asked.

"Without a doubt, sir. The scum even has the guild's tattoo on his arm."

"Noah wanted everyone to know who was behind this. That bastard is getting more brazen every day."

"There's more, sir," another soldier said. "Without the strangers here, you would surely have taken that arrow through the back, and this thief would have escaped."

"You're saying you weren't up to the task of running down one thief?"

"Not this one, sir. He was fast, like animal-fast. The boy caught him with his chain thing and had him beaten and begging for mercy before we even caught up to them."

Corliss looked from Goodwyn to Urus and back again, his face somber. He put his hands on his hips and paced back and forth, looking to his men for advice and getting only shrugs in response.

"It appears as though I owe you my life, and after accusing you of being assassins. I let my feud with Noah cloud my judgement and I apologize."

"Why is Noah trying to kill you?" Urus asked.

"That, young man, is a long story, and one I will share with you this evening after I take care of some business. The church maintains a small hostel not far from here. I will see to it that they provide you both with a fresh bath and something to eat. Perhaps then you can tell me about your gray-skinned friend with white eyebrows."

Chapter Eleven

Cailix sat in the corner of the small room on the second floor of the inn, knees tucked into her chest, staring through the darkness at the bed and the creature sleeping within.

So careless, she thought, a satisfied grin parting her otherwise grim face.

Deep in thought, she rubbed the bumps on her knees, scars left over from the burns inflicted by one of her former caretakers. She didn't know what to make of Anderis. At times he seemed like the strongest, most powerful person she had ever encountered, and yet he often made the most foolish of mistakes that even she, a mere child in his eyes, would never make. She was better than him, and she was going to show him just how much.

He clearly had the power and blood supply to have whisked them across the countryside with magic, but instead he opted for a tedious horseback journey, where he could drone on about the intricacies of blood magic and its uses. He thought himself a teacher, and her the rapt student.

Instead, she had been soaking up the knowledge, learning how to use blood magic not so that she could be his faithful apprentice, but so she could become even more powerful than the teacher, and end his life in the most humiliating and painful way possible.

She had never seen Anderis use his own blood for power, but she had been practicing it ever since that day she killed the rabbit in the shadow of

Mount Kebel. She bit a small piece of her fingertip and, in the presence of just the one drop of blood, all it took was a fleeting thought and the iron shackles binding her wrists liquified, dripping to the floor.

Two soft steps across the woven carpet later and she was within striking distance of the beast. He had taken her protectors away, removed her from the safety and security of the most stable home she had ever known. But in the process, he had also unleashed her true power, given her the means to fend for herself. Now, no matter where she was or how alone she might be, she would always be strong and safe, and that was what mattered to her most.

Fueled by her rage, in her heightened state she could sense the nature and strength of every living, blood-pumping creature nearby. She could feel the slow pulse of those sleeping, the weak pulses of the aging, and even the incredibly strong pulse of the horse in the stable.

She looked down at the knife in her hand. She wasn't even sure how it got there, only that she wanted a knife and now she had one.

Leaning over the bed, holding the knife inches above the quiet, sleeping neck of a man she at once despised for his actions and admired for his power and knowledge, she knew it would take but a twitch to plunge the knife into his neck. She could set his still-pumping blood on fire and walk away as though nothing had happened.

She had all the power, all the advantage, and she couldn't bring herself to use it.

A quick death while he slept was too good for Anderis. After all, she had more practicing to do, more training to wield and focus her power. Then, when the time was right, she would challenge her master and defeat him, showing him how powerful she really was.

Cailix gently left the knife on the pillow beside Anderis's head and walked out of the room.

CHAPTER TWELVE

The voices would not relent. They were everywhere.

Everywhere Murin turned he heard people talking and shouting, haggling and bickering. It was insufferable. Worse than the voices, though, were their *thoughts*.

Well beyond earshot, Murin sensed the minds of everyone nearby. It took too much concentration to block out all their thoughts in the midst of such visual and aural chaos, so he suffered through the endless prattle.

In every direction people worried about money, thought about sex, plotted against their neighbors, dreamed of greatness, and pondered a million more utterly useless things.

He should have stayed where he was. Back in his lab, with his books and his research, alone without another active mind for a hundred miles. It was quiet, then. Lonely, but quiet. It was an exile he deserved and he was starting to miss it.

He made his way through the market, the exertion of keeping the thoughts of the herds of simple minds at bay making him sick. He ignored the stares and sideways glances from the locals. This was the price for doing as he was told, for keeping his distance and not interfering. The world was as it was because of him.

He stepped in front of one of the few locals who hadn't turned away at the sight of him. At least back in Kest, many of the minds were shielded by some awful-smelling local herb they chewed like it was candy. Here, it was as if everyone's mind was shouting at him.

"I mean you no harm; I simply seek directions," he said. "I need to know where I can procure the most potent of your local opiates."

The confused man shrugged without saying a word.

Murin probed the man's mind, but there was no recognition there, no meaning associated with his words.

"Dens of iniquity," Murin offered, still unsure of what the people of Waldron might call such places.

The man shook his head. "Say what you need, friend, and I can point you toward it."

"Tell me where the most villainous scum of this city go to spend their money."

Shocked, the man took a step back. "You'll be wanting the warrens, then. Follow this street through the market. At each fork head downhill until you're going down the back slope of the mountain and into the first tunnel. You'll know you're there when you want to turn and run back."

"Thank you," Murin said, bowing slightly. He shrugged into his cloak despite the sweat and headed off in the direction the man pointed.

"Stranger, you may be a big grey slab of freak, but nobody in their right mind goes into the warrens without an army behind him," the man called after him.

"Thank you for the advice," Murin said without turning back, crossing the market in just a few of his long strides.

He wove his way through the city, at first trying to stay out of people's way, but it proved easier simply to charge through the middle of the streets and let the locals step aside to let him pass. These people had probably never ventured far outside the city and had never seen anyone who didn't look like their neighbors.

If only they knew he could hear their thoughts, the vile things they thought about his skin color, his size, or just the fact that he was a stranger. It was hard not to be bitter in the presence of such hypocrisy. What people claimed to be on the outside was never the same as what they truly were on the inside.

Except for the Kestian boys.

While Urus's mind yet remained closed off somehow, Goodwyn was a rare example of a young man with no pretense, no airs, no layers. He simply was what he appeared to be and Murin had to respect that, though the boy still held a few things back.

After a long walk on the slippery and damp stone walkways that refused to be coerced into a straight line, Murin finally stood atop a steep slope, gazing down at the entrance to a tunnel, not much more than a rotting archway below a run-down wooden shop.

Here there were no stone buildings, just darkly painted and stained wood homes that leaned inward over the street, lit torches hanging from sconces even by day to push back the fog that clung eternally to the back side of the mountain.

He didn't know how people tolerated it; the sun either piercingly bright or hidden behind clouds, the air so damp you could drink it yet so hot one might actually long for the winters of the north.

Thoughts of thievery, murder, and all manner of foul things washed over him like a rising tide of scum as he ducked into the tunnel. Amazingly, there were more minds crammed into the warrens alone than in all the rest of the city. For every mind bent on villainy, he sensed two minds filled with despair, clinging to hope for scraps of food and shelter for their children.

This was the other reason he had stopped traveling so many years ago. Each place he visited had a shiny veneer covering a festering, rotting core, just like so many of the people who lived there.

He had only gone a few feet when two armed men detached from the shadows and blocked his path.

"State your business or turn back, stranger."

"I seek the pipes. Opiates," Murin said. Such feeble minds, he thought, like little worker bees that mindlessly went from task to task without a thought or care in the world. "You will let me pass."

"Sure thing," the weak-minded men said, stepping aside. The only clue they would have about what had really happened would be a splitting headache when they woke up in the morning.

Murin had a chance to sift through their minds as he walked by, knowing what they knew, feeling what they felt. It nauseated him, but he had learned in his travels that digging through the garbage every once in a while could result in something useful.

He crept through the warrens, navigating the maze with ease, using the thug's knowledge as a guide. It took him longer than expected, as though the simpleton's perception of the size of the warrens was warped somehow.

He emerged on the other side of the tunnels on a vast cliff shelf, surrounded by sculpted stone walls. The plateau was filled with clusters of tents and ramshackle buildings spread out among a few well-built three-story homes that seemed like palaces in comparison.

Passing through a shanty town with open cooking pits, blazing fires, and barely standing wooden homes, Murin wrinkled his nose at the smell but finally found what he was looking for. It was a large tent with four thick stovepipes sticking up through slits in the canvas, the unmistakable sweet odor wafting out with the thick, white smoke.

He lifted a tent flap and stepped inside, nearly doubled over to avoid putting his head through the tent roof. A round, bearded man in brightly colored, loose-fitting clothing eyed Murin up and down.

Now this is a man with secrets, Murin thought, taking stock of all that remained hidden behind the man's bright blue eyes.

"I don't care how big or small or what color you are so long as you can pay. If you can't, then you got troubles, bud."

Murin reached into a hidden pocket in the lining of his cloak and withdrew three gold coins, tossing them to the den master. "I need a private tent and the strongest concoction you have."

Astounded, the man stared at the gold and back at Murin. "Bud, for this much you can have all my tents. My friends—an elite group of which your deep pockets have made you a member—call me Noah. Follow me."

Murin followed him through another flap into an empty, adjoining tent. Plush, multicolored cushions lined the floor. In the center sat a giant glass bowl with several hoses dangling from it, giving off little puffs of smoke, looking something like a smoldering octopus.

The owner bent to drop a black brick into the glass bowl, then stoked the fire underneath, also adding some water to an adjacent glass bowl connected with more tubes.

The people of this world never ceased to amaze Murin; endless in their capacity to invent ways to kill each other and themselves, yet so stunted in their ability to use that same ingenuity to better their lives.

"That is the strongest you have?" Murin asked, his willpower almost at an end, the incessant nattering of the swarm of minds around him chipping away at his sanity.

"Fella, this stuff could put a pair of horses into a three-day slumber. This is my best stuff, imported all the way from Kanzibur."

"Leave me then," Murin said.

"I'll make sure you aren't disturbed. The tent is yours for the night. Enjoy," said Noah, ducking out through the tent flap.

Murin lay down across the pillows and took a long, deep pull from the pipe, awaiting the blissful quiet that he hoped might come.

As the owner had promised, his eyelids grew heavy within seconds of the first pull, the din of the minds around him beginning to dull even with the second inhale.

For the first time since he had encountered the shamans of Kest, and only the second time in the past three months, Murin slept.

"Wake up," called the voice.

Murin ran the back of his hand across his damp forehead, disgusted by the sweat and even more annoyed at hearing another voice. He willed the voice away and rolled over.

"I said wake up, you oaf," the voice persisted.

Murin sat up, the effort making him nauseous.

"Shut up, whatever sort of hallucination you might be," he said to the apparition on the other side of his closed eyelids.

"You think me a hallucination, do you? It will take stronger stuff than this world has to cloud that mind of yours," the voice said. It sounded familiar; like someone he used to know from a time long gone.

It cannot be, he thought.

"Oh, but it is," the voice answered.

Murin opened his eyes, struggling to adjust even to the dim light of the smoke-filled tent.

"Timoc?" Murin said, rubbing the sleep out of his eyes, squinting through the smoke at the shimmering, translucent shape of a man sitting cross-legged on the pillows across from him. The figure was nearly as tall as himself, with grey skin and bright purple hair in a simple grey hooded robe. "This is not possible. You cannot be here."

"Physically, no. Have you forgotten all about astral projection, old friend?"

"You should still not be able to reach this world," Murin said, slowly regaining his senses. Thankfully, he couldn't yet hear the minds of the people in the warrens.

"The first of the vertices has been destroyed. The ward has weakened."

Murin straightened. "Impossible; I just left that vertex yesterday. It was well guarded. And you're not here. This is all just the drug affecting my mind."

"Deny it all you want, but the first vertex has been destroyed and here you sit, lying in a drug-addled stupor in this cesspool. Were you not listening? The first vertex has fallen, and the ward is weakening. The mere fact that I can project into this world should make you wet your pants with fear, old man."

Murin leaned back and stretched, as if being called an old man made his muscles cramp up. He chuckled. "You will never guess who I found while locating the first vertex."

The translucent image of Timoc said nothing.

"A sigilord and a quiver, neither of whom have the faintest idea of their power or potential."

"Now you really are hallucinating. The sigilords have been gone from this world since the end of the Fulcrum War and the Age of Power."

"Some of the old blood must still persist after all."

"Murin," Timoc's image said, leaning forward, "the universe isn't like it used to be. Things have changed. We can no longer sit idly by and watch."

"You know what interference has cost me—cost us all—in the past."

"And you know all too well the price of doing nothing," Timoc retorted.

"Do not *dare* bring that up." Murin bristled. "I did what I could. I went to warn the people who live above the first vertex. They are the most fierce, most battle-hardened people on this world. If they could not stop the Order then I doubt any can."

"The Order? Those blood-drenched madmen still remain, after all this time?"

Murin nodded. "There are only a few, and they have but a fraction of their former power. They play games of politics and power to manipulate the new races into doing their work for them."

"You can't let them destroy another vertex. There must be one near you; that's how I can project into this realm. You have to find it and move it."

"I will not interfere again. I cannot. The cost is too high."

"Murin, don't you think three thousand years of penance is enough? This is bigger than your guilt. If I can project through the ward, then so can others, others who can help the Order tear down the rest of it."

Murin looked up at his old friend and one-time student. He had been consumed by his own guilt and his self-imposed exile, too consumed to see all the possibilities. If the Order destroyed the vertices, the consequences would be unimaginable.

"Moving the vertices won't stop them," he said. "The Order doesn't care about what gets between them and the vertices, they will lay waste to this whole planet."

"Master, you have to stop the Order. The last time we stayed our hands and let things take their natural—"

"Enough, I remember what happened," Murin snapped. "No army can stop the Order, Timoc,"

"If you have a sigilord and a quiver at your side, you don't need an army."

Murin looked up, suddenly aware of multiple presences approaching him. These were disciplined, focused minds. They were carrying out orders; soldiers or some other form of local law.

Before Murin could stand up, the tent flap opened and a trio of soldiers wearing shiny, bronze-colored armor ducked inside, their pointed helmets and floating cloaks making them look like decorated birds.

The leader of the trio flipped his helmet up and stared at Murin for a moment before speaking. "My name is Knight Marshall Corliss, and I should be arresting you. Unfortunately there's no law against what you're doing down here, since technically we aren't within city limits. I am a little surprised to see you here, however."

"Surprised to see me? Why?" Murin replied in fluent Erubis, the local language. He didn't know it normally, but since the drug was already wearing off, he had picked it up from nearby minds.

"I've had my men searching all the reputable inns and hostels for you. Imagine my surprise when you turn up down here while I'm looking for thieves," Corliss said. "I promised your friends I would look for you."

"My friends?"

"Two scary-looking dark-skinned boys from Ehmshahr."

For the first time in as long as he could remember, Murin smiled.

Chapter Thirteen

Cailix sat in the pub in the basement of the hostel, facing the exit, her back to a corner. Instinct told her this was the safest position to take up in a strange place, and there was no place stranger than this. Part of her regretted leaving Anderis, but only because there may yet have been something more she could have learned from him. Part of her also regretted not killing him when she had the chance.

But being free of that creature and on her own, in control of her own fate, was more important.

She smiled a little, imagining the look on his face when he awoke with the knife on his pillow, a clear reminder that she'd had the power to kill him and let him live.

Waldron was every bit as hot and sticky as Naredis had been cold and unforgiving. The sun had been down for hours, yet still she sweltered.

The room was quiet for the most part. A few older men carried on in the local tongue, arguing about the game they were playing with stone pieces on a painted game board. Others took their supper in silence, pondering their meals, trying to avoid staring at the strange boy who sat at the bar.

Cailix may have been a stranger from far to the north, but this young man exemplified the word *strange*. At least with the clothing Anderis had provided, she could blend in relatively well. The stranger who people could not stop ogling sat reading a book and serenely eating cookies, but there was little he could do to avoid standing out.

His skin was the color of the briene foreman's drink with a drop of milk, his eyes the color of pure amber, his long, shoulder-length hair as black as night. His arms were so thick with muscles she wondered how he could move them, and, over the protests of the innkeeper, weapons poked out of his clothing like seedlings pushing through fresh topsoil.

Of course, someone who looked like that eating cookies was just the finishing touch on the bouquet of strange.

Cailix watched him sipping his drink, fascinated by the contradiction of this brutal warrior drinking tea with honey like a handmaiden. Maybe where he came from, the tough men drank tea and all the dainty women drank the hard stuff from the cask. She wondered if there even were any dainty women where he came from.

One thing she had learned in her travels with Anderis—one of the many things she would take away with her when she rid herself of him—was that the idea of *normal* changed with who you were and where you came from.

It also changed with how much power you could wield.

A trio of boys spilled through the entrance, laughing at some inside joke, pushing and shoving each other and generally being the typical annoying creatures who were too old to be boys and not mature enough to be men.

They stopped short when they saw the stranger sitting at the bar, gesturing at him and whispering to each other.

She gripped the little dagger hidden in her coat sleeve. She knew their type, old and strong enough to create mayhem and too stupid to decide against it. They pointed, each daring the other to approach the stranger, that glint in their eye that flitted between malicious and mischievous intent.

Finally the tallest boy puffed out his chest, gave his companions a few punches in the shoulders, and approached the bar.

* * *

Urus stared into the bottom of his hot tea, his mind wandering. How Goodwyn had been able to sleep was a mystery. They were alone, halfway across the world from home, and had no idea where Murin was or how they could get back. Hell, they didn't know if there was even a home left waiting for them if they could get back.

He hated this place. He hated Waldron and the wet, smelly air and the way people stared at him. Most of all he hated that Uncle Aegaz wasn't there.

The people here didn't smell right. Back in Kest, everyone smelled of the spices they used in the food; mostly the dried red pepper Kestians called the "devil's cinnamon". He hadn't noticed the change in smells until he arrived in the city where everyone smelled of wet earth, sweat, and pungent perfumes to cover up what the soaps couldn't clean.

Urus studied the book on the counter before him. Wrinkled, aged leather cradled the old, yellowed pages in a soft, maternal embrace. The gold clasp taunted him, begging him to find a way to open it.

He lay his hand across the symbol in the lock. Without his willing anything to happen, the blue smoke drifted up from his hands and the warmth surged from his fingertips, through his shoulder, and down his spine. It hurt a little, like flexing a cold, sore muscle.

The clasp sprang open. Urus cast a furtive glance around the room, checking to make sure no one had noticed the blue glow, then opened the book.

The pages smelled old and dusty, but then he had always loved the smell of books and the stains they made on his thumbs after a long night of reading great tales of adventure. The first page was indecipherable, written in some unknown language. The second was equally opaque, as was the third.

Urus flipped through the book, picking up speed as he scanned for something that he could read. Finally, about halfway through the book, he found a page written in ancient Kestian, a language every Kestian boy was taught and every Kestian boy thought was dead and useless. He could imagine the "I told you so" look on teacher Garish's face if he could see Urus now, reading ancient Kestian.

The passage read:

118 Deborg's Reign 27
Today we repeated the experiment again. Only two of the sigils glowed in
response to Serbis's touch. We still struggle to discover the meaning of the symbols. It
has been three weeks since the arrival of the stranger who says the obelisk is one of
five points. He says they are like keystones to a building that exists outside this
universe. He calls people like us, people who can activate the stone, Radixes.

125 Deborg's Reign 27
Tragedy and heartache. Serbis's lad, Inox, was playing in the obelisk chamber
as we repeated our experiments to no avail, when he touched one of the symbols and
vanished.

Deborg's Reign, Urus thought. *Emperor Deborg ruled the deserts when Kest*
was nothing more than fence posts and tents, 800 years ago.

He closed the book and stuffed it back into his vest as a young man
plopped down at the bar next to him, a wide grin on his face. His cheeks were
flushed, probably from drinking somewhere else earlier. If it was more hard
drink he was after, surely there were better places to get it than the lonely
church hostel common room.

"The winds blow good fortune our way, it seems. We thought we might
never see you again, stranger," said the boy. His lips made strange shapes that
didn't look like any language he knew, but somehow Urus still knew what the
boy had said.

It took him a moment, but he finally recognized the boys as the ones who
earlier had ended up on their backs, bruised, shamed, and ultimately punished
by their commander.

He said nothing and took another sip of his tea. He had seen enough
bullies in his time to recognize their look; that pent-up anger that might
explode at any moment. It was a kettle, seeking any excuse it could find to
boil over.

"You don't stoke a fire with lamp oil," Aegaz used to say, one of his many
lessons about how to deal with bullies. When he was younger, it seemed as if
Urus had trouble with a new bully practically every day. The lesson was to not

ever give that bully's fire an excuse to explode.

"Knocking down innocent cadets is thirsty work, eh?" the boy asked, nodding toward the pewter teacup, barely turning his face enough to allow Urus to read his lips.

"You struck first," Urus said aloud in Adosian. "I apologize for the misunderstanding."

The boy at the counter doubled over laughing. "You hear that, boys? The wittle baby said we attacked fiwst," he said, mocking Urus's awkward speech.

His friends also started laughing, mocking, and pointing—all gestures Urus had grown up with. His blood boiled, repressed anger at a childhood of bullies welling up inside him.

He grabbed the bar counter and squeezed until his knuckles were as pale as the boys' skin. *Of all the nights for Goodwyn to decide to turn in early!*

"That's enough, Victor. You would do well to remember that this hostel is still run by the church," said the barkeep, his apron a canvas painted with a rainbow of stains.

"And you would do well to remember who my father is, barkeep," snapped Victor.

At this, the man wiped his hands on his apron and quickly found a place further away to clean.

"I am sorry about this afternoon," Urus said.

"Oh sure, now that your friend isn't around to keep you safe, you talk up peace and apologies."

Urus ignored the comment and returned his attention to his teacup, anything to avoid eye contact with the bully. He slouched, his posture submissive and weak. He didn't want to challenge him, and the boy was clearly looking for a rematch.

Out of the corner of his eye, he caught a glimpse of a young woman sitting in the shadows in the corner, her red hair and bright blue eyes visible even in the dark. She was staring right at him, probably thinking about how weak he was, about how he should be handling this bully situation better. Despite being fully clothed, it still felt as though everyone could see the brand on his chest, the symbol of his failure.

"I'm talking to you, stranger," Victor said, shoving Urus's shoulder. His cohorts laughed the whole time, standing between him and the door. There was no way he would be able to leave the hostel unchallenged.

Urus continued to ignore them.

"I said, I'm talking to you!" Victor punched him in the shoulder this time.

Again, Urus paid him no mind, taking another sip of his tea, choking back the anger and sadness churning in the pit of his stomach.

"Are you deaf?" Victor shouted, this time punching Urus in the ear.

Urus's mind reeled. In his mind, he screamed, allowing all his pent-up rage and fear to surge out of his mouth like some kind of emotional vomit. On the outside, he stayed still, barely reacting to the blow and the little trickle of blood dripping from his ear.

Again Victor punched him in the ear.

Urus could take no more. He snapped.

His mind tried to retreat, to hide from what was happening, but there was no refuge. There was no safe place to hide, nothing he could do to stop the memories from bubbling to the surface like so much flotsam and jetsam from the wreckage of his early childhood.

Urus sat cross-legged on the floor, playing with a little soldier made of burlap and stuffed with straw. Swords made of twigs were sewn to its puffy, fingerless hands.

Hugo was his name, and he was a mighty warrior; the mightiest, in fact. Urus grinned down at him and giggled. Despite looking as fat as the baker and as funny as a jester, Hugo could vanquish any foe, be it human or dragon or troll. Urus had drawn a name sign on Hugo's burlap chest, a symbol that looked like four swords, crossing in the center. Everyone needed a name sign, especially heroes like Hugo.

It took skill to work Hugo's legs across the floor while still swinging his swords around, but Urus was up to the task. Hugo leapt across the partially eaten meat pie Momma had made earlier. It was a cold mountain fortress now, and Hugo conquered it with ease.

Urus laughed as he made Hugo do a little victory dance atop Fort Meatpie. He looked around the room for his next conquest. There was always Momma's boots. She loved it when he played by her feet while she sharpened her blades or made armor or sewed things. She was always sewing or sharpening things.

Next to Momma and her boots sat a table filled with treasures to plunder, but Papa hated it when he got the table messy, or spilled something, or worse yet, broke things.

With the table option out, he set his sights on Momma's boots, slithering across the floor on his stomach, following Hugo on his trek across the vast stone wilderness as he ducked under swooping dragons and sent flames bursting from his magical swords.

He looked up and gave Momma a smile, and she smiled down at him from her comfy chair, her lap filled with strips of treated hides, ready to be made into armor or sheathes or whatever else people wanted. Momma was the best at making things and could make anything anyone wanted. After all, she had made Hugo.

Hugo was nearly there, about ready to dive over the bubbling pitch swamps to the safety of Momma's boots, when Urus felt his shirt collar tighten. He couldn't breathe and gasped as he was lifted off the floor. He lost his grip on Hugo while spinning around mid-air.

He hung there, dangling in his shirt like meat on a hook in the cold rooms below the palace kitchen, staring into his father's angry eyes.

"Just because you live in a palace doesn't give you the right to waste food," he snapped, pointing at Fort Meatpie, which had fallen victim to Hugo's trek across the floor.

"I'm sorry, Papa," Urus started to sign.

His father clapped a cupped fist over Urus's ear, hard. His head hurt as if his brain was bouncing around inside his skull.

"You talk to me like everybody else."

"I didn't mean to ruin the meat pie. It got cold and I wasn't hungry," Urus said aloud, finally allowed to stand on his own feet. Papa never signed; he didn't even know how.

"Well, you're gonna go eat it, and finish every crumb right up off that floor you ungrateful demon."

"Yes, Papa," Urus said, bowing his head and taking a step toward the mess.

He hadn't gone more than a step when his father slammed a clenched fist into his ear, knocking him to the floor. Urus struggled for footing but his father lifted him up again, spinning him around.

A warm, thick trail of blood oozed out of his ear.

"The demon in you may have taken your ears, but he hasn't taken your manners. You go apologize to your momma."

Urus looked up at Papa, not sure why he should apologize to Momma. This delay cost him a punch to the other ear. Now both ears bled, and the pain was excruciating.

He looked over at his mother, giving her a pleading look. She was a strong warrior; one of the strongest in Kest. She should be able to defeat the smelly, dirty man who had sired him.

She returned his look with a sympathetic smile but did nothing. She didn't even stop sewing. How could she let him do this? Maybe on the inside she felt the same way Papa did, that there was a demon in him. Maybe they both hated him and she didn't stop papa because she felt the same way.

Even in a house with two parents and in a palace full of people, Urus was alone.

"I'm sorry, Momma, for wasting food," he croaked, barely able to make a noise through all the pain and the mucus running back down his throat.

She smiled again, looking as though she might cry, but no tears came. She just turned away and kept at her sewing.

He went to go pick up his mess when the punch hit the side of his head between his temple and ear. It sent him sprawling to the ground, scraping his bare knees on the stone.

Finally, unable to stem the tide any longer, he wept. The tears streamed, and he did that scary thing where it felt like he couldn't catch his breath, like a stutter but with tears and spit dribbling out of his mouth. His bawling was embarrassing, and he was sure if he didn't cut it out his father would come and hit him again for crying. This time he didn't care. Papa could hit him all he wanted and it wouldn't hurt more than he hurt right now.

He let the tears flow as he crawled over to Fort Meatpie. He scraped the bits of cold food off the floor and into his mouth, swallowing hard, trying to get the dirty food down between sobs.

A real warrior, a true fighter like Hugo, would have drawn his mighty sword and cut Papa down and run; run out into the desert and kept on running, living the rest of his life searching for adventure instead of being a punching dummy for that terrible, foul man.

But Urus was no hero; he was no warrior. He couldn't defeat Papa and escape, and so he kept crying, accepting a future of eating cold meat pies off the floor while his father beat him.

Urus stood up from the bar and took a step back, part of his mind pulling out of the memory but the rest staying there, surrounded by the pain. He turned, rubbing the blood from his ear, remembering the many times his father had hit him there.

He looked at the person responsible and saw Papa standing there, a wicked grin on his face, smelling of ale and dirt. Urus studied his arms while Papa and the two boys with him kept on laughing. They were strong arms, much stronger than he remembered them being. These were arms like Hugo's, the arms of a warrior who could strike Papa down.

Urus spun, instinct driving his body to twist and direct the force up from the spinning ball of his foot, through his hips, up through his tensing torso, through his shoulder, along his arm, and out through his fist.

A surge of blue light erupted from his fist as it slammed into Papa's chest. Papa sailed back across the hostel like a leaf caught in a breeze, crashed onto a table and tumbled backwards over it onto the floor.

Papa's friends rushed Urus from the side but it didn't matter. He was Hugo now, not Urus. Hugo the mighty warrior knew exactly what to do and could do it without thinking.

Papa's friends closed the gap in two quick paces, reaching for little daggers hidden in their belts. Urus stepped toward them, slamming his right elbow into the man on the left then striking the other in the back of the head with his elbow's backswing.

He swept his leg and dropped the one on the right easily, then punched the other in the chest. That same burst of blue light bloomed out of his hand, heat searing from his fingertips to his shoulder.

Urus ignored the two boys and stalked over to the table, now in tatters, where Papa had fallen. The broken man was gasping for air and struggling to get to his feet.

Urus unhooked the mace from his belt and squeezed it hard. He imagined what it would be like to hit Papa in the ear with a mace, to finally be rid of Papa and his punching and hating, to pay him back for everything he'd done to him and Momma.

He hefted the mace over his head and was ready to strike when he felt a pair of hands grab his wrist.

"Stop!" a girl shouted into his face.

Urus blinked.

The girl from the corner had her hands clamped around his wrist.

"Who are you?" he asked.

"My name is Cailix," she said, "What's more important is who that is on the floor—or rather, who it isn't."

Urus looked down at Papa. He looked so helpless, far from the towering brute he remembered.

"You yelled at him, called him Papa," Cailix said. "That boy isn't your papa, he's a stupid bully. You don't want to do this."

"Yes, I do," Urus said. "I want Papa dead, to be free of him forever." His head hurt and he felt tired, his vision blurry. Part of him knew that he was standing in a hostel in the middle of a strange land, half a world away from Kest, but part of him felt he was still in his boyhood home, weeping on the floor and eating cold meat pie.

"That's not your papa," Cailix said, still gripping his arm. "You don't want to kill anybody, not like this, not a stupid kid. You're not the type, I can tell because I know the type and you're not it. You wouldn't be able to deal with the reality of it when you woke up tomorrow."

Urus turned and looked at Cailix, then back at Papa, except it wasn't Papa anymore. This time it was Victor, the bully and shamed cadet. Urus knew what it was like to be shamed. He knew what it felt like to be defeated in front of his friends, and he definitely knew what it felt like to want revenge.

Uncle Aegaz said that revenge is for the weak, that it turns a man all black and dead inside. Urus already felt black and dead inside, and he felt ashamed of what he'd done to the bully and his friends, what little of it he could remember.

He relaxed, lowered his mace, and hooked it back on his belt.

"Good. Now you'd better get out of here before the barkeep calls the watch," Cailix said.

Urus turned to leave but stopped, a thought suddenly occurring to him, a gnat that had been chewing on his neck all night until finally it had become so annoying he couldn't ignore it.

"How is it that everyone here knows Kestian?" he asked.

"Kestian? I was going to ask why you were speaking Naredan."

Bizarre things with languages like that had only happened once before, and could only mean one thing.

"Murin is here," he said.

CHAPTER FOURTEEN

Urus froze as the door burst open and Corliss and two of his men filed into the common room, blades drawn and at the ready.

"For once you show up early!" shouted the barkeep. "I was about to send a man to fetch you. This kid is making a mess of my bar."

Corliss took in the scene, eyebrows slowly rising and mouth dropping. "What in all the hells happened here?"

Urus looked from Corliss to the defeated young soldiers, to Cailix, and back, "I can explain," he said aloud.

Corliss blinked. "I knew you were lying before. You can speak Erubis!"

"You're both speaking Naredan," Cailix interjected, her lips moving in flawless Kestian.

Corliss shook his head and paced around the common room. After several laps around some tables, he turned to the barkeep and said, "I am sorry for any trouble the boy has caused you. I will be bringing him before the duke."

Urus's heart raced. A little scuffle like this was hardly a matter for someone like a duke. In Kest, the emperor never got involved in trivial matters like this.

"The duke? You're going to bring me to the duke over this?" Urus gestured toward the boys. "They're not even hurt that badly. We did save your life, that has to count for something."

Corliss spun toward Urus, looking truly angry for the first time since they had met. "It looks like you've nearly killed one of my cadets. You seem to have made a habit of assaulting my trainees."

"Pardon me, sir, but—" Cailix started.

"Who in the hells are you?"

"No one of concern, sir, but you should know that your cadets started it. They taunted him until he had no choice."

"There is always a choice, young lady," Corliss said. He straightened and sighed, then turned back to Urus. "I was on my way here to find you to bring you to the duke long before any of this happened."

"If I'm not to be punished for this, then for what?" Urus asked aloud. This time, even he wasn't sure what language came out of his mouth. Murin had to be involved in this somehow, and hopefully that meant he was nearby.

"You aren't to be punished, Ehmshahran. We have far bigger problems to deal with, and you and your friends appearing just before these problems is something we need to discuss."

"What kind of problems?"

Corliss looked around, making sure the barkeep was out of earshot. "An army camps at the base of the white mountain. We are besieged."

"An army?" Urus wondered if the Order was controlling this army the way they pulled the puppet strings of the armies that attacked Kest.

"So the briene have arrived then," Cailix said more as a statement of fact than a question.

"Girl, what could you possibly know of this?" Corliss demanded.

Cailix said nothing, glancing casually about the room as though she were the only one there.

"Just as well you don't answer me here. This is a discussion best had in private with the duke. Whoever you are and whatever you know, you're coming with us now, girl."

Corliss led them out of the hostel, again apologizing to the barkeep and assuring him that the crown would compensate him for any damage and lost business. For a warrior, Corliss seemed to do a lot of placating and licking of wounds. He wondered if Aegaz's job was like that—spending more time pleasing people and tending to their needs than actual military business.

Leadership didn't seem quite so appealing as it once had.

They walked in silence, making their way through the city, snaking between pools of lamplight as they climbed higher up the mountain toward Waldron's center.

Urus exchanged a few glances with Cailix, trying to figure out what lay beneath that cold stare of hers, but she neither said a word nor revealed anything in her gaze. Who she was or why she had talked him out of killing that boy remained a mystery.

It didn't matter who she was; she knew he thought the boy was his father, and she knew he was going to kill him. Most importantly, she had saved him from himself, from living with the guilt of doing something for which he could never forgive himself.

They crossed over a massive stone bridge guarded by a half-dozen men, marking the transition from the main part of the city to the political center where the duke's private residence, the courthouse, and the council chambers sat: smooth, polished stone reminders of where the true wealth and power of the city lay.

"What about Goodwyn?" Urus finally asked Corliss.

"More likely than not, your friend is bored to tears awaiting our arrival in the council chambers. Before I went to fetch you I sent men to escort him as well."

"Why do you think this army has anything to do with us?" Urus asked.

"You show up here, claiming that your home was attacked by four armies, and then not a day later, my scouts report campfires from the mountain base all the way to the coast."

"It doesn't sound like a coincidence."

"No. No, it does not," Corliss said, picking up the pace a little.

It took them until the full height of the moon to finally reach the outside of a castle, by the looks of it one of the oldest structures in the city.

"This is Castle Durgas, named for the nomadic tribe that first settled in the mountain caves," Corliss said. "They're the ones who started carving this castle right out of the mountain itself." He ushered them through the narrow opening beneath the portcullis. "The duke's private residences are up the hill to the left, the public audience chambers down to the right. Where we're going is where the nobles manage the city's daily affairs."

They walked past even more guards, across an open courtyard, and through huge iron doors into a giant, vaulted-ceilinged room where plush, cushioned seats arranged in a semi-circle sloped downward to a dais on a large platform. Brilliant, oversized lamps hung from the ceiling and walls. The finely polished white marble floor cast back the lamplight back up at the ceiling.

This is where the business of an entire city takes place, Urus thought. He'd seen every room of the palace in Kest and knew where all of that city's business happened, but somehow it seemed to carry more weight in a city like this; a strange city where he hadn't grown up down the hall from the emperor's private chambers.

"This is it," Corliss said. "The heart of Waldron."

Down the stairs, just in front of the dais, two figures sat bathed in shadow. They stood as the group proceeded down the gleaming steps. The quartermasters had a saying for floors like this: "Boots on marble carry the walking dead." In other words, nobody wearing boots ever sneaked up on someone on a marble floor.

The figures climbed steadily up out of the shadows to meet them, both taller than Urus, one much more so. As they stepped into the light cast by the lamps overhead, the shadows peeled back to reveal Goodwyn and Murin.

"Urus!" Goodwyn shouted, his mouth barely visible in the dim light. "Guess who Corliss found?" He gestured wildly at Murin as though they had been reunited with some long lost friend. Murin was no such thing, and had a lot to answer for.

Urus sped down the stairs to stand face-to-chest with Murin. "You used us to get to the vertex. We looked for the vertex instead of staying to fight for Kest. For all we know, Kest could lay in ruins right now. Everyone—my uncle —could all be dead. You may even be the reason Kest was attacked in the first place!"

Murin blinked, slowly. Those bottomless pit eyes crept downward toward Urus but he said nothing.

Corliss gripped his shoulder and spoke. "You best put aside whatever issues you might have between you. Duke Pemor will be here shortly and this is no time for bickering."

As if on cue, a door shaped like the wood paneling on the wall behind the dais opened, spilling more lamplight into the chamber. A man in a dark purple robe, a bright red jerkin, black tights, and polished black boots, strode onto the platform.

Urus had to stifle a laugh, and he could see Goodwyn was having the same trouble. This was a duke? The man looked like a jester. He wore no armor, carried no weapons, and his hair was preened and shampooed and had obviously never felt the touch of sweat or dirt. His hands were covered in ornate, gold and silver rings inset with huge, colorful gems.

Corliss approached the dais and bent to one knee in front of it. He looked back, waving the others on to do the same. Goodwyn and Urus took a knee next to Corliss but Murin and Cailix merely stood.

"Rise," said the duke, flashing an irritated look at Murin and Cailix. Urus could've sworn the duke spoke Kestian.

"Corliss, please tell me the whispers I hear in the dark about an army at our doorstep are just rumors."

"I'm afraid I cannot, my liege," Corliss said, standing.

"Let's have your report, then."

"My liege, early this evening my scouts reported large campfires at the base of the mountain. I sent some men up to the roost to investigate. With their scrying lenses, they could see the flames of war camps all the way to the coast."

The duke gasped and took a seat on the large chair behind the lectern. "That's not possible. You can't see campfires on the coast from here."

"No, but you can see a forest being burned," Cailix said, stepping forward.

Urus had almost forgotten she was there. She had a way of blending in that would make the stealthiest of Kestian warriors jealous.

"Who is this little waif, and why does she address me out of turn? We have rules in a civilized society, girl."

"Answer the duke's question," Corliss said. "I've been dying to hear the answer to this myself."

"My name is Cailix. In the time spent with my former…custodian, we have encountered the briene before. They burn down entire forests to provide fuel for their war machines."

"The briene?" Duke Pemor exclaimed. "No one has seen them for a hundred years. For all we know, they died out in their caves and there is nothing left of them."

"They are quite real and quite alive," Cailix said, without using any formal address for the duke. She talked to him in that same calm, steady manner she had used with Urus earlier.

"Corliss, have your scouts actually seen any of the enemy?"

"No, my liege. We can count the fires and guess their size, but from the roost we can see nothing but shadows moving in the firelight."

"What numbers have you counted?" Duke Pemor asked, stroking his white beard, resting his elbow on the soft armchair cushion.

The idea of a cushion on a chair seemed ridiculous to Urus, but so many things about Waldron seemed ridiculous that he was learning to accept that everything here was strange.

"We count two hundred fires at the base of the mountain, another two hundred leading from here to the coast, and, as the girl points out, a few blazes that could only come from something as big as a forest fire out near the coast."

"This is troubling indeed, though I have no doubt that our defenses will hold. Attacking Waldron is folly, no matter what number the enemy brings to bear," said the duke, standing up and pacing between his chair and the lectern.

"We need to organize a scouting mission, to get closer to the enemy, to gauge their number and makeup," Corliss began. "And these boys here think they may know why the enemy is after Waldron."

The duke stopped pacing. "Oh? More young strangers? You are full of surprises tonight, Knight Marshall Tudell."

Urus stepped forward and bowed slightly, careful to treat this noble with more respect than had Cailix. "My Lord, my name is Urus Noellor and my friend is Goodwyn Stom. We are from Ehmshahr."

The duke whistled appreciatively. "A long way from home. Let us skip the usual formalities and you can jump right to the part where you tell me what you know about the motives of this briene army."

As quickly and with as few words as possible, Urus stumbled over the story, starting with the arrival of the four armies at Kest and their escape, finishing with a narrative of the stone slab that dumped them onto the white mountain road.

"There is another vertex somewhere near here, probably in the mountain caverns below the city, the ones hewn by the Durgas. This is what the briene seek, but they do so under the heels of the Order of the Sanguine Crystal," Murin added.

"How will that effect their tactics, Corliss?"

"If there is any truth to this story, sire, then the briene will care little for our soldiers. Their aim won't be to occupy the city, it will be to destroy it."

The duke resumed pacing, his face troubled. "This situation is dire," he said, nervously rubbing his hands together. "My constable and war advisor is returning from a diplomatic trip to the crown city and, if my own sources at the gates are reliable, he has arrived and should be here any moment. We will wait and hear his counsel on this matter."

"But my liege, we need to act now," Corliss pleaded.

The duke whirled. "I said we will await my advisor. In the meantime, you and these others may wait here. You know where to find the food and drink. If you're lucky, there may even be a few sweets left over from today's sessions."

Corliss bowed. "Of course."

He turned and led everyone up the stairs, Urus following last to make sure he could see everyone. He didn't like how dimly lit the place was, even with all of the lamps and sconces. The room had narrow vertical slits in the stone walls, but at this time of night they seemed to swallow light rather than admit it.

There were trays of bread and pastries and pitchers of ale left over from the city government sessions earlier that day. At the sight of the food, he realized just how hungry he was. He felt more hungry than he had in a long time, and ended up fighting with Goodwyn over the last few cake squares.

One hand still clutching the sweets, he approached Murin, turning him to make sure he could see his lips.

"We're way past your secrets and holding back from me. I want to know what's really going on here and I want to know now," he signed, which allowed him to keep chewing the piece of bread he had just stuffed into his mouth.

"What do you mean?" Murin asked.

"For starters, I want to know why when I speak, people hear their native language, and I can read lips of people speaking languages I've never seen before. Don't deny that isn't your doing."

Murin grinned. That expression still seemed alien on his grey-skinned face. "Do you know the phrase 'quantum entanglement'?" he asked, but didn't pause long enough to let Urus answer. "No, of course you would not. It is part of what happened when you invaded my mind in the dungeon in Kest. You have inherited a power you cannot possibly imagine and have no way to control or harness. You are like a cauldron of pitch near an open flame."

Urus flinched, remembering the damage he had caused in the hostel and how close he had come to killing someone. *Like pitch near an open flame, indeed,* he thought.

"None of that makes any sense at all," Urus signed, stuffing pieces of cake into his mouth while Murin spoke.

"You saw the blue light again tonight. You used your power," Murin said, watching Urus eat and looking at his hands full of food. It wasn't a question.

Urus looked away, ashamed of what he had done, afraid of what he might have done had Cailix not been there.

Desperately wishing to change the subject, he turned to Corliss. "How many ways are there in and out of the city?"

That question had been nagging at him since they talked to the duke.

Corliss smiled, clearly amused by Urus's talent for holding so much food and still managing to talk or sign. "To get in? Just the one, the road where we met. It's possible to climb down through the mists on the back side of the mountain, but it's dangerous and definitely can't be used to enter the city."

"If that's the only way in, then how did the duke's constable get past the briene army to get here?"

Corliss dropped his drink on the table and turned to look back down at the duke, seated in his chair, casually sipping from a silver wine chalice, his mind lost in thought.

Murin gripped Urus's shoulders. "I cannot believe no one thought of that sooner. The constable would have had to go right through an army spread across a hundred miles of forest."

"Why don't we just ask him?" Goodwyn said, pointing to a silhouette that had just stepped into the light of the door behind the dais.

The new arrival, presumably the constable, was tall and wore a bright white robe, his short hair barely reaching to the cowl. Urus thought it odd that a man with a military rank would wear a robe, but he figured it must be another cultural difference between Kest and Waldron. After all, their duke dressed like a feastday turkey.

Corliss and the others started down the stairs toward the dais as the constable spoke with Duke Pemor. As Urus took the first step, he noticed Cailix withdrawing into the shadows again, the look of fear on her face at odds with her usual stoic countenance.

Urus took a few more steps down toward the dais when it dawned on him that the look on her face hadn't just been fear. It was recognition.

She knows the constable!

"Corliss, please bring the visitors here so they can tell Constable Anderis what they know of this new threat. I am particularly curious as to what the young woman knows about the briene," called the duke, the constable still whispering in his ear.

"As am I," said Anderis with a wry grin, his eyes focused directly on the shadow in the back of the chamber where Cailix had been standing before she disappeared.

Murin straightened and reached into his robe. "Surely you are not Anderis Slakenwood of the Order of the Sanguine Crystal? I saw that creature die three millennia ago."

"Appearances can be deceiving, Arbiter. You of all people should know that," Anderis replied, a knife appearing in his hand as he seized the duke. "And if you move on me I will slit the duke's throat."

"What are you doing?" demanded Pemor, eyes wide with shock and fear. "Release me!"

"I know you're there, Aerlissa," Anderis called to the darkness, again looking to the back of the room. "After all that I have taught you, all that I have done for you, you betray me like this by siding with the enemy? And that bit with the knife on my pillow, that was priceless. You made me so proud."

Instinctively Urus flexed his fists by the mace handles at his waist, waiting for a chance to use them. He hoped someone else would take care of this constable first, though, saving him from the fight. His mind flashed back to the boat in the cistern below Kest; to when he froze and almost let the invader kill him. He wondered if the same would happen the next time he faced an opponent, or if the mysterious blue light would kill his enemy or his friends. It was all just too much to think about.

He wished Uncle Aegaz were here.

It suddenly hit him that Murin had said three *millennia*. They were three *thousand* years old? That couldn't be possible. He must have misread Murin's lips in the dim light.

"How could you betray us like this?" Corliss asked, sidestepping along the edge of the dais, his curved sword drawn.

"Betrayal requires that my allegiance belonged to this rathole to begin with," hissed Anderis, tightening his grip on the duke and pushing the blade up into his neck, drawing a small bead of blood.

He bent closer to the duke's neck and sniffed. "You smell that, apprentice? That is the smell of power; power that you will never have. The real betrayal here is what you have done to me!"

"Let him go, Anderis, you've got nowhere to go," Corliss yelled.

"You have no idea how wrong you are, Knight Marshall," Anderis said, a wicked grin spreading across his face.

He squeezed the duke's neck with one hand and pulled the other back to strike with the dagger.

"No!" Cailix shouted, leaping from the shadows onto the dais, a dagger in each hand.

Ignoring her, Anderis sliced open the duke's throat, sending a spray of blood across the dais and onto the front row of seats. He pushed his victim to the floor and rubbed his hands in the duke's blood.

Cailix pounced, landing on Anderis's back. At this, everyone rushed the platform. With the duke down, Anderis had lost his hostage. Murin leapt up first, followed by Corliss and Goodwyn, all with weapons in their hands. Urus arrived last.

Paying the girl no heed, as Cailix plunged her little knives into the man's back Anderis's lips moved while he smeared the blood on his face and chest. If he felt the stab wounds, he showed no sign of it.

Just as the group reached striking distance, with Goodwyn's suzur already flying through the air, Anderis vanished. There was no smoke, no flame, no fanfare, just the absence of Anderis.

Cailix dropped to the floor and ducked as Goodwyn's bladed chain flew by, a mere hair's width from her head.

"Where did he go?" Cailix asked, looking up at Murin.

"How did he do that?" Corliss and Goodwyn asked at the same time.

"I think you have some explaining to do," Murin said to Cailix.

Corliss stood over the dead duke, shaking his head. "I think you all have a lot of explaining to do."

CHAPTER FIFTEEN

Urus watched in silence as Corliss's men carried away the wrapped corpse of the duke.

"We have to get to the roost," Corliss said.

"What's up there?" asked Goodwyn.

"If that traitor Anderis has been working with the briene all along, and they are planning to attack, then they know everything about Waldron's defenses and the devil only knows what other surprises Anderis left behind. I need to see this army for myself."

"What about the duke?"

"There is nothing we can do for him now. What we need to do now is defend this city and keep its people safe. Come with me, all of you." Corliss led them out of the council chambers and across the main courtyard to the courthouse.

Urus and Goodwyn followed him through a several large assembly rooms, the last of which held a small door that led into a narrow back hallway. Murin and Cailix took up the rear of the procession of foreigners.

Corliss stopped in front of a small, uninteresting wooden door and turned to the group, "It's going to be a long, painful climb to the top."

Urus exchanged a look with Goodwyn but said nothing.

"By the time we get to the top, I expect to be fully informed on just who in all the hells you are," Corliss said, pointing to Cailix, "and how you came to be that traitor's apprentice. And I want explanations for everything else that's happened here tonight. If I don't get my answers, I may just push you off the roost myself. The fate of my city is at stake, and I will brook no evasions or half answers. Am I clear?"

Urus nodded, as did the others. Even Murin seemed a little intimidated by Corliss's newfound determination.

"All right then, let's go." He opened the door to reveal an iron spiral staircase and started climbing.

It was Murin who spoke first. "I will ask, then. Cailix, how did you come to be the apprentice of a blood mage?"

"Someone had better explain to me what a blood mage is," Corliss snapped.

"Cailix," Murin said, "answer the question."

Urus held onto the railing with both hands so he could twist around to look at the person talking. It was awkward and nauseating to try to read lips while ascending the staircase, but he wasn't about to miss a word of this.

"I was a ward of the monks in Naredis," she said finally. "Anderis and two others came and killed everyone but me. I fought back, so Anderis thought I was interesting. I think he saw me as a pet."

"What were they looking for in Naredis?" Murin asked.

"Something called the Woan Map. They found it, but it turned to dust after they broke the wax seal."

"That was no wax seal, that was a sigil ward," Murin said, his eyes wide. "After all this time, to think that the Woan Map was real. That explains how the Order knows where to find the vertices."

Cailix shrugged. "They covered it with blood before the map crumbled. They made a new map out of the blood. I went with them after that."

"Those men are murderers. Why would you do such a thing?" asked Corliss.

"Because the monks were all dead. I had no way of surviving there in the cold, and I thought I might eventually be able to kill Anderis if I stayed with him."

Urus watched as she described what had happened, her face calm and distant as usual, as though she were merely describing what chores she had done. Even Kestians didn't talk about vengeance with such coldness. He found it a little scary.

Corliss had been right. The staircase seemed to go on forever. As Cailix spoke, they had climbed up through a stone tower that rose above the city. Corliss lit a torch as they rose above the tower and the stairs wound up into the mountainside like an iron screw boring through the stone.

"So what are the briene doing here?" Corliss asked. "What do they want with Waldron and what does that have to do with you and the constable?"

"The Order of the Sanguine Crystal, a cult of the last remaining blood mages, seeks the five vertices," Murin replied, a bit breathless. "The Woan Map contained their locations. All the evidence points to there being a vertex here in Waldron."

"A vertex?"

"Like a door, but not a door. It can be any shape, though most are slabs of stone with carvings on them. Each vertex is a fixed point in multidimensional space. It exists both in our universe and in another. They also act as wards, preventing anyone from crossing between."

"First your companions appear out of nowhere and tell me that magic is real," Corliss sputtered. "Then you show up and my superior officer turns out to be a…a blood mage who murders the duke. Now you tell me that there is another universe? Do you have any idea how absurd that all sounds?"

"To be precise, there exist a countably infinite number of universes," Murin began. "As to the vertices, they were set in place three thousand years ago to put an end to a brutal war that nearly destroyed this world. The Order is trying to destroy them."

"Why?"

"So they can escape," Murin said without further explanation.

Corliss looked up and wiped the sweat from his brow, the only time Urus had seen him sweat, despite the oppressive heat in the city.

"We're almost there," he said.

They trudged on in silence until finally they reached a metal hatch. It took both Murin and Corliss to push it open.

They filed out onto a small plateau of rough white stone just below the mountain's summit. Urus stood up, stretched, and sucked in the cool air. At this altitude, the cool, dry air was much easier to breathe and certainly smelled a lot better than it did in the city.

Strong winds buffeted them from all sides, the churning currents swirling constantly around the summit.

"What do you expect to see from up here?" Urus asked.

"Nothing," Corliss said with a grin. "This is where we will jump."

Urus swallowed hard. "Jump?"

Corliss pointed at a pair of wooden trunks behind the hatch they had come through. "Each of you put on a windrunner cloak. Make sure you fasten the cords tightly around your wrists and ankles. If one of those slips off while you're gliding, you'll make for one hell of a stain on the forest floor."

Urus put his on first, a little disappointed that the smallest cloak was the one that fit the best. The cloak felt clumsy, and he was sure he appeared ridiculous in his Kestian leathers with a black cloak that looked like cloth stretched over a spiderweb.

"I think it works like a bat's wing," Cailix said, fastening the straps of her cloak.

"From a really big, ugly bat," Goodwyn joked. No one else laughed.

"Remember when I told you we teach our cadets to glide by pushing them off the perch? I wasn't joking," Corliss said, flapping his arms to demonstrate how to make the cloak billow out in the wind behind him.

"What are we supposed to do now?" Urus asked.

Corliss turned around, showing off the back of his cloak. It shone bright yellow, glittering in the darkness like a lamp.

"Sunstone!" Urus and Goodwyn exclaimed.

Corliss nodded. "It costs us a fortune to import from Ehmshahr. They mine it in Tanis and ship it out of Blackport to us in bricks. We crush it into a powder and use it in the dye for the outside of the cloak. You'll be able to follow me as I descend, while I will still appear as nothing more than a shadow to those on the ground."

"That's brilliant," said Urus, marveling at the workmanship and thought that had gone into the cloak. "In Kest, the central buildings and walkways are made of sunstone so they light up at night without torches."

"You have entire *buildings* made of sunstone? Now *that* is truly amazing," said Corliss. "When we're done with this terrible business, I would give everything I have to see a sight like that."

"Speaking of this terrible business," Murin interjected, "I assume you have some sort of plan?"

"Almost at the bottom of the mountain, a short distance from the road, there is a flat mound of earth that juts up from the forest floor. The forest is covered with them, but this one will give us the perfect vantage point to get a closer look at our enemies."

"You really expect us to be able to fly from this perch down to a hill without killing ourselves?" Goodwyn asked.

"Yes." Corliss said, "It's easier than it looks. If you spread your arms and legs wide, you will glide slowly down. Lean or roll in the direction you want to go, hug yourself with your arms to drop like a stone."

"Why would you want to do that?" Cailix asked.

"When there are invaders on the road, that's how we attack them."

Urus and Goodwyn gave each other a look. Their first encounter with the Waldron cadets had been less than impressive, and they had mistakenly assumed that everyone in Waldron was as bad at combat as those boys. Imagining Corliss and his men diving a few thousand feet and attacking at that speed gave Urus a newfound admiration for them. They might have a different way of fighting than the Kestians, but it could be just as effective.

"We should be looking for the vertex, not wasting our time with a scouting mission," Murin said.

"Your concern may be with some magical trinket, but mine is with the safety of my people. I need to find out what we're up against so I know how to prepare. If you really feel like your time would be better spent elsewhere, then you are welcome to go back down the stairs."

Murin frowned but didn't move.

"As soon as I jump, each of you will also jump," Corliss instructed. "The safest thing for you to do is mimic my every move; roll and tilt the way I roll and tilt. Don't think about the height or your speed, just focus on the back of my cloak."

Everyone nodded, though Urus was already focusing on the height. He knew how fast one could fall from the top of even a small building like a palace, but falling from the summit of a mountain, that was just madness. Calix, to his annoyance, seemed eager and excited.

"Everyone step up to the edge here," Corliss said.

Urus moved to the edge and peered down into a deep abyss of dark blue and black shadows barely illuminated by the full moon. The last time he stood at a precipice like this, he'd been ready to end it all and hoped he would not survive. Now he looked down and feared death. He wanted to live; he wanted to live to see his uncle again, to help prevent Waldron from suffering the same fate as Kest, to find out more about his power and if it could be used without hurting people.

"Just one question," he said to Corliss. "Once we get down there and we've gotten a look at the enemy, how are we going to get back up here?"

"Trust me, I know the way back up. As I said, we do this all the time," Corliss replied. "Ready?" He waited for a few nods, then spun and leapt from the edge of the cliff.

Urus watched as the Knight Marshall spread his arms and legs wide, the sunstone-imbued cloak blooming into a wide yellow circle that shrank rapidly until moments later he was little more than a yellow dot like a firefly flitting about.

Murin jumped next, then Goodwyn. He looked over at Cailix, unsure if he should go first, but she made the decision for him and jumped first. He stared at the descending fireflies, petrified with fear.

He took a deep breath, bent his knees, then pushed off, leaping into the air thousands of feet above the ground, certain that he was doing the single most foolish thing he had done in his life.

As he fell he wanted to flail, to swing and flap his arms about as panic set in. Finally he gritted his teeth, locked his knees and elbows and spread them as wide as he could. The cloak billowed and jerked against his limbs as it caught the wind.

He could barely see Cailix below him, but he could make out enough to tell when she tilted or spun to one side or the other. Heeding Corliss's advice, he ignored the wind blasting into his face, the feeling of his last meal struggling to work its way back out of his stomach, and focused only on the yellow light of Cailix's cloak.

He fell for so long that he worried they must have missed the ground somehow and were falling into hell itself. For a few blissful seconds, he felt he was flying like a bird. It was exhilarating, while it lasted.

Just as he felt his resolve waver and the urge to flap his arms and panic returned, several yellow lights appeared out of the darkness below.

The lights formed a circle, and as Cailix landed below him in the center of the circle, her light moved to the outside as well. They were guiding him in to land on the mound, illuminating a landing circle with their cloaks.

He twisted and angled his way into the circle, still unable to see anything but the lights. He saw the grass with just enough warning to get his hands and knees out in front of him, ploughing into the dirt.

Hands grabbed his shoulders and legs as he rolled, picking him up and keeping him from dropping off the edge of the mound. He looked around, seeing the same look of elation on their faces that he felt within. Once he'd gotten over the fear from the fall and relaxed, he really had felt like a bird.

"That was amazing," Goodwyn signed, dropping to his knees. He motioned for Urus to do the same. Everyone crouched except Corliss who lay on his stomach facing the campfires, fires that erupted from everywhere in the dark forest below. There were hundreds of them, huge bonfires fueled by freshly felled trees from the smell of them.

"Except for the part where we almost died, yes, it was amazing," Urus signed back.

"You seem to be quite the natural flyer," said Murin.

Urus could see that Corliss had started talking, but the Knight Marshal faced the campfires and his mouth was obscured. Urus crawled up next to him, tapped him on the shoulder, and pointed at his ear.

"Oh, sorry," Corliss told him. "I was saying, I've never seen anything like this before. If each of those fires is at the middle of a battalion with the companies circled around, like we would do, then there are easily fifty thousand soldiers in that forest."

"That's not just a single army, that is the entire host of the briene," Murin said. "Every last man, woman, and child would have to be there to mount a force of that size."

"Why would they all come?" Corliss asked.

"The women and children maintain and prep the machines."

"What kind of machines?"

"Look there." Murin pointed past a particularly large fire. Glowing molten red in the moonlight lay a giant sphere with thick steel spokes jutting out of it and all sorts of strange platforms and railings bolted on. "That is just one of their siege engines, powered by steam. The briene likely brought a dozen or more with them."

"There are other kinds of machines, too," said Cailix. "They have winged machines they call buzzwings, chariots that pull themselves with steam-driven wheels, and even more strange weapons for the soldiers. There's also a big golden ball that Anderis had them make just for him."

"What does it do?" Corliss asked.

Cailix shrugged.

"Nothing good," Murin added.

"There's something else," Cailix said. "Try not to kill the briene. Anderis and the blood mages fed them lies to drive them here."

"Lies are their trade, Cailix," Murin said. "War is upon us, there is nothing we can do about it now."

As Urus's eyes adjusted to peering through the moonlight between the fires below, he noticed more details, and worse, more terrible machines and structures.

He focused on giant tubes he saw arrayed on the ground. Little shadowy silhouettes hovered around them like bees tending to a hive. The tubes ran like tentacles from machines of all shapes and sizes, connecting up to huge iron towers.

"What are those towers, the ones with the tubes?" he asked, sitting back on his heels as the others also sat up to face each other.

Murin followed Urus's finger down to the forest floor and stared silently for a moment before answering. "Those towers are supplying fuel to the other war machines. That kind of technology should be beyond the briene. It should be beyond anyone from this world for the next two centuries."

Urus had no idea how to respond to that. Murin seemed more strange every time he spoke. All this talk about three-thousand-year old wars and technology people shouldn't know about was as frightening as it was confusing.

Urus had liked it better when things were simple and clear, when he was just a culled and life was bleak, but predictable. He scanned the towers up and down, following the tubes like the bronze ones that fed the gas lamps in Kest. They ran up the side of the towers and connected to metal casks surrounded by more gears, pulleys, and cables than he could count.

That was when he decided to do something truly foolish.

"I can destroy the fuel towers," he said.

"The hells you can, boy," Corliss replied with a mix of shock and amusement on his face. "Did you not notice the entire nation of enemy soldiers surrounding them?"

"I know I can do it," Urus said. "I can get up inside the tower and ruin it. Without the fuel, the machines stop working. It'll be just like clogging the gas lines for the lamps in the palace in Kest."

Corliss stood up, hands on his hips. "It may be possible to bring down one of those towers, but you'll have to get to it without dying first."

Urus wasn't going to back down. "You may think I'm just a kid, but I know I can do this. I know I have a better shot at this than I do fighting on an open battlefield."

Goodwyn stood up next. "Count me in," he signed, then spoke aloud. "If Urus says it can be done, it can. He may not be fast with a sword, but figuring out how things work, that's what he does."

"This is a fool's errand," Corliss said. "You'll never survive and I won't be responsible for your deaths."

"With all due respect, Knight Marshall, you're not responsible for us at all," Urus answered. "If we choose to go on this fool's errand, that's our choice and our right." He forced his gaze high, standing his ground even though part of him wanted to agree with Corliss and go run and hide.

Murin and Cailix rose, Murin with a wide grin on his face, the widest Urus had ever seen on him.

"The boys may have something here," the old man said. "Taking out those fuel towers could cripple their army, and a few quiet warriors in the dead of night stand a better chance than a thousand under the midday sun."

"I'm going too," Cailix said.

Goodwyn held up his palms. "Now hold on just a second; Urus and I can handle this."

"Wyn, she kept me from making a terrible mistake back at the hostel. If she wants to help then I owe her that much," Urus signed.

"I'm not going to get you to change your minds, am I?" asked Corliss.

Urus, Goodwyn, and Cailix all shook their heads.

"I can't believe I'm saying this, but you only get one chance to surprise them, so you'll need to take out both fuel towers at once."

Urus looked at Goodwyn, wondering if this was one of those times when he knew what to do ahead of time.

"She should come with me," Goodwyn said, as though reading Urus's thoughts.

"You don't think I can take out one of the towers on my own?" Cailix huffed, hands on her hips. She had as much fire in her as a Kestian.

Goodwyn smiled. "It's not that. I just saw the way you went after that constable, and whenever Urus and I pick teams, I get to pick first, so you're on my team."

That seemed to satisfy her. Goodwyn always knew what to say and how to say it, even if it was a complete lie. Urus saw something in Goodwyn's eyes that told him there was more to his reason than that.

Corliss pointed off into the darkness. "If you get a running start and jump into a glide southeast, away from the fires, you should be able to land in the deep trees where the army hasn't cleared."

"We split up when we land, make for the towers, destroy them, then make our way back here without being killed or spotted?" Cailix asked.

"Simple," said Urus, trying to lighten the mood a bit.

"You'll need a weapon," Corliss said, offering a large knife to Cailix.

She shook her head. "I'll manage."

"This is the stupidest thing we've ever done," Urus signed to Goodwyn.

"Until the next time," he replied with a grin and walked to the far edge of the plateau, readying himself for the run.

Chapter Sixteen

Urus watched Cailix take up a spot next to Goodwyn as she double checked the clasps on the windrunner cloak.

Urus joined them, his stomach twisted in knots, sweat dripping from his forehead and palms.

"Ready?" Goodwyn asked.

"No," Urus replied. For the second time tonight, he was about to jump headlong into darkness, where he would most likely end up dead or mutilated.

"Corliss and I will have a distraction ready when we see the towers fail," Murin said. "We will be here when you get back and pull you back up to the plateau."

"And if things go horribly wrong?" Urus asked.

"Then we improvise. Make for the road and get as high as possible."

"Enough talk, let's do this." Cailix broke into a sprint and sped across the grassy plateau. Without missing a step she leapt into the air, spread her arms and legs like a gleaming yellow bat, and sailed off, away from the enemy camps.

Urus and Goodwyn exchanged a look, then both dashed for the edge. Unlike Cailix, Urus did miss a step, slipping on the damp grass, flying into the air, and, for a moment, dropping like a stone. But he quickly regained his wits, spread his limbs and turned his free fall into a rapid glide toward the glow of Cailix's cloak.

They soared through the air, and despite feeling as though he might crash and die at any moment, Urus was getting used to it and even starting to like the exhilaration; the speed and the wind in his face. Never would he have experienced anything like it in Kest.

Suddenly, Cailix's cloak folded in on itself and dropped out of the sky below the tree line. Urus aimed for that spot, but didn't want to risk dropping as fast as she had. He maneuvered around the first treetop, bounced off a branch, and ricocheted his way from tree trunk to tree trunk all the way to the forest floor, flapping and struggling to avoid falling at full speed. He rolled to his feet just as Goodwyn dropped from the sky onto an oversized fern.

"We'll be ready on our tower when you do whatever you're going to do," Goodwyn signed.

Urus nodded.

"Just remember what the battle masters say: Never take a step forward without planning two steps in retreat."

"We've lost our minds, you know," Urus said.

Cailix joined them, seeming perfectly relaxed. "Do you want to die trying to stop something worth stopping, or live knowing you never did anything worthwhile?"

"That's something my uncle would have said," Urus said.

"Be careful," Goodwyn grasped the inside of Urus's arm.

"You too," Urus said, returning the gesture.

He stood for a moment and watched as Goodwyn and Cailix disappeared into the thick forest, barely enough room between tree trunks for the two of them to squeeze through. Goodwyn led Cailix into the forest, turning abruptly without warning the way he had led Urus through the dungeons in Kest.

Urus took a deep breath, let it out, and rushed forward, angling away from the path the others had taken. He was thankful for the moonlight; otherwise he would have run headlong into just about every tree in the woods.

It took a while to work his way around to the side of the giant fuel tower without getting too close to the camps. Kestian warrior training in the desert had not given him much practice running through rain forests.

Crouching behind the undergrowth between a pair of trees, Urus peered over at the fuel tower. It was a massive thing, a dark tower of iron and steel and wood with serpentine tubes coming and going in all directions, plugged into cauldrons and boxes. After a while, he discovered where the tubes ultimately started, a central hub filled to bursting with gears.

That's it, he thought. *If I take that out, I kill the tower.*

A small clearing lay between the safety of the wood and the tower, with relatively few patrols crossing through. Whoever these briene were, they didn't look like fighters and they certainly didn't know how to secure their own assets. Overconfidence always meant one of two things: either foolishness or the enemy was powerful enough to justify it. Urus hoped it was the former.

He watched the patrols, counted off the seconds between each, and found an opening where the back of the tower would be unguarded long enough for him to cross the clearing. Waiting until the last guard was out of sight, Urus sprang from the brush and ran as hard as he could.

No women or children, he thought, remembering Murin's words about how the families maintained the machines. That must not have applied to the fuel towers.

Running at full sprint in the humidity, wearing the awkward bat-cloak, was difficult, but still he managed to take the clearing in short order. He clambered up the iron supports on the back of the tower and finally slid into a shadowy spot about halfway up before the first patrol returned.

Directly above him lay the central hub of gears, each grinding and spinning at a different speed, each a different size and lubricated with dark ooze. The gears pushed the fuel through the tubes, so if he could break the gears, it could be days or even weeks before they could use the tower again.

Checking to make sure there was no one above him, he pulled himself up to the next level and crouched, carefully watching each cog and wheel. He followed them, one after the other, until he located one point that, if broken, could cause all the others to fail.

He checked the other tower—no alarms, no fighting, no bodies falling from the scaffolding. This was a good sign.

Urus unhooked a mace from his waist and held it right above the key point in the network of gears. He paused, closed his eyes, and signed a prayer to Ishimani, asking for her strength and fortitude.

Heat surged through his fingers, radiating out from the palms of his hands and into his arms. As he gripped the mace, it felt as if the blood in his veins had been switched with hot water. He saw the glowing blue wisps of smoke drifting up from his fingers, but this time his mace glowed just as brightly.

A mix of fear and elation surged through him, along with the heat from the power, presumably the power of a sigilord if Murin was right. All that power and no one to teach him to use it, no way to control it, and no way to know if he would hurt someone with it.

What a waste of a gift, he thought. *I was definitely the wrong person to get this power.*

For now, he was glad it had come to him when he needed it. With renewed confidence, he plunged the haft of the mace into the gap between the two main gears he had spotted earlier. He waited a moment to make sure the gears stopped, then dropped to the level below.

He didn't want to be anywhere near the tower when those gears finally broke.

He waited at the tower's midpoint, his heart pounding in his chest, his slick palms barely able to keep a grip on the steel girders. He knew he didn't have long before the trap sprung, but he had to wait for the patrol below to leave.

He watched, gritting his teeth at the little brienes' slow footsteps. Finally the patrol walked out of sight and Urus dropped from one level to the next, dropped to another and another, landing in the clearing ready to run.

He ran with every ounce of strength and speed he had left and leapt from the clearing into the woods, rolling into the brush and behind a tree. Still trying to catch his breath, he felt the earth shake.

Flaming debris flew past him into the woods, setting the brush on fire. Huge lengths of tubing flapped and bounced through the air, flames jutting from both ends like some kind of mutated, beheaded dragon.

He risked a glance around the tree to see the tower in flames, metal supports buckling and pieces of it popping and shooting everywhere. His plan had worked far better than he could have imagined.

Now all he had to do was get back to the plateau without being killed by the flaming debris or any soldiers, though the briene were surging toward the tower from all directions, not paying any attention to the forest.

As soon as he recovered enough to breathe again, Urus sprang up and ran deeper into the forest, taking an even wider route than he had last time, careful never to backtrack over his own trail in case it had been discovered by a sentry.

He didn't have time to look back to see how Goodwyn and Cailix were doing; he was too concerned with running and not falling. A moment later he got his answer. Mid-stride, a rush of hot air picked him up and threw him into the side of a tree like he was nothing more than a twig.

Wincing in pain—he felt he had a couple of broken ribs—he looked back at the towers to see the second one had exploded. Where some of Urus's tower still stood smoldering, the other had been blown completely apart, littering the entire camp and much of the nearby forest with flaming parts.

Chaos marred the camps and the briene were running around, at a loss for how to react.

They don't act like any military I've ever seen, Urus thought. They might know how to build weapons, but they lacked the organization and discipline of a true army.

He pulled himself up with the help of a low branch, then ran as fast as he could, but with his injuries it wasn't much more than a hobble. He kept running until skidding to a halt at the forest's edge, where a vast clearing separated him from the plateau where he hoped to find Murin and Corliss.

Urus didn't have a chance to figure out how to get across the clearing. The landscape exploded in brilliant light on the far side of the plateau, a spectacle of bright yellows and oranges with flashes of white. The air reeked of burning dead wood, smoke, and the acrid odor of a blacksmith's furnace, probably coming from all the hot metal.

To his left, under the flashing lights and the glow of the nearby fires, he saw thousands upon thousands of briene, all of them scurrying this way and that with their soot-covered aprons and their strange helmets and goggles.

It was now or never. If he waited too long, the camps would regain order and he would be square in the middle of an enemy army with no way out.

Shaking his head at the sheer stupidity of everything they had been doing lately, Urus again sprinted from the safety of the forest, out into the clearing.

He hadn't gone more than a few strides when the sky above the clearing erupted in bright white light. Still running, he looked up to see torches burned as bright as the sun, floating down from the sky, carried by giant white tarpaulins spread wide, almost like white windrunner cloaks. He was curious about the flares, but not curious enough to stop running.

Urus didn't need to be able to hear to know that there were briene charging his way. He could smell them on the wind and feel them pounding the earth beneath his feet.

There was nothing else to do now but run, and run hard. He was too far into the clearing to race back to the forest. He had to make it to the plateau and then try and glide across to the mountain road.

A blast of wind from behind knocked him to the ground as he neared the center of the clearing. Instinct told him to lie flat. Obeying that instinct he slid across the freshly cut brush, just as a massive bronze wing sliced through the air above his head.

He scrambled to his feet to see a huge bronze bird pulling up high into the sky, preparing to come around for another dive. Urus looked around for someplace to run or hide and found nothing except the sight of thousands of approaching soldiers.

Again he ran, biting back the pain in his ribs and legs.

The bronze bird swung around and dove straight for him.

Urus remembered slogging through the water in the cavern below Kest, remembered hesitating and almost getting killed because he wouldn't act. This time, Goodwyn and Murin weren't around to save him.

Act or die. React and you're already dead.

He reached for the mace on his right hip, only then remembering that it was gone. Still running, he unhooked his other mace and kept an eye on the metal bird plunging out of the moonlit sky and the small silhouette of the briene piloting it.

As it drew closer, Urus ran in a crouch. Just as the bird reached its lowest point, Urus dove, spinning onto his back before he landed. He reached upward and grabbed hold of the bird's metal talons as it flew over. The jolt of the rapid climb through the air nearly knocked him off, but he managed to cling to the underside of the metal beast.

It soared up and rolled around again, making for another pass at Urus's last position. The pilot must not have known what had happened. That gave Urus just enough of the element of surprise to climb up from the talons, clamber over the right wing, and leap for the pilot's seat.

This time there was no hesitation; this wasn't like the boat. He swung his mace, slamming it with full force into the briene's chest. The pilot flew backward but not out, as a thick fabric strap kept him fastened to the seat.

Urus punched the smaller man in the face as he reached for the control stick, then cut the strap. He waited until the bird flew over another high plateau and dumped the pilot out where the fall wouldn't kill him.

Slipping into the pilot's seat, he studied a mesmerizing display of knobs and gears, all arranged around a single metal rod jutting up from the floor. He had seen the pilot holding the rod and so he did the same.

It didn't take him long to figure out that the rod worked a lot like shifting his weight when using the windrunner cloak. Urus banked hard to the right and swung the flying machine back around toward the rendezvous point on the plateau.

Flying the metal bird was even more exciting than gliding using the cloak. He could fly up or down or in any direction and he felt safer sitting inside the bird's metal head than he did gliding in the open, exposed and vulnerable.

It took only seconds to get back to the plateau. He flew low to the ground but saw no one, not even Murin or Corliss. They must not have been able to make it back from wherever they had been when the explosions started.

Urus veered off and headed for the road carved into the mountain, all the while looking down at the chaos of the camp. As he settled into an easy course, still not sure how to control the speed of the bird, he risked a quick glance behind him.

He was being followed.

Two more giant metal birds soared down toward him in fast pursuit. Urus pulled back on the stick to try to get higher. He pushed pedals on the floor and spun gears and knobs, but nothing, not even his repeated pounding and kicking, made the bird fly faster.

As he approached the mountainside, he saw four silhouettes running up the road, one over a head taller than the rest. *That must be them.*

Urus rolled the aircraft toward the mountain, then pulled back on the stick again, climbing higher and higher. The other two birds easily swung up behind him, closing the distance until they were only a few feet behind him as the birds soared straight up.

He looked back past the giant metal tailfeather that controlled the bird's direction, down at the briene pursuing him, and an absolutely insane idea came to him.

He gripped his mace, rolled up and out of his seat, and slammed the mace into the tail, pushing off of the bird with his feet. His bird spun and smashed into the other two, sending a giant wreck of bronze and steel spinning down toward the earth.

Urus spread his arms and legs as he fell, the cloak billowing up and catching him. He soared down past two switchbacks in the road and then, mimicking the landing he'd seen Corliss and the others perform, he leaned back and folded the cloak inward as his feet hit the ground, running off the extra momentum.

Exhausted, bruised, and in pain, he collapsed on the road just as the others came up around the switchback.

"Urus!" Goodwyn called, running to his side.

Urus sat up, waving Goodwyn off. He clutched his ribs, but he could still manage. Barely.

"That was some spectacle down there," Corliss said, "With those towers down, we might stand a chance against them."

"No," Murin said, shaking his head sadly, "we do not stand a chance. With those towers down, we have just enough time to try and get the townspeople to safety. The briene likely have many more of those towers in reserve. We have bought some time while the briene bring up the reinforcements."

Urus pushed off a knee, grimacing as he stood, and looked over at Cailix. Her clothes were soaking wet, as was her hair, and there were dark smudges on her face and hands.

"It's all right," she said, noticing his gaze. "The blood isn't mine."

"All of that is blood?" Urus gave Goodwyn a questioning look. They would definitely have to talk about this when they got back to the city.

"You said there was a second way out of the city, but it was dangerous. Too dangerous for civilians?" Murin asked Corliss as they started up the road again, supporting Urus's weight between them.

"There are tunnels that lead to caves you can take to the other side of the mountain. It's a treacherous road to get anywhere safe, but it's possible."

"When we get back to the city, you'll need to order everyone to evacuate." Though Corliss was now in control of the city, Murin's grimace made his statement more an order than a suggestion.

"There is one small problem," Corliss said.

"And that is?"

"The tunnel to the other side of the mountain is controlled by Noah, the head of the thieves' guild and the man who has been trying to kill me."

"I may be able to help with that," Murin said with a grin. "He and I are apparently friends."

Chapter Seventeen

Draegon Asurnios surveyed the battlefield, his cloak billowing in the dry desert heat that carried the stench of war: a potpourri of blood, rot, and burning embers. Thick black smoke drifted over the red-orange sand from the fires of the camps, burning boats, and flames still raging within the walls of Kest.

He wiped his face, scraping the insufferable sand out of the scars in his cheeks and his mustache. He could not wait to be done with this miserable place. He was the first, the first of all of them. He remembered the day he had discovered his powers as though it was yesterday, even though that day was over five thousand years gone.

He had seen it all and survived everything imaginable. He was one of the few who remembered what the world looked like on the brink of destruction, humanity about to become extinct. That was the height of the Age of Power, when the worst of the fighting between his kind and his ancient enemy had nearly destroyed everything. The scar it left on the universe could still be felt by those who knew what to look for.

He stood there on the dune, surrounded by tents and commanders from the four armies at his command, and surveyed the siege before him. These people didn't know war, not real war like he had seen. They didn't know power. If they had seen even half of what he remembered, they would turn and run, never again to take up the blade.

He chuckled aloud at the thought.

A blond-bearded, bare-chested general with as many scars as muscles stepped out from one of the nearby tents, a lit pipe in one hand and a mug of ale in the other. Tattoos and war paint decorated his body from neck to toe.

"My men grow restless, Draegon. Where is all the limitless plunder, the riches and bounty of women ripe for the taking you promised us when we signed on for this? I didn't drag my army this far south for some fool's errand."

How dare the pathetic creature speak to him so!

Draegon answered without taking his eyes from the smoldering city on the horizon. "Remember your place, Kraedd. I promised you a quarter of the haul from the city after you took it."

"And so where is our share?" Kraedd asked, gesturing at the city.

Draegon scowled at him. "Your men sacked the city, but you fell back. In fact, all of the armies fled. You stand around outside, waiting like vultures for the enemy to die."

"You can't blame us for that, mage. Those desert savages closed the gates after we took it. They trapped ten thousand of my men and just as many from the other armies within. You can't imagine the bloodbath. The soldiers are cut off from command, fending for themselves in small units in a city they don't know."

"And what of the Kestians now?" asked Draegon.

Another commander stepped out from the tent, a fair-skinned man with long black hair and tight-fitting armor, his hand resting on the hilt of a broad sword.

"They hide in the nooks and crannies like insects fleeing the light," he said.

Kraedd nodded. "It is madness. I have never seen anything like it. They have besieged the besiegers. Our men trapped inside cannot get out, and the savages appear out of the sand like scorpions when we try to take a gate to rescue them."

"You got yourselves into this mess, you can get yourselves out," Draegon said.

"No way, mage. You're going to conjure up something to get my men out of that city, or to get reinforcements in. Blast the gates open wide or something."

Draegon spun and grabbed Kraedd by the throat, lifting him off the ground and high over his head. Without a word he crushed the man's windpipe and let him drop to the ground in a lifeless heap.

"Any questions, Commander Elwin?"

"None," replied the remaining commander.

"I am finished here. My companions have accomplished their goal. If you wish to retreat and cut your losses now, there will be no reprisal from me."

"Understood. And if we stay?"

"Then if you manage to clean the rats out of their holes, whatever riches remain are yours for the keeping, including whatever is left on the bodies of the other armies."

Elwin nodded but said nothing.

"Before you decide, bring me the turncoat. I wish to speak with him before I leave this foul place."

Elwin nodded and plodded awkwardly over the loose sand, down the dune and into a larger, rectangular tent.

Draegon turned around and smiled. There, hovering a few feet above the sand, were the translucent images of four of his long-lost brethren, those he had not seen in the flesh for several millennia.

"With this vertex destroyed, our ability to reach into this plane grows stronger," said one of the nearby shimmering figures.

"Waldron should be under siege as we speak. That vertex should be destroyed in a matter of hours," Draegon said.

"Have you determined the locations of the others?" asked another of the apparitions.

"My apprentice was able to copy the Woan Map before it crumbled to dust. We have the locations and are massing resources as needed. We have gathered a navy to reach the last vertex."

"Timing is everything, as you know, Draegon. We will not get another chance like this for a very long time."

"I am aware of the timing. Know your place, Esseril. I am the one who figured out when the time would be right in the first place. Have there been any stirrings from our old enemies?"

"None," replied one of the figures. "your notion that they were wiped out entirely by the Fulcum War may hold true. Surely they would have felt the breaking of the wards and come out of hiding if any of them yet lived."

"Stay vigilant; they may yet remain and are just waiting to strike,"

Draegon said.

"There is another matter," whispered a pair of robed, translucent figures in unison.

The Meretho twins, thought Draegon. On their own they were utterly useless, but together they possessed the gift of prophecy and foresight. Power like that was always wasted on the dimwitted or undeserving. "What matter?" he asked.

"We appear to have failed to account for temporal shift. The vertex stones are no longer in the same place as their anchors within the quantum foam."

"So destroying the stones isn't enough?"

The twins shook their heads. "We will need a chain reaction of splitting atoms to tear the bonds with the anchor. An impact that tears at the fabric. Only then will the vertex be truly destroyed and the tether cut, taking the ward with it."

"There isn't enough blood of potency on this planet to create that kind of explosion," Draegon snapped.

"No, but there is something we have never tried. There may yet be another way—" The ghostly figures stopped and peered over Draegon's shoulder.

Two soldiers pushed one of the dark-skinned savages up the dune, his hands bound, and shoved him to his knees before Draegon. A single tail of black hair dropped to his shoulder from a topknot on his otherwise bald head. Chains of bone hung from his neck and waist.

"Why are you treating me like a prisoner? Anderis and I had a deal!" sputtered the fool. Traitors were all the same, Draegon thought. If a man could betray his own kind to your benefit, he could easily betray you to his own. Never trust a traitor.

"I believe Anderis held up his part of the bargain. Your life was spared."

"I was supposed to remain in Kest to rule!"

"Then why did you leave?"

"I killed the emperor with my own hand," he spat. "and I nearly killed the Commander of the First Fist. You should be rewarding me. You owe me!"

"Nearly? You're telling me that you let the city's highest ranking soldier escape?"

"Yes; well, no, not intentionally. His men are the ones organizing the resistance. They're calling it a reverse siege. They're all mad; they actually think they will prevail. The shamans loyal to me have been rounded up and thrown in dungeon cells."

Draegon gave a bored sigh. "None of that concerns me anymore. Now that I have what I want, Kest is just another worthless, pathetic city filled with weak, powerless little people."

"Anderis and I had a deal," the prisoner insisted. "You have to honor his promise! I am Kebetir, the High Shaman, not some common citizen!"

"I was just about to speak with Anderis. Perhaps I will mention your concerns to him," Draegon said. He beckoned to a soldier.

"Get a bowl," he said, and the man ran off to obey. The soldier returned and placed the bowl on the sand in front of the shaman.

"A blade," Draegon said, holding out his hand.

"What are you doing? You can't do this to me!" the shaman cried in an embarrassing display of weakness and fear.

The soldier put a sharp dagger in Draegon's hand. Draegon sliced across Kebetir's throat, and the soldiers held his head back, pumping his blood into the deep bowl below.

Draegon dipped his finger into the wonderful liquid and swirled it about, muttering the ancient words of power as he drew energy from the blood and focused it, bent it to his will.

A moment later the pool of blood lost its color and then seemed to disappear altogether, acting as a window to some other place, a dark, candlelit stone room. Anderis's head appeared gazing down into the bowl.

"Master," came his voice, a moment after his mouth moved in the pool.

"Anderis, I trust you have news for me. I would hate to have wasted all this blood merely for smalltalk."

Anderis hesitated, his gaze shifting for a tiny moment. It wasn't like Anderis to look anxious. Something was definitely wrong. He had better not have failed him already, because Draegon wasn't above killing his own apprentices to make an example of them.

"Master, there is much news, and some of it disturbs me," he said.

"What of the vertex?" Draegon asked, impatient.

"The briene are ready. They bring their siege engines upon Waldron at first light."

"After that business with the Woan Map, this had better go perfectly. I want that vertex destroyed tomorrow. You need to inspect the vertex yourself. I need to know if temporal shift has pulled the anchor away from the stone."

"It shall be done, master."

"Now, what is this news you hesitate to deliver?"

"My pet betrayed me. She has sided with the locals. She even tried to kill me."

"This is hardly newsworthy, Anderis. It would be newsworthy if she had succeeded in the attempt. I have warned you about keeping pets before."

"She has tremendous potential."

"Get to the point, apprentice."

"She and others sabotaged some of the briene siege equipment last night. Nothing that will stop the siege, but it may take a little longer now."

"I am still waiting for the part where any of this becomes relevant to me."

"Master, one of the people she is with…he is an arbiter."

Draegon took a step back from the bowl, shock running through his system, squeezing his lungs tight. "Impossible, they were all killed or shut on the other side of the vertex wards."

"Apparently not this one, master. And there is more."

Draegon dismissed the news with a wave of his hand. "Even if there is an arbiter, he cannot interfere; it would violate their oath. And besides, they were invaluable to our cause during the war, so why are you concerned?"

"Last night, before the raid on the briene, I felt something, something I haven't felt in ages."

Draegon seriously considered whether he should jump through the pool and strangle the incompetent bastard himself. "Out with it, Anderis, before I kill you out of impatience alone."

"It was a sigilord, master. There is a sigilord in Waldron."

The news hit Draegon square in the chest. His heart stopped and he gasped for air.

"Also impossible," he managed to say after taking a deep breath. "After the arbiters sealed the vertices under the terms of the so-called treaty, we killed every last sigilord and all of their sons and daughters, their spouses, and even their dogs."

"And yet that is what I felt. The sigilord was in the room with the arbiter and my apprentice when she betrayed me. The sigilord's presence was weak, tiny, but he was there, in that room, somewhere."

Draegon straightened and forced himself to take a deep breath. This could not be possible. There was no way it could be true. But if there was even a slight chance it was true...

"So, *apprentice*, you are telling me that there is a sigilord, an untrained rogue blood mage, and an arbiter all in Waldron, and they might be working *together*?"

Anderis nodded on the other side of the rippling pool.

"The wards are still up," called one of the floating spectres behind him. "The sigilord must have been born to this world. He is without a teacher or any knowledge of his birthright. He will be harmless."

"The sigilord may not have access to the sigils, but the waif already knows too much, thanks to your bumbling, *apprentice*," roared Draegon. "She is dangerous, and with him nearby, she could prove lethal."

"What are your wishes, master?" called Anderis from the pool.

"This changes everything. This is now more important than the siege. The briene can finish their work without you. The girl cannot be allowed to tap the sigilord's power."

Draegon bent over the bowl and glared into the eyes of his apprentice. "Kill her, but leave the sigilord to me."

CHAPTER EIGHTEEN

Urus sat on a bench in the corner of a brightly lit room in a Waldron barracks, leaning against a cold stone wall, staring at nothing in particular. Again his thoughts returned to home—if there even was a home—and his missing uncle.

But how much of a home could it be now, anyway? He'd been branded to be shunned by everyone in Kest, only grudgingly fed and clothed like a prisoner. Despite the crowd of soldiers in the room, his best friend standing nearby, and his newfound companions, he felt truly alone.

Even at his lowest point, standing on the palace rooftop, looking down at the escape death might bring, he'd still had Aegaz and a city he loved, even if that city thought nothing of him in return.

A hand waving in front of his face brought him out of his reflection.

"We need to treat your wounds, sir," said the soldier, still mostly in his nightclothes.

Why would he call me sir? Urus thought.

"I'm fine." Urus dismissed the offer with a wave of his hand.

"The Knight Marshall insists," he replied.

"I said I don't need any help," Urus said, straightening. Sitting up sent pain shooting through his chest, radiating out through his broken ribs.

Nobody needs to see what's under my armor, Urus thought. *Nobody here knows that I'm not a real warrior.*

"Sir, let me just get your armor off and I can dress the wounds and set your ribs."

"No!" Urus shouted. He tried to stand up to get away, but doubled over in pain. It hadn't been very long since he'd hit those trees, and the pain was getting worse with each minute.

The next face he saw was Goodwyn's, helping him back up onto the bench. "Let him tend to your wounds, you stubborn ass."

Urus lacked the strength to resist any further. He leaned back and looked around the room. Murin stood in a corner, saying nothing but taking everything in. Corliss barked orders at soldiers as soon as they arrived, continuing a half dozen other conversations over a table full of maps as soon as they left.

The barracks door swung inward, admitting a tall, barrel-chested man in plate armor with a sword slung over each hip. Stains and scratches marred nearly every inch of his gear.

Now this is a man who knows how to fight, Urus thought. *Though the heavy armor makes him slow and easy to defeat.*

"Captain Rhygant. Did you stop at the baker's for a nice sweet roll on your way here?" Corliss snapped, not looking up from the map-covered tabled.

"Sir," the captain said with a bow. "I've been seeing to the defenses. Lieutenant Vidiam has been organizing the men into companies while I have been readying the ballistae."

"And?"

"We're low on stones. We may end up hurling goats and laundry baskets by day's end of the first battle," Rhygant said with a sigh.

"Noted." Corliss pivoted his attention from a map of local geography to a diagram of Waldron's inner structures.

Cailix sat on a bench across the room from Urus, dressed in clean linens, eating an apple while being helped on with a suit of padded leather armor. She seemed as distant and unaffected by all of this as Murin.

Pain seared Urus's neck and shoulders as the soldier unstrapped the stiff leather plates.

"So what now?" he asked, hoping to take the focus off of himself.

Corliss looked up from the table. "Now you let my man tend your wounds before one of those broken ribs pokes a hole in your lung."

With the leather vest out of the way, the soldier grabbed the soiled and bloody sleeves of the acolyte's tunic and pulled it off.

All eyes in the room turned to him, the commanders straightening at the table, eyes wide and jaws dropping. They stared at his brand.

"What in the name of the gods did that to you, son?" Corliss asked.

Urus stared at the floor, biting back the tears he felt welling up inside. The brand on his chest was shame enough; he wasn't about to let anyone see him cry over it.

"Rhygant, stop staring," Corliss chided.

"Sorry sir, I just—" Rhygant said, unable to keep his eyes from the symbol on Urus's chest. There was something different about the way Rhygant looked at it. The glint in his eyes wasn't one of shock, but something else entirely.

Gritting his teeth and taking a deep breath, Urus tried to speak, but his throat tightened. He knew he would burst into tears if he opened his mouth.

Instead, mouth still clenched shut to block the tears, he signed to Goodwyn, who translated aloud, "It's the mark of the culled, those found not worthy and skilled enough to be true Kestian warriors."

"They burned that mark onto you like that because you weren't a good enough warrior?"

Urus nodded.

"Well if that isn't the biggest pile of manure I've ever set foot in." Corliss leaned forward on the map table with a look of disgust on his face, glaring across the room at the scar. "You're a better fighter than half my men. Hell, you blew up a fuel tower, jumped off a flying bird machine, and took out two briene pilots at the same time. How could they find you not skilled enough?"

"I failed their tests," Urus signed again, the emotional and physical pain still too much for him to speak. "I never passed the blindfighting test, and I scored lowest on all of the others."

Corliss gave Urus a deep, appraising look. After a long pause, he stood up and said, "Seems to me that you've got skill to spare, son, so if you failed those tests, maybe there was another reason."

Urus didn't get a chance to ask what he meant by that, as a pair of scouts charged into the room, both shouting and gesticulating. Even with Murin in the room, if Urus couldn't see their lips, Murin's strange language tricks didn't seem to work.

As the scouts delivered their reports, each of them turned and stared at the brand on Urus's chest. Ashamed, he wanted to go hide somewhere that no one could see him, but the poultice Corliss's man was rubbing into the bruises felt too good to refuse.

"They've broken camp. They are massing and bringing up more battalions from the coast," Corliss said, turning to Murin. "I need to know what this army will do. Will they try to starve us out? Will they come at us in waves? I need something so I can prepare my men."

"They will certainly not do anything to delay. This army is not here for conquest," Murin said, scrutinizing the maps. "They do not want land or power or title. They are here because the Order has manipulated them—lied to them, twisted their motivations, and convinced them that they fight a just cause. The Order wants the vertex destroyed, and they mean to lay waste to anything between them and their goal."

Murin stood up from the maps, stroking the few stands of white hair that passed for his beard, and asked, "Have you sent word to the king?"

Corliss nodded. "I sent word as soon as the fires were spotted, before last night's little adventure. Even if the fastest of my falcons makes it, the king's forces will take at least a week to get here."

"A week?" said Urus. "Isn't the king here in Waldron?"

Corliss waved Urus over and pointed to a spot on the map. Despite his body's complaints, Urus stood up and made his way to the map table. Corliss's physician followed, pasting more sticky goo onto Urus's wounds and wrapping them tightly with bandages. He didn't recognize any of the words on the map.

"This is Waldron here. We're just a ducal seat, and a small one at that." Corliss slid his finger across the map, north up through a forest and out over plains to rest on the image of a great castle, "Here is Niragan, the capital of Acederon, our kingdom."

Urus was stunned. The idea of the leader of a city not actually being in the city seemed—unthinkable. He could not imagine the emperor trying to rule Kest from some remote mountaintop. No one would stand for it.

"The king rules Waldron from that far away?"

"Not just Waldron, but Prilameth," Corliss touched a separate dot on the map as he listed off each city name, "Ethiral, Trienn, Alleigan, Jorelith, and all the farms, villages, outposts, and roads in this circle."

"I've never heard of such a vast kingdom before," Urus said.

"Waldron and the other cities have sworn fealty to the king. In exchange we get safe passage on the roads, commerce free of tariffs, and the security of the kingdom."

"If it takes the king a week to come help, that doesn't seem like much security."

"This is an unusual case. No army this size has ever before massed within the kingdom borders."

Urus turned and his ribs stabbed at him. The physician helped him on with his padded leather vest and cinched it up tight. It hurt at first but eventually the pressure holding the poultice felt good.

The Knight Marshall lifted a sword from brackets on the wall. It was much wider than the usual blades, forged from thick steel and somewhat longer than a typical broadsword.

"This was made by the best blacksmith in the city," Corliss said, admiring the blade like a proud father. "It swings as heavily as a two-handed sword, but has perfect balance. He swears it will cleave through just about any armor. Hopefully this will help ease the loss of your maces."

Urus took the weapon and held it with one hand. Corliss was right: the heavy weapon was perfectly balanced, the broad blade great for parrying. He ran a finger along the blade, satisfied when the thin edge easily drew blood.

He noticed Cailix staring at the blood. He wiped the blade clean, then sheathed it and winced through the pain to strap the sword to his back.

"It's a fantastic blade, thank you very much."

Corliss nodded. "All it needs now is a name. In Waldron, all commissioned soldiers name their weapons."

Hugo, Urus thought, in honor of the doll-hero his mother had made for him when he was a boy.

"The weapon suits you, Urus. Big, bulky, awkward," Goodwyn said with a grin.

Urus ignored the joke. He couldn't stand around in the barracks anymore. Despite the size of the room, it felt too dark and closed in, and he needed some fresh air, or whatever passed for fresh in this part of the world.

He pushed through the door and stepped out onto the stone balcony overlooking one of the main streets of the city.

What he saw shocked him to the core and filled him with sadness.

Women and children filled the streets, more than he thought could possibly live in a city this size. The women carried sacks on their backs or dragged trunks behind them on wheels while the children clung to their favorite toy or clutched a beloved blanket, toddling along behind their parents in lines like little ducklings.

They were fleeing the city, heading for the warrens and beyond while every man capable of bearing a sword stayed behind. Corliss and his men would try to keep the briene army at bay long enough to get the women and children to safety.

Such a strange place, Urus thought. *The women and children flee rather than fight*. No Kestians ever fled from a fight.

He stood watching the looks of despair on the women's faces and the children crying, the word 'Papa' on their lips. Those old enough to know what was going on futilely tried to comfort the younger ones.

Goodwyn gripped his shoulder, giving him an excuse to look away from the sad scene. Rhygant stepped out of the barracks, followed by Murin, Corliss, Goodwyn, Cailix, and several of Corliss's men. They stood on the balcony surveying the exodus below.

"This isn't what war is supposed to look like," Urus signed to Goodwyn.

"It is for the losers," he replied.

Urus stood in silence for a moment, letting that statement sink in.

"I want to help keep them safe, to defend Waldron," Urus said to Corliss.

"No matter what your people thought of your skills, I know my men would be glad to have you and your friends fight at their side. The heavens know we could use all the help we can get."

"We have a more important task ahead of us, Master Corliss," Murin said.

"What could be more important than defending this city and protecting those people down there?" Urus said. "I'm not going to run while another city gets attacked like we did at Kest."

"Have you not been paying attention? There is far more at stake here than Waldron or Kest. You cannot possibly imagine the atrocities that will befall this world and others should the Order succeed in destroying the vertexes; there are no words to describe that horror."

"So we're just supposed to go off and leave these people?" Urus asked aloud, fists clenched.

"If the Order succeeds because we stayed behind to slay a few briene and perhaps save one or two lives, then the fate of the entire world will be our fault, and trust me when I say tell you that you cannot fathom that kind of guilt."

Urus remembered the ocean of guilt and pain that washed over the shores in Murin's mind when the two had shared that awkward moment in Kest's dungeons. What could fill a man with such anguish?

"So what would you have us do then?"

"We must find the vertex before the Order does."

"Have you any idea where this thing might be, or even what it looks like?" Corliss asked.

"Only that it will be in the oldest part of the city. It could be anything—a stone slab, a wall, anything on which the ancient sigils could be etched. The writing will look freshly chiseled though it was carved in a time when this mountain was nothing more than a refuge from the weather for nomads and travelers passing between the old kingdoms."

Murin leaned against the railing, a hand clutching his forehead, eyebrows furrowed.

"What's wrong?" Cailix asked him.

"There are too many people here; their minds assault me with ceaseless prattle. I do not have any of the herbs used by the Kestian shaman nor anything else that can dull the noise."

"You can hear their thoughts?" Corliss asked the question Urus had been itching to ask.

Murin gave a slow nod.

"My men and I are going to lead the citizens down to the warrens to make sure they don't have any trouble with Noah and his thugs," Corliss told him. "Once we see them safely in, we'll be heading for the Sky Gate. You can decide then whether you're staying with us or whether you're going after this vertex."

"I want to go with Urus and the gray man to find the vertex," said Cailix.

"No way," Goodwyn said, stepping close and towering over her. "You put your lot in with that blood mage who killed the duke. You're not coming with us."

Cailix's eyes flared, but she spoke calmly. "I used him to stay alive, then I turned on him as soon as I could."

"You're not coming with us," Goodwyn said.

"Yes, she is," Urus said.

Goodwyn just turned and stared back at Urus.

"I know you don't trust her," Urus signed so no one would overhear. "But I do. If she wants to come with us, she can."

Goodwyn shrugged. "If you say so. But I still don't like it."

The group, accompanied by a detachment of Corliss's men, made their way out of the barracks and down to the street below, called Tannery Row by the locals. Despite the fact that no one was working that day, it still smelled as bad as its name implied.

They joined up with the procession of refugees and weaved their way to the front. Urus hated the idea of heading in the opposite direction of the fight—again. The notion that there was a fate worse than losing another city to siege scared him to his core. After seeing what the blood magic could do, he didn't want to imagine what horrors awaited them if they failed.

They walked in silence at the head of the crowd, slowly making their way out of the more prosperous sections of the city, then heading around the curve of the mountain and down the slope toward the entrance to the warrens.

"If this thing you seek is as old as you say it is," Corliss said, breaking the silence, "and it's down in the old caverns below the city, then there is someone who might be able to help you find it."

"Who?" Murin asked.

"Noah." Corliss snorted. "That scum knows every inch of the inside of the mountain below Waldron."

"How are we to find this Noah?"

Corliss stopped short and held up a closed fist. The soldiers behind him turned and stopped the throng of civilians.

"I don't think finding him is going to be a problem," he said, pointing ahead. Down the road, just before it passed under the bridge marking the unofficial start of the shanty towns and slums that were the warrens, stood a bearded man in a brightly colored shirt and matching pants.

"That is the man who operates the opium tent where you found me, Master Corliss," offered Murin.

Corliss simply shook his head and sighed.

"I won't speak to the Knight Marshall," called Noah. He appeared to be alone, which seemed odd, given Corliss's description of him. Urus suspected there were thieves hiding around every corner.

Corliss stood still, folding his hands over his chest, "Look at the people behind me, Noah. You would drag them into our petty feud?"

Noah said nothing.

Murin was about to take a step forward, but Urus felt compelled to do something. He had seen enough of this kind of bickering between the shaman and warriors in Kest. The two of them would never settle this on their own. They each had too great a personal stake in the argument.

He took a few steps forward and shouted down the street, "Will you speak to a stranger then? One with no claim in this quarrel between you and Corliss?"

Goodwyn shot him a warning glance.

Urus kept walking so he could get close enough to read Noah's lips.

"You speak our language, but you slur it like a drunken child. Are you a drunkard, then, stranger?" asked Noah.

Urus studied the leader of the thieves' guild. He was an average man. He had no scars or markings, his beard was nearly trimmed, his hair cut short. He was a little round but not an overly fat man. If anything, Noah looked a little *too* average. Everything about him seemed to be deliberately insignificant.

"He is deaf and was born as such," Murin said with remarkable diplomacy, given his attitude toward the emperor back in Kest. "He does not speak as clearly as others. I can assure you the boy is no drunkard."

"I was talking to the boy," Noah snapped, walking closer to Urus so they could talk without shouting. The idea seemed foolish to Urus, since Noah's volume didn't matter at all. "That true? You deaf?"

Urus nodded.

"Well, I suppose given your company that may be a blessing. That way you don't have to listen to Corliss's shrill cry, and the gray opium fiend has a voice as deep as a thunderclap."

Urus ignored the comments. "The city is going to be attacked. We need to get these people to safety."

"Oh, I know all about the little people and their crazy machines at the bottom of the mountain. That was quite a display you put on last night."

Urus blinked. Noah was definitely more well-informed than Urus had expected. Corliss had warned that he was not to be underestimated, and now Urus understood why.

"I will let these people into the warrens and will even provide guides to get them down through the tunnels and out the other side of the mountain," Noah paused, holding up an index finger. "On one condition."

"My head is staying firmly attached to my neck, if that's what you're thinking, Noah," said Corliss, stepping closer to the conversation. The men behind him bristled.

Noah ignored the remark and turned back to Urus. "I want a full pardon. If this city isn't a smoldering ash when the enemy take their machines and go, I want to walk the streets of Waldron as a free man."

Now Corliss bristled. "Absolutely not. You're a king among criminals. Not a single crime happens in this city without you being involved somehow."

Noah grinned. "Ever stop and wonder about that, Knight Marshal? I don't just control the crime in Waldron, I control Waldron itself. You may think you're the law and order around here, but you're only the law. *I'm* the order. I maintain the even balance. Without me, this city would plunge into anarchy."

Corliss's face reddened with anger and his fists clenched. "That's absurd! You're nothing but a—"

Urus cut him off. "Gentlemen! There's an army approaching, and there are thousands of civilians behind us in need of safety. Can you put aside your bickering for their sake?" Urus snapped. He had seen countless petty arguments while watching his uncle work, and heard tales of even more that the emperor had settled. He felt a little disappointed to see that such arguments persisted even this far away from Kest.

"The boy is right," Corliss said.

"I'll still need a pardon before I take this flock off your hands."

"Knight Marshall, we need to get the citizens to safety so we can get back to the city's defenses," Rhygant urged.

Corliss gripped the hilt of his sword and gnashed his teeth together, a pained look on his face. "All right. It sickens me to my core to do so, Noah, but the safety of these people is what's important here."

"Fine, my men will—" Noah stopped short, jaw dropping as he stared up into the sky.

Urus turned to look. Dozens of the briene mechanical birds swooped down low over the road. Briene tossed little black clay pots from the front-shielded cockpits in the bronze bird heads. As the pots shattered, thick, black smoke billowed up. Within seconds half of Waldron had been swallowed in the dark cloud.

Urus drew Hugo, again appreciating the expert craftsmanship that had gone into its making, waiting for one of the birds to drop within attack range. Just seconds later, a silhouette of a giant bird glided through the dark smoke then burst out, its gold and bronze feathers gleaming in the sunlight. Urus dodged to one side, swinging and slamming the flat of the blade into the back of the pilot's head.

The briene sagged in the cockpit, and the bird-machine smashed to pieces against the stone cliff that formed one side of the road to the warrens.

"This is going to be a bloodbath! The civilians are exposed and we can't defend them from the air!" Corliss shouted. "Get them to the warrens!"

Urus looked but couldn't find Murin, Goodwyn, or Noah. *Probably knee-deep in briene corpses by now*, Urus thought. Through the thinning smoke, hundreds of panicked people ran, the women snatching up their children and making for whatever cover they could find.

Urus studied his hands, wrapped tightly around the hilt of his sword. He could try to use his power, to summon the blue smoke and use it against the briene like he had against the bullies in the hostel. But what price would he pay? Could he control it? Would he hurt his friends instead of the briene?

Cailix stepped out of the smoke and grabbed his arm. "I need some of your blood."

Urus gaped. "You need *what*?"

"No time to explain, but those women and children are going to die if you don't give me some blood. It's okay, I just need a little."

"I'm not giving you any of my—"

"Now!" she demanded, pulling a dagger from her sleeve. "Or I'll take it by force!"

Urus relented, figuring that donating his blood voluntarily would be much less painful than Cailix taking it. Sheathing Hugo, he grabbed her dagger and pressed the edge of the tip into his finger just deep enough to draw a bead of blood.

Cailix snatched the knife back and gripped his hand. She squeezed his finger, forcing more blood to the surface.

Out of the corner of his eye, Urus could see a towering shape rushing toward him through the smoke, hands flailing. It could have been Murin, but he couldn't see through the smoke to read his lips.

Cailix rubbed each of her fingertips in the blood dripping from the wound.

Now the flailing silhouette jumped up and down as it raced toward them. *What in the hell is wrong with Murin?* Urus thought.

Each of Cailix's palms were now coated in red, as were her fingertips. She turned to the chaos in the smoke cloud, the metal birds diving and looping over the crowd like a swarm of bees over a field of flowers.

Murin finally emerged from the smoke, shouting, "…your blood!"

Cailix thrust her hands forward, and wind surged down from the mountainside, slamming into the road like a hurricane. In an instant the smoke was gone, revealing the few civilians in the road who hadn't found cover pressed face-down against the cobblestones.

"No!" Murin shouted, somehow still standing against the gale.

Cailix turned her attention to the gleaming bird machines. She flung her hands outward and, one by one, little tornados spun up out of nowhere, sucked the machines into their vortex, and flung them out over the side wall, where Urus imagined they shattered into pieces as they tumbled down the mountainside.

The tornados exploded out of pockets of air everywhere over the city, some ripping rooftops off buildings, others sucking gaping holes out of walls.

Stones and debris flew in all directions, smashing into buildings and sometimes even people.

Moments later, Cailix and Urus stood by the entrance to the warrens, looking up at the road. A few puffs of smoke lingered over the stone as frightened mothers and children emerged from crevices and alleyways, escorted by Goodwyn, Corliss, and his soldiers. Thousands of little gears, springs, and chunks of metal littered the roadway, along with the rest of the debris from the tornados that Cailix had summoned.

She turned to meet Urus's eyes. "You have potent blood, Urus."

"And your aim is terrible," he answered, pointing at a group of citizens digging out of a pile of rubble. Thankfully all of them seemed to have survived with just cuts and bruises.

The others approached, all staring at Cailix. Even Corliss marveled at the girl. *Was that fear in his eyes?*

"Before you boys arrived here," he began, looking at Urus, "I would have bet my mother's life that magic was nothing more than a myth. Since then I have seen men vanish into thin air, and now a girl who can use blood to summon storms. It was luck alone that kept the innocent citizens from being caught in the debris."

"I tried to warn you, Urus. You should not have let her use your blood," Murin said.

"Why?"

"Why do you think the blood mages tore this entire world apart, hunting down every last sigilord they could find during the Fulcrum War?" Murin demanded, not pausing long enough to let anyone answer. "In the hands of a blood mage, sigilord blood is a…there is no word for it. It is a super catalyst. With sigilord blood, a single blood mage can wipe an entire army from the earth. Once the blood mages discovered this, the sigilord genocide began."

"I had no idea," Urus said. He felt terrible. He saw how much power Cailix could wield and also saw how many innocent people got hurt as a result.

Is my power the same? He wondered. *Will I hurt people like this if I use my magic?*

"The damage here is not the worst of it, Urus," said Murin, again as though he could read his thoughts. "The Order now knows for sure that there is a sigilord here, and I'm sure they had someone watching. They know what you are now. This changes everything. The Order will stop at nothing to have your blood. They have not tasted that kind of power in three thousand years."

"What do we do now?"

"We must flee. Your presence here is a danger to this city. But first, we must find the vertex; our time has run out."

"I'm staying with Corliss," Goodwyn said.

"What? Why?" asked Urus, stunned.

"Because this is what I was meant to do. I'm a soldier, and a damn good one. I belong on the front lines with Corliss, keeping this city and these people safe. You and Murin and Cailix, you have...magic things that need doing, and to be honest, I want no part of it. I'll take my suzur over blood tornados any day, though I do hope you find the vertex and can get it away from the briene and the Order. We'll buy you as much time as we can by keeping them outside the city walls."

"But—"

"There is no time to argue, Urus. We must go, now," Murin urged. "Cailix, if you want to come with us you must do so under the condition that you will never ask Urus for his blood again. In fact, you must promise not to use blood magic at all. You are meddling with powers you cannot possibly comprehend."

Cailix took a step back. "I—"

The air beside Cailix warped and bent the way air shimmered above a smokeless fire. In an instant, Anderis appeared standing beside her, as quickly as he had vanished the night before. He covered Cailix's mouth, closed his eyes, and vanished.

Cailix and the blood mage were gone.

CHAPTER NINETEEN

Cailix groped in the darkness, fumbling over wooden boxes and bits of junk she couldn't identify, her wrists and ankles bound with thick rope.

The stench of wet wood and straw assaulted her nose, her nostrils burning as they filled with the odors of soaps, spices, salted meats, and a dozen others that blended into an indecipherable stink.

She lay still, taking it all in. Movement in the pit of her stomach made her queasy, a gentle rocking that, were she not a prisoner in this foul place, might have been comforting.

I'm on a ship, she thought. *This isn't good.*

She felt pretty confident that she could escape from just about any prison Anderis put her in. The problem with escaping from a ship was that she was surrounded by water with no way of knowing how to get to the nearest shore.

Scraping her knees on the floor and loose bits of wood and metal, she crawled through what she figured was the cargo hold. It took a moment before she realized that she was wearing a dress.

That bastard changed my clothes, she thought. *When I find him, I'm going to bleed him just like he bled Brother Toyce. He'll even be alive long enough to see the spell I cast with his own blood!*

Her head bounced off of something wooden, stopping her blind foraging.

"Ow!" she said aloud, regretting it instantly. Motionless and holding her breath, she waited for a guard to arrive to investigate the noise. No one came.

She probed the inky black with her hand, feeling the shape of a narrow wooden ladder, and got a splinter in her palm for the effort. This time she winced, but held back the urge to yelp.

Someone's got to come down this thing eventually, she thought as she curled up under the back side of the ladder. As she waited for the inevitable arrival of some lackey ordered to check on the prisoner, she busied herself with untying the ropes around her ankles. With her hands still bound, it took longer than she hoped but eventually she freed her feet.

The wait seemed to take forever. To keep her muscles from cramping she stood, stretched her legs, then crouched back into position. At last a beam of light burst into the hold and Cailix finally saw the layout of the place. Barrels, stacked chests, and nets filled with unlabeled sacks littered the floor, along with tons of other junk.

The fat form of a sailor stepping down the ladder nearly eclipsed all the light of the opening, the man barely able to squeeze himself through the hatch.

She hunkered down, holding her breath. Each step the man took bowed the strained crossbars. Even his boots looked as if they were ready to burst at the seams.

She waited until he lowered his left foot, just before it would have landed on the rung in front of her. Striking with vicious speed, she reached out with her bound hands, grabbed the boot, and wrenched it to one side as hard as she could.

Bone broke as it twisted in ways the fat man's body couldn't handle. His mouth opened to scream, but she had already sprung up and around the ladder and clamped her hands over his mouth, wrapping her legs around her victim like a constricting snake.

Barely able to support his own weight and only having one good leg, the fat man pitched forward into the cargo hold with Cailix on top of him. He writhed and struggled beneath her but stopped after she rammed her elbow into his face a few times.

She searched his massive girth for a knife, digging through his pockets and coat until finally she found a small blade sheathed in the boot she had twisted. A noise overhead sent her dashing back into the darkness of the cargo hold.

Once out of sight of the hatch, she held the knife between her feet and sawed the rope around her wrists against it until it snapped.

She was free. Well, somewhat free, anyway. At least she could use her hands and legs. All she needed now was a little bit of blood and she might be able to get out of this mess alive.

"Baris?" called a voice from above the hatch.

Cailix crouched further into the shadows, tucked behind two large barrels.

"Baris, you big oaf, answer me."

Cailix rolled the knife's pommel in her hands, rocking back on the balls of her feet, ready to pounce.

"Oy, Baris, you fall asleep down there?" called a new voice this time.

Two men climbed down the ladder, one after the other, both much thinner and far more muscled than their predecessor.

This wasn't going to be easy.

If she had been stronger, she would have dragged the fat man's body into the darkness to buy some time, but he was just too heavy. And he smelled. Really bad.

"It's Baris!" shouted the first man down. "He's been attacked!"

There goes the element of surprise, she thought.

"The girl's loose in the hold," the other shouted up to the deck. "Get the net!"

Cailix held her ground, knowing that moving would give away her position. All she had to do was cut one of them with her knife and the advantage would be hers. Of course, she had no idea how many men there were up on the deck, or how far away from the shore they were, but she tried to focus on one impossible hurdle at a time. She could cut herself as well, but she didn't know what other challenges lay ahead, and she needed to conserve her power.

"Come out real nice like, girl, and we won't spill your guts all over this hold," called the first man with a sadistic grin, drawing a curved, rusty blade with a hook at the tip.

"Yeah, give yourself up and we won't have to kill you," said his companion. Both men were dressed in stained leggings, boots, and equally dirty shirts. She was thankful they were too far away to smell, for they glistened from head to toe with dirty sweat and heavens only knew what else.

If she was a prisoner on this boat then someone, probably Anderis, wanted her alive. Despite their threats, these thugs wouldn't kill her. Hopefully.

Cailix dashed from her hiding spot, ducking and rolling as one of the men tossed a clay pot at her. As she stood up from the roll, she leapt at the nearest man, hands and feet ready to strike.

He was so surprised at the offensive that he took a step back and bumped into the ladder. Cailix plowed into him, wrapping around his shoulders.

She lifted the knife over her head and thrust it down, expecting a gusher of red liquid to come out of her victim's neck. Instead, he knocked her arm to the side with his head, then punched her in the stomach.

The knife clattered to the ground as she fell back. Before she could recover, both men were upon her, punching her in the stomach and sides.

Where Anderis won't notice, she thought. She'd been punched like that before at many of the orphanages. The workers there liked to beat the kids, but didn't want to lose their jobs by bruising them up so much they couldn't work.

A net dropped from above, and with the skill and ease of expert fishermen, the men trussed her up in the net, cinched it tight with a pair of thick knots, and hung her from a hook lowered through the hatch.

"Haul the little brat up. If the wizard wants to keep her a prisoner, he can do it without her damaging our cargo," shouted one of the men, checking the back of his head for blood.

She kicked and screamed, tugging and pulling on the net to no avail. The more she fought it the more entangled she became.

Bright daylight hit her as she was winched up into the warm air to dangle a few feet above the deck. All around her, sailors hanging from the sails and riggings stopped to stare. Armed mercenaries, and more sailors walking the deck, all turned to see the fresh catch as she cried and squirmed.

"Let me out or I will kill every last one of you!" she shouted.

The men burst into a chorus of laughter, a deep-throated, uproarious noise that filled her with shame.

Nobody laughs at me, she thought. *I'll make them all pay. I'll show them how powerful I am and that I can take care of myself. They don't frighten me.*

"Absolutely fantastic," called a familiar voice from the foredeck. It was Anderis. "Child, you are the most remarkable creature I have ever laid eyes upon."

Anderis stepped lithely down the stairs and past the mainmast to stand just below her, thumbs stuck in the top of his bright red captain's coat with long tails. In that outfit with his black breeches and high boots he looked every bit the dignified gentleman, the opposite of the monster he really was.

"Here you are in the middle of the ocean, trapped on a ship filled with blood mages and mercenaries who would just as soon toss you overboard as help you, and yet still you fight. Still you try to escape. Such a remarkable creature you are, Aerlissa."

"My name is Cailix, you bastard!" she snapped, still fighting against the grip of the net. From her vantage point, dangling above the deck, she could see nearly everyone on the ship. She counted a crew of twenty veteran-looking sailors, another dozen mercenaries who looked as though they could barely tie a knot let alone manage a ship, and at least four other blood mages standing about in their white robes looking down their noses at the inferior folk around them. Despite Anderis's ridiculous attire, there was probably a real captain somewhere, the one who gave the real orders and held the respect of the crew.

She spotted two more ships on the horizon, barely more than little white splotches floating on the blue-green sea.

Way too many to kill, she thought. *I'm going to have to get off this ship and swim for it.*

"Cut her down and toss her in the fish trough," Anderis said, pointing at a long, high-sided tray filled with salt water that the fishermen used for dumping and sorting their catch.

They opened the net, and she dropped into the puddle of water with as much gentle grace as a dead fish. She sputtered and coughed, flailing about for purchase on the wet, slimy wood.

As she managed to sit upright, two men grabbed her arms and held her still. She spit a mouthful of salt water into her nearest captor's face. His look of surprise at seeing this little female prisoner resist was priceless. If she was going to die today, she would take that memory with her to the afterlife, giggling all the way.

Anderis came to stand over her, his narrow, old-looking form blotting out the midday sun. "My master thinks I should have killed you. He thinks I should have killed you where I found you in Naredis."

"Your master?" Cailix smiled sweetly, remembering the pockmarked mage she'd seen in the pool of briene blood. "I didn't think you took orders from anyone. I thought you took what you needed. Surely no one is more powerful than the omnipotent Anderis?"

Anderis reddened and bent closer, whispering in her ear. "I suffer the presence of a master so long as he furthers my aims. You should know exactly what that feels like, Aerlissa."

He straightened and raised his voice, ensuring that the nearby blood mages could hear him. "You and I are so much alike. It is a shame it had to end this way. You could have been something truly amazing."

"Fight me without your cronies and I'll show you just how amazing I can be," spat Cailix.

Anderis threw his head back and laughed. The sailors ignored the spectacle and went about their business, while the mercenaries simply gripped the hilts of their swords in case the annoying brat got loose.

"You really think you learned everything there is to know about being a blood mage from our short time together?" Anderis waved over one of the mercenaries. "Bring the slaves."

The man nodded and disappeared through a hatch in the aft deck.

"Mage, must I remind you how much those slaves cost me?" a voice boomed from the captain's quarters as the door swung wide.

"You will be more than adequately compensated, Captain."

"I'd better be. I'm losing more than enough money on this fool's errand as it is," the captain bellowed, a giant of a man with an equally robust beard. Were it not for a few pieces of jewelry and the expensive saber he wore, he would have looked just as dirty and ragged as the rest of the crew.

Pirates, thought Cailix. It looked as though they had picked up slave trading as a side business. Pirates and mercenaries, people who didn't need convincing to do the Order's fighting. All they needed was money.

A few moments later, the mercenary climbed out of the other hold, followed by a line of men shackled to each other at the ankles with iron chains. Each man was dirty and naked save for short breeches, hunched over and barely able to walk. Time spent crammed into the hold weakened the slaves, and she had heard that the longer they spent on a ship the less they were worth when brought to market.

Clearly Anderis had no intention of selling them.

"For example, Aerlissa, I never taught you this little trick," he said, a proud grin on his face. "Drain the trough."

The sailors did as ordered, and the water spilled out of the trough onto the deck. The mercenaries holding her pressed down on her neck and tied her hands to the trough's support legs. It took all her strength to crane her neck and look her former mentor in the face.

He pointed at the first slave in the chain, and the man dropped to his knees, mouth agape, gasping for air. When Anderis clenched his fist, the man doubled over in pain, clutching his stomach. He spasmed violently, thrashing about on the deck, shrieking like nothing she had ever heard before.

"Pay attention, apprentice," Anderis said. He clenched both fists then clapped them together. As his fists touched, the slave exploded. It wasn't like a cannon explosion, but it was the closest description her brain could call up. The slave's skin vanished. One moment flesh and bone flapped on the deck like a fish out of water, and in the next, red mist filled the air as though the ship had sailed through a fog of blood.

The blood fog swirled into a vortex like the tornados she had conjured back in Waldron, spinning itself into the trough. It took only a few more seconds for everything the slave once was to collect as a pool of blood as deep as her waist. Everything that man was and had ever been now collected in a puddle around her.

She had seen all kinds of violence and had imagined visiting every kind of punishment on Anderis; had even seen her previous caregiver bleed out before her eyes, but nothing could compare to what she had just witnessed. She wanted to throw up.

She felt her stomach heave and her throat open but she resisted, fought with everything she had not to give that man the satisfaction of seeing her weakness. Swallowing back the bile, she faked a bored, blank look and stared back at Anderis, showing no reaction.

"Now do you see the power you could have had? If only you hadn't betrayed me."

Cailix said nothing, feigning disinterest.

"Since you chose to betray me when you had the freedom of choice, I am going to take that away from you. I am going to bind you to me, and you will no longer have a choice. You will do everything I say and, more importantly, kill whomever I ask you to kill." Anderis dipped his hands in the blood at the end of the trough.

"Prelate, the master said she must be killed," urged one of the other blood mages.

"The master does not always know best. If we kill her then we waste all of her power. Bind her, and she becomes our weapon to do with as we please."

They nodded. "Perhaps it is better this way. We can certainly use all the weapons we can get."

"He will see the brilliance of my plan soon enough." Anderis leaned forward and cut his wrist with a fingernail, adding a few drops of his own blood to the mix. "And now for your blood, my dear."

The soldier to her left pulled a small knife from his belt and grabbed her arm. She struck as he took a step closer for better leverage. She lunged to the left and bit down on his arm, ripping a chunk of flesh right out of it.

She couldn't use her hands for the blood power, so instead she sucked a mouthful of blood from the mercenary's arm. In her mind, she imagined the blood heating up and becoming as hot as flame.

She spit the blood in the man's face and, as she imagined it, the blood burst into flames and the mercenary raced across the deck, screaming, engulfed in dark, blood-red fire.

Shrieking, the burning mercenary jumped overboard, splashing into the ocean, a thick black puff of smoke rising from the water.

"Gag her!" Anderis yelled.

Hands grabbed her from all sides and pushed her face-first into the blood pool. Her mind sought the power of the blood in the pool around her but found nothing, as if it wasn't there. It smelled and looked like blood, but it carried no power for her.

More hands lifted her head up and stuffed a wadded-up rag on a rope into her mouth and cinched the gag tight. Ropes drew her arms back and bent her back at a painful angle.

"Another trick you never learned, apprentice, is that the blood in which you now sit belongs to me. You might as well be still sitting in ocean water for all the good it will do you."

A knife pierced her thigh, squirting her own blood into the vermillion mix. All she could smell was its pungent, metallic odor. She could barely see, struggling to blink the blood out of her eyes.

"You know what I'm going to enjoy most?" Anderis asked, pressing a bloody fingertip to her forehead. "That you will be aware of what is happening the entire time and completely unable to do anything about it. You will see and remember everything I make you do."

"You'll never control me," Cailix said, hoping he couldn't hear any of the doubt creeping through her veins like a plague. The only thing she could imagine worse than dying out there on that boat was living as Anderis's unwilling slave. It would be the ultimate humiliation, and all of her work to gain power and control would have been for nothing.

She hadn't come this far just to lose control now.

Anderis plunged his hands into the trough as the mercenaries tightened their grip. He chanted in a language she had never heard him use before. Up until then, she'd assumed it was all just triggered by thought.

I should have waited before I betrayed him, she thought. *There was so much more to learn!*

His voice rose in pitch and volume, then fell into a deep rumble that barely sounded like words at all. His muscles spasmed, his face twitched, and she half expected to see a demon or something crawl out of his mouth, he looked so bizarre. She studied his every move, fascinated by the ritual and the power required to complete it.

Tremendous gusts of wind blasted into the ship's sails, all of which were at full sail, driving the ship through the churning water. Clouds formed directly over the ship, smothering the sunshine and blanketing the boat with a chill air.

Anderis's head jerked forward, a triumphant, exhausted look on his face.

"Arise as my new thrall, Aerlissa," he said, spreading his arms wide, proud of his work and gesturing at it for all to see.

"Go piss yourself!" Cailix spat, shocked that she had enough free will to do so. She couldn't help but smile.

"What?" Anderis shouted, nearly falling backwards. "How is this possible? Ruorg, what did you idiots screw up this time?"

"Nothing, prelate. I felt the binding flow between you. It should have worked," Ruorg said, the shortest and widest of the white-robed hench-wizards Anderis always kept nearby.

"I guess you're not as powerful as you think you are. Maybe you're just losing potency in your old age," Cailix taunted him with a sneer.

Anderis leaned forward and backhanded her across the face. It stung, but she enjoyed being able to get under his skin and drive him mad even more. Even if he hit her, it was because *she* made it happen. She was in control again.

"You cannot even begin to comprehend my power, whelp," Anderis said, then whirled to face his fellow mages. "How could the binding fail? Could she have cast some kind of immunity before we took her out of the cargo hold or taken something to pollute her blood?"

The three men made their way across the deck to stand before their leader, their eyes downcast and faces filled with fear. Clearly they didn't find Anderis's impotence as amusing as she did.

"Prelate, there is no such spell. There is no way to ward oneself against the binding," said one mage.

"There is one way," said Ruorg, hesitating a little and avoiding Anderis's eyes.

"What? Tell me, how could she resist the spell?"

"Well," Ruorg stammered, "the only known immunity to the binding spell is if it is cast upon a blood relative."

"The only way she could have resisted the spell is if she was your—" another mage began.

"Daughter," Anderis finished.

Chapter Twenty

Urus tugged on Murin's sleeve, waited for him to turn, and signed, "Which way?"

Murin looked left and right, peering down the tunnels. The hallway in which they stood was carved smooth with barely a single visible tool mark, as was the branch leading left. To the right, the way looked carved with rough tools, the stone glistening with rivulets of water dripping down the sides.

"This way," Murin said, ducking into the older tunnel to the right. "We follow the tool marks through the ages, from the recent to the old to the long-forgotten."

Urus followed. The tunnel descended around a precipitous curve into the darkness. Within just a few steps, Urus could barely see his hands before his face, the ambient light from the hallway above almost gone.

He pulled up, frozen with fear.

Murin turned and signed. Urus had to struggle to make out the shadows of the man's enormous hands against the darker shadow of the surrounding cave. "Keep moving, we have no time to squander."

"I can't," Urus signed, "I can't go through the pitch black, not again."

Murin sighed. "Think about seeing the world through my eyes and the bond will take care of the rest."

"What bond?"

"The bond you created when you entered my mind back in Kest," Murin signed, the blurry, jerking movement of his hands reflecting his impatience and frustration. "Quantum entanglement. Do you remember nothing I say?"

Urus had no idea what any of that meant, but he was growing accustomed to that feeling, so he put his doubts into the back of his mind and tried to imagine what the world looked like from inside Murin's eyes. No doubt everything would look smaller from that height.

A rippling rainbow of color splashed over the scene, deep reds and blues spilling as though from some unseen dye vat onto the rock. When the fresh colors bled away, the vista remaining was a thing of wonder. The rock surface luminesced with hues of blue such as he had never seen before, with Murin awash in deep reds and oranges. He looked down at his own hands, similarly pigmented in reds and oranges.

"What is this?" Urus signed, spellbound by the colors in his hands and the contrail of fading yellow left behind as he formed signs in the air.

Murin smiled. It was a rounded brush stroke of yellow in the middle of his orange-tinted face.

"You are seeing through my eyes. You see temperatures, red for hot, blue for cold, and different mixtures for everything in between."

"This is the most amazing thing I have ever seen. Do you see like this all the time?"

"Only when the need arises," Murin signed.

"Fantastic," Urus whispered.

"Marvel later, we must be off." Murin turned and forged further into the mountain.

Urus wondered if the sigilords could change their vision, or if all they could do was make blue smoke or hurt people.

Curious, he tugged Murin's sleeve.

"What now?" he signed, irritated.

"I want to know about the sigilords' magic," Urus signed.

Murin threw up his hands in exasperation. "If I have to stop and turn around every time I talk to you, the Order will find the vertex before we get to the bottom of this hallway."

The insult stung. He knew it was a burden for people to stop and look at him in order to talk, but most of the time people pretended otherwise, putting on a show to avoid hurting him.

"I am sorry," Urus signed.

"Do not apologize, simply use your thoughts," Murin said.

Urus gave him a blank look, unsure what he meant.

"I thought I explained this already. Think what you want to say, but think it *at* me. No need to waste time with primitive communication methods."

Like this? Urus thought, *at* Murin.

Precisely; now let's get moving, came the response, a strange thought that felt like it came from his own mind, but different somehow. It felt like when he read the lips of the Bormesh twins back home. They both moved their lips exactly the same way, but he could still tell the difference between Abel and Obel without knowing exactly how.

They continued further down into the mountain for a long time without saying—or thinking—anything else.

Urus finally mustered the courage to ask again, *What do you know about the sigilords' magic?* It was amazing to be able to ask a question to someone's back and to get an answer, without reading lips or signing!

They reached the end of the slope, and Murin paused briefly to inspect the rock on two different forks in the tunnel. He stroked his almost nonexistent pure white beard for a moment then departed down the left tunnel.

I know very little of how it works. Until I met you, I believed the sigilords long extinct. Their power was that of space and time, and I do not have enough time to explain the science that proves how nearly unstoppable such a power can be in the right hands.

Faced with another fork in the passage, Murin ducked into an even smaller, much less refined shaft leading to the right and even further down. They had been walking downward for so long that Urus wondered if they were still in the mountain or below it.

So they just made blue flashes like I do? he asked, still coming to grips with the idea of being able to communicate with thought alone; no one making fun of his speech and no tradesign.

Not blue, no. The sigilords would draw ideograms—sigils—in the air, imbuing them with their power. They combined sigils to produce effects. They called it sigilcraft. I have seen more wonders in my lifetime than you can possibly imagine, and yet there is still nothing that can surpass the spectacle of a sigilord in his prime, wielding the raw, unfettered power of space-time itself.

Urus thought a moment, letting the image of a sigilord blasting a battlefield with raw power percolate in his mind. *That sounds…dangerous,* he thought.

Murin stopped short and turned around, giving Urus a long, appraising look. *Dangerous indeed. So dangerous that the arbiters believed sigilords should not be allowed to exist.*

Movement caught Urus's eye. In the distance he could see several small, faintly reddish shapes that blended with the cold blue of the wall in a way he hadn't seen before.

What's that? he thought.

Murin turned and looked, holding up his hand to signal Urus not to move. *Those are people, on the other side of some thin cave walls, I do not know how many.*

We can see them through the stone? Urus asked.

Murin nodded. *If the wall is thin enough, yes. Follow me, quietly.*

Murin led them through several narrow, low corridors, some small enough that they had to crawl over the damp rock to get through. They stopped and knelt, Murin listening to the conversation that was lost on Urus. A tall, skinny shape seemed to argue with shorter folk, their gestures frenetic. *Briene and a blood mage,* he thought.

Precisely, Murin thought in reply. Urus jumped a little, forgetting that Murin was listening to his thoughts.

What are they saying? Urus asked.

They are here looking for the vertex. The briene are dating rock samples, looking for the ancient tunnels.

Urus shifted his weight to avoid cramping. *They're headed in the same direction we are, down into the oldest part of the mountain.*

Then we follow them and stop them before they destroy it. We can stay far behind them without them noticing.

They crept further into the depths of the mountain, the cool damp air of the higher shafts replaced by hotter, much more muggy air. They kept far back from the group, only turning a corner after the others were barely visible through the cave walls.

The briene seemed fine moving through the dark caverns, but the blood mage must have had trouble. A small orb of bright red heat hovered just over his shoulder. Urus could see the ripples of colored heat it cast on the ground and against the nearby stone.

After seeing the world through Murin's heat-eyes, he would never look at it the same way again and he wasn't sure he wanted to. He wished Aegaz could see this. He would have been just as awestruck.

I am sure your uncle is alive and that the heads of Kest's invaders lie atop pikes on the nearby sand dunes, Murin projected into Urus's mind, sensing Urus's emotions as well as his thoughts.

Before Urus could reply, he saw the briene and the blood mage stop short, the hovering ball of heat pulsing brightly.

They've found something, Murin and Urus thought to each other.

Can you hear them? Urus asked.

It is the vertex. We must strike now. Kill the blood mage before he can cast a single spell, understand?

Urus nodded and drew the heavy, two-handed sword from his back. It occurred to him that if the cave wasn't wide enough, he would have to stick to stabbing attacks, as there might not be enough room for slashing.

Murin ran, through the tunnel, back hunched over, a knife in each hand and Urus followed close behind, his sword pointed away and behind him. The last thing he wanted was to impale Murin from behind if he skidded to a halt.

An image appeared in Urus's mind—it was the path ahead, as seen by Murin. Without projecting any words, Urus absorbed the plan. Murin conveyed the route through the caves and where the blood mage would be standing. The feeling of urgency coming from the grey man was unmistakable; if they didn't kill the blood mage in the first strike, the first spell he cast could obliterate them all.

Seconds passed in what felt like hours as they surged through the passage.

They emerged into the chamber where three small briene stood with the blood mage who, despite his height, was still a hand shorter than Murin. Urus followed in the footsteps he had already seen as through retracing the steps of a dream. He leapt for the red-orange shape and, unlike in the boat in the cistern below Kest and the road leading to Waldron, he didn't hesitate.

He thrust the massive sword forward through the man's torso, planted his feet, and swung the man, still impaled by the sword, into the rock wall. The impact was so powerful that bits of rock crumbled to the floor. Murin sprang forward after the impact, thrusting both knives into the blood mage's heart.

Urus spun and grabbed two briene heads, bashing them together. They slumped to the ground as an ice-blue blade flew across the room into the forehead of the remaining briene. Urus watched as life's bright red-orange heat started to drain from all four men. Just like that, it was over, and they had killed them all.

Will yourself to use your own eyes again. Heat will be of no use to us reading the sigils on the vertex, Murin thought.

Urus closed his eyes, did as he was told, and opened them again to near total darkness. A small flame erupted from a red stick Murin took from the body of one of the fallen briene. His heart ached with a feeling of loss, as though he were diminished without the enhanced colors of the heat-eyes. The world seemed dull and empty by comparison.

Mourn not, for the Infrasight is at your call any time you will it, Murin thought, again sensing what Urus felt. While Urus liked the ease of communication, this new relationship with Murin felt a little too intimate. He liked the privacy of his own mind.

Urus stood over the blood mage's lifeless body, lit by the flickering light of the strange briene torch. Unlike the mage who killed Waldron's duke, this one didn't wear magician's robes. Instead, his body was wrapped in a skin-tight leather suit fitted with little puffy pouches from neck to ankle.

Blood packs, Murin thought. *The blood mages who do the real fighting, not like that coward Anderis, use those to carry blood. Their body heat keeps the blood warm and ready to use as a reagent for their spells.*

Remember what Corliss said about me? asked Urus. *About how there was another reason I failed the gauntlet tests?*

Urus sensed Murin's agreement without Murin needing to describe it in words.

He was right. I failed because I don't want to be a warrior. He pointed to the blood mage's body. *This isn't who I am or what I want to do.*

A surge of pride rushed from Murin through to Urus. It was a potent, intoxicating feeling. He had never known what it felt like for someone to be proud of him before, not even Uncle Aegaz.

Perhaps there may be hope for you yet, young man. The insatiable thirst for blood, power, and victory over one's enemies is what started the Fulcrum War, and what nearly destroyed this world.

Before Urus could think to ask what that was, Murin responded.

The Fulcrum War began three millennia ago as a feud between the blood mages and the sigilords. Once the blood mages discovered the potency of pure sigilord blood, the war turned to genocide, the blood mages hunting the sigilords nearly to extinction for the power their blood contained. The war virtually destroyed this planet before the arbiters arrived and, with the help of a single sigilord named Komindus, created the seals binding the five vertices.

Urus was about to ask another question when Murin continued, sensing the question before it was asked.

The few sigilords who survived, only a handful if I recall, fled to another universe, and this world and the universe in which it resides was sealed off from the others when the last vertex was put in place. The Fulcrum War ended, and after all this time this world has still not fully recovered from the damage it caused.

Urus stared at the stone slab in the center of the chamber, the vertex he hadn't noticed until then. Etched sigils that looked as though they could have been carved that morning covered its surface.

So if the blood mages destroy all the vertices, they'll break all the seals and then what? he asked.

Then they will escape this universe and find other worlds, worlds filled with millions of people rich in potent magical blood. They will harvest these worlds like corn fields and reap unstoppable power. It will only be worse if they take your blood with them. The devastation left in their wake will be unimaginable.

Urus studied the cavern ceiling and the narrow columns that lined the passages and shafts leading in all directions like holes in a block of cheese imported from Milof.

Can we bring the mountain down around this chamber to keep them out? he asked.

That is about all we can do. It will delay them while the briene excavate the rubble. I can find a weak point, Murin thought, heading off down a shaft, one hand holding the briene torch, the other hand pressed against the ceiling, palm up.

Urus followed to stay in the light now that his vision was back to normal, running his fingers along the rock surface. Unlike the caverns above, these walls were dusty, warm, and riddled with sharp, jagged crystals.

He stopped, something tingling in his fingertips. Curious, he pressed his hands close up to the ceiling. Faint, rumbling vibrations transferred from the rock to his palms, like they did when he felt approaching horses in the stones of the streets of Kest.

Murin, they're coming, he thought.

Murin halted. *What? Who approaches?*

Probably the briene. Hundreds of people running in the caves above us. I can feel it in the rock.

Murin disappeared down a corridor framed by a pair of stalactites. They dodged and weaved through the caves, heading away from the vertex stone slab. He reached an opening with five different shafts extending from it and spun, finger pointed at one stalagmite that had joined with a stalactite to make a tapered column.

There, Murin thought. *Use your power and destroy that column. If you punch it as hard as you can, your power will shield you and keep the stone from shattering every bone in your hand.*

That's comforting, Urus thought.

You cannot doubt it or hold back, or it will not work. Punch the column with all your might and it will bring the caves down around the vertex, Murin projected.

What about us? Or the people fleeing Waldron for the far side of the mountain?

They will be fine. They're too far away and much too high to be affected. Us, on the other hand, I am not so sure about. But this must be done. The Order cannot break another seal. It would be like letting loose an insatiable predator among countless worlds filled with defenseless cattle.

Urus wasn't ready to die, not now. But if he was going to die, he would rather it be trying to save people than wasting his own life by throwing it off a roof.

He nodded resolutely and stood before the column. He could now feel the vibrations of the approaching host of briene pulsating up through his boots. He took a step back, readied himself in attack stance, made a tight fist, and closed his eyes.

Urus struck, his fist lashing out before him, using the rotational energy of his body like an uncoiling spring, exploding into the stone column. He felt the impact and braced for the pain he was sure would follow.

There was no pain; just that same quick pressure followed by a snap like the one that happened when breaking practice boards back in Kest. His bones were intact and the column lay not just in shards, but pulverized nearly to powder.

Run, urged Murin's mind. *We have started an earthquake.*

The cavern shook and pieces of stone tumbled away from the ceiling. Murin and Urus sprinted out of the chamber, back down the shafts through which they had come. Before they could reach the vertex chamber, a group of briene spilled into the cave, weapons at the ready, seemingly unconcerned with the mountain collapsing around them.

With the same stance and clenched fist he had used on the stone column, Urus punched the first briene with every ounce of power he could call forth. A blue light erupted from his fist and the briene flew back, smashing into his companions and hammering them all to the ground.

Before Urus could attack again, Murin was upon them, snatching up their unlit torches and stuffing them into his robe. Then he ran for the vertex room.

Appalled but unable to do anything about it, Urus followed.

They got to the room housing the stone slab as more debris fell from the ceiling.

We must flee or be buried here, Murin thought.

If we go, the blood mages get the vertex.

They will get it whether we die here or not. If we live, we may yet still stop them at the next vertex, and the blood mages will not get your blood, Murin thought. He pointed pointing to the sigil on the slab identical to the one Urus had touched before in Kest, the one that had brought them to Waldron.

Urus stepped to the slab and held out his hand. He looked back over his shoulder to see swarms of briene surging out of side tunnels and making for their position. In seconds they would be overrun.

He pressed his palm to the sigil. A warmth filled his hand and extended up his arm.

The world vanished in a burst of blue fire.

CHAPTER TWENTY-ONE

Goodwyn Stom stood on the small ledge on the cliff, overlooking an ocean of puffy clouds stretching from horizon to horizon. Infinite, perfect blue filled the void above. The sharp cliffs poked up through the clouds like cloven hoofs, piercing the veil of a thick, white sheen.

Clouds are supposed to be above, not below, thought Goodwyn.

Soldiers clung to every inch of usable rock on either side of the road and all along the ramparts. Wrapped in their windrunner cloaks, steeling themselves against the buffeting winds, they looked like a cast of falcons, each claiming a tiny piece of the rock for their nest.

It was all so beautiful, and he knew that it wouldn't last. They were under attack, and soon blood would run thick, staining the pristine cliffs with the inevitable aftermath of war.

I wish Therren could see this, he thought.

Absently he stroked the smooth bronze pendant hanging from his neck. Urus had teased him that it might have been a gift from one of the many girls who sought to court him. Goodwyn smiled at the thought, remembering the night he got it.

***

He'd been sitting cross-legged atop an ale barrel, his back against the cool stone wall of the tavern, his gaze transfixed on the beautiful orange glow of the palace. The sunstone stood out like a bright star in the night sky, even from the far edge of town where he waited.

"Wyn," came a whisper from the dark.

Goodwyn grinned, immediately recognizing the young man's voice. "All good."

Therren Muldown stepped out of the shadows in the alley behind the tavern, his shadowy form gradually solidifying into the shape of a tall, strong, short-haired young man as he drew nearer the lamp hanging from the corner of the building.

Kest's graduating class certainly had better warriors, stronger arms, and faster runners, but none of them could compare to Therren. The two always seemed to know how the other was feeling, and what the other needed to be cheered up.

Therren leapt up onto the barrel next to Goodwyn's, mouth parted in a huge smile as he did so. He was an insufferable showoff, but Goodwyn loved that about him. With another deft maneuver, he spun and dropped into a cross-legged position.

"So tomorrow's the big day," said Therren, reaching for Goodwyn's hand. Goodwyn took it.

"Sure is," Goodwyn replied, an electric rush surging from the touch of Therren's hand, through his body and to his feet. His heart quickened.

The two turned to face each other, clutching each other's hands tighter.

"I can't wait. Watching you with the suzur is like being next to a master painter or something," said Therren.

Goodwyn blushed a little, hoping the dim light would hide it. From the glint in Therren's eyes, he knew the light had concealed nothing. "You're biased."

"That doesn't change your skill. Tomorrow all of Kest will get to see it. I'm so proud of you, Wyn."

An awkward moment of silence passed, Therren shooting furtive looks to the left and right.

"It's okay, there's no one around," Goodwyn whispered.

"We can't be sure. If someone sees us, doing…this, we'll be culled, just like Urus—or worse."

"Nobody's going to see us." Goodwyn reached up to touch Therren's cheek.

They leaned in to kiss each other, tenderly at first and then, as Goodwyn's pulse quickened and lungs contracted, he pulled Therren closer.

They stared into each other's eyes for a moment after the kiss and then Therren broke the silence, reaching into a pouch hung from his belt, "I brought you something."

"You didn't need to—"

"Nonsense, you know I did," Therren said. As he dug through the pouch, he added, "Have you told Urus yet? About the First Fist?"

Goodwyn and Therren had both been chosen for the First Fist, an honor bestowed on only the best graduates.

"No, I just haven't found the right time."

"You haven't found your balls, you mean." Therren chuckled, pulling something out of the pouch wrapped in a swatch of cloth. "If he finds out from his uncle, or during the ceremony, he's going to bust a blood vessel."

"You're right."

Therren beamed. "I'm always right. Now promise you'll tell him before the ceremony or I'm not giving you this."

"Promise," said Goodwyn, making an "x" with his arms across his chest in the traditional warrior's salute.

Therren unwrapped the item and held it out for inspection. Hanging from a golden chain was a miniature bronze suzur, its chain coiled like a snake ready to strike, a small green gem nestled in the center.

Goodwyn was stunned speechless, barely able to breathe.

"Well, put it on, let me see it on you."

Goodwyn slipped the chain over his neck and let the pendant hang over his linen shirt. He rubbed the gem with his thumb.

"It's beautiful."

***

"Beautiful, isn't it?" Corliss said, bounding over to Goodwyn's side, his feet as stable as a mountain goat's.

Goodwyn just nodded, still taking it all in, heart aching as he thought about Therren, wondering if he was even alive after the attack and if they would ever be together again.

"It's a shame that war has come to smear blood across a view as majestic as this," Corliss added with a sweep of his arm toward the vista.

"I'm sorry."

"This is not your doing, son. You can't blame yourself for surviving the attack on your home, and your arrival gave us precious early warning to prepare."

"How will it all start?" Goodwyn asked. He'd been through countless drills, read thousands of accounts of battles and skirmishes, and memorized hundreds of strategies, but nothing had prepared him for standing up on that cliff, waiting for the enemy to arrive.

"It's hard to tell. Nobody alive here has experience fighting the briene. If I were them, and had their crazy machines, I would send them in first, try to scare us off the wall and cliffs. Then, once we're running from their flying machines, take the gate. And then I would rush in with the infantry and take the city square by square."

"Have you taken many cities before?" asked Goodwyn.

"Only one, but I've defended more than enough, including this one."

"Do you think we can hold them off, to buy Urus and Murin enough time to do whatever they need to do?"

"What happened to your friend, anyway?" Corliss was clearly changing the subject.

"What do you mean?"

"He is an amazing fighter, even by your standards, and his presence on the wall here could turn the tide of a battle. Yet he goes in search of some magic door."

Goodwyn thought about it for a moment and then answered. "Urus is the best fighter I've ever seen. If he wanted to, he could even defeat me. But his heart isn't in it. I don't think it ever has been. He may be a fighter, but he's not a warrior, if that makes any sense."

Corliss nodded. "He may be on a wiser path than the rest of us, then."

"I asked if you thought we could hold them off," Goodwyn repeated, still fascinated by the cliffs and the thousands of soldiers perched on them.

"No, we can't," Corliss said simply. "Hopefully your friends will find what they need down below the city and find it soon. With their numbers, the briene could overrun our gates in a matter of hours."

The blast of a horn cut through their conversation. Another echoed the same tone, then another, until the whole city reverberated with the bass tones of battle horns.

"They've started their approach," Corliss said.

They waited in silence for several minutes. Goodwyn gripped his suzur hilt until his knuckles went white, pacing back and forth as much as the narrow walkway on the cliffside would allow.

Movement in the clouds before the sky gate alerted everyone. At once, the raven-shaped silhouettes on the cliffside stirred, all eyes on the road below.

"Look, there!" shouted Captain Rhygant, pointing at a dark wedge shape creeping up the road, emerging from the thick fog.

They watched as the dark wedge pushed forward toward the gate. As it moved further uphill, Goodwyn could see individual shapes.

*Shield*s, he thought. They were advancing under the cover of a roof of kite shields.

"With all their flying machines and steam cars and cutters, this is how they come at us? Hiding from archers under shield?" Corliss exclaimed, leaning back and grabbing his stomach as if to hold the laughter back.

"It's a good tactic," Goodwyn said. "They could get all the way to the gates without losing many of their men."

Corliss whirled to face Goodwyn, mouth spreading in a wicked grin. "What makes you think the only threat to them is from *above*?"

The Knight Marshall stood, watching the wedge of shield-bearing briene approach the gates, his hand held aloft in a clenched fist. Just as it seemed as though the briene would reach the gate, he dropped his fist.

Horns blew and others echoed the call, but this time with a higher pitch than the first warning blasts.

"Watch," Corliss said.

All throughout the phalanx of armored briene, chaos erupted. Shields dropped, blood shooting from beneath them and splashing across the road. Within minutes the briene line had broken. As the invaders turned to retreat back down below the cloud layer, arrows thunked into their backs.

It was then that Goodwyn saw them: slits in the road just wide enough to let hooked spears through. Those spears sawed down the enemy front lines and those who didn't die by the first strike bled to death minutes later.

Before long all that remained before the sky gate were bodies, abandoned shields, and blood stains.

"That was just a test," Corliss said. "Next time they'll throw everything they have at us, including whatever bird machines they have left."

"Knight Marshal!" shouted a nearby soldier.

Goodwyn turned to see a large group of briene re-emerge from the cloud. They carried neither shield nor sword. Instead, they walked in pairs, carrying litters between them.

They're gathering their dead, Goodwyn thought.

"On my command," Captain Rhygant barked.

"Wait, you can't attack them like that!"

"They lay siege to the city, Goodwyn. We are defending ourselves," Corliss said.

"This is not your fight, boy," Rhygant snapped. "If they come back up that road, we will cut them down."

"They're unarmed!" Goodwyn shouted, grabbing Rhygant's arm, keeping him from giving the order to fire.

"They're the enemy!" He wrenched his arm free and thrust his fist down. Again horns blared, commanding an attack. Rhygant spread his arms and legs, his windrunner cloak billowing up behind him, then leapt from the cliff.

"And they deserve your respect!" Goodwyn shouted, leaping after him. Soaring straight for the briene, he glanced back to see Corliss and a dozen others leap from the cliff after him.

They shouted something but he couldn't make out what. All he could hear was the sound of wind rushing by and pounding at his ears as he plummeted for the sky gate.

He landed with his legs already down and pedaling. Lurching forward, he barely managed to keep his balance. He skidded to a halt right before the first pair of briene litter-bearers.

Rhygant wheeled on him, grabbing his neck. "Listen to me, you savage runt, this is war. You're not going to stop it."

Rhygant let go, then punched Goodwyn in the chest, knocking him backwards and sucking the wind out of him. The man hit harder than Urus, which was impossible. *Nobody* hit harder than Urus. Goodwyn dropped to his knees and watched as Rhygant swiveled and approached the briene litter-bearers.

"Stop!" Goodwyn shouted, but it came out as little more than a croak.

Goodwyn watched, helpless, as Rhygant pulled his swords and cleaved the first of the little men in half. The briene dropped their litters and stood transfixed in shock. What happened next seemed to take forever, every detail of it burning into Goodwyn's mind forever.

The captain reached down and buried his arms in the bloody entrails of the briene. As he stood up, the blood burst into flame, immolating his body with blood-red fire. Whips of red fire cracked forth from Rhygant's hands, engulfing two more briene in fire. The burning men screamed and flailed as they dropped to the ground.

That's blood magic! Goodwyn thought.

Finally able to breathe, Goodwyn leapt forward, unleashing the suzur as he did. The thought that Rhygant was a blood mage fueled a white-hot rage within him.

Rhygant laughed as he engulfed another briene in blood-fire. So consumed was he with growing his power by attacking the defenseless men, he had no idea the suzur was coming when it sliced his right arm off. Goodwyn yanked the handle, pulling the chain back, and the return pull of the weapon ripped off Rhygant's right leg. The blood spurted wildly from the severed arteries, catching fire.

Goodwyn stood over the smoldering body of the blood mage, cursing himself for not marking him as a traitor sooner. The blood mages were determined to use the briene to destroy Waldron, so Goodwyn had to be more determined to stop it.

He looked at the goggled faces of the briene who stood, staring at the burned bodies of their men, thankful that he didn't have to look them in the eyes. A tear escaped his eye, pain and disgust welling up within him. His power to see things before they happened hadn't given him a single glimpse of what Rhygant was or that he was going to kill those briene.

What kind of people can sacrifice an entire civilization and start a war just to get some stupid object? Goodwyn thought, spitting on Rhygant's charred body.

Corliss and a dozen other men came up behind him, watching the briene remove the bodies of their dead.

"Kestians respect their enemies. Our code demands that enemies be afforded rights. One of those rights is the right to their dead," Goodwyn said, too furious to look at Corliss. If Therren were there, he would lose his lunch, witnessing such a dishonorable display of warcraft.

"I didn't know that Rhygant was one of them, one of the blood mages," Corliss said.

"No, but you were going to let him order the slaughter of innocent briene just the same."

Goodwyn spun and stared long and hard at Corliss before speaking, "You clearly know less about war than I thought."

Corliss looked stricken. A moment passed before he spoke again. "We'd best get back up to our perch before the next wave."

"I will face the enemy here," Goodwyn told him. "Your men are better trained at flying and more suited to fighting the bird machines. I prefer to stay down here where I know which way is down and which is up. Besides, I can't put a stop to this war from up there."

"There's no stopping this, son. Not after what's happened. I've got a company of men who aren't using windrunners. I'll send them out," Corliss walked toward the gate.

Goodwyn made no reply, staring into the whitish-blue mist hovering over the road below.

"Goodywn," Corliss called.

Goodwyn turned.

"Good luck. It's a shame I have to learn so much about a grim topic like war from one so young."

"War is only grim when fought without honor," Goodwyn said, then turned back to await the next wave of briene.

"If only all of our enemies felt the same," he heard Corliss mutter as he made for the gate.

Goodwyn didn't have to wait long for the next wave.

The screeching of the bird machines above accompanied the belching flames of wheeled furnaces below. Seconds later the road erupted in briene, a swarm of charging bodies overtaking every inch of flat stone.

It was a foolish strategy and would get many of their number killed. They charged at full speed, axes, picks, spears, and swords raised high, exposing their torsos as easy targets for Waldron's archers.

Of course, once the Waldron and briene lines clashed, the archers would stop firing and all plans and tactics would descend into pure chaos. Goodwyn's teachers used to say that the art of war was in learning how to accept that all of your planning meant nothing once the first drop of blood was spilled.

Goodwyn slung back the suzur's chain when his first target was still nearly a hundred meters away. He swung it overhead, building up momentum, twice before his target arrived. He knew where the briene would be and when, and his suzur gladly met the victim at the appointed time and place, hitting his helmet. Goodwyn deliberately held the weapon in check, not killing the briene.

The Waldron host piled onto the road behind him, meeting the briene surge head on. The sound of steel clashing against steel echoed off the cliffs. "*The Battle Ballad*", Battlemaster Kurd used to call it. The rhythm, that unmistakable ebb and flow of swordplay, took on a dark, musical quality that Goodwyn would never forget. It was at once the most terrible and most beautiful song he had ever heard. It was the music that drove a Kestian's heart, or so the Kestians said. Goodwyn had his doubts.

He had little time to contemplate anything other than the fight at hand. He wielded the suzur with a lethality like never before. Before one target had even been cut down, his body was already twisting and coiling, ready to unleash his weapon upon the next target, and the next, and the one after that. He tried to avoid killing the briene, but there were so many of them, their numbers overwhelming. Someone was going to die, and Goodwyn wasn't ready to die yet.

He worked his way forward through the throng like a farmer shearing wheat with his scythe. Scores of briene fell to his blade before ever getting a strike close to him. He cut such a wide path of death through the enemy that the Waldrenes fighting beside him pulled back and to the side, else they too might get cut down like so much grass.

The sight was dizzying, but he fought to stay focused. He never saw where his targets were, only fuzzy outlines of where they *might b*e. The stronger the image, the more likely his target was to end up in that spot. It was as though he was fighting a battle two seconds in the future, and everyone else was stuck in the past.

For what seemed like hours, he threw his suzur into, through, and around his enemy. To anyone other than Goodwyn, it might've appeared as though the briene were hurling themselves at the suzur rather than the other way around. Goodwyn was only barely aware of the battle being waged in the skies above him. The briene on the ground simply didn't stand a chance.

Until *he* arrived.

For a moment, he was just another ant in the swarm, a target who would eventually meet death at the hands of his suzur. Goodwyn swung, twirled, and performed his dance of death, unaware of this briene.

After he fought his way through a few more crowds, a nagging feeling tugged at him, raising the hairs on the back of his neck. Someone hadn't been *there* when the suzur flew. Goodwyn had missed, and not just once.

It was then that he noticed that most of the briene had withdrawn. Goodwyn actually had to twist to avoid the stab of a blade that would eventually make its way through his circle of bloodshed. Then he dodged another, then another.

Before long, the only two people fighting on the road were Goodwyn and the other briene. Everyone else was either a corpse or a spectator, Waldrene or briene. An eery silence had fallen upon the road, the only noises that of Goodwyn, his opponent, and their weapons.

He let loose with a vicious thrust, aimed for where he knew the victim's face would be. Just to make sure, he leapt through the air, kicking out at another spot his victim might be. To Goodwyn's shock, the briene dodged in an unexpected direction, rolling under the flying blade and then dodging his kick.

This put Goodwyn on the defensive, struggling to avoid a flurry of blows while he yanked the chain to summon his blade.

This can't be happening, he thought. He had never been unable to see where an opponent would strike. No one had ever been able to move in a way that eluded Goodwyn's senses.

Could this briene be a quiver? Or maybe he's like Urus? Goodwyn thought, stumbling back, resorting to using his boot dagger to deflect blows as his opponent easily ducked under and leapt over the suzur's long-chain attacks.

The faster the briene attacked, the more glimpses of future possibilities Goodwyn saw. The man was everywhere; his short, wiry little briene silhouette appeared in nearly every direction. *How could someone have so many possible attacks?*

Still being pushed back, Goodwyn did the one thing he knew would be the most unpredictable. He sought out the one spot in his enhanced vision where the briene did *not* appear, and he swung for it, with as much speed and power as he could muster. He flung the suzur ahead of his own leaping kick, in a direction his senses told him the briene would never choose.

As expected, his blade swung wide of the target, but it did so because the briene dodged toward Goodwyn's kick. He landed the kick squarely in the briene's chest, sending him flying back onto the road, sprawled on his back and gasping for air.

Goodwyn recovered, running to stand over the briene. Without having to look, he knew that the entire battlefield was watching. They had all stopped fighting and had become spectators in the match between him and this mysterious little briene.

Kestian code called for killing him. Any true Kestian warrior would have slit the briene's throat by now to set an example. A demonstration like that could be used to convince an enemy to give up their dreams of victory and to walk away. Goodwyn had been forced to memorize dozens of historical battles that had been won by such a demonstration.

There had been enough bloodshed already, and Goodwyn was determined to stop this pointless war. He reached down and offered the man his hand. Gasps escaped from both the briene and the Waldrene hosts.

To his surprise, the briene took it and stood up. Goodwyn and the briene stood in silence for a moment. He wondered what the other man was thinking, if the briene truly knew anything about honorable combat or whether there was an archer ready to put a bolt through Goodwyn's chest any second now.

The briene bowed slightly, pressing a closed fist into an open palm. It looked a lot like one of the many Kestian warrior salutes, signifying a combination of both power—the clenched fist—and control—the open palm.

Goodwyn returned the bow and watched as the briene host simply turned and walked back down the road. It was then that he noticed the sun was almost below the horizon and the clouds were painted orange and purple with the rays of the oncoming sunset.

"You battled that briene for more than three hours," came a voice that answered his unspoken question. It was Corliss.

Goodwyn turned to see hundreds of Waldron soldiers, all standing in awe. They were sweaty, bloody, and haggard. Behind them, other soldiers were hauling away the bodies of the dead. There were so many bodies they had to carry them two or three to a litter.

Having fought an honorable battle didn't make that sight any easier to take. Goodwyn felt sick.

"What..what happened?" he asked, barely able to get the words out through a sore, clenched throat. His body ached, his toes, his fingers, and everything in between. He collapsed onto the ground before anyone could answer.

Corliss knelt beside him. "You fought hundreds of them. No one could get near you without dying. It was a sight to behold."

Goodwyn threw up, the vomit spilling onto his shirt and burning his mouth.

All those dead bodies, all those people he had killed. It was the Kestian way, and all of Kest would treat him like a hero, sing songs of his victory and write books about this battle alone. But at what price? Maybe Urus had been right all along. Maybe standing on a hilltop, looking out at a battlefield covered with the bodies of your enemy, wasn't the way things were meant to be. Or maybe that was the *only* way of things, and Urus had it wrong.

But still, he had turned the tide of the battle. He had won the day for Waldron, and because of him maybe even bought Urus and Murin enough time to do…whatever it was they needed to do.

Waldrene soldiers brought him some water and helped him to his feet. He was covered from head to toe in bruises and would likely be all shades of yellow and purple by tomorrow.

"Goodwyn," Corliss said finally, "I've spent my whole life thinking that magic was a fairy tale, the stuff of children's stories. After seeing what the blood mage and that girl could do, I still wasn't convinced any good could come from magic. Watching you fight today, watching you fight a man for hours like that, showed me that maybe some good can come from it. The men, they all saw it. You're a hero; you saved the line and the city."

"I killed hundreds of men, Corliss. The only thing that makes that heroic is the honor of the battle, the *code*. Without that, without honor, it's all just murder. And for what?"

"You saved lives, and Urus and Murin are safe. You did what needed to be done, as did we all."

"The briene will be back at dawn; I haven't saved anything yet," Goodwyn said. "I sure hope Waldron has good ale, because I could use a—" He stopped short, staring up into the sky.

Three massive balls of fire shot down from the stars above, trails of flame and debris streaking behind them, as though heaven itself had fired a catapult, launching chunks of hell through the air.

Corliss gasped. "What in the name of the heavens are those?"

"We have seen stars fall from the sky before in Kest, but they were only tiny little streaks of light. Nothing like this."

A loud bang echoed against the cliff face, knocking the Waldrenes to their knees, followed by another, and a third thunderous roar and crackle as the nearest of the three fallen stars struck some distant target.

Each of the balls of flame crashed into the earth, sending up a huge, billowing cloud shaped like a mushroom. Each explosion came with a piercing flash of light that hurt their eyes even from this distance.

A moment later the earth shook, splitting off chunks of the mountain from the cliff face and hurtling them down into the road. Cracks appeared in the ground, in the stone of the sky gate, and in homes and buildings throughout Waldron.

When the ground stopped quaking, many of the soldiers exclaimed that the Gods were angry.

"This has nothing to do with the Gods," Corliss shouted, standing up and squinting into the distance. "I don't know where those impacts were, and it's hard to judge from so far away, but I would bet that one of them came down in Ehmshahr."

"Ehmshahr? That's where Kest is," Goodwyn said.

"And I don't think these were just random falling stars, Goodwyn."

Goodwyn thought about the vertices, and how Murin had said there were five of them: one of them below Kest, one below Waldron, and three more in locations described by some old map.

"Do you think the Order knocked those stars out of the sky and used them to destroy three of the vertices?" Goodwyn asked.

"If so, then fighting off the briene is the least of our problems."

CHAPTER TWENTY-TWO

"Foreman, the general brings news of the battle," the general blurted, not waiting for a response before taking his ease in a chair across from his old friend's desk.

The foreman sipped at his mug of blute, savoring every drop of the glowing red brew, a tea made from a naturally fluorescent algae that only grew in the puddles ringing his home town of Mog. The sweet-smelling steam drifted to his nose and filled his mind with images of home.

Home felt so far away, memories of the faces of his family already fading.

"So the briene should be through to the inner keep by nightfall?" the foreman asked, cradling his mug with both hands.

The general, a stout man wrapped in tight leathers, shifted uncomfortably in his chair. He was strapped from boot to gauntlet with little daggers and pouches filled with tricks that might come in handy in a battle. Aside from the blade, the general was probably the fiercest warrior among all the briene, and the foreman's best friend. After a pause, he answered, "Well, not exactly."

"What does that mean?" asked the foreman, finally looking up from his drink. He regretted it instantly, for now he could see the stacks of paperwork piling up on his desk, and the stacks of other matters piling up in front of the desk, and pretty much everywhere else in the command post.

"The Waldrenes have provided more resistance than the blood witches said they would. They are fierce warriors, not intimidated at all by our technology. They fight with—" the general stopped.

"They fight with what?"

"Honor," he said.

The foreman slammed his mug down and bolted up. "Honor? Those dogs flood the caves with their dams, they steal the children in the dark of the night to put them into their labor camps, and they make ready to lay waste to briene homeland. How could they possibly fight with honor?"

The general shrugged. "Had the general not been there to see it with his own eyes, he would not have believed it. There was a blood witch among them. He killed three medics before one of the Waldrenes killed him."

"A blood witch attacked the briene? And a Waldrene killed him?" the foreman asked.

The general nodded.

"It's got to be a ruse of some kind. They are playing the general for a fool, hoping the general will fall into their trap. The general will see."

"Perhaps," the general mused. He rubbed his thumbs against his fingertips, a nervous habit he only did when something was bothering him. "Has the foreman any more blute?"

The foreman smiled a little and stepped to the kettle over the fire behind his desk to pour his friend a drink.

"So," the foreman began, handing his friend a mug, "how goes the battle then, with these so-called honorable fighters?"

"The sky gate has yet to be breached. The battle waged long until the sun hung low in the sky. The blade accepted a *fein dur* from one of Waldrene heroes, the dark-skinned giant who slew the blood witch."

"A fein dur?" asked the foreman. He had never heard of an outsider issuing a hero's challenge before, let alone someone who wasn't a briene. These Waldrene seemed nothing like what the blood witches said.

"It lasted for hours. The Waldrene was victorious and spared the blade's life. The Waldrenes allowed a retreat to renew the fight at dawn."

"None of that makes any sense, General."

"No, it doesn't. And there's more."

"More surprising than Waldrenes fighting with honor while blood witches attack us?"

The general swallowed, hard. He looked troubled, his yellow eyes watery, as though holding back tears.

"Much."

"Out with it then," prodded the foreman.

"The foreman needs to see this for himself."

The foreman straightened. *What could possibly be so bad?*

"Show the foreman."

The general and the foreman grabbed their mugs of blute, and the foreman followed his friend out of the office. They weaved their way through the caves, slowly winding around the underground foundry until they reached the surface.

"This way." The general pointed to the west, off into the forest.

"What is it the general intends to show the foreman?" asked the foreman.

"It really would be best if the foreman saw it personally."

Grudgingly, the foreman bit his tongue and followed in silence as he was led into the forest along a narrow game trail barely visible in the dusk light. After a few furlongs, they crested a small rise to stand before a watering hole, probably used by the same animals that made the trail.

The watering hole had been drained, only to be replaced with thick, dark purple blood. Hanging from hooks knotted into ropes crisscrossing over the pond were hundreds of briene. They hung upside down, each with a cut across their abdomen and inner thigh, drained of every ounce of their life's blood.

The foreman dropped to his knees, salty tears rushing down his cheeks, over his thick mustache, and into his mouth. He wrung his hands, pleading with the gods to provide him with an answer for the horror before him. No answer came. No solace came from the prayer, no explanation, just death and violence.

Death and violence visited by the blood witches.

Without getting up, through sniffs and sobs, he barely managed a question to the general. "When did this happen?"

The general turned and coughed, unable to look at the scene, "Briene only discovered the bodies moments before the general visited the foreman's office. The blood is—" He swallowed, choking back bile, "—still fresh."

"The blood witches did this. All this time, the briene have been supplying volunteers to be taught their technology, their knowledge of steam and metallurgy. Instead the blood witches have been slaughtering innocent brothers and sisters to cast their blood-spells."

"The briene are betrayed, foreman."

The foreman stood and stomped away from the pool. "And they will be avenged, General. Cut the bodies down so they can be given a proper burial of stone and fire."

He stormed down the game trail and out into the clearing, a wide swath torn through the forest to fuel their war machines, war machines attacking an enemy whose only crimes were angering the blood witches.

How could the foreman have been such a fool? he asked himself, still weeping.

He gazed up to the heavens. "Why, God? What have the briene done to deserve this?"

In response, the heavens opened up and spat forth three giant balls of flame. At first it looked as though they were falling as softly as a feather, but he knew enough to know that was his mind playing tricks on him.

The stars are falling, he thought. *Surely this is a sign.*

"Foreman!" came a shout that shook him from his prayer, though he couldn't tear his gaze from the falling stars. "Foreman!"

"What is it?" asked the foreman without looking down.

"Riders approach from the southeast, perhaps twenty," the soldier replied, arriving to stand by the foreman, also craning his neck to stare at the spectacle in the sky.

"Riders from the southeast? The Waldrenes would never be foolish enough to attack our rear with only twenty men."

"They aren't Waldrenes. The riders look like the *fein duras* who fights for Waldron."

The foreman tore himself away from the falling stars to confront the soldier. "What?"

"The riders. They are dark-skinned giants."

* * *

"As you wish, master," Anderis replied into the blood-filled trough.

Cailix hung on her side, wrapped in a fish net, gagged and trussed up a few feet above the deck. After Anderis's spell had failed, he had taken his rage out on her, beating her like a butcher tenderizing a cut of meat. She winced at the memory of the blows raining down on her face and body. Everything hurt. Her bottom lip was swollen, and she imagined her right eye must look like a blueberry pie by now.

Anderis turned from the trough and stepped over to Cailix, his hands folded behind his back and a disgusting, smug grin on his face. She imagined what it would feel like to cut that head from his neck. *We'll see if he's still grinning when I'm done with him*, she thought.

"In case you have any aspirations for escape, let me dash those hopes for you now. It seems your sigilord friend did not survive the briene assault on Waldron, nor did anyone else for that matter. It was a bloodbath." He smiled. "You might have enjoyed that part."

She wriggled and kicked, screamed behind her gag. Her tears dripped onto the deck below. She wasn't supposed to cry—strong women didn't cry. She had lost people before, caretakers and food providers mostly, and hadn't shed a tear at their passing. So why would the death of people she barely knew bother her? Perhaps it didn't, and she was only crying because of the beating. *That's got to be the reason*, she tried to convince herself.

Anderis's smile widened. He was enjoying this, making her show weakness in front of all these men and mages.

"Have you anything to say?" Anderis asked. "Here, let me." He reached through the net and removed the gag.

She coughed and tried to spit at him, but she failed to muster the saliva needed. Her mouth was sticky and dry and tasted like other people's blood. Useless, impotent blood.

"Why haven't you killed me?" she asked with an itchy, dry throat.

Anderis blinked. *He's hiding something*, she thought.

He recovered quickly, but not quickly enough that she didn't notice. If they had been playing at cards, she could have bought a castle with the winnings.

"Because the blood in your veins is mine," he answered, "and that makes it powerful. Think of your skin like the walls of a bank. I keep you around in case I need to make a withdrawal, and as long as you keep making more blood, I can keep making withdrawals."

"What if I were to kill myself to deprive you of your bank?"

"Why do you think you are wrapped up like a dead fish, my dear?" Anderis grinned again. "I am protecting my investment."

"Who was she?" Cailix asked, trying to change the subject, and more importantly, stall for time until she had a plan.

"Who was whom?"

"The woman you raped to make me. Surely no one would've given themselves to you freely," she said, leering, hoping the insult would make him angry—angry enough to make a mistake.

He pivoted and walked toward the captain at his great wheel, calling back to her, "The truth of it is I haven't the faintest idea. She was probably some bar wench who caught my fancy one night. It's a miracle she survived the encounter at all, let alone carried you to term."

If it's possible to kill someone twice, I'm going to do that to him, she thought.

As Anderis reached the captain's wheel, Cailix could make out some of their conversation.

"…until we reach the island?" Anderis asked.

"We should be there at the dawn of the third day from now, sir mage," replied the captain.

"And you say there are a few thousand people there?"

"Aye sir, could be as many as ten thousand if you count all the inland farmers and the fishing villages."

"That should be plenty," Anderis replied.

"For what?"

"Just be ready to earn your pay, Captain, and make sure a skiff is ready for me at dawn tomorrow with a few oarsmen," her former master replied.

They're going to kill the people on that island like they are no more than a herd to thin, just for their blood, Cailix thought. Her mind again turned to escape.

Mercenaries paced back and forth across all the decks, some of them still getting seasick over the gunwales. She counted six blood mages, all of whom were assembled up on the foredeck, gesticulating to each other and at the ships beyond them, a large naval fleet. The ships were of different sizes and shapes and flew different banners. *More pirates*, she thought.

She had been submerged in useless blood, unable to cast a single spell. She wondered if her own blood would be as ineffective. All she had to do was twist around in the net enough so she could get her teeth close to her arm.

"Aerlissa," Anderis called, turning back from a conversation with the captain. She froze, hoping he hadn't noticed anything. "Do you want to see a demonstration of the true power of the Order of the Sanguine Crystal?"

She said nothing.

"Keep your eyes to the sky." he pointed upward. "Shortly, you will see what we are really capable of."

A moment later the sea crackled with a thunder unlike anything she had heard before. It was a terrible boom that sounded as if a god had reached down and broken the sky itself. Two more booms filled her ears and made them ring.

Everyone on the ship looked up, mesmerized by what they saw. Three flaming cannonballs, bigger than she could imagine, streaked out of the sky. They separated and each took its own course, screaming toward the earth.

Nobody was watching her.

Cailix writhed and spun until at last she could reach her shoulder with her mouth. She bit into it and stifled a scream. She sucked at her own blood until she had a mouthful, then, imagining the same flaming blood she had used on one of the sailors before, she sprayed it in a broad mist onto the ropes.

They caught fire, the multicolored flames licking at the higher ropes as they raged upward and across the net. Cailix kicked and clawed, pulled and stretched, hoping that the ropes would give way before her escape turned into a cremation.

A swath of net snapped away and her legs dropped out beneath her. She fell through the net to her shoulders, then stuck, face to face with the searing flames. She held up her arm to shield her face and her skin bubbled and burned. With another fierce twist, she shrugged into as straight a line as possible and slipped through the hole onto the deck.

All hands on the ship still stood transfixed by the falling fireballs. Cailix ran for the nearest gunwale, nearly falling as pain wracked her legs and torso. The sailor who stood between her and the ocean never saw her coming. She yanked his knife from his belt, slit his throat with it, then pushed him overboard and plunged into the water alongside the dying mariner.

* * *

Urus had taken a breath, at first inhaling air, then finishing with saltwater. When he opened his eyes, the cave chamber with the inscribed stone slab and the horde of oncoming briene was gone. There was nothing but darkness: cold, wet, salty darkness.

His ears and head hurt, and his chest felt as if it was being crushed by a boulder. The pain was unbearable, worse than when his ears would get punched by his sire as a sick punishment for being deaf. He choked on the salty water and swallowed some of it. He wanted to open his mouth and gasp for air, but he was aware enough of being underwater to resist that urge, as such a gasp would be the end of him.

There's something very wrong with a Kestian meeting his end by drowning, he thought, struggling to figure out which way was up.

No one is meeting any ends here, came another thought. It was the voice of his own mind, but it had that strange tinge to it. It was Murin.

A hand pushed up into his armpit, another pressing against his back. Urus's fingertips tingled, as did his toes. He felt dizzy and his eyelids grew heavy. He longed to take a nap.

Enough of that, Urus. Swim up or you will be that Kestian who drowned in the ocean, Murin said within his mind.

Urus tried. He kicked his legs back and forth and lashed out with his arms. He was a terrible swimmer, as anyone who grows up in a desert should be. Kestians didn't swim in water; they saved every last drop for crops and drinking. One might as well have been swimming in an ocean of gold.

At some point he was vaguely aware of the fact that he had stopped paddling. Then his arms stopped moving, and the world went black, even blacker than the salty depths of the ocean.

A slap across the face jolted him awake, and he threw up bile and saltwater. His head was above water.

Can you tread water? asked Murin.

"I think so," Urus replied aloud, still not used to communicating with thought instead of his hands, which were currently occupied trying to keep himself afloat. He looked around to see Murin before him, casually treading water as if he could do that all day without fatigue. But that was all there was —in every direction there was nothing but ocean, an infinite blue expanse with no land in sight.

"Where are we?" he asked.

Murin squinted up at the sky and swished left and right in the water. Urus had no idea what he would be looking for, there were no landmarks in the endless water, just clear open sky that met the horizon in every direction.

Murin thought, *We're clearly in the middle of the Faernath Sea.*

"How can you tell that?" Urus asked. "And more importantly, where is that?"

"I have neither the time nor the energy to explain how I know. Suffice it to say that we are roughly two days journey by ship—a fast one at that— northeast of Waldron harbor."

"There's nothing out here. Why did we end up here when we traveled through the vertex?" Urus asked, his legs and arms starting to settle into a synchronized rhythm, though he was sure he was going to have to discard Hugo and the rest of his heavy gear soon.

"Do you know anything about n-dimensional geometry?" Murin asked.

"Of course not," replied Urus.

"The vertices are unique in that, in order to form a barrier between universes, they must exist in multiple universes at once. The stone slabs are really just anchor points for the real vertex, which we cannot see."

"What does all that have to do with us floating in the middle of an ocean?"

"Everything, boy," Murin said. "The vertices are millennia old. Over the ages the universes have changed position relative to each other…drifted in the quantum foam where both universes reside. That means the stone slabs and the real vertices are not in the same place relative to each universe any longer. That is why we did not appear at Waldron's vertex and why we are not standing before a stone slab now."

"So where is the stone slab?" Urus was going to ask even more questions, like *What in the hell is a quantum foam?* but stopped short when the sky erupted with flame. He felt pressure against the inside of his ears and could see waves forming on what used to be the calm surface.

He and Murin both stared, slack-jawed and in awe, at the flaming orbs dropping out of the sky.

The heavens are falling, Urus thought.

Not quite, but an altogether appropriate analogy, Murin replied. *Asteroids, pulled from a safe orbit around this planet. The amount of blood it would have taken the Order to discover and compel those rocks is mind-boggling. In fact, I am not sure it would have been possible on their own.*

A wave of emotion rushed from Murin to Urus, a gut-wrenching swirl of despair, hatred, and anger.

"Why would they knock rocks out of the heavens?" Urus asked aloud.

They've discovered the same temporal shift we have. They know destroying the stone is only part of the task. They need a much more potent weapon, something like the destruction of a falling asteroid.

They watched in silence, horrified. The asteroids streaked out of the sky, leaving a contrail of rock and a thin streak of what looked like clouds behind, highlighting the path to destruction like the stroke of a devil's paintbrush.

As each massive rock slammed into the earth, pulsating rings of light flashed outward from the impact spot; then a cloud of smoke and ash shaped like a monstrous mushroom appeared. Even from as far away as they were, the ocean churned in response, whitecaps forming on the surface as far as the eye could see.

Murin spun around to face Urus. *Urus, one of those asteroids may have hit Kest. There would be nothing left, no life of any kind, not even the tiniest of creatures. Nothing for miles.*

Nothing? Urus thought of Uncle Aegaz, who he had last seen battling that traitor Kebetir. Goodwyn wasn't in Kest, but there were thousands of innocent people there. They had culled him, but that was the Kestian way, and they didn't deserve to die.

Tears welled up in his eyes and ran down his face. *All those dead people*, he thought.

Murin grabbed Urus by the shoulders, somehow keeping himself afloat with just his feet.

"More people will die if we do not stop the Order. We have to protect the next vertex," Murin said.

The fifth vertex, actually, came the thoughts of yet another person in Urus's mind.

Without warning or fanfare, a purple-haired, grey-skinned man in robes appeared, hovering just above the surface of the water. While he seemed real, he also had a ghostly visage, and Urus could still see the ocean through the man's shimmering form. He looked as if he could be the purple-haired ghost of some relative of Murin's.

"Timoc?" Murin exclaimed. "How are you able to appear like this, to a non—" Murin stopped, glancing at Urus, "To someone not like us?"

"The vertices have been destroyed, all but the last. The membranes are coming closer and the barrier is almost gone. It will only be a matter of time before those less powerful than I figure out a way to make astral projection work in this universe. In fact, agents could already be at work from across the divide even as we speak. The Order may already have help."

Murin shook his head and sighed. "The Order pulled asteroids from orbit and dropped them on three vertex sites. The fourth, Waldron's vertex, must not have shifted and was destroyed in the earthquake after we fled."

"Asteroids, you say? Well, that is unexpected. Even if they had a river of blood to fuel a spell like that, they would have needed help from compatriots on my side of the divide. Unless they had a sigilord with them. Or maybe, no…no, that wouldn't be possible."

"The only sigilord on this world is with me," Murin said, his face grim.

"And the quiver?"

"He fights for Waldron."

Where is the vertex? Urus asked, thinking to himself and hoping this Timoc creature would understand. His throat was still tight with the pain of thinking of Kest being destroyed in a single death blow.

Timoc turned and regarded Urus with a distant expression. *Curious that you are in my thoughts. I only intended to appear to our friend Murin here, but… oh my…oh, this is rich!*

Timoc burst into laughter, holding his gut and bending over. Urus wondered if the laughter sounded as irritating as the man looked.

Let me congratulate you on making a pet of my former teacher. This is truly a day to remember.

"A pet?" Murin snarled. "The boy asked you where the vertex is and you play foolish games?"

"Oh, this is no game," Timoc said. Urus could read his lips, despite not knowing what language the man was speaking. "The boy has made you his familiar."

"He *what?*" Murin shouted. "That is not possible. I am no one's familiar, I am Murin of the House Futanishar, Viceroy of the Second Legion of Arbitration, and Dean Emeritus of the Academy of the Magic Sciences! I am no *familiar!*"

"Nevertheless, a sigilord boy has made you his familiar. I can feel the bond even from here, and I am literally worlds apart," Timoc said, still chuckling.

"We will discuss this later, Timoc. Much, much later."

"Where is the vertex?" Urus demanded, splashing water through Timoc's diaphanous form.

It is somewhere beneath you. If my guess is right, you are floating above the remains of the ancient city of Vultara. It is the only place where there could be a nearby vertex, and the only explanation for how I could have found Murin across the divide.

"Beneath us?" Urus asked, incredulous.

"Yes, about five hundred meters," Timoc replied, the smile vanishing from his face. "Under the sea."

Chapter Twenty-Three

"How are we going to get down there?" Urus asked, his arms and legs growing weary from treading water with his soaked clothing and Hugo strapped to his back.

"I might be able to hold my breath to get down there," Murin said, "but even though the sunken island is more shallow than the rest of the sea, the pressure in the ruins would crush us both to death."

"You are a sigilord, a master of space and time," Timoc told Urus. "There must be a sigil you can etch to ferry you both down to Vultara. If not, you'll both drown out here and Draegon will win, and set out to bleed both our universes dry."

"Who is Draegon? I thought Anderis ran the Order."

"Draegon Asurnios is the head of the Order of the Sanguine Crystal," Murin said. "Anderis is likely just a lieutenant, though if given the chance, I am sure Anderis would kill Draegon and take the Order for himself."

"Urus, have you cast even a single sigil?" Timoc asked.

"I don't know. I might have once, the night before Murin arrived in Kest. But I don't know what I did or how."

Timoc's insubstantial form made a clucking noise. "All that power and no one to teach you how to use it."

"I could try. I could try and make a sigil that could get us to the bottom."

"No, it is too dangerous," Murin said, brow furrowed with that same paternal look Aegaz got when Urus did something foolish. "You have no idea what might happen if you cast the wrong sigil, or worse, fail to cast a sigil properly."

"Look around us, Murin. We are about to drown in the middle of the ocean with no one to help us, not a ship or shoreline in sight. I would rather die trying to help than die a slow death doing nothing."

Murin and Timoc both grinned, the expression looking alien on both men. "Your uncle would be proud, Urus."

"What do I do?" Urus asked.

"Neither of us has ever worked alongside a sigilord," said Murin. "All I know is what I have read in ancient books. First, focus on what you want to happen. Then cast a sigil in the air, imbuing it with your power."

"How do I know what sigil to use? I don't know any."

"Try something old, the older the better," Murin said, finally starting to show signs of fatigue from treading water. "Pick from the oldest signs you know in the oldest version of tradesign you can remember. It is likely that tradesign evolved from the the sigils themselves."

Urus thought about it for a moment. They needed to breathe underwater, like fish. Maybe there was a sigil that would let them swim like fish. He concentrated on an image of them swimming like fish and signed the tradesign word for *fish* in the air.

The blue light and smoke appeared, drifting from the ends of his fingertips. As he signed *fish*, the blue smoke hung in the air, retaining the shape of the symbol.

It's working! he thought.

Moments passed, but nothing happened. Urus sighed and was about to try something else when a small fish leapt out of the sea, shot water from its mouth, then splashed back below.

"Try again," Murin urged.

Urus thought about the problem again. They needed more than to be able to swim, they needed air to breathe and to withstand the pressures of the deep that would otherwise crush them below. He focused on the need for a bubble of air, pictured it in his mind, and signed the oldest tradesign symbol for *air* he knew.

The sigil hung in the air, floating above the water, little droplets of blue ooze leaking out of the symbol and into the water. Gusts of wind buffeted them from all directions. The sea churned and heaved, and they rode up and down on foamy waves.

A swirling gust sucked them both out of the water, hurled them into the air and dropped them down hard against the sea. Urus marveled at the pain in his back from hitting water. How could something as soft as water hurt so much?

Timoc shimmered and reappeared above them, looking concerned.

"I am unharmed. Urus?" Murin asked.

"My back hurts, but I think I'm all right."

"The wind was a good idea. Now you need to control it, make the air into something that surrounds us so we can go below."

"I am starting to see why the blood mages hated the sigilords so much," Timoc said. "Magic with no reagent? They would covet that kind of power above all else."

"Just because we cannot see it does not mean there is no cost," Murin answered. "There is always a price to pay for power. Energy, magical or otherwise, cannot be created, only repurposed. That power comes from somewhere, and that is what the arbiters feared most about sigilcraft."

Urus thought about the problem again. He pictured him and Murin floating in a sphere of protective air, descending into the black depths of the ocean. He took a few slow, deep breaths, hoping that his own calmness and sense of control might transfer to whatever the sigil conjured.

This time he remembered an even older word, a sign that referred not to air in general, but to one of the four elements once thought to be the stuff of which all things were made. After one more breath, steadying himself by keeping the kicking rhythm with his legs, he cast the sigil.

The sigil hung in the air over the water, and this one did not drip or leak. It had clean, crisp edges and seemed to glow brighter than the others.

The ocean dropped out from underneath them, as thought someone had pulled the plug on a bathtub in Kest. They fell toward the hole and the hole fell ahead of them, so they kept falling.

Down they went, falling as though through nothing but air. It reminded Urus of the leap from the top of the palace in Kest; his stomach rolled and his insides felt like they would fall out through his mouth. He flung his arms and legs wide, like he had with the windrunner's cloak, trying to keep from flipping over.

The water continued to recede before them. Urus risked a glance behind him and saw the ocean closing in above them. Finally his stomach settled and the falling sensation stopped. The water still churned above and below, and they yet raced toward the ocean floor, but he no longer felt like he would end up splattered into pieces on some coral reef.

We should slow down, Murin thought.

I don't know how to— Urus started to reply, but cut short when they landed on the ocean floor, standing up straight and unharmed.

They stood on a plateau of rock. To their left the ocean dropped off into pitch darkness, while to their right, the broken stone remains of an ancient city spread out farther than they could see. Judging by the height of just the broken towers and pillars, the city must have been magnificent in its prime, taller and bigger even than Kest or Waldron.

A stop that quickly should've killed us, Urus thought.

Not if you weren't moving to begin with, came a thought from Timoc, who reappeared before them.

What does that mean?

"Have you ever—" Murin began, a look of pleasant surprise on his face. He gazed up and marveled at the dome of air extending around them, sea water rippling softly around the edge. "Have you ever taken a carpet or blanket and whipped it, just to watch the wave ripple through it?"

Urus nodded, still taking it all in. He was on the bottom of the ocean, breathing air, admiring the ruins of an island city that had sunk before the earliest history book was written.

"Sigilords were masters of space-time," Timoc continued, finishing Murin's example. "Rather than moving through five hundred meters of water, you bent space-time and simply sat on top of the ripple in the carpet until you reached the end. You didn't move…space did."

"Why did it feel like I was falling then, at the beginning?" Urus asked.

"Because you are like a baby playing with knives and torches," Murin continued. "You have had no guidance, no teacher. You are stumbling blind in the darkness."

Urus wondered if that was how he had survived the fall from the roof of the palace. Maybe he hadn't fallen at all, but instead, bent the space between the roof and the ground, folded it like a piece of parchment.

Precisely, remarked Timoc and Murin's minds in unison.

There are only a handful of people in this world who can even hope to grasp that concept after years of instruction, Timoc added, *and you understood it within seconds. You have inherited your forebears' innate grasp of space and time.*

"Anderis and Draegon no doubt know how powerful you can become," Murin said. "They will seek to convince you join them, or simply take your blood and give you no say in the matter."

"Timoc, since you have no body, you can search the ruins faster than we can," Urus said.

"Indeed I can, young sigilord," Timoc said with a bow. "I will start at the perimeter and work my way in and meet you two in the center square. There is a lot of stone to search here, worn and softened by thousands of years underwater."

"I don't think the writing on the vertex stone will be worn," Urus said. "It looked freshly carved on both of the stones we've seen so far."

"An excellent point." Timoc shimmered and then disappeared.

Urus turned to Murin. "Let's go. The air dome should follow me. I think."

"How reassuring," Murin replied, mustering a smirk.

They walked along a broken cobblestone road, making their way through the darkness around wide rectangles edged with marble that could have been gardens or the foundations for homes, Urus couldn't tell which.

They came upon a stone pedestal along the side of the road. A red crystal hewn into a diamond shape sat atop the pedestal. Etched into the column were four little dots that came to a tapered head. They looked like the little flames from the tips of candles.

Urus reached out and pressed his palm against the flames. They came to life, turning a bright yellow, and the red crystal on top lit up. The crystal on a pedestal a short ways down the road flared to life, then another, and another. The path toward the city center lit up in glowing red.

The scene Urus saw next would be forever etched in his mind as one of the most beautiful things he had ever witnessed. The darkness of the ocean pulled back from the city as tall buildings, brilliantly carved spires, railings, and walkways all lit up in a rainbow of colors. It looked like the sunstone buildings of Kest at night, but brighter and with a myriad more colors.

Ah, much better, came a distant thought from Timoc's mind.

"Astounding," Murin said. "After thousands of years, it takes but a single touch to bring the city back to life."

"Now we don't have to use the infer…" Urus struggled to remember the word. "Infar…"

"Infrasight," Murin corrected.

Urus looked up and watched the blackness give way to a light blue that reflected the many rainbow hues pushing outward from the city. It was then that he noticed the ripples of the water that used to be close overhead now hovered on the city's edge.

"The air dome," Urus pointed. "It's bigger than the city now."

"You must have activated a sigil that protects the city, like the one protecting us."

"You didn't tell me that Vultara was a sigilord city," Urus said.

"I knew that some sigilords once called it home, but I knew nothing of this. Outsiders were not exactly welcome here."

In awe of what lay before them, Murin and Urus continued on the road toward the city center.

Urus reached into the pouch in his wet leather armor and withdrew the little black diary. Sweeping his hand across the clasp, it flashed blue for a moment then snapped open. Urus barely noticed the pain in his arm this time.

To his surprise, the diary was undamaged by water. The pages were intact and even the ink on the paper was dry. Maybe the sigil on the lock did more than just lock the book; maybe it protected it as well?

"What is that?" Murin asked, tapping Urus on the shoulder.

"It's a journal I found in the vertex chamber below Kest. I can't read half of it, but some of it is in ancient Kestian. The entries I can read were written by people who call themselves *radixes*."

"That is a word I have not heard in an age. A radix was someone who was connected to the same source of power as the sigilords, but could not control or harness it themselves. During the Fulcrum War, the radixes fought alongside the sigilords against the blood mages using weapons etched with sigils of power."

"Like a magic infantry?" Urus asked.

"Just so."

I grow tired and can no longer maintain my projection. I will rest and return as soon as I can, master, Timoc thought. *May knowledge be your steed and wisdom your reins.*

Thank you, old friend, Murin replied.

They walked around more of the rectangles and down streets in varying stages of decay. Gradually the buildings around them grew taller and showed less evidence of destruction. Urus couldn't help but chuckle as they came to the top of a stone bridge.

"What is it?" Murin asked.

"I just think it's funny that we're on a bridge that should ford a stream, yet we are hundreds of fathoms into the deep."

"Find merriment where you can, Urus. I fear the worst is yet to come."

"You couldn't just fake a little optimism?"

They crossed several more bridges over chasms that were probably part of the city's original irrigation system. Surrounded on all sides by undrinkable saltwater, an island like this would have to catch its water in a cistern like Kest's.

They stood in the city center, looking up at the glowing statues of heroes or gods or goddesses, whose identities they could only guess. The figures rose from the ornately marbled square and loomed above it like guardians, their hands outstretched, palms first.

"If this was a sigilord city, would they hide the vertex stone where no one could find it, or put it on display, give it a place of honor?" Urus asked.

"You are only the third sigilord I have met, which is two more than nearly every other creature on this world. What would you do?"

Urus turned a full circle, studying the buildings that faced the heart of the city, arguably the most important buildings on the once-thriving island. If he was a sigilord, and he had created a city this amazing and put a vertex in it, he would have put the vertex somewhere special. But not special like the statues of heroes guarding the square, special with a different kind of reverence.

A museum, Urus thought, stopping mid-spin to face a wide building fronted by ornate, fluted columns of black and green stone, its brightly colored walls carved with intricate pictures depicting all sorts of scenes, from battles to rituals to who-knows-what else.

"I would put it in a museum," Urus said.

Without waiting for Murin, Urus started for the building that looked more like a museum than any other he had seen so far. They rushed up the stairs and slipped through a narrow opening between two collapsed stone doors.

The inside of the building was as black as night.

Let me try something, Urus thought.

He concentrated on the outcome he desired—illumination—and allowed the power to flow through his hands as he signed the tradesign word for *light*, a quick double-shake of his left hand twitching his four fingertips to represent the flickering flames. The gesture reminded him of the carved candle flames they had encountered upon first entering the city.

The sigil floated in the air before them for a moment before the room exploded with brilliant white light with a faint tinge of blue, like white light filtered through a blue crystal.

"I wonder why the sigils are always blue," Urus said.

"Until meeting you, I had not seen sigilcraft practiced up close and paid little heed to the color of it. A great and intelligent question, however one to which I do not know the answer," Murin replied. "We should split up. Convey your thoughts to me if you find something."

Urus nodded and clambered up a mostly intact nearby staircase while Murin headed off into the depths. It seemed that Urus's light filled the entire museum and wasn't limited to just where he stood.

The museum fascinated Urus. All around him were unimaginable things. There were machines that looked even more deadly than the ones used by the briene, yet they had to be thousands of years older than the flying birds he had fought or the siege engines they had sabotaged. There were things that must have been weapons because they were placed nearby swords and shields, but he had no idea how they were supposed to work. Some looked like crossbows, only there seemed to be no place for bolts.

He passed through the weapons room into a chamber that reminded him of the room in the top floor of the palace back in Kest. It was filled with carvings of stone animals and plinths supporting empty metal frames, whatever animals they held up having long since decayed.

All along the walls in the menagerie room stood suits of armor, each one unique and still glinting with polish as though they had been forged just yesterday. Urus wondered why there was no dust or cobwebs or damage from the sea water. One statue in particular, an obsidian four-armed suit wielding four curved blades with spiked pommels and blade guards, caught his attention.

What kind of creature needs a suit of armor with four arms? He reached out to touch the shiny metal plates. He had seen plate armor before, but this armor was made of so many reticulated plates they could easily have doubled as dragon scales.

As he touched the suit, one of its arms stretched out and grabbed Urus's wrist.

He leapt backward, yanking his arm free. The suit of armor stepped forward, spinning its blades and dropping into a perfect forward stance, feet spread just wide enough to expose a minimal target with maximum balance. Not only was this armor moving, but it had been trained how to fight. If it weren't for the clearly vacant helmet, Urus would have believed a real person lived within the suit.

Urus drew Hugo from his back and relaxed into nearly the identical stance.

Murin! Urus shouted with his mind. No reply came.

The suit of armor seemed to pause for a moment, as if waiting for something. Urus, too, waited, neither advancing nor retreating.

Murin, this thing is alive! he mind-shouted again, also with no reply.

The armor took a step forward, each of its lower arms sweeping to the side while the upper arms each spun their blades into a flower spin.

Urus took an involuntary step back, watching with fear and awe as this four-armed metal thing showed off with all the talent and style of a solo performance at a Kestian graduation ceremony.

The demonstration stopped and the armor leapt forward, slicing out with all four swords. Urus dodged to the side, evading two and parrying the others with a sweep of Hugo's broad blade.

Thinking and planning vanished, replaced entirely by instinct and muscle memory. Urus was barely able to manage a single thought over the next few minutes as he struggled to avoid being impaled. Further and further back the armor pushed him, knocking him over statues and sending him tripping over platforms.

Urus leaned back, letting two blades slide just a hair away from his chest, then spun toward the armor, getting between it and its swords. He slammed into it shoulder first, knocking it back onto the floor.

Murin, I'm fighting a living suit of armor! he managed to think while the creature recovered.

Urus went on the offensive, swinging Hugo with one hand while grabbing, punching, and throwing with the other. For all his sword's strength and sharpness, it could not cut through the enemy armor. It bent and warped and chipped, but nothing slowed it down.

He wasn't sure what good it would be to cut through the armor; if there was nothing living within it, how would he even kill it?

Then an idea came to him. All he needed to do was buy himself a few seconds to put down his sword, and hopefully not be cut into a dozen tiny pieces during that time.

He unleashed a flurry of quick, strong attacks and finished them up with a sweep, knocking the armor down. He turned and ran as fast as he could, spun back around, and leapt backward, shocked to see the armor already up and gaining ground on him.

Still in the air, Urus cast the *air* sigil, not the older elemental version but the newer, unstable one that had nearly killed them on the surface. He slammed back-first into a wall, the air emptying from his lungs. The blue sigil couldn't hold its shape and just seemed to leak everywhere.

He ducked just in time to avoid a quadruple sword attack that cut deep grooves into the wall.

So I guess sigilcraft doesn't work while moving. Fantastic, he thought, rolling away from the armor, halting, then re-drawing the sigil in the air. He finished the sigil just as the suit of armor leaned in for the killing blow.

Two blades sliced through his leather armor on either side of his chest, the other two just missing his legs. He screamed as the blades tore shallow cuts in his skin. As the armor readied its swords to decapitate Urus, the air in the room grew chill. Gusts blew in all directions and from all directions, quickly gathering into a swirling vortex. The wind slammed into the suit of armor, picked it up, and then shredded it, sending all of its small pieces of plate mail clattering against walls and to the floor, embedding some into nearby statues.

That wind could give one of Cailix's tornados a decent fight, Urus thought.

He stood up and checked to make sure his wounds were as shallow as they felt. Unfortunately those were the ones that hurt the most. The battlemasters always used to say that it wasn't the painful wounds were the worst, it was the wound you couldn't feel that would kill you.

Murin? Urus called out with his mind. Again no answer.

As Urus sheathed Hugo, movement caught his eye. A piece of armor stuck in a stone statue vibrated. Others on the floor started to shake then, and in an instant dozens of pieces slid across the floor into a pile. The pile quivered and then jumped up, reforming into a suit of armor. A moment later, the remaining pieces freed themselves from the statues and flew into place on their host, now a fully assembled suit of armor.

Seriously? Urus thought. Covered in sweat, exhausted, and in pain, he again drew Hugo and braced for battle. The shining black armor approached, swords at the ready.

As it drew near, instead of assuming a battle stance, it stopped. A gleaming green sigil appeared on the chest plate like a flaming brand. Urus thought of the scar on his own chest where he had been branded as a failure, as a culled, unfit to be a warrior. He almost chuckled, wondering what Battlemaster Guren would think to see him now, standing off against a magical four-armed knight.

The sigil did look like a brand, an image of some kind of antlered animal like a deer. As quickly as it flared to life it disappeared. With its chest back to its normal black color, the knight took a knee and bowed deeply.

Murin, you have got to see this, Urus thought. He wondered what Murin could be doing that was so important he wouldn't reply. It was a scary thought, so he pressed it from his mind.

Urus relaxed his stance and sheathed Hugo. The knight stood up and sheathed its swords, the scabbards on its back custom-made for four blades. Urus couldn't resist the temptation and so leaned forward and peeked inside the thing's helmet.

It was empty, as he expected.

The other suits of armor in the room peeled away from the walls, fifteen in all, each a different style and make of armor. They all flashed the same stag sigil and bowed before him. They stood at ease, as though awaiting orders.

This will do nicely, Urus thought, a grin spreading across his face.

There were no other exits from the room, so the only way to go was back toward the entrance.

"Well, let's go then," Urus said aloud, waving the soldiers on. Somehow they seemed to understand, nodded, and followed him out of the hall.

He rushed down the lobby's main stairwell to see Murin standing on the other side of the entrance, staring up into the ocean. It still felt odd to be looking up into water rather than sky.

He slipped through the opening and stood next to him.

"Why didn't you answer me?" Urus said aloud.

Murin turned. "I discovered a few chambers that were shielded from arbiters and that must have blocked your thoughts. Did you have any trouble?"

"No, not really," Urus said with a smirk. At that, a steady stream of animated suits of armor poured out of the museum entrance to take up defensive positions around Urus. "Wait, why would there be rooms shielded against arbiters? And you need to explain what an arbiter is."

"Simulacra? How did you manage that?" Murin asked, changing the subject.

"Is that what they're called?"

"Did they ask you if you were friend or foe?"

Urus blinked, his thoughts returning to the confrontation. He remembered the odd pause before the knight attacked. Had it been talking to him?

"It didn't occur to me that they might have been talking to me."

Murin nodded and appraised the squad. "Impressive. Those will come in handy."

Urus gazed up in the direction Murin had been looking. *What did you see?*

Pulsing colors, each followed by a popping noise. I fear the dome has been breached.

Urus met Murin's somber gaze, "Breached?"

"The Order is here."

CHAPTER TWENTY-FOUR

Goodwyn winced as the healer stretched the bandages tight around his bruised ribs. In truth, he was bruised pretty much everywhere, but he felt good. He felt alive. The smells around him seemed deeper, the colors more vibrant, and, unfortunately, the suffering of the people around him more palpable.

He turned to the torchlit courtyard, giving the healer access to more wounds so the man could work more slimy concoctions into his skin under fresh bandages. Fires burned at the top of nearly every tower; thatch roofs that hadn't disintegrated entirely burned slowly to ash. All around, stone spires and towers that weren't hewn from the mountainside had been toppled. Rubble littered the courtyard and virtually every street in Waldron from the sky gate to the warrens.

The briene war birds had decimated the city, even though the Waldrenes had won the engagement on the road before the sky gate. It would be dawn soon, and with it would come another wave of briene. He and Corliss harbored no illusions about what was coming next—it would be quick, brutal, and contain everything the briene could deploy.

Corliss approached and grunted as he sat down on the flat piece of a smashed gargoyle that used to overlook the parapets on the north wall. He carried a tray filled with bits of meat, bread, and fruit.

"Eat," Corliss said. "We haven't much time to regain our strengths."

"My jaw hurts," Goodwyn replied.

"Shall I have one of the duke's kitchen staff pound it into a paste for you?" He chuckled.

Goodwyn grabbed a roll from the platter, tore it into pieces, and started to pick at it. He knew he needed the strength but he wasn't hungry. His mind was elsewhere, wondering what had become of Kest, whether Therren still lived, and if Urus had survived and accomplished his task.

There was so much at stake. This wasn't like the war drills they taught in Kest that were more like fun camping adventures than real war. They trained to survive sieges and plan tactics in waves and prepare for long battles, but there was no training that could have prepared him for actually being in battle and, worse yet, knowing that men had died fighting alongside him, knowing that he had killed so many.

"There you are, master Corliss," a man said as he approached the courtyard, looking as tattered and weary as everyone else in the city. His brightly colored tunic and loose pants were stained with dirt and blood, his beard coated with stone dust. His bright blue eyes stood out against the rest of his smothered appearance.

"Noah," Corliss said without looking up from his platter. "I'm too tired to let you kill me right now."

"Knight Marshall, you flatter me," Noah replied, taking a seat on the cobblestones nearby, but not too close. "I have news from the warrens."

Now Corliss and Goodwyn both looked up.

"I took a group of my men and we led a group of your soldiers down into the warrens to look for the boy and the grey man."

"And?" Corliss asked.

"There was no sign of the boy or his freakish friend. We did, however, run into a horde of briene down there. They were chiseling and hammering and working all kinds of tools into the stone. They collapsed half the mountain in on the lower caves. Would have taken the whole city had we not stopped them."

"No sign of bodies or blood?" Goodwyn asked, standing up, exasperating the healer still working on his back.

"We found a few bodies, but they weren't briene or your friends. One corpse wore a suit filled with little blood pouches," he turned to Corliss. "The little buggers put up more of a fight than we expected, but we finally routed them. You can thank me when all of this is over."

"Huh," Corliss said, but looked pleased. "This is good news, Goodwyn. Your friends may have found what they were looking for."

Goodwyn nodded. "I hope so."

The next few hours felt like days as the soldiers tried to get as much rest as possible, many sleeping wherever they were standing when they ran out of energy—against walls, on tables at the inns—but most of them near their posts and ready to return to battle a moment's notice.

Goodwyn made his way to the gate to stand beside Corliss outside the city and await the coming dawn and next wave of briene attack. He wasn't going to hide, nor was he going to do battle in one of those flying cloaks. No, his place was right on the front line.

"You fought bravely yesterday, with honor and more skill than I have ever seen," said Corliss. "No matter what happens, I consider it an honor to have fought beside you."

"The honor was mine, Knight Marshall." Goodwyn gave the customary response. In truth, Corliss hadn't behaved honorably at all. He had disrespected his enemy, something no Kestian would ever consider.

"No, it wasn't. I was going to slaughter those briene fetching their dead. You were willing to die for their rights, to die for the rights of your *enemy*. I learned something about myself yesterday that I cannot easily forgive."

"It is all sand on the wind now," Goodwyn said.

Together with four hundred soldiers outside the gate, they waited.

Dawn brought with it thick clouds covering the road leading to the sky gate. As the clouds encroached upon the feet of the waiting soldiers, the first of the dark silhouettes appeared below. Then another, and another, until the clouds darkened with the shapes of small armed men, marching steadily upward.

Behind them, as their forms solidified and they emerged from the clouds, materialized the looming shapes of great machines.

"Hold fast, men!" shouted Corliss, drawing his weapon. Goodwyn readied the suzur and put some distance between himself and the others, lest they become accidental casualties of his long strike.

The marching army appeared downhill only a few hundred meters away and then stopped. Two figures stepped forward out of the crowd, both with their arms spread wide.

"What kind of trick is this?" Goodwyn asked.

"Be ready for anything," Corliss said, just loud enough for Goodwyn to hear. "I don't like the looks of this."

Once the two figures were out of the clouds, Goodwyn recognized one of them immediately. The taller of the two wore a dark green suit of leather armor, which stood out against the pure black clothing of all the other briene. He also wielded a much bigger, specialized sword. Goodwyn recognized the sword as well. It was the briene he had dueled with for several hours the day before.

"The briene wish to speak with the *fein duras*," shouted the shorter of the two, who looked just like any of the other briene, except that he seemed to be wearing rugged clothes rather than battle-ready armor.

Corliss took a step forward, his sword still at the ready. "I am Knight Marshall Corliss Tudell and I am charged with the safety of Waldron and all its people. If you wish to speak, you can do so with me."

"The foreman and the blade will only speak with the *fein duras*, though you may accompany him if you wish," replied the shorter briene.

"I do not know this fein duras you speak of," Corliss replied, his stance relaxing a little. The shorter briene had no weapons and the green-suited one's sword remained sheathed on his back, their goggles pulled back so Goodwyn could see their eyes for the first time. They had brilliant, almost glowing, golden eyes.

The green-suited one pointed at Goodwyn. "That is the fein duras, the champion who fights for Waldron's honor. The blade and the foreman would speak with him."

"Where is this blade and foreman, then?" Corliss asked.

"This is the foreman," replied the shorter one, pointing to himself. "And this is the blade." He indicated the one in the green suit.

"These people get stranger every time we encounter them," Goodwyn murmured.

He took a few steps toward them, and they formed a group of four in the middle of the road.

"Fein duras." The foreman bowed. "The foreman has heard that the fein duras and his people fight with great honor."

"Thank you." Goodwyn bowed slightly. "As do yours. I apologize for what happened with the litter-bearers. We did not know we were betrayed until too late."

"This is why we have come to discuss matters with you. The briene are a peaceful people—" Corliss interrupted him with a stifled snort. "—unless provoked."

"The briene were struggling to survive, dying out," continued the blade. "Until the blood witches came."

"Blood witches? You mean the Order?" Goodwyn asked.

Both men nodded. "They came and offered the briene knowledge. They showed the briene ways to improve how to harness steam, ways to build better, to manufacture things to trade with other cities to get food and other things the briene lacked. That knowledge saved the briene."

"What does this have to do with Waldron?" Corliss asked.

"The blood witches told the briene that the Waldrenes were ruthless savages who would take briene resources, destroy briene cave homes, and run briene out of the kingdom. They said that the Waldrenes were without honor, and the briene believed them. The briene had to believe them; the blood witches saved the briene."

"So you waged war upon us based on the word of forked-tongued devils like the blood mages?" Corliss snapped.

Goodwyn held out a hand, trying to calm the Knight Marshall. "Corliss, remember that your own duke heeded the counsel of a blood mage too. And we don't need to mention what happened with Rhygant."

"The blood witches can be very persuasive, and they gave the briene many gifts—gifts that saved the lives of thousands of the foreman's people," the foreman said, his eyes wet with tears held in check. "The foreman discovered that the blood witches had killed hundreds of briene and used their blood for something terrible."

"The foreman and the blade think the blood witches may have used briene blood to make the stars fall yesterday," the blade added.

"They have persuaded other armies to do their bidding as well," Goodwyn said. "Four armies attacked my home before I fled, no doubt promised mountains of gold or other gifts in return for laying waste to my city."

"Yes, we heard this same story," said the foreman.

Heard the same story? How, from who? Goodwyn thought, his mind racing.

"What is it you want then, foreman?" Corliss asked.

"Forgiveness," he replied.

"Forgiveness? That's it?" Corliss asked, sheathing his sword finally.

"No," replied the foreman. "We also want revenge."

Hooves clopping on the road echoed up from below the cloud layer, interrupting the conversation.

"I didn't know the briene had cavalry," Goodwyn said.

"The briene do not. Horses are giant, smelly animals, get lost in caves. The friends of the fein duras are arriving," said the foreman, revealing the tiniest hint of a smile for the first time.

"My friends?" Goodwyn asked, peering into the mist.

A moment later shadows of men on horses pushed aside the clouds— shadows of tall men, not briene. More horses galloped into view until there were twenty in all. Goodwyn's heart skipped a beat as they trotted to a halt on the road and he could see them clearly.

Each of the dark-skinned riders wore a red tabard emblazoned with a white fist. Beneath that they wore the light-colored, finely stitched and riveted leather armor that could only be made by the finest Kestian craftsmen. It was the First Fist of Kest, and on the lead horse rode none other than Aegaz Noellor, their commander.

"The gods be praised!" Goodwyn shouted, tears running down his cheeks.

He raced down the hill as Aegaz dismounted. He slammed into his commander's chest just as he hit the ground, lifting the unsuspecting man with a back-crushing hug.

"Easy, boy, you'll crush the life out of me," Aegaz said in Kestian, wheezing a laugh.

Goodwyn set down his commander and perhaps a more attentive father than his own sire had been.

"There's so much to—" He was about to unleash an assault of words explaining what had happened since he had left Kest when he saw another of the First Fist dismount, a handsome young man with short cropped, dark hair and brilliant brown eyes.

"Therren!"

The two ran to each other and embraced. Then, realizing that all eyes were upon them, they separated and gave each other a traditional warrior's greeting with arms clasped together up to the elbows.

"I, uh," Goodwyn stammered. "It is good to see the colors of the First Fist again."

"These men of Ehmshahr arrived last night, in search of two boys, one of whom fit the description of the fein duras," called the foreman as the First Fist gathered in closer to the discussion.

"How did you find us? How did you even get here so quickly?" Goodwyn asked, his mind reeling with questions.

"Quickly? Why, it's taken us nearly seven weeks to get here," replied Aegaz.

"Seven weeks? That can't be right. Urus and I only arrived here a couple of days ago."

Aegaz shook his head and smiled. "I remember each day of the journey from Kest. We left a city under siege to come find you boys."

"How did you find us?" Goodwyn asked.

"I was able to unlock one of the journals in the room where you three vanished. In it I found this," Aegaz said, pulling a scroll from one of his saddlebags. He held it up. "Where are Urus and the grey-skinned stranger?"

"That is a very long story, but they are gone. I suspect they went to the location of the next vertex, but I have no idea where that would be."

"Well, I might." Aegaz unfurled the scroll, revealing a detailed map with hundreds of landmarks and annotations. He ran his finger along lines leading from a spot that marked Kest to Waldron and then followed a line out into an area labeled as the Faernath Sea.

The blade and the foreman pressed in closer to study the map, though from the looks on their faces it seemed as though they had seen it before.

"That's out in the middle of the ocean. How are we going to get there?" Goodwyn asked.

Aegaz smiled but said nothing, instead turning to look at the blade and the foreman.

"This was the purpose of our parley this morning, fein duras," said the foreman. "The briene wish to make amends to the people of Waldron and to those who defend it. The briene will repair every stone taken down, once the task is done. The briene wish to exact revenge upon the true villains, the blood witches. The fein duras and the Waldrenes have the same goal, no?"

"Indeed we do," Goodwyn replied. "I mean to see the heads of all of the blood mages on pikes and to help Urus stop them from destroying the fifth vertex."

Aegaz stared down at Goodwyn with an appraising, surprised look. "Much has changed since you left Kest."

"You have no idea, Commander. You have no idea."

"Well then, you can tell me all about it on our way down to the briene ships. They are ready to take us all, including as many of Waldron's army are able, out to meet the blood mage's navy."

"The briene have ships?" Goodwyn asked.

The foreman and the blade exchanged mischievous looks. "The briene adapted some of the techniques the blood witches provided in ways the blood witches did not expect," the foreman said. "nor did the briene share those adaptations with the witches."

"So after attacking my city, laying siege to it, and killing my people, you want me to just give up, to walk away and pretend as though nothing happened here?" Corliss snapped.

"No, Knight Marshal. The blade and the foreman want to help hunt and kill the blood witches," said the blade. "All of them."

Corliss looked at Goodwyn, Aegaz, the rest of the First Fist, the briene army, and then finally back at his men, all standing at the ready, awaiting a battle with the briene they all knew they would have lost.

Then he nodded resolutely. "I can have a group of men ready within the hour."

Chapter Twenty-Five

Cailix pushed off the rocks and spat out seaweed. The blood from the unfortunate sailor who had been foolish enough to stand between her and freedom had been enough to cast a spell that sent her soaring through the water like a bird would through the air.

She rubbed the bump on her forehead and checked to see if it was bleeding. Somewhere on her escape from the blood mage pirate navy, she had slammed head-first into something big and heavy. Being knocked unconscious seemed to be the only explanation for her current situation; washed up on the rocky shore of a lighthouse keeping watch over the bay.

Cailix took stock of her surroundings, looking for potential danger. She was standing on a manmade stone platform in the middle of a bay, over which a bright red lighthouse kept vigil. Fishing boats crammed into the bay and the harbor within. Vessels of all shapes and sizes dotted the ocean beyond.

The whole place smelled of salty seaweed and decaying fish. She walked around the base of the lighthouse to face the bay, looking for a way to get inland. Without any blood to spare for a spell, she might have to swim for it.

Walking down toward the water, still rubbing her head, she nearly stumbled over the nest of a sea bird. Two chicks lay sprawled out on the rocks, chirping for their mother, while another sat oblivious and content, napping in the warmth of the nest made from straw and bits of broken shells.

She bent to the two little birds and watched them crying, struggling to move. Their little legs were bent at odd angles and one chick had a broken wing. Neither would ever be able to fend for itself nor would the mother bird carry that burden.

They were going to die, and do so slowly. Cailix reached out and quickly snapped the two chicks' necks. She cleared away some rocks and dug two little holes in the sand below. She buried the birds, shedding a tear for each. It felt odd to cry, an alien feeling to her.

Seeing those helpless little birds hurt her more than seeing the people in Waldron fleeing their homes, seeking shelter from the coming siege. *Is that normal? Why do I care more for the plight of these birds than I do for people?* she wondered.

Because people will betray you, she answered herself. *Animals operate on instinct alone.*

She cracked open a few mussels and scooped the meat into the nest with the remaining little bird. He awoke from his nap and started probing the food with his beak. Satisfied the little thing would be all right until his mother returned, she waded knee-deep into the water and started waving her hands.

"Ahoy!" she shouted at the closest boat, a wide, flat thing piloted by a single fisherman. "Ahoy there!"

"Who's there?" called the man, standing up in the boat and shielding his eyes from the sunrise.

"Please, sir, can you ferry me to the harbor?" she yelled to him.

"Only if you can swim aboard and don't mind settin' on a pile of gloomfish. That's all I got room for, young miss."

"Thank you!" she sprang into the water and swam out to the boat. Either she had misjudged the distance or the energy she had, because she was exhausted by the time she made it to the boat, so much so that the fisherman had to haul her aboard.

The man hadn't been joking about not having much room. The boat had four large square bins, each filled to overflowing with stinky fish. After the fish, there was enough room for the captain, the sail, and the tiller.

She took a seat—wincing as she did so—on a bin of slimy fish, their dead mouths bent into a sad looking frown. *Maybe that's why they call them gloomfish?*

The fisherman—a man who looked more like he'd been carved out of a piece of sunburned stone with a beard than made from human flesh—laughed a deep, roaring laugh. Until then, she didn't really think fishing was something that would build a person up like a fighter or a blacksmith.

"Little lady, the look on your face—hell, just the look of you as you sat on my haul of gloomfish, will keep me laughin' clear through next week."

Cailix gave him a look. She didn't like being made fun of.

"Oh relax, miss. I ain't laughin' at you, just laughin' in your direction."

She harrumphed and folded her arms, realizing how difficult it was to maintain dignity sitting on a fish pile.

"What's a young woman doing sopping wet and alone out on the lighthouse point?"

"My business is my own, sir," she replied. The defensive reaction was a reflex, like a flinch. She wouldn't get far if she kept up that kind of attitude. "I'm sorry, I-I'm just not used to strangers being helpful."

The fisherman considered her, his gaze softening. "That's okay, lass, no apology needed. The accommodations aren't exactly first rate." He nodded at the fish with a smile.

It was a kind, gentle smile, without an agenda or hidden motive. It was just a simple smile. She had only met one other person who was on the surface exactly what he was within, and Urus might now be dead. The only hope she had that Urus was alive was that news of his death had come from Anderis, and that man was a liar to the core.

"By the by, my name's Hutcher, and don't worry, I won't ask you yours," said the fisherman.

"Who rules this island?" she asked Hutcher as he maneuvered the boat between the larger ships and toward a long pier off to the side of the main harbor. He might be a nice man, but she didn't just volunteer her name to anyone.

"Aldsdowne has no ruler; we're just a small island. This place ain't no place, it's just some place between places. Only us fishermen, farmers, and traders are fool enough to stay out here."

"Is there no garrison here? No law?" she exclaimed. Anderis's captain has said there could be as many as ten thousand people on the island. The idea of all those people with no one to rule over them seemed outrageous. How had the place not descended into anarchy?

"We're not part of any kingdom, so no nation leaves a garrison. As for the law, we have a constable and he's got some men who help him, but they mostly keep the traders in line, checking scales and running scammers off the island and such. If someone breaks one of our rules, we stop trading with them and they lose out."

"No king? No lords and ladies and dukes or castle?" asked Cailix, wide-eyed.

Hutcher chuckled. "No miss. We got us a nice small island here and we love it, so we keep it in line ourselves. We don't need no fancy lords or ladies to tax us or tell us how to live our lives."

They pushed up to the pier, where Hutcher cast a loop of rope around a moss-coated pole and pulled the boat in close. "Out you go, miss. Just watch you don't slip on the pier; it's slicker than my pile o' fish."

Cailix clambered up onto the pier. Turning back to Hutcher, she asked, "Where can I find the constable?"

"This time of day? He'll probably be down in Lucien harbor, the next bay south of here. That's where the big ships put up for a couple days on big trips. Like I say, Aldsdowne ain't no place, it's just between places. Why all this fuss about law and garrisons and such?"

"How far?" she asked, her mind already planning the conversation she might have with the constable.

"If you start walkin' now you can get there just after lunchtime. Just take the main road south. It'll turn east along the southern shore; then you can't miss it. Now, I reckon you have a right to your privacy, and I been nice about it, but now you're gonna tell me why you need to see the constable." Hutcher hopped out of the boat with a grace that belied his girth.

"The island is in great danger, Hutcher. There's a navy coming this way, and they don't mean to take prisoners."

Hutcher laughed, drawing a few curious looks from nearby fishermen busy unloading their own hauls. "Nobody attacks Aldsdowne, girl. We got nothin' worth stealin' and we got no throne to occupy."

Cailix gave him her most intense look, hoping it would impart the seriousness of the situation. "Nevertheless, a navy approaches and everyone on this island is going to be slaughtered unless I can speak to your constable."

"I see," Hutcher said, resting his palms on his hips. "Well, you best be going then, if you hope to catch him still in Lucien."

"Thank you again, sir," she said, then jogged up the pier, turning right at the end and making her way out to the main road. She glanced back once as she ran and saw Hutcher shaking his head and chuckling to himself.

He doesn't believe me, she thought. *If the constable doesn't, this island, and who knows how many other nations with it, are doomed.*

As she ran, pacing herself so she wouldn't get tired too soon, she marveled at Aldsdowne's beauty. The rolling hillsides that sloped down toward the coast burst with brilliant greens and short, puffy trees. Here and there shards of white stone peeked out, wearing thick patches of dark grass like a hood. Even the road was pleasant, a wagon-worn track through the low-lying ranges between hills.

Further up into the hills and away from the coast, shepherds tended to their flocks of sheep, dogs yipping and racing back and forth to keep the animals in check. Up on the road the sea breeze still smelled of saltwater but didn't carry with it the stench of decaying fish.

She ran until well after what she thought should have been lunchtime, her stomach turning in on itself with hunger. She tried but couldn't remember the last time she'd eaten anything, or drunk anything other than sea water.

As she crested a ridge playing host to a flock of geese, her feet felt as though she had run them into bloody stumps, and her knees and back ached. Weak and lightheaded, she kept moving forward out of momentum and determination and little else.

On the other side of the ridge, the bright green hillside sloped down toward the southern shore of the ocean. It appeared as if a small army of merchants and craftsman had lain siege to the hill and taken it as their own. Tents and campfires dotted the hills, and huge roped-in squares contained all manner of crafts and handiworks. Everywhere she could see people were buying and selling wares, laughing and smiling and playing music.

And cooking!

Her mouth watered.

The crowds, and more importantly the food, drew nearer as she stumbled her way down the slope. Her knees gave way a few times, and she hit the ground, rolling. One time she didn't bother trying to get up because rolling down the hill on her side was easier than walking.

With the last of her strength near the end of a roll, she pushed off the ground, teetering up onto her feet. As she did, her eyes met those of a man and his wife, who looked up from their struggles with a defiant lamb that had no interest in being sheared. A moment later, a young man and woman appeared from within a tent with concerned looks on their faces.

It was the last thing she saw before dropping to her knees and passing out.

***

"Young lady?" called a woman's soft, gentle voice.

Cailix rolled to the side of the cot on which she lay and retched, but nothing came out. There wasn't enough in her stomach to throw up. She didn't know where she was or why, and that uncertainty scared her beyond belief. She had to get out.

"Miss? Can you hear me?" came the same woman's voice again.

Cailix blinked and looked around. She was in a small, whitish tanned-hide tent. From the size and shape of it, it was probably one of the hundreds of merchant tents she had seen on the hill. An older woman with a kind smile hovered over her, wringing her hands with worry. A short, stout man with a gray beard loomed behind her, pacing. She heard two more voices whispering behind her.

Instinctively, she took note of the small fish knife on a table within arm's reach. From the whispers, she knew roughly where the other two people were, a girl and a boy, she guessed. She also knew about how tall they would be.

Without hesitation, she lunged for the fish knife, rolled to the side, then leapt over the cot, grabbing the boy by the waist and holding the knife to his throat.

It smells so good, she thought. She could smell the boy's blood through his skin, feel it pumping through his veins. She could feel the power it would grant her. All she had to do was poke one tiny little hole in his...

"Woah there, girl," said the man, his voice every bit as friendly and warm as the woman's. There was definitely something strange about these people.

Nobody is this nice, she thought. *They're up to something.* Anybody that nice had to be working some kind of angle or scam.

"You're safe here, dear one," the woman said, holding her hands up palm-out in a pacifying gesture. "We saw you runnin' down the hill all dirty and bruised up, wearin' a slave tunic."

Cailix risked a moment to look down at her clothes. She no longer wore the prisoner's garb Anderis and his men had given her on the ship. Instead, she wore a bright blue dress with silver filigree worked into puffy short sleeves and around the waist. It was the most gaudy, pretentious, beautiful thing she had ever seen.

Stunned, Cailix said nothing. She just looked up and stared back at the family. The girl and boy both appeared to be the same age as Cailix, and she had no idea how old the parents were. Old was old, and she couldn't tell the difference between the various types of old people.

The girl, still standing close to the boy, smiled wide. "It's one of my best. Do you like it? I like to wear it at carnival and when Ma and Pa take us up north to the city. I think it suits you nicely."

The girl gave Cailix and appraising look. She seemed genuinely proud of the dress.

"My name's Drayna," she said. "And that's my brother, Bayard. And these are our parents, Ma and Pa."

The woman chuckled, a gleam in her eye as she looked at Drayna. It was a loving, maternal look. Cailix felt ill and wanted to cry.

"My name is Orla, and this is my husband, Woss," she said. "Please, dear, put the knife down and let my boy go. No one in this tent is going to harm you. Come now, give us the knife and we can get some food in your belly. You must be starving."

Cailix felt her resolve fail. All her instincts told her to run, or to stand her ground and keep her position of strength. She couldn't allow herself to be vulnerable. She had to keep her back to the wall and her eye on the exits. She had to survive. She had to eat.

The blond-haired girl with piercing, almost ghostlike blue eyes, kept smiling, her head tilted to the side slightly. Cailix had seen that look before. It was *pity*. The girl actually felt sorry for Cailix. But why?

The boy, his brown hair smelling of saltwater and farm animals, seemed calm. His pulse had only quickened a little. He wasn't afraid. He knew Cailix was going to put the knife down.

The food did smell amazing. They had some kind of meat stew simmering over the fire just outside the tent. Out of the corner of her eye she spied a basket filled with biscuits and rolls.

She couldn't take it any longer. Cailix dropped the knife and made for the freshly baked breads. She grabbed a roll with one hand and a sweet, sticky bun with the other. If she could have crammed them both in her mouth at the same time she would have.

"There now," comforted Orla, patting Cailix on the back. "Take your time, dear, or you'll make yourself sick again. Come, let's have a sit by the fire."

Cailix barely noticed the family at all, so consumed was she with stuffing food into her mouth. At that moment her mouth seemed like an annoying barrier that just slowed the food down on its way into her belly.

Orla sat her on a log in front of the fire and wrapped her in a thick wool blanket. It scratched at her neck but it was warm and smelled nice. Bayard and Drayna took seats on a log on the other side of the fire. Woss continued pacing, still not saying anything other than stopping a few times to whisper in Orla's ear.

Cailix stared at her dirty hands as she chewed and watched big droplets of water splash off the bread. At first she thought it must be raining, but then she noticed that only her cheeks were wet. Like a wound that only hurts after you see how much it bleeds, Cailix let it all go. All the pain, the hurt, the sadness, the loneliness—it all came rushing out in sobs and tears and sighing shudders.

"Oh you poor thing," Orla said, scooting in next to Cailix. "Let's get some supper in you, and then if you're up to it, you can tell me about it."

"Flupper?" Cailix spat, shooting crumbs into the nice woman's face. "Supper!" The tears stopped. She had important things to do and couldn't be bothered with weakness right then.

"What of it, dear?"

"I'm late! I need to find the constable!" She bounced up, shedding the blanket.

"What do you need the constable for? Did something happen to you? Is that why you're all alone out here?" Orla asked.

"I'll bet it was slavers," Drayna said. "You saw the way she was dressed, I bet she escaped from a slave ship."

"Or pirates!" Bayard added, intrigued by the drama.

Orla hushed her children with a wave of her hand and a clucking noise.

"Unless he got himself waylaid somewhere, the constable's long gone by now," Woss said, finally standing still, his arms folded across his chest.

"I need to find the constable now. This island is in danger!" Cailix said.

"Nobody would bother attacking this island, girl."

"I know, 'This ain't no place but a place between places'" she mocked, quoting the fisherman.

Woss grinned. "So, you've met Hutcher then."

"This is serious. Which way to the constable? I don't have time to explain."

"We're not going to bother the constable with the ramblings of a half-starved waif," Woss said.

"Woss!" Orla scolded.

"What? The constable won't sound the alarm without cause. We all know what happened last time."

"Alarm? What alarm?" Cailix demanded, grabbing Woss by his vest.

"Nothing, girl. Forget I said anything. You need to calm back down and get some food in you. You're delirious and imagining things."

"If you don't get me to the constable or sound an alarm or do *something*, everyone on this island is going to die!"

These people are so stone-headed. They'll never listen to me!, she thought.

"And who would want to attack this island?" Woss said with defiance, hands on his hips.

"People who can do this." She spun on her heels and found the lamb, sheared and tethered to a post near the tent.

This is okay, she told herself. *This lamb's going to end up as someone's dinner anyway. I need to do this to show them what's coming. This is not like what Anderis did. I am not like him.*

She felt the blood course through the veins of the little animal. Cailix called to the blood, controlled it, manipulated it. Without touching it, it was hers, and she could do with it as she wished.

She clenched her fists and the lamb exploded into a cloud of red mist.

"By the heavens!" Woss shouted. Orla staggered back, crossing herself with some kind of religious warding Cailix had seen the monks use before. Drayna shirieked, and Bayard stood still, his legs crossed.

He's pissed himself, she thought. *What is wrong with these people?*

In the cool blue twilight by the shore, dozens of people screamed. Those screams drew more people out of their tents, who also screamed when they saw what was happening.

"Where is the alarm?" Cailix demanded. She turned her hands over into little cup shapes. The swirling mist of lamb's blood spun like a tornado, hovering just above the ground.

Woss said nothing, but pointed to the hilltop behind them. Barely visible in the dim light was a pyramid of stacked wood and kindling. *They probably light that when the lighthouse fails,* she thought. *That'll do for now.*

She sent the blood cloud soaring up the hillside. As it flew higher, she vibrated the blood droplets faster and faster until, just before reaching the hilltop, they burst into flame. A moment later the signal fire blazed to the sky, casting a flickering orange glow on the hillside. Before she could decide on her next move, another signal fire flared to life further down the shore, and another on an inland mountaintop.

That should get the constable's attention, she thought. *Hopefully it won't get me killed or thrown in jail.*

"Do you believe me now?" Cailix asked the stunned family, expecting them to flee in terror, to run from her power. Instead, they stood their ground. Orla and her daughter gazed back at her with even more pity than before.

"Oh you poor, poor girl," Orla said. "What have they done to you?"

CHAPTER TWENTY-SIX

Goodwyn squinted back at the face in the wall mirror, convinced that it couldn't possibly be his own. It had grown black with stubble on the cheeks and jaw, but remained smooth under the nose. The deep eye sockets seemed to have sunk further into the stranger's face, casting dark shadows below the eyes. Once-straight long hair now rebelled, bunching into little waves and curls.

The man staring back at him wasn't the same boy who had left Kest only a short time ago.

Goodwyn grabbed the de-thorned cactus leaf from the edge of the water-filled basin, crushed it, and spread the icy cold goo on his stubble.

"You're really going to shave that off? I like it," Therren said, his smiling face appearing in the mirror.

"It doesn't look like me," Goodwyn said, dunking a sharp dagger in the water.

Therren strode up behind Goodwyn, rested his hands on his hips, and gently kissed the back of his neck. "But it gives you such a handsome, rugged edge."

Goodwyn smiled at his friend in the mirror. Nothing made him happier than having Therren back, but everything was all so…different. He felt like he was living a different life now, and everything from Kest—from *before*—

belonged to someone else.

"Therren," he said, turning to face him. His pulse quickened, and he felt short of breath—exhilarated. "Everything's different now. All I want is to go back to that night, the night you gave me this." Goodwyn lifted the locket that hung from his neck.

"Our first kiss," Therren said softly.

"We can't go back."

"I know, Wyn. Believe me, I know. We don't even know if there's anything left of Kest to go back to," Therren said, taking a step back. He gazed into Goodwyn's eyes for a moment.

"You've changed, Wyn."

"What do you mean?"

"I don't know, but your eyes are different. They don't look so...Kestian."

"What does Kestian look like?" Goodwyn asked. He didn't need to ask. He knew what was missing; he could feel that a part of him would never be the same.

I don't want to fight any more, he thought. *How can I be a Kestian and not want to fight?*

"You don't have 'the look'," Therren said. "What battlemaster Kurd called 'the warrior's soul'; the killer instinct you can see in a man's eye."

"If that's what Kestian looks like, then maybe looking Kestian isn't such a good thing." Goodwyn sniffed back the tears he could feel begging to be let out. "You haven't seen what I've seen, Therren. The bodies, the dead people, and not just the warriors—little children, women who aren't trained to fight, people who just happened to be standing in the wrong place when the side of a building exploded. There is nothing to love about war, no pride in having a killer instinct. Yesterday we were killing the briene and today we're all on the same side. It's all so senseless."

"Maybe Urus is the luckiest of us, then. He never had the bloodlust."

"Maybe—" Goodwyn started, but the floor jerked one way and then the other, knocking both of them to their knees. A horrific metal-grinding sound came from the hall as the floor and walls vibrated and shook loose bits of dust.

"What's going on?"

"I think we're moving," Therren replied, helping Goodwyn up.

Goodwyn frowned. "How can we be moving? Steel bunkers don't move. I followed Aegaz and the foreman into this building from the caves."

Therren grinned wide. "Wyn, this isn't a building. It's a ship!"

"A ship made of steel? That's ridiculous. It would never float!"

"Come on, I'll show you!"

Before Goodwyn could argue, Therren grabbed his hand and yanked him out into the hallway. A moment later they were sprinting through corridors lit by eerie blue orbs jutting out of the ceiling, Therren giggling like a little kid on his way to the next adventure.

I don't know if I'll ever laugh like that again, Goodwyn thought, trying to soak up as much of his friend's joy as he could before the bloody memories came crashing back.

After descending several staircases and charging through corridor after corridor filled with briene and the occasional First Fist warrior, they skidded to a halt in front of a thick, black steel door.

"Down here?" asked Goodwyn, still catching his breath. "Shouldn't the deck be up?"

Therren beamed, barely able to contain himself.

"Oh, the deck is above us, but that's not where the captain pilots the ship!" Therren spun a wheel on the door and pushed. It swung inward, revealing the most incredible sight Goodwyn had ever seen, and that was no small feat considering the things he had seen lately.

The door led to a steel catwalk, with staircases leading up to other raised walkways that encircled the room and down to more walkways below, each dotted with stations manned by briene pulling levers, spinning wheels, and peering into tubes of all shapes and sizes. A wall of glass stretched across the front of the room, and on the other side gleamed the bright blue hue of ocean water. A school of fish darted back and forth, curiously inspecting their side of the glass.

"What...how is this...where are we?" Goodwyn was so stunned he didn't even know what questions to ask.

Aegaz, Corliss, the foreman, and the man the foreman called "the blade" all stood before a large table, peering into the ocean waters.

"We're underwater, Wyn! This ship doesn't sail on the water, it sails *under it*!" Therren was practically bouncing. "Can you believe it? All that water, and we're inside it and still dry!"

The men at the head of the chamber turned, Aegaz flashing him a reassuring smile. "The foreman says we may be able to catch up with the blood mage navy by dawn," he said.

"The blood witches underestimated the briene," said the foreman. "The briene learned things they did not intend to teach."

"How are we moving? Why don't we sink? How can we stay dry in here?" Goodwyn blurted, unable to contain his curiosity and shock.

The foreman beamed, "The briene can teach the fein duras about waterbird ships if the fein duras teaches the blade how to use that weapon." He pointed to the suzur coiled at Goodwyn's waist. Goodwyn hadn't even noticed it and didn't remember putting it on.

Maybe I haven't changed after all, he thought, frowning at the weapon. There were still marks on the chain and blade where the blood had been so thick, the stains refused to yield.

"Why don't you have names?" Goodwyn asked. The question had been nagging at him ever since their first encounter.

"The briene have names. The foreman's name is the foreman, the blade's name is the blade, and the fein duras is the fein duras."

"That's what you do, not who you are," Goodwyn said.

"They are the same, are they not?" replied the foreman.

That's a great question. Can there really a difference? he thought.

"What does fein duras mean?"

"Honor fighter," replied the blade, speaking for the first time.

Is there such a thing? Can a killer really have honor?

Goodwyn climbed down the steps to stand next to the others, feeling dwarfed by the massive glass wall. "Don't you need the sun and stars to know where you're going?"

"The navigator knows where the ship goes, where it has been, and where it is now," replied the foreman, pointing at a briene busily staring into a pair of tubes and turning knobs.

Corliss stepped around to the other side of the table, its surface covered with little wooden carvings of ships, boxes, and a few other things Goodwyn didn't recognize.

"The Order, as you call them," he said, nodding to Goodwyn, "as far as we know, has eighteen ships. Our scouts managed to get a good view of them before they pushed out of the harbor."

"And?" Aegaz asked.

"There are at least three white-robed men on each of the ships, and they are filled to the gunwales with soldiers."

"The entire Order must be out there on those ships," Aegaz said.

"If the last vertex is out there, that makes sense," Goodwyn said. "It's the only thing that matters to them now."

"Urus is out there somewhere too, and we can't let the blood mages reach that vertex before he does," said Aegaz.

"Foreman," said the navigator, finally looking up from his tubes.

Everyone turned to watch as the foreman stepped over and peered into the tubes, wincing as he saw something he didn't like. The fact that there was anything at all to see at the bottom of a tube should have surprised him, but Goodwyn had stopped being surprised by these people ever since he saw the first flying metal bird.

"The blood witches make wind with sorcery," said the navigator.

"How do you know?" Corliss asked.

"The sails are pushed near to tearing, yet the sea birds have no currents on which to fly."

"Can I see?" Goodwyn asked. The foreman nodded, and Goodwyn ran over, peering into the mysterious tubes.

It looked like a reflection in the shaving mirror, only instead of seeing his black stubble he saw a fleet of ships at full sail far off in the distance.

"How far out are they?" he asked without looking up.

"If the briene burn all of the fuel as fast as possible, and the blood witches keep up their pace, this fleet can catch them by daybreak, but—"

"But what?"

"But that is all there is," the foreman said. "When there is no more fuel, these ships will stop. No amount of wind can push these ships through water. If the briene have not overtaken them by then, it will mean failure."

Aegaz clasped a hand on Goodwyn's shoulder and squeezed. Goodwyn stood up and noticed that all eyes were on him.

"We will make them pay for what they did to Kest, and we will find Urus, alive," Aegaz said.

"And for what they did to Waldron," added Corliss.

"For the blood witch treachery and scheming that brought the briene and the Waldrene to war, there will be payment due," said the blade, who nodded to the foreman.

Goodwyn crossed his arms over his chest. "So how can we make these ships go faster?"

CHAPTER TWENTY-SEVEN

"How did they know we were here?" Urus asked. "We're at the bottom of the ocean."

"The Order has access to artifacts and relics older than most history texts. It wouldn't have taken them long to compare the Woan Map with old maps, leading them to Vultara," Murin answered.

"If we don't get to that vertex before they do, it won't matter."

"And if you do?" Murin asked. "If you do find the vertex, how will you keep the Order from destroying it as they did the others?"

"I'll think of something," Urus replied. "You need to stop being such a pessimist."

"He has always been like that," Timoc said, his thoughts intruding on Urus's mind. Timoc's translucent image stood at the top of the entrance stairs to the museum. "Ignore him, he is a cranky old man."

Murin's expression did indeed seem cranky. "Now is not the time for levity, Timoc. We must delay the order so Urus can find the vertex and think of something."

"Well, you know that you and I are useless in the presence of sigilord magic, so the boy has a point," Timoc replied. "Three of our Sanguine Crystal friends have arrived. They are weaving their way to this spot now."

They must think the vertex is here in the city center as well, Urus thought, knowing he didn't have to speak aloud. *What other building is a building of reverence, a place to put honored things?* He scanned the central square.

"I assume you already checked the museum?" Timoc asked.

Urus nodded. *Not a museum, but the mausoleum!* he thought, pointing to a smaller building between the museum and a wide building with a columned facade. "Not honored things, but honored dead, maybe?"

"Check it out," said Murin. "We will try and delay the Order."

"One man and a ghost? What will you do? You should take my simula… simulo…suits of armor," Urus said.

Timoc laughed. "Murin isn't just some weak—"

Murin cut him off. "You'll need them with you, and we don't know if you can control them at a distance. Just get into the crypts and look for the vertex. We are running out of time."

Urus nodded, willed his little company of knights to follow him, and ran for the crypts. Murin ran in the opposite direction while Timoc's apparition flowed behind him.

The crypt doors proved to be no match for the combined strength of the metal soldiers, who broke the left side completely off its hinges. Once inside, Urus was able to use the same sigil as before to illuminate the interior with a bluish glow. The warm pain from using the sigil magic was starting to feel good, and that worried him.

A thought occurred to him suddenly.

"Show me the vertex," he said to the knights.

They didn't move.

"Go to the fifth vertex," he said.

Again, they did nothing.

That would have been too easy, he thought, and started moving along the outer wall of the foyer, looking for any of the symbols he had seen on either of the other vertices.

"Guard the door, then," Urus said.

At once, the group took up positions to secure the entrance. Two of them even picked up the heavy stone door and slid it back into place as best they could. Two more climbed nearby stairs to take overwatch positions.

How can they possibly know how to do all this stuff without brains? Urus thought. *Maybe they're borrowing mine, because that's what I would've done if I were them*. It was getting too damn crowded in his brain, with Murin and Timoc talking to him and now these knights borrowing his tactical knowledge.

Satisfied that the knights would keep the place secure while he searched, Urus crept further into the tomb. It was a morbid place, with death everywhere he looked. Some walls had bunks cut into the stone where skeletons lay exposed, while others hosted row upon row of iron doors that must have held more important dead people.

He wondered who got to decide who rotted on a stone bunk and who got to rot in a nice iron tube. The more he came to know of other civilizations, the more bizarre he thought they all were. Kestians burned their dead and returned the ash to the desert, to hopefully one day smother future enemies.

I wonder if the Waldrenes or Vultarans would think we're the bizarre ones.

He continued further into the tomb, discovering that the small building was nothing more than a cap atop a vast network of catacombs below Vultara's center. After clearing the first level, he found a stairwell down into the second level.

As he descended the lower level bloomed with light, and Urus exhaled with relief. He remembered back in Kest, running through the dungeons in the pitch dark with nothing but the chain on Goodwyn's suzur to guide him. At least here he would have some light.

On this level the dead were afforded even more luxurious accommodations. They each had full-sized doors that led into small apartment-like chambers. Each of those had a foyer, marked by a plaque, and then the burial chamber itself, containing a stone sarcophagus in which lay the body of an ancient Vultaran.

The plaques didn't bear words, but sigils that Urus guessed were like names, and then below that maybe a description of that person's deeds in life. He couldn't tell, at least not until he got to the third tomb.

In this one, he recognized two sigils from his book. He pulled the book out and flipped through the pages until he got to a chapter that looked exactly like the plaques on the walls. The name-sigils were identical. Below that, in ancient Kestian, the book read: "Stebin Ombish, Fourth of the First, Master of the 9th Circle."

There was some more writing he couldn't translate, followed by "killed in the Fulcrum War holocaust."

If this was the same Fulcrum War that Murin had talked about, this man had died thousands of years before and might have been one of the last sigilords, if he was a sigilord at all. Urus hated not knowing anything about sigils or sigilords. He hated not knowing the answers to puzzles.

For good measure, he ran his hands over all the sigils on the plaque just to be sure none of them did anything special, then stepped back out into the hallway. He hurried through the remaining rooms on that level, keenly aware of the precious little time he had left.

He found another staircase going down, and instead of taking the stairs he hopped up over the railing and dropped to the level below, letting the time pressure rush him into making careless mistakes—careless mistakes that a true Kestian warrior would never have made.

Urus crept through the ever-shrinking corridors, wondering if only the corpses of long-dead sigilords populated the catacombs. Perhaps he had chosen wrong, and there was no vertex down there.

He shrugged off his doubts and kept going, determined to search every inch of the tombs. His determination did not last long. After just a few more minutes of searching, the corridor came to an abrupt end.

There was no door, no opening, or even as much as a crack in the dead end, just a confusing jumble of raised lines and swirls chiseled out of the stone. The relief carvings bore a similar style as the name-sigils on the rooms above, but none of it made any sense; none of the lines seemed to connect to each other.

Murin! Urus called out with his mind. No response came. He was going to have to figure this out for himself.

Urus inspected the lines on the wall more carefully. The more he looked, the less random it all seemed. Certain shapes and curves repeated themselves, and he saw the same line strokes and carvings in several places. On either wall to the side of the dead end, raised lines of shaped stone lifted out of the smooth rock wall, stopping short at the corner.

I wonder if it's just a crazy sigil, Urus thought, and pressed his hand against one of the lines, calling forth his power. Instead of glowing like a sigil, a square section of the wall slid to the right, changing places with the adjoining square section.

Urus stepped back and exclaimed aloud, "A puzzle!"

Finally a puzzle I can solve, Urus thought. He took a few more steps back and looked at the wall from the new perspective of a riddle that needed solving. He scanned the lines on the side walls, noting how they stopped abruptly in the corners. *I'll bet if I make the lines connect, the door will open.*

He approached the puzzle wall again, and blue smoke poured from his hands as he shifted and rearranged parts of the wall. The pieces had no seams and there were no cracks or any other evidence that the stone could be moved.

"Masters of space and time" is what Murin called the sigilords. Urus was finally beginning to appreciate the depth of power those people once had, and why the blood mages wanted it for themselves.

Urus lost himself, and all sense of time, in the puzzle. He had gotten nearly all of the lines to match, but he realized a crucial mistake too late and had to undo most of his moves and start over. Finally after spending far too much time on the puzzle, the four lines that grew out of the side walls crisscrossed in an intricate weave across the dead end wall, resulting in an amazing sigil.

A moment later the sigil flashed blue and the wall simply vanished. It had been a locked door after all and the sigil had unlocked it. Urus felt as proud of himself as he had the one time he had managed to navigate the network of gas lamp pipes to find the source, except this time he hadn't gotten stuck between walls with only Goodwyn, some rope, and a jar of wax to pull him out.

Fingers still surging with the heat of his power, he pulled Hugo from its sheath, thankful for its protection. He thought back to the real Hugo, the doll who had been his lone childhood companion for so long. He remembered Hugo's name sign, the four crossed swords on the straw doll's chest. He pressed his fingers to the blade and that same name sign flashed blue then cooled, leaving the etched image of crossed swords in the center of an outline of a doll scored into the metal.

Urus had no idea what he had just done to his sword, but there was no time to find out. He had to find the last vertex.

As he stepped across the new threshold the darkness receded, replaced by a soft green glow. The dome-ceilinged, circular chamber held a single coffin in the center. Aside from the sarcophagus, the room held no other furnishings or decorations. not even a single sigil was carved into the walls.

Urus was about to approach the casket when he noticed blood beginning to drip from the ceiling. At first it was just a few drops, then a steady stream, finally it looked like a river of blood poured through some unseen opening in the dome. The pool of blood rose from the floor, assuming the shape of a tall, thin man. A moment later, clothes and human features appeared and the blood splashed back to the floor.

The tall, white-robed man stood in the center of the blood pool, a wicked smile on his scarred, pockmarked face.

This must be Draegon, the man Murin said Anderis wanted to succeed as ruler of the Order, Urus thought.

"I am indeed Draegon, leader of the Order of the Sanguine Crystal, Blood Mage of the 13th circle," Draegon said aloud, his smile spreading over impossibly white teeth.

He can read my thoughts, Urus thought. He had no idea where Murin or Timoc were, and his protective knights were too far away to do any good. He was all alone and he had to come up with a plan soon. *If he can see inside my mind then I'll have to make sure he likes what he sees.*

"I believe I have you to thank for removing the ward that protected this chamber," Draegon said with a wry grin. "Without your help, I could never have penetrated that wall."

Fear and panic surged through Urus. Had he really just helped Draegon find the fifth vertex?

"Come closer, boy, I would see the annoying little creature that has been nipping at my heels all this time."

Urus took a few steps closer, tightening his grip around Hugo's hilt.

"I'll take that," said Draegon. Hugo escaped Urus's grasp and flew into Draegon's hand. "Such an impressive and heavy weapon. This must have been forged for a giant!"

Alone and unarmed, Urus channeled all of his hatred for the man and all he had done, hoping his opponent would sense it.

"You think me evil, do you?" Draegon said, taking the bait.

"You destroyed my homeland, killed all of my people and countless others in other cities and Ishimani knows how many others died in what's left of

Waldron by now," Urus said through clenched teeth.

"How many people have the Kestians killed in battle? How many died in the Fulcrum War on both sides? When will you foolish people understand that there is no good or evil. There is only what we need and that which opposes our needs. I oppose your needs, so you think me evil. You oppose mine, therefore you are evil."

"I'm not evil. I'm nothing like you." Urus stalled for time until he could find an opportunity, hoping the rage and hatred on his mind would keep Draegon from seeing what else he was thinking.

Draegon raised an eyebrow, then smiled. The leader of the blood mages covered his mouth with his hand and spoke. Urus couldn't read his lips and Murin's translation power failed him.

"You have been reading my lips, haven't you? You're deaf, and quite talented at hiding that fact. A deaf sigilord!" Draegon said with a laugh. "A more rare creature does not exist in the universe. Next you'll tell me that you rode here on a dragon or that your sigils are blue!"

To avoid reacting to Draegon's mention of blue sigils, Urus recalled as many powerful, overwhelming, and terrible memories as he could, hoping to flood Draegon's mind with distractions. He focused on his deafness and dredged up traumatic memories, some he'd thought long forgotten. He remembered his sire pounding his ears until they bled, his peers teasing and taunting him because of his speech problem and deafness, and his lack of the true Kestian killer instinct.

Unable to hold back the flood of emotion, Urus dropped to his knees and wept. He wondered if Draegon was in his mind, somehow, rooting around for bitter memories.

"How could one with so much power have led such a terribly painful life?" Draegon asked. "Life is not about right or wrong, good or evil. It is about those who have power and those who don't. Had you known how to use your sigil power, you could have shown those children that it was they who were weak and helpless. I have many powers, including the power to cure your deafness."

Urus looked up at Draegon, a man who could likely kill him with a single thought. Urus had never thought about what it would be like to be able to hear, only what his deafness had cost him over the years.

"You can?" he asked. Urus had to struggle to keep hold of that tiny thought in the back of his mind that reminded him of what he was doing without letting Draegon see it. The idea that someone could cure his deafness tugged at his heart.

"That and much more. I can give you control of your power. I can teach you, you would have the so-called Kestian killer insti—wait! What have we here?" Draegon gasped, stepping closer to Urus.

"Where?"

"Deep in your mind, buried way in the back where no one could ever see it," said Draegon. Urus panicked. Had he caught on? Did Draegon know what Urus was planning?

"What? What is it?" Urus asked.

"A memory so terrible that your mind sealed it away, where not even you would find it, yet it is at the core of who you are and who you have become. Oh, I must see this memory," Draegon said, coming even closer. He stood over Urus and placed his hands on Urus's head.

This is it, this is my chance. All it will take is one strike, Urus thought.

"Come, see what I see, Urus. See why you should join me, let me cure your deafness and unleash your true power," Draegon said. A jolt of heat rippled from his neck to his toes. Urus blinked and the world in the stone chamber was gone, replaced by his childhood home. He stood in the corner of the main room, watching in horror as the memory unfolded around a tiny, younger version of himself.

***

Young Urus sat on the floor, his legs crossed as he rocked himself back and forth, the motion a poor substitute for his absent mother's embrace. In the weeks before her death, she had only rocked him like that a few times, but he remembered each one: the warmth of her shoulders, the firm but comforting pressure of her hand on his back, the soothing vibration that came from her throat as she sang him to sleep. He wanted that warmth, that comfort, but he knew he would never again feel that safe or that loved.

Tears spilled onto Hugo's chest as he held the doll. His sire had thrown the doll away a dozen times, but each time Urus managed to find it, and each time he had gladly endured the beating he got for fishing the toy out of whatever sewer or hole into which the angry old man had tossed it.

Urus watched as the tears absorbed into the crossed swords drawn into the ratty cloth material. He wished that Hugo was a real warrior who would come and save him from his father. Without his mother around to temper the man's foul moods, Urus felt like a training dummy, enduring punches and kicks day in and day out, his wounds healing only so that they could be reopened again.

A throbbing pain erupted in Urus's left ear. He rolled to his side, covering his head with his hands. Blood gushed from his ear while his father kicked him in the stomach and stomped on his knees and feet. His father rolled him over and held him down so he could punch the other ear. Urus's vision blurred, and the pain in his head was so intense he was sure he was going to black out.

He didn't even know why his father was angry this time. It didn't matter —the man always found some excuse to be angry and to take that anger out on Urus. Through a mix of blood and tears, Urus looked at Hugo sprawled out on the floor: the warrior hero that was, at least in Urus's dreams, everything that a Kestian warrior should be.

The blows hit him in so many different places Urus could no longer tell what his father was hitting him with, or where. Everything hurt, or bled, or both.

"Save me, Hugo," Urus whispered to the doll with the last of his energy, reaching out and touching the crossed swords on the doll's chest with a bloody finger.

A rush of heat and pain flowed down his finger, through his wrist and up to his shoulder. A thin, blue tendril of smoke drifted from his fingertip into the symbol on Hugo's chest. The symbol flashed blue and then faded.

Massive hands as thick as stone hammers clamped onto Urus's neck and lifted him up. Urus looked down into his father's face as he choked, flailing and struggling for just a single gulp of air. The man's face contorted in a rictus of anger and hatred. Urus gasped, certain he was about to die.

As Urus looked down on the face of his killer, a father who had rejected him since birth, a blue shadow formed behind his attacker, coalescing from puffs of smoke drifting up from the floor—drifting up from Hugo the doll. Ghostly blue hands gripped his father's neck and squeezed.

His father's hands spasmed, and Urus dropped to the floor. He looked up and wiped blood and tears from his eyes, unsure of whether he was hallucinating, dreaming, or already dead.

The translucent blue form squeezed at his father's neck, pushing the man to his knees. His father choked and struggled, spittle and drool dripping from his mouth. Urus watched, horrified but also not intervening. Even if he could have, he wasn't sure if he wanted to save his father from the blue creature.

Only a few short moments later, his father dropped to the floor, lifeless and twisted. Urus stood up and looked at his blue savior. There, in its chest among wisps of blue smoke, hovered four crossed swords made of pure, brilliant blue light.

***

"You killed your own father." Draegon released his grip on Urus's head.

"No!" Urus shouted, tears rushing down his cheeks. "No, that's not possible! I couldn't kill him or anyone else!"

"You sat back and watched while your creation, your *power*, killed your father. Do you still think good and evil are the only distinctions? Friend or foe? Right or wrong? You think yourself a good person, yet you killed your own father. How does one rationalize such a thing?" Draegon said.

Urus struggled to come to grips with the memory of Hugo—or some sigil-powered version of Hugo—killing his father. It didn't matter that his father was about to kill him, all that mattered was that he had killed his own father. His power had killed his father, and he didn't how many people he might kill in the future.

"Let me cure your deafness, let me show you how to control your power, let me show you how the arbiters and the sigilords treated the blood mages the way your father treated you. With control of your power, you can be sure you won't hurt the innocent. Join us, Urus, and you will never again know loneliness or despair or weakness."

"Prove it," Urus said.

"Prove what?"

"Prove that you can cure my deafness, that you can teach me to control the power."

"And in return for these gifts?" Draegon asked.

A childhood of hurt and pain, anger and rage flashed before his eyes and, hopefully, before Draegon's as well. Urus tugged at every emotion he had, relived every memory in which he had failed, where he had been shunned by the Kestians, where his deafness had brought him nothing but suffering and despair.

"In return, I will join you," Urus said, hoping that Draegon's thirst for power would blind him long enough to hide the lie while he waited for Draegon to reveal a weakness.

Draegon smiled and stepped closer to Urus. "The power of a sigilord, in my hands at last. I haven't wielded the blood of a sigilord in three thousand years. I can almost taste it!"

He cupped his hands over Urus's ears and muttered words in a language Urus couldn't lipread.

At first the incantation seemed not to have worked. Then...*something*... came rushing in. He didn't know what it was, but his mind felt assaulted. Stimuli that he didn't recognize invaded his mind from every direction.

The world was awash in it, things he had never experienced and had for which he had no reference. It was like the vibrating floorboards during a bard's performance, only now everything vibrated—the walls, the floors, his hands, even Draegon. The world was filled with painful, overwhelming vibrations.

The pain in his head grew to be too much to bear. A wave of dizziness hit him first, then nausea. He bent over, vomited, and then the world went black.

CHAPTER TWENTY-EIGHT

Cailix paced, fists clenched, muttering about indecisive old people.

"You'll wait while we decide just what to do with you, girl," the constable snarled through a puffy beard that threatened to swallow his rose-colored face. He had the shape of one of the fat, abusive land-owners in Naredis but carried himself like a just, righteous man. She just hoped he would figure that out for himself before it was too late. "You're lucky we haven't thrown you in a stockade."

"Calm down, Ben, we're not accusing the girl of anything." Orla, the kind matron of the family on which she had intruded, spoke softly. "Speaking of which, we don't even know the girl's name."

"My name is Cailix," she said, feeling at once stupid and vulnerable for having given her real name.

"And what a pretty name that is. Is that a Fedigan name, or Bruhan perhaps?" Orla asked, placing herself between Cailix and the makeshift council that included Ben, the constable; Hutcher, the fisherman; and a handful of pike- and axe-wielding farmers and merchants.

Cailix stopped pacing, stunned. "I-I don't know," she said. She didn't know whether Cailix was her given name or just the name given to her by the first of many fosters who had taken her on as a burden.

"Orla, it's obvious you've got a soft spot for the girl, but you need to let the men take care of business here," Ben said.

"And what business is that, this business that can only be done by men?" Orla demanded, hands on her hips, a wooden soup spoon still inexplicably in her hand.

"She exploded a lamb to light the signal fires, woman. This is serious."

"Oh, it's quite serious. You think if she could explode a lamb she couldn't explode you, Ben? This girl's in trouble and she's trying to save this island, so you need to quit your old man fussing, grow yourself a pair of walnuts, and do something."

Cailix was really starting to like this woman. She was as full of fire and spirit and energy as she was of motherly kindness. She had never encountered anyone like that before.

"You can't talk to me like that, Orla, I'm the only law this island's got."

"Ben, quit flirting with Orla and let's take a vote on the matter," said one of the farmers in the little council huddled around a large bonfire they'd built just down the hill from Orla and Woss's tent. A young man—his son, presumably—stood just behind the farmer, unable to take his eyes off Cailix, big brown eyes that reflected the firelight and seemed to match his blond hair perfectly.

"If she's lying, then she's a witch and she just sacrificed a sheep," one of the men said, stuffing some tobacco into his pipe.

"It was a lamb, you idiot," Orla shouted.

"If she's telling the truth, she's still a witch, but she's the least of our problems," another said.

"If she's telling the truth, we need to figure out how to protect the people of Aldsdowne," Hutcher said, looking across the fire at Cailix.

Cailix shrugged into Orla's embrace as the woman wrapped her in another blanket. She grabbed another biscuit when she thought no one was looking and shoved it into her mouth.

The moon was nearly full overhead, the night half gone. Anderis's navy would be within range of the island tomorrow.

Woss glanced from Cailix up to the moon and back. "You boys better figure out what you're going to do quick. The night's not gettin' any longer."

"We can't fend off a navy, lest we drive 'em off by throwin' spice barrels and dead gloomfish at 'em."

"We could hide."

"Where would we go, Abe? Look around. We're on an island," Hutcher said. "We don't have enough empty ships to carry all our people off to the north and away from the navy."

"So it seems like you all agree she's telling the truth about this navy coming our way," said Ben.

"Maybe Cailix knows how to stop them," said the farmer's son, forcing an awkward smile in her direction.

Cailix couldn't figure out what his angle was, why he was smiling.

"Colin, stay outta this. This is grown men's business," scolded the farmer.

"I don't think we can take the chance she ain't tellin' the truth," Hutcher replied.

"We need to start preparing now!" Cailix shouted.

"Hush now, girl, let us handle this," said one of the farmers.

"My name is Cailix, and I would let you handle it if I thought any of you oafs were capable!"

One of the farmers picked up his garden hoe and stepped around the fire, muttering, stomping, and making a big show of being a big strong man.

Oafs indeed, she thought. *They don't have a whole brain between the lot of them.*

"Someone's gonna have to teach you the proper way to behave 'round your betters, little miss!" grumbled the oaf.

"When I see any of my betters, then I will gladly await such a lesson." Cailix reached out, still able to draw some power from the lamb's blood, and lifted the oaf into the air, dangling him there like a helpless fly caught in a spider's web.

"Cailix, you put that man down right now!" Orla demanded.

Never before had she cared about any orders any adult had barked at her. She complied when it suited her needs, complied when it was necessary for her survival. But to comply because she cared about the other person's opinion? *Never.*

Cailix let the oaf-man drop.

"Orla, you keep that witch on a leash till we figure out what our next move is, understand?" said the farmer, Colin's father.

"Yes, Rowden," Orla said in a sweet, demure tone.

She pulled Cailix aside, sat her down, and whispered in her ear, "You and I both know these dunderheads need a good kick in the arse to get them going in the right direction. Problem is, they're too stubborn to admit it. You need to ply them, treat 'em like stubborn mules. Get them to think it's their bright idea, and they'll take all the credit but do 'zactly as you want 'em to."

Cailix's eyes widened. This Orla was an amazing woman. She could survive, and she was in control, but she didn't have to fight for her control; she got it with her brains and cunning. The best part was that she was in control even when everybody else thought they were in charge.

Maybe a good strategy is as good a power as the blood magic, she thought.

"Watch and learn, sweetie," Orla said.

She stood up, approached the fire, and stoked it. She leaned in to stoke the fire again and slipped, tripping over something. Rowden reached out and caught her just in time.

"Lord above, woman, you need to be more careful."

"I'm sorry, I'm just frazzled, all this talk of witches and invasions and navies. It's more than an old woman like myself can take."

"Don't you worry, nothing's going to happen to Aldsdowne."

"It's just, well, you've seen what the girl can do."

"Yes, I have," Rowden said, the pitch in his voice rising a little.

"Well, she's barely an apprentice. The people who took and slaved her, well they're the really dangerous ones. If you think explodin' lambs is terrible, just you wait till they get here."

She's amazing, thought Cailix. *This idiot is falling for it, buying into Orla's poor defenseless scared woman act.*

"How many of them did she say there was?"

"The girl says they got eighteen ships, with three witches on each ship," Orla said, just loud enough so the others would overhear.

That was all it took. Cailix could have shouted the same words at the top of her lungs and the men wouldn't have cared, but coming from Orla the way it did, they all stopped talking.

"How many witches and ships?" Hutcher asked.

"Eighteen ships, with three blood mages on each, four on the lead ship," Cailix said, trying to keep her tone as soft as Orla's had been.

"What if we just surrendered?" Rowden asked. "We could let them have what they want from the island and then they would leave. Other kingdoms have come and gone when they found out we have little to offer them."

Cailix stood up, her fists clenched. She looked at Orla and Woss and took a slow, deep breath before she spoke. "They don't want the island, they want you. They use blood for power, and they need the power to finish what they're doing, to destroy something big. They'll bleed the island dry like you were nothing but cattle."

"She's joking, right?" asked one of the farmers.

"What I did to that lamb, that's what they'll do to every man, woman, and child on this island."

"How can we fight a power like that?" another farmer asked. "Garden tools and bread are clearly not going to do any good, and none of us are soldiers."

"We could dig in, fortify ourselves?"

"You mean hide," Hutcher said. "If they can turn you into a bloody fog, they can find you hiding under a barn."

Cailix waited, tapping her foot, but biting her tongue and waiting for someone, anyone, to ask the right question.

"Girl," said Hutcher.

"Cailix," she offered, calmly, even with a hint of a smile.

"Cailix. You escaped from these people, and you made it all the way to this island to warn us they were coming. What would you have us do? How would you fight them?"

Cailix stifled a grin. *It's about time they came around. It would've been easier just to beat them into submission, but Orla's way may have its merits.*

"That depends," she said.

"On what?"

"On how many farm animals you can get to the southwest shore before dawn."

CHAPTER TWENTY-NINE

Goodwyn lay on his hands and knees, dry heaving, wondering when the ship would stop moving. He'd lost track of whether they were moving up and down or side-to-side, it was all the same to him. The stomach of a Kestian warrior had no business in the belly of a steel ship in the middle of an ocean.

He tried—carefully—to get to one knee, then climbed up the wall, hugging a lit sconce as though without that grip he would fly off in any direction.

A knock at the door startled him. He let go of the sconce, lost his balance, and fell back to his knees.

"Come in," he coughed, feeling as though the mere effort of talking might make him vomit.

Therren strode through the door carrying a large flagon, his usual grin brightening his face.

"You look terrible," he said.

"Thanks," Goodwyn replied, clinging to the floor as though his life depended on it.

"Try some of this." Therren sat down on the floor nearby. "It's a tea the briene make. They're giving it to all of us 'sand people'. That's what they call us, you know. Sometimes they call us giants. Can you imagine that? Us, giants?"

Goodwyn crawled closer, grabbed the flagon, and took a few gulps. The concoction tasted terrible, like boiled dirt. He didn't care. It could taste like boiled underclothes and he would drink it if it made his stomach feel better.

"Why are we bouncing around like this?"

"It's almost dawn and the fleet has come up to the surface. The waters are rougher on the surface than they are down below."

Goodwyn choked down another few slurps of the disgusting brew. "Can we go up top? I need some fresh air."

Therren clapped him on the shoulder, which made Goodwyn's stomach churn. "That's why I came to get you. We're gathering up there. Corliss, Aegaz, and the briene are working out an attack plan."

"What do we know about naval attacks? Kestians don't even build ships," Goodwyn commented, climbing up Therren to get to his feet this time.

"I don't know, but they want all of us up there."

Therren helped Goodwyn to the door and turned to face him as they stepped into the hallway. He bent close for a kiss, but Goodwyn held him away.

"We can't do that here; there're too many people around," he said. The defeated look on Therren's face hurt him, a lot more than he thought it should.

He grasped Therren's hand, tightly. "I don't know who or what I am anymore, Therren. Everything I grew up believing just seems so wrong now. I don't feel all that stable, and that's not just because I'm seasick. You're the only thing I'm sure of right now. You have to believe that."

Therren nodded and squeezed Goodwyn's hand in return. "I suppose I should go on ahead. Are you okay following?"

"Yeah, I'll be right behind you."

Goodwyn watched as Therren left, listening to his boots clatter against the metal walkway. The whole world was in chaos and they were about to fight a naval battle—Kestians, fighting in a navy!—and he just wanted to be with Therren and leave it all behind.

"Is Therren the mate of the fein duras?" asked a familiar voice from behind him.

Goodwyn spun to see the blade, by all respects a tiny little man, but easily the most formidable fighter he had ever encountered.

"My mate?" Goodwyn asked, unsure what to say.

"Yes, mate. Partner for life. Has the fein duras chosen a mother for the children yet?"

Goodwyn took a step back. *Mate? Children? What in the hell is he talking about?*

"When the briene choose partners that do not produce children, it is an honor for others to volunteer to bear children on their behalf," said the blade. "Do the sand people have similar customs?"

"No, no we don't. I'm afraid the sand people wouldn't understand how Therren and I feel about each other."

The blade smiled and clapped Goodwyn affectionately on the shoulder, an action that actually required a hop on the little briene's part. "Come, the blade will discuss this on the way up to the deck. The blade is sure that any briene woman would be honored to bear the children of the fein duras and heart-mate Therren."

Goodwyn gaped at the little man and swallowed down a wave of panic.

They made their way topside, with the blade going into excruciating detail about marriage ceremonies, how briene couples chose surrogate parents, and the fact a briene woman carried a child for eleven full months before giving birth. A briene child was such a rare blessing that when a briene mother became pregnant, her entire village would pamper and protect her and provide for all her needs, including the birthing itself.

Goodwyn listened intently, trying not to throw up or stumble. Thankfully, the entire trip passed without such an embarrassing event.

Maybe that nasty tea does work. I hope they've got enough for the return trip, he thought. *If we survive, that is.*

They climbed a set of stairs and stopped before a circular steel door.

"Before we go up," Goodwyn said, giving the blade an intense look, "you can't tell anyone about Therren and me. The Kestians, the sand people, they wouldn't understand. It could be…bad for me. For us."

"The sand people are a strange people, but the blade will keep the fein duras secret. But when the fein duras and heart-mate decide to have children, the fein duras must let the blade know. The blade will find a most suitable mother."

"You need a better name, something other than 'blade,'" Goodwyn said, ignoring the comment about bearing children. "A blade is a tool you use to kill, or a tool you use to survive, but it isn't who you are."

"The blade is the blade, there is no other name," said the blade as he used two big wheels to push the door in and roll it to the side, revealing a narrow cylindrical chamber with a ladder leading up.

They climbed the ladder, stepped up through another hatch, and Goodwyn found himself standing on the vast, flat metal deck of the briene ship. Dozens of briene stood up on the deck, where Aegaz, Corliss, Therren, and the foreman waited near the front edge.

The rest of the fleet appeared as dark shadows bobbing up and down on the rough, dark seas, all bathed in the bright pre-dawn moonlight.

"If this wasn't about to be a battlefield, it would be beautiful," Goodwyn remarked, marveling at the moonlight reflecting off the ocean's surface.

"It's the battle that makes it beautiful, soldier," laughed one of the nearby Kestian soldiers. It seemed like just yesterday that Goodwyn was one of them, and felt that these were his people. Now, it was as though he looked at some foreigner from a distant land, someone with whom he had nothing in common save skin color and ancestry.

"That's them." Corliss pointed to a cluster of shadows in the distance to the northeast.

"What's that beyond them?" Goodwyn asked. "The dark outline on the horizon."

"That's Aldsdowne, a waypoint for trading and traveling ships. Most of the trade ships making their way to Waldron stop at Aldsdowne first."

"Is that where the fifth vertex is?"

"Could be," Aegaz answered. "They've brought their entire fleet to that island for a reason."

"Is there anyone defending the island?"

"No; technically Aldsdowne isn't even part of a kingdom. It has no protectors," said Corliss. "We need to take out that fleet's biggest advantage —the mages."

"Can we get close enough to attack without them knowing?" Goodwyn asked the foreman.

The foreman smiled up at Goodwyn. "Not with these slow ships, but maybe with those." He nodded past Goodwyn's shoulder.

Behind them the briene moved out to the edge of the platform while huge square sections of metal sank into the ship below. Loud grinding and clanking noises followed; then the square metal blocks returned to the deck, each carrying a briene flying machine.

Goodwyn and Therren rushed to inspect them.

"These are amazing, like machines out of some fantastical tale from a book," Therren said.

"Urus flew one. Actually, he flew one, crashed it, then jumped onto another one while they were still flying," Goodwyn said, enjoying the memory.

"Urus? Urus-the-*culled* did all that?" Therren said with an equally big grin.

Goodwyn shrugged. "He's full of surprises lately."

"These are equipped with spear launchers," the foreman explained, inspecting each of the machines, taking a moment to caress the metal as he walked by each of them. "The blood witches need time to make the blood magic. If the attack is quick enough, the blood witches will die like any other man."

The foreman gave everyone a quick demonstration of how to operate the flying machines, then stepped to the front of the platform. "There is enough fuel in these to get to the island and back, but no more. Get within range, skewer the blood witches with the spears, then return. Any blood witches left alive will surely use blood power to try to shoot the briene and sand people out of the sky."

Each of the other platforms seemed to be getting the same speech from each of their commanders. Members of the First Fist, Goodwyn and Therren included, jumped into flying machines on every platform, as did the briene and Corliss's men.

"May the blood of our enemies run beneath your boots!" Aegaz shouted to the First Fist. They replied with enthusiastic shouts of "For Kest!"

"For Kest!" Goodwyn shouted, though it felt a little half-hearted. This was for far more than Kest. If Murin was right, the whole world was at stake if the Order should succeed. He just hoped that Urus and Murin were alive and keeping the fifth vertex safe.

The foreman gave the signal, and the fleet of metal birds took off. At first

269

Goodwyn almost crashed into the water, but managed to pull the bird's beak up just in time. Then he somehow got going the wrong direction and had to swing back around to catch up to the others.

He settled into formation just behind Aegaz and Therren, each piloting their own birds.

Warriors born and bred in the desert who see one rainstorm a year, and we're flying over an ocean in metal birds. Nobody back home will believe this, Goodwyn thought, then remembered that likely there was no home left, no one there to appreciate what was happening.

As they flew toward their target, the first orange and yellow tinges of the sun broke over top of Aldsdowne, their trip strangely quiet save for the buzzing noise of the birds.

"The noise is too loud!" he shouted ahead to the others. "They're going to hear us coming!"

Therren heard him and relayed the message, which got passed to others in their group.

Aegaz turned back and signaled him, jabbing his finger at the target twice. It was too late to back out now; they had to attack even if the enemy could hear their approach.

A bright yellow flash of light erupted from the island. At first Goodwyn thought it was the sun peeking between mountains, but the light came from the near shore, not from the horizon beyond. A moment later another flash lit up the shore. Then another, and another.

The flashes turned into balls of fire, soaring up from the shore into the air above the Order's ships.

The Order responded with a similar volley, huge balls of flame launching from the decks of their ships and arcing high into the sky over the ocean between the island and the navy.

"Now! Hit them now while they're busy!" Goodwyn shouted, and pressed down hard on the foot pedal that controlled the bird's speed. He pointed the nose of the bird down a little and aimed for the nearest ship, which still seemed small and distant from that height.

Who in the hell is throwing fireballs at the mages? Goodwyn wondered. *Could it be Urus, or maybe Cailix?*

The sky over the shore lit up with hundreds of little suns. As the fireballs launched from the shore collided with the ones launched from the ships, bursts of light preceded deafening thunderclaps. It was like a dozen winter's-long-night celebration fireworks displays, all happening at once.

Falling now more than flying, Goodwyn pushed his bird as fast as it could go toward the nearest ship, which was the furthest from the shore. A fireball slammed into the ship to the left of his target, shattering the deck into a thousand flaming splinters. Burning bodies flew in all directions, including a few white-robed mages. Pieces of wood bounced off the metal hull of the bird, and Goodwyn had to duck to avoid losing his head.

He could see the blood mages on the ship in front of him now. They stood on the foredeck, chanting something while holding hands. The foredeck was slick with blood, and the bodies of sacrificed sailors lay strewn about, broken limbs sticking out at terrible angles.

He aimed the bird's nose down just a bit more, then pulled back on the lever to release the spears. They shot from springs in the bird's talons. Two shot straight through the blood mages' backs, pinning them to the ship. The other sank into the back of a mage's thigh.

Goodwyn veered off to the left and pulled up. He looked back to see how the others were doing. Metal birds buzzed around ships, diving and launching spears onto the decks. Some spears hit, others missed. There were definitely going to be enough mages left to retaliate.

He angled his bird back toward the briene fleet, a cluster of flat black lines floating on the water in the distance.

Therren pulled his bird up into formation alongside Goodwyn's craft.

"How many?" Therren shouted. Goodwyn replied by holding up three fingers.

Therren held up a single finger, a disappointed look on his face.

A ball of flame shot past them from below, followed by several more. The mages were retaliating, and the briene birds were out of spears.

Goodwyn swerved to the right just as a fireball rushed toward him. He easily avoided two more, then put the bird back on course toward the briene fleet.

Those fireballs are too slow to hit anything, he thought, but the comfort was short-lived. He looked back to check on Therren and saw his friend's bird spiraling toward the ocean, its wings ablaze.

"Therren!" Goodwyn shouted, banking the bird down and back toward the spot where he knew his friend was going to splash down. Therren jumped out of the bird and landed in the water on his back while the bird broke apart into pieces against the the rough surf.

Goodwyn swung around and flew over Therren, who wasn't moving.

"Therren!" he screamed, then pulled up to come around for another pass.

The battle raged all around him, volleys of fireballs launched by the magical archers on the ships toward the island shore and the briene birds. The Order was fighting a battle on two fronts, and the initial bird attack had decimated their numbers. Whoever had engaged the Order from the island had saved the battle.

As he came around for another pass, Therren splashed and sputtered.

He slowed the bird down as much as he could and lowered the talons until they skimmed the ocean.

"Grab the claws!" Goodwyn shouted.

He soared up to and right past Therren. Therren reached out but his timing was off, and he missed the chance. Even flying as slowly as the bird could go, it was still much faster than a sprinting horse.

Goodwyn came around again for another try, this time so slowly the bird barely managed to stay aloft. He knew exactly when Therren would need to raise his hands to be able to grab the talons.

"Wait for it!" he shouted. A moment later, "Now!"

Therren reached up, grabbed the claws, and hung on. Goodwyn pulled the bird up and again aimed it toward the briene fleet, trying to get out of range of the mage fireballs. He reached down and hauled his friend up into the cockpit.

"I was about to drown," Therren said, still coughing up sea water.

"I would never let that happen," Goodwyn said.

"Are we the last ones out?" Therren asked.

Goodwyn turned in his seat, looking back. What he saw terrified him more than the sight of his friend nearly drowning or the dozens of near collisions with fireballs. A wall of water taller than the highest ship mast rolled toward the Order ships. His jaw dropped.

"What?" Therren said, turning to look. "Pull up! Pull us up, now!"

Goodwyn yanked up on the control stick, but the bird wouldn't lift.

Black smoke puffed out from under the wings and the little metal needle for fuel pointed to the carving of an empty jar.

"It's almost out of fuel, and it won't go any higher," Goodwyn said.

They looked back in horror as the wall of water swallowed five of the Order's ships, breaking them apart like children's toys. The wave surged toward them.

"Make it go higher!" Therren yelled, also grabbing the control stick. Instead, the bird's nose started to dip toward the water.

"Hold on tight!" Goodwyn pushed Therren down into the empty space near the pedals in the cockpit. He grabbed the rails on the cockpit edges and closed his eyes as the wave hammered into their helpless craft.

Chapter Thirty

Urus steadied himself on all fours, looking down at the stone floor. Noise was everywhere and everything made it—the stone, the door, and of course Draegon.

How do people deal with this? I can't think with all this noise! Urus thought.

He looked up to see Draegon inspecting Hugo, running his finger down the long, flat side of the blade, opposite the side with Hugo's name-sign etched into it.

"So how does it feel to be able to hear?" Draegon asked. His voice cracked and sounded like there was something stuck in his throat. *Does everyone sound like this?*

"It hurts. Everything is so...loud," said Urus.

"You will get used to the noise, just as you will get used to the other change I have made to you," Draegon said, cracking a wide, wicked grin.

"What other change?"

"You didn't actually think I believed your nonsense about joining me, did you?" Draegon snapped, his expression changing, his face filling with rage. "Playing me with the sob story of your sad, pathetic childhood so I might believe you would join me freely...for what? So I let my guard down long enough for you to plunge your sword into my gut? Boy, I have not remained alive thousands of years to be fooled by some pathetic little untrained

274

sigilord."

"What did you do to me?" Urus struggled to his feet. The room still seemed to wobble and the way the walls repeated everything he said disturbed him.

"I would never risk that you would hand over a power like yours voluntarily. I bound your blood to mine when you let me cure your disability. You submitted to me, which is all I needed to take your power. You are mine now, sigilord. I *own* you."

"Never!" Urus shouted and leapt forward, hoping to strike before the blood mage could summon his power.

Draegon held out a hand and Urus stopped in mid-air, frozen in place hovering inches above the ground.

"As I said, I own you. Your blood is mine to do with as I please. You will be an endless source of power to me. I could slaughter an entire city and consume all of its blood and still not even come close to the power you have granted me."

"I won't let you do this," Urus mumbled, struggling to open his mouth.

"Really?" said the mage, still smiling wide. He knew he had won and was relishing the victory. He wiggled a finger and, in response, Urus's right arm snapped completely backward, white bone jutting out from his elbow. "Leeching the power from stupid sigilords like you is what I live for. It really is a shame that you're the only one left."

The pain was unbearable. Urus's eyes rolled back into his head and, just as he felt the bliss of unconsciousness take him, his eyes flared wide again, forced to feel every bit of pain.

"I can also control whether you pass out or not," said Draegon. "Don't think for a second that I can't inflict unspeakable pain upon you, for as long as I see fit. Now, let's see about destroying this last vertex, shall we?"

An image flashed into Urus's mind, a single sigil—a spiral with four lines coming out of the center. *Where did that come from?* Urus wondered. He had never seen the symbol before.

Draegon beckoned Urus's helpless body and in response Urus floated toward the center of the room. Blood dripped from his arm and the pain was more than he could bear, yet Draegon kept him conscious. Shock and pain wracked his entire body.

Urus hovered over the coffin, a simple stone box with a forged steel shield adorning the top. It was a kite shield with a riveted reinforced border and etched patterns all along the outside. In the middle of the shield was a single symbol—four opposing triangles that overlapped in the middle, all surrounded by a circle with an inner circle around the triangle points.

It was the Kestian brand for one of the culled.

"That's impossible," he said out loud. *How can this symbol be here? These people died thousands of years before Kest, why is that symbol the same?* Urus thought, his mind racing. Somehow the symbol had survived throughout history, inexplicably coming to be used by the Kestians as a symbol burned into the chests of failed warriors.

"What's impossible?" Draegon asked, glancing back and forth between Urus and the sigil on the shield.

Could this be the vertex? he asked himself. All the other vertices had been big slabs of stone, or made to look like doors. They were carved with inscriptions and writing from top to bottom, some of also appeared in the book he carried.

"Once I force you to cast the destruction sigil, the last ward will be down and we will be free," Draegon said.

There has to be a reason for this, Urus thought. *That symbol, it's not a coincidence that I'm the one that found it. It has to be meant for me.*

"It isn't just meant for me," he said aloud. "That symbol *is* me."

As if in response to the realization, the sigil on the sarcophagus sprang to life, glowing bright blue. Heat filled his chest and the scar from when he had been culled also luminesced, the scar tissue on his skin heating up like it had the day he had been branded. Compared to the pain in his arm, the burning sensation was almost pleasant.

"Stop it! What are you doing?" shouted Draegon. He cast his arm wide, flinging Urus across the room, slamming him into a wall.

It was too late. As the light faded from the sigil on the casket, so too did the sigil. The metal shield's surface was now smooth and polished, with no trace of the sigil etching. The culled brand on Urus's chest brightened, burning the symbol into his shirt.

"A blue sigil? That…That's not possible!" Draegon fumed, so enraged that spit frothed from his mouth, his hands twitching.

What's so important about blue sigils? Urus wondered.

He didn't know how, but Urus knew that he and the fifth vertex had been joined somehow. It had become an inseparable part of him. The scar tissue on his chest, the symbol of a culled unworthy of being a Kestian warrior, now felt as though it weighed more than a suit of plate armor.

He laughed, which made him cough blood up against the wall. "I guess if you want the fifth vertex destroyed, you're going to have to kill me. It's a shame you have to give up using me as your sigilord marionette to do it."

"No!" Draegon shouted. "This isn't possible, you can't have used your power, your body is under my control! How did you do that to the vertex?"

The blood mage stalked across the room, his face flush with anger, fists clenched. Urus immediately recognized the look in the man's eyes. Draegon was furious, and he was about to take his anger out on Urus. Urus mentally braced himself for what he knew was coming, unable to brace himself physically.

"I may have to kill you, but I don't have to do it quickly. I will break the final ward, but not before I take my time slowly breaking you!" Draegon leapt into the air and landed on Urus's chest. A flurry of furious stomps on Urus's stomach followed. Unsatisfied with the pain he was causing, Draegon got down on his knees and punched Urus in the face, over and over until Urus could barely see. He felt his jaw detach from his skull, dangling loose, tethered only by skin and muscle.

With what he was sure was his last breath, Urus looked toward his sword and whispered through broken teeth, "Save me, Hugo."

Urus endured a few more punches to the face and chest, then the blows stopped. A strange sound filled the room as a wind blew against his face. He struggled to open his eyes, only managing to get one open. Through puss and blood, Urus managed to get a glimpse of the action.

Hugo—the ghostly blue phantasm whom he had once summoned to kill his own father—stood beside him, holding the screaming blood mage aloft in its smokey blue grasp.

Draegon bled from fresh cuts and, as each new drop of blood touched the air, it floated up off his skin, formed into the shape of a spear, caught fire, and shot straight toward Hugo. The blood-fire passed through the creature as though he weren't there. Unaffected by Draegon's magic, Hugo countered each attack with a punch to the mage's face.

The blood mage began an incantation, despite his throat being slowly crushed by Hugo. Draegon's control of Urus's actions lapsed as he focused solely on the spell that would likely banish Hugo.

Unable to summon the physical strength to attack the mage, Urus remembered the image of the destruction sigil that flashed through his mind, the one Draegon was going to force him to cast to destroy the fifth vertex.

With his one good hand, Urus urged the power through his fingers as he etched the sigil in the air. *How would a blood mage know about a sigil like this?* Urus wondered, but put the thought out of his mind so he could stay focused on his sigilcraft. He still didn't know the extent of the dangerous side-effects of casting a sigil incorrectly.

Hugo vanished suddenly and Draegon dropped to the floor. The mage whirled, flashing a bloody, victorious grin at Urus. With a dismissive wave of his hand he flung Urus back against the far wall.

But it was too late. Urus had finished casting the sigil, a spiral with a decreasing radius with four lines drawn into the center. It hung in the air, solid and bright, glowing blue.

Draegon gasped as his body twisted and contorted. Bones snapped, blood streamed from open wounds as the mage's limbs folded in on themselves. Draegon continued to compress and fold into himself, shrinking until a few seconds later, nothing remained of the leader of the Order of the Sanguine Crystal.

A moment later, the uncontrollable torrent of stimuli that had come with his newly granted hearing vanished. The silence of his deafness smothered him just as he was finally allowed to slip into blissful unconsciousness.

CHAPTER THIRTY-ONE

Cailix stood on the shore, oblivious to the oncoming tide, hurling massive balls of bloodfire out at the ships in the bay. The rush of power that surged through her was intoxicating. She didn't just feel in control, she felt invincible —not only did she control her fate, but she could affect the fate of others. This was what true power felt like, and she didn't want to let go of that feeling.

She watched with detached focus, like an observer watching a game of stones, noting the positions of all the pieces in play. Her opponents' pieces were pirate and mercenary ships controlled by blood mages, but the game board had obeyed her every command…until they arrived.

At first they looked like a flock of gulls, circling the ships, awaiting their next meal. Then the shapes grew larger and the sun glinted off their bronze hulls.

The briene? Here? she thought, still throwing as many fireballs as she could, consuming the blood of the gathered livestock at an astounding rate. If she didn't stop soon, the island would die of starvation rather than at the hands of the Order. *Sheep can be replaced*, she rationalized, hoping she was right.

"What are the briene doing here? And why are they fighting the blood mages?" Cailix asked aloud.

"What, dear?" Orla asked, standing amid the gathered council of leaders of the island. They huddled behind a livestock fence, watching in terror as sheep after sheep exploded into a bloody mist, caught fire, and then soared out over the coastline into the naval battle beyond.

"Nothing," Cailix said.

The blood mages answered her volleys in kind, returning a salvo of a dozen fireballs for each of hers. She stood knee deep in water and the coastline was nothing but sand and shells for hundreds of yards up the slope, so most of the fireballs landed nearby with little effect.

Fatigue gripped her, urged to her to give up and sit down and rest. Her mind and soul were ready to quit and she had nothing left. Her fingers and toes tingled and her head was light. She didn't have much time left, so she was going to have to make her last attack count.

With one stroke she consumed all of the blood of the remaining livestock.

So... much... power!

She could barely contain it all, feeling she might burst from the amount of power that flowed through her. Yet she craved more, she *needed* more.

She channeled all of that power into the water at her feet. The water swirled and churned, then lifted over her head. The higher the wave grew, the more water it sucked up in its wake. At her command, the wave rose and rolled backwards, out into the bay, taking all of the water underneath with it.

The tidal wave rolled higher and higher, churned faster and more violently, leaving nothing but barren shoreline in its wake. It crashed into the first of the pirate vessels, ripping it apart, rending it into nothing but broken planks and splintered masts.

It hit another ship, then another, and another, until the wave finally crested out in the ocean, with an ear-splitting crash that made a thunderclap sound like a whisper. She hoped that somewhere amid the flotsam lay the body of her nemesis, and, inexplicably, her father.

But hope was for fools, and she knew it. Without seeing his body, she wouldn't truly believe he was dead, and she wouldn't be satisfied. Father or not, she meant to see him die, at a time of her choosing, in a way that *she* controlled. She wasn't going to let Anderis win.

Thoughts of killing Anderis faded along with her consciousness. Her power spent, she dropped to her knees and fell into the returning tide.

Cailix awoke in Orla's arms, the woman spooning a thick broth into her mouth, whispering encouraging words in her ear.

"Orla," Cailix said after taking in a big gulp of the soup.

"Just call me Momma, dear," Orla said, rocking Cailix back and forth like a babe. "You rest now; you must be exhausted."

"So tired," Cailix managed between sips of the broth.

"You exploded a whole herd of sheep, plus a few cows and all the pigs on the island. I imagine that has to take its toll," Orla said with a smile. "Not to mention all those fireballs and that wave."

"What happened? I remember the wave crashing, but that's it." Cailix sat up, finally taking in her surroundings. She was sitting on the grass at the top of the shoreline, looking down at the wreckage coming ashore. It littered the beach as far as she could see in both directions.

"You saved the island," came a deep voice that seemed familiar, but she couldn't place it.

Then Colin stepped into view, smiling at her. It was that simple farm-boy who seemed infatuated with her.

"The boy's right," another voice said, approaching from behind. This voice she recognized; it belonged to Woss. "I wouldn't believe it if I hadn't seen it with my own eyes. I suppose I have to start believin' in fairytales, boogey men, and dragons now, too."

Woss seemed genuinely flustered by the events. Witnessing a magical display like that had challenged everything he believed in, Cailix realized. But he also seemed like a strong man, and he would eventually get over it, she thought.

"Were there any survivors?" Cailix asked. "Did any of the mages come ashore?"

"No, dear, no survivors that we've seen," Orla said in a comforting tone, trying to spoon more soup into her.

Cailix tried to stand up, failed, and then managed the feat on the second attempt.

"There's a chance he survived then," she said softly, not realizing everyone else was listening.

"Who, dear?" Orla asked.

"The man who kidnapped me, tried to enslave me, tried to kill me, and tried to kill everyone on this island. My father."

At that, everyone tried to find something else to do or somewhere else to be.

Cailix stood for a while, taking in the scene before her, assessing the destruction she had caused. It wasn't just the sheer number of animals she had disposed of as fuel for her power. She had also decimated an entire naval fleet, using nothing but her own power and livestock.

What must it have been like during the Fulcrum War, when the blood mages used sigilords as their fuel? she thought. Just a few drops of Urus's blood could have supplied all the power she needed to summon that tidal wave. The devastation caused by the Fulcrum War, the number of innocent people who must have died, was incomprehensible.

"Orla!" came a shout from the beach head.

"Orla, we found survivors!" another man shouted, appearing on the shoreline from around a bend in the dunes.

She really does run this place, Cailix thought, smiling. The men hadn't called for the constable or any of the council members, they'd called for Orla.

Cailix stumbled and crashed her way down the sandy shore to where they had dragged two survivors out of the water and lain them on a section of torn decking from one of the ships. Colin, Orla, and Woss all trailed after her. Part of her hoped one of them was Anderis, so she could kill him personally.

She was disappointed and relieved to see that both of the survivors had dark skin and were tall, strong warriors. Both lay on their sides, retching saltwater onto the sand, propped up and being aided by a group of fishermen.

"Urus!" she shouted, seeing the array of weapons scattered around the two dark-skinned boys. "Urus!"

One of the boys rolled over and squinted up at her. It was Goodwyn, Urus's friend. He had never seemed to warm up to her, not that she could blame him. The night they'd sabotaged the fuel towers, Goodwyn had watched her gut a briene alive and use his blood to set fire to the tower. Since then, he had kept a distrustful distance from her.

"Cailix," he sputtered. "Where's Urus?"

"I thought he was with you," she said.

"Enemies approaching!" shouted one of the fishermen, pointing off shore.

Cailix spun to see a dozen rafts, each carrying a group of briene soldiers, as well as several dark-skinned Kestian warriors and Waldrene soldiers. *What in the hell happened while I was gone?*

"Those aren't enemies, they're briene," she said. "They were helping me fight the Order's ships."

Goodwyn tended to his friend while the fishermen and farmers helped pull the briene rafts up to the beach, creating quite the unusual gathering of soldiers and island natives. And Cailix. She didn't fit into any of the groups and stood off to the side, watching as the soldiers discussed the battle, looks of relief and happiness on their faces. She didn't know if she would ever be on the inside of such a group or share in those looks of mutual enjoyment.

"Who's Urus?" Colin asked. "You were calling his name earlier, hoping he was one of the survivors."

Cailix sighed. "Not now, Colin," she said, and walked past him up the beach, toward the bowl of Orla's soup that still called to her.

She sat down on the scrub-grass next to the bowl and plunged the ladle in, then dropped the ladle on the ground when the air on the beach where she'd come from rippled and warped, the image of the sand and the water beyond it bending and shifting, as if someone was stretching a painting.

Then, out of that distorted painting of the scene before her popped a dozen figures. They simply appeared, and then the strange warping effect stopped, a rush of sea water exploding outward onto the sand around them. Ten brilliantly colored suits of armor stood on the beach, two of them holding Urus upright next to the grey-skinned man.

Cailix yelped and raced down the beach.

She ran to Urus and hugged him, squeezing as tightly as she could. She didn't care if he was going to return the gesture. He was the only kindred spirit she had, and she had thought him dead. Finally something good had come of all this, a reason for her to smile.

Her smile disappeared when she felt warm blood drip from Urus's face onto her shoulder and he dropped to the sand in a heap.

"Oh no!" she shouted and knelt over him. "Is he alive?"

"Barely," Murin replied coldly. "But for how long I cannot say. I fear he spent the last of his energy getting us here."

At this, the suits of armor each bent to one knee and planted a sword in the sand in front of them. Crowds of people and soldiers of all sizes and colors gathered around the scene.

Cailix looked down at the broken, nearly dead boy laying on the sand. His branded scar had been burned into his shirt, blood glued the shirt to the scar below. Bone stuck out from his arm, and his face was barely recognizable as human. The bottom half of his mouth didn't even seem to be attached.

This poor boy had been through unimaginable torture, and this was just the beginning. As she looked down at him she couldn't help but think of the little birds in the nest she encountered when she first arrived on the island. Two had been so weak or injured that they would have been a burden to the other, and she'd killed them to ensure the strong one survived.

She could do the same for Urus. She could end his suffering. Even if he managed to live through this, his life would be an endless struggle, she knew that now. It was the burden of having such power. She could spare him a lifetime of constant struggle, loss, and suffering. All she had to do was end it right here, and his pain would be over just like the sickly little birds on the rocks.

She leaned over him and stuck her finger into one of his open wounds, in search of fresh blood.

"No, Cailix, don't!" Murin shouted.

Maybe life is worth the struggle, she thought.

"What are you doing to him?" Goodwyn yelled. "Leave him alone, you're going to kill him!"

Cailix ignored everyone and watched as the blood on her fingertip—the still-warm blood of a dying sigilord—disappeared, absorbed through her skin and converted into raw power.

She closed her eyes and let the power take over, sensing all of his wounds.

So much pain, she thought. *So many wounds! How did he ever survive this?*

"In Hol's name," she heard Goodwyn say. His gasp was followed by sounds of shock and amazement from the other onlookers, but she didn't stop to open her eyes. She had too much work to do.

One by one, her mind and her power sought out Urus's wounds.

So many wounds! What had he been fighting? She wondered.

The power surged through her into the wounds, closing holes, mending muscles, sealing broken bones back, and reattaching parts. A loud crack accompanied the mending of his elbow as it snapped back into place. She felt the muscles reshape around Urus's bones. She also felt some of the agonizing, searing pain that Urus had felt when receiving those wounds. She had no idea how he had managed to survive.

She didn't remember finishing the work before she slipped into a deep sleep.

She awoke in the middle of the night, surrounded by campfires and dozens of little groups of soldiers of every shape, size, and race all discussing the day's events. Words like "fireball" and "witch" dominated the conversations.

Cailix leaned forward, steadying herself.

"Easy now, dear," Orla said, propping her up and stuffing a hot bowl of soup into her hands.

"Urus," Cailix said, her throat dry and itchy. She couldn't remember the last time she had been that parched or ravenous. "Did he survive?" she asked then downed the bowl of soup in a single gulp, dividing the portion equally between her mouth and her clothes.

"Ask him yourself," Orla said, gesturing to a shadow approaching from around one of the camp fires.

"Urus!" Cailix jumped up and rushed to him, squeezing him, hard.

"Easy now, you're going to break all the bones you healed." Urus met her gaze. Something deep behind those dark brown eyes had changed, but she couldn't put her finger on what exactly. "Orla told me everything," he said.

Only when he took a step back to gape at her did Cailix imagine the sight she must have presented, with her red hair flying wild and her ruffled and stained bright blue festival dress.

She blushed, hoping he didn't notice in the dim light of the beach fires.

"Cailix threw fireballs and giant waves at the blood mages from the shore," Goodwyn said, coming to stand next to Urus, his usual distrustful stare replaced with a look of appreciation. She had to admit she liked the change. These people felt like family to her, but the good kind of family, not the kind of family that hits you or hurts you or discards you like so much trash, but real, good family.

"You do know how to make an entrance," said a tall man who looked like an older, graying version of Urus, spinning Urus around so he could read his lips. Aegaz nodded to the unmoving suits of armor standing vigil nearby. "The knights were a nice touch."

"Uncle!" Urus shouted and hugged the man.

"I would have come by sooner, but I felt you could use some rest. It is good to see you up and walking, we were all worried."

After a long time, Urus finally peeled away, tears flowing. "Uncle, there is so much I need to say, so many—"

Aegaz held up a hand. "There will be plenty of time for that. But for now, what happened with the vertex? Did you save it?"

Urus stared down at his chest and absently ran a finger along the burned outline of the vertex sigil on his shirt above where Cailix knew the culled brand lay.

"I think so," he said.

"What happened with the Order?" Goodwyn asked.

"I killed Draegon, the head of the Order," Urus answered.

Cailix grinned. With Draegon dead, it would be that much easier to hunt down and kill Anderis.

"What do you mean you *think* you saved the vertex?" Aegaz asked. "Murin, what happened?"

"I honestly am not sure," Murin replied. "Urus should explain."

Cailix was as happy that there was finally a question to which Murin did not know the answer as she was that Draegon was dead.

"The Order is gone, so they won't be going after the vertex. Draegon wasn't able to destroy it because I was able to move it."

"What are you talking about? Where is it?" Goodwyn asked.

Urus pulled himself up to his full height and answered quietly. "I *am* the fifth vertex."

EPILOGUE

Urus sat on a large piece of driftwood, watching the soldiers relax and celebrate around the bonfires that ran up and down the shore. The sun had almost set, but the men were hungry, thirsty, and in need of a release, to revel in the fact that the fighting was done. He marveled at the way the last remnants of the sun glistened off the motionless suits of armor, still kneeling in the sand.

He watched Goodwyn, Therren, and the other First Fist gathered around their own fire. Aside from Goodwyn, they seemed like strangers. The Kestian soldiers all had that look in their eyes, that steely gaze of a true Kestian warrior. He couldn't imagine that there was ever a day when he had envied that look, when all he wanted was to be such a warrior.

He stood up, groaning against the aches and pains that still remained after Cailix had healed him, and walked down to the water, admiring the colors of the sunset rippling on the calm seas, seas that had been raging with battle just a few hours earlier. It was funny how nature could return to such a natural state of beauty as soon as people left it alone.

He sighed, picked up a flat shell, and skipped it along the surface of the water.

A second shell bounced along the water's surface, following behind the one he had thrown. Urus turned to see his uncle approaching.

"So much water," Uncle Aegaz signed. "Isn't it beautiful?"

"You can't drink any of it," Urus replied. "It makes you sick."

Aegaz laughed. "That doesn't make it any less beautiful."

"What good is water you can't drink?" Urus signed, turning away from the ocean.

"What's wrong?" Aegaz asked.

"What good is power you can't use? Or power that hurts people if you do use it?"

"It's like any tool, I suppose," Aegaz began. "You can use it to tear down or to build up. Everyone hits their own thumb with a hammer before they learn how to use it."

"But this isn't like hitting my thumb," Urus said. "When Cailix doesn't control her power, buildings collapse, tornadoes run wild. I-I did things. When I use my power, people get hurt. People die."

Aegaz stroked his beard, then signed, "People die in war, Urus, you know that."

"What about my father?" Urus asked. "Did you know what really happened to him…what *I* did to him?"

"When I came and found you that day, and I saw your father there," Aegaz signed. "I figured he had boxed your ears one too many times and finally got what he deserved. Your sire, my brother or not, was a cruel bastard, and my only regret is not taking you away from him sooner."

"It was the sigil power," Urus signed. "I summoned something with it and it killed my father."

"Urus, you need to understand that—" Aegaz stopped short, staring off into the distance. Urus turned to see the source of his uncle's fixation.

A swirling vortex of light hovered just above the sand. Out of it stepped four men, each wearing armor unlike any he had ever seen—blacker than the blackest night but thin and somehow reflective. It gleamed and reflected the light of the vortex. A fifth man stepped out, a man in simple robes with a red sash. His gaze was fixed on Urus, and he ignored all others on the beach. The four men assumed guard stances next to the portal.

Urus took a step back, drawing Hugo. After what he knew about Hugo and the sigil on the blade, the sword seemed heavier now.

Aegaz drew his sword and Goodwyn and Therrin appeared at his side. Before the robed man could take another step, Urus felt Murin's presence directly behind him.

"Stay back or we will cut you down, stranger," Aegaz said.

Urus felt Cailix put a reassuring hand on his back. He hadn't even seen her approach.

"You will do no such thing, radix," replied the man in fluent Kestian. He turned his attention again to Urus and asked, "Are you the sigilord?"

Tell this man nothing. Murin's thoughts entered Urus's mind. *He is an arbiter, and nothing good can come of this meeting. Say nothing.*

Urus did as he was told and did not reply to the man's question.

"That is fine, you do not have to answer. I know you are the sigilord. You positively reek of it," said the man, looking down his nose at Urus. By this time most of the briene and Waldrene soldiers had gathered observe the commotion.

"You have no jurisdiction here, Arbiter," Murin said. "I know your oath, and you cannot interfere with the natural course of things on this world."

"And I know you, Murin Elimhaer of Futanishar, Viceroy of the Second Legion of Arbitration, and Dean Emeritus of the Academy of the Magic Sciences. Your past service with the arbiters will garner you no favors here."

"What is your business here?" Murin demanded.

"The sigilord has violated the Continuum Protection Act. He is to be brought back to Almoryll for judgement and sentencing."

"What is the cont...protection act?" Urus asked, unable to reproduce the word he had read on the man's lips.

It is a law the arbiters passed to justify their inaction during the Fulcrum War as they watched, and often encouraged, the blood mages' genocide of the sigilords, Murin projected in Urus's mind. *They justify their right to persecute those who wield more power than they do.*

"It is a law that prevents the use of unsanctioned sigilcraft. It preserves the balance and punishes those who would set the balance out of order," said the arbiter.

"You and your laws have no jurisdiction here, Arbiter," Murin repeated.

"Oh, but I do, and *you* have no say in this matter, *former* arbiter Murin," the man said. He reached out and touched Urus on the shoulder. The beach, the water, the people, the entire world vanished.

www.ingramcontent.com/pod-product-compliance
Lightning Source LLC
Chambersburg PA
CBHW020242180626
46810CB00006B/2330